"Robson skillfully builds a believable world . . . [a] solid page-turning debut." —*Publishers Weekly*

"Be prepared. You aren't going to want to put the book down—it's too much fun!" —Urban Fantasy Reviews

"A new great series, and I really can't wait to have more now!" —Between Dreams and Reality

"Pumped with adrenaline . . . beyond entertaining. . . . I can't wait for book two." —Talk Supe

"This is an exciting and refreshing debut, and I can't wait to see what's next for this series!" —My Bookish Ways

"[W]hen it comes to romance, [Celia] has a refreshing innocence that is sure to delight readers."
—*RT Book Reviews*

The Weird Girls: A Novella

"Absolutely phenomenal." —Nocturnal Readings

"It kept me on the edge of my seat."
—Urban Fantasy Reader

"Sure to be a great new action-packed urban fantasy series. I can't wait to hear what other craziness these four sisters will find themselves in." —Readers Confessions

"Wonderfully imaginative. . . . I can't wait to see what happens next to these sisters. Something tells me it's going to be a wild ride." —She-Wolf Reads

The Weird Girls Series by Cecy Robson

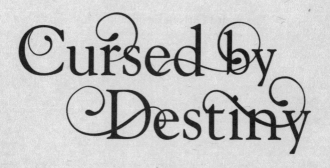

Cursed by Destiny

A WEIRD GIRLS NOVEL

CECY ROBSON

A SIGNET ECLIPSE BOOK

SIGNET ECLIPSE
Published by the Penguin Group
Penguin Group (USA) LLC, 375 Hudson Street,
New York, New York 10014

USA | Canada | UK | Ireland | Australia | New Zealand | India | South Africa | China
penguin.com
A Penguin Random House Company

First published by Signet Eclipse, an imprint of New American Library,
a division of Penguin Group (USA) LLC

First Printing, January 2014

Copyright © Cecy Robson, LLC, 2014
Excerpt from *Sealed with a Curse* copyright © Cecy Robson, LLC, 2013

SIGNET ECLIPSE and logo are trademarks of Penguin Group (USA) LLC.

ISBN 978-0-451-41675-9

Printed in the United States of America
10 9 8 7 6 5 4 3 2 1

To my children, my sunshine in the rain and my stars in the sky. Mommy loves you. And to my mother-in-law, Shirley, who always treated me like one of her own.

ACKNOWLEDGMENTS

To have one person help me bring out my creativity and give it life is a tremendous blessing. To have an entire team available leaves me blessed beyond words.

First of all, many thanks to my editor, Elizabeth Bistrow, who not only jumped on the crazy train known as Cecy Robson, but boarded with a smile, and purchased a few extra tickets so Claire Zion and the staff of Penguin Random House could ride along. Thank you, everyone, for your participation in the book-birthing process. Another "weird" novel is born!

To the artists and model, I could have never imagined more beautiful covers. Thank you for your talents and collective vision for my world. You are amazing!

To my agent, Nicole Resciniti, who is more family than friend, and the person who fights fang and claw for me. Nic, thank you for always laughing at my jokes—even the bad ones—and for caring with all of your being. I would be lost without your honesty, intelligence, and heart.

To my husband, Jamie: Babe, where would I be without your loving arms, your devilish grin, and your horrifically bad recaps of classic songs? Thank you for lifting me with your words of support and for laughing at me when I really need to be laughed at. I'll love you forever.

To Pat Cicci, a beautiful woman who gave life to one of my dearest friends, Marifran. I'll remember her gentle words and kind heart always. She laughed at my silly antics and sarcastic humor, mostly because she enjoyed the happiness that laughter brought her, and because she enjoyed life. Heaven has a new angel, one that will watch over her husband, Frank, her children and her grandchildren, and offer them hope and love in times when they need it most. May God bless her.

To my Weird Girls fans, thank you for your loyalty and for spreading the word about my series. I'll tell you this much: The best is yet to come!

CHAPTER 1

Master Vampire's Estate
Tahoe City, California

"Are you ready, Celia?"

Misha's voice was nothing more than a seductive whisper. It made me breathless. "Yes."

His gray eyes wandered down my body. "Are you sure you can handle it?"

"Yes."

"*All* of it?"

I shot him an exasperated look. "We're no longer talking about the scrimmage, are we?"

He let out a deep sigh. "No, but perhaps we should continue."

Misha gave the order in the form of a subtle nod. Ten of his vampires attacked me, the thirst of the hunt shadowing their overly eager faces. It was hard not to rely on my claws. The vamps fought dirty, and they didn't hold back, but hell, neither did I. My body slid lithely across the hardwood floor of the dojang, just when two vamps tried to tackle me. They slammed into each other—hard, like two boulders colliding.

The moment I kipped up to my feet, three more advanced. I punched, kicked, and maneuvered my way around them. It was grueling and my animal instincts propelled me into overdrive. Yet my innate need to survive and the long months of extensive martial arts training paid off. The overly obnoxious and excessively tanned vampires dropped with a skull-pounding crunch against the hard floor while I continued to hold my own against the rest. It wasn't easy. Liz, Maria, Edith Anne, and Agnes Concepción were especially vicious. For she-vamps who bounced around in Catholic school uniforms all day, they sure were a mean bunch.

Maria threw back her dark hair, her Brazilian accent thick and dripping with spite. "Did you get an invitation to Aric and Barbara's wedding, little tigress?"

That was low, even for Maria. "That's none of your business." She hadn't even hit me yet, but I knocked her out with an uppercut to the chin just for being a bitch.

Liz jumped over Maria's body, pouting her perfectly plump bottom lip as she advanced with all the grace of a starving cheetah. "What's the matter, Celia? Are you mad that you're not good enough to marry that werewolf?"

My hackles rose. Liz had hit a raw nerve. "Mention Aric one more time and you'll be gumming your next meal."

Liz smiled, peering down her nose at me. "*Aric.* There. Now what—?"

Liz's fangs landed somewhere near Misha's feet. He rolled his eyes. An entranced maid silently appeared and swept the pointy canines into a pan.

Edith Anne crouched into an attack stance. "Damn. You're an angry little shit."

I growled at Edith, blocked her strike, and wrenched her arm behind her back. She hissed and snapped her fangs at me. I silenced her with an elbow to her temple. The sickening snap almost made me feel bad. Almost.

Maria stirred as she regained consciousness. I was still ticked at her for mentioning Aric's wedding, so I knocked her out again with a kick to her face. My sudden bitterness overwhelmed me and made me lash out at two male vamps who'd struggled to their feet.

My foot nailed the first vamp in the jaw, but his pal struck me across the face before I was able to plant both feet. I whirled in the air three times before crashing on my back. *Crap.* He leapt into the air with his fist reeled back. I rolled away—*fast.* He grunted upon impact, lodging his hand through the floor. My heel found the back of his neck before he could jerk his arm free. The pop of his vertebrae and limp form told me he wouldn't be getting up anytime soon.

I panted and spun around, swearing under my breath. The vamp could have easily busted my jaw. I knew it, and so did the next two vamps who rushed me.

I couldn't heal like *weres*, but damn it, I was just as strong and just a little faster. And unlike *weres*, I could *shift* underground and come up completely unscathed. I spat out some blood and used my resentment against the remaining opponents.

I held Agnes and Edith with my feet pressed against their throats, taking care not to protrude my back claws when they grabbed my ankles and tossed me. I flipped back and landed in a crouch. Maria regained consciousness again, and tackled me from behind. I yelped as fangs dug into my skin, piercing my flesh like sets of scorching needles. The scrimmage ended and the pain receded before I could tear the Prada-worshipping leeches off.

Edith and Agnes visibly shook as Misha laid into them. "Celia belongs to *me*," he hissed. "You are never to taste her."

I frowned. "I'm not yours."

The vamps ignored me. "I didn't drink her blood, Master. I swear it," Edith Anne whimpered.

Agnes cowered at his feet. "Neither did I, Master. Not even a lick."

I rubbed my face. The Catholic schoolgirls and I weren't exactly buddies. In fact, we barely tolerated one another. That didn't mean, though, that I wanted them turned into clumps of dust. I strode to Misha's side and grasped his elbow, halting his tirade. "Misha, it's fine. They only bit me. On the shoulder and . . ." I turned to look at my backside. "Damn it, Edith—you bit my ass?"

Edith shuffled back and forth, looking at her feet. "Sorry, Celia. It was an accident."

Her wicked smile and flirty wink told me otherwise. Misha glared with the might of his master badassness. "Leave *now*."

The so-called Prince of Darkness knew how to clear a room. There was a slight breeze and the whole lot of them vanished—as in hauled serious supernatural tail. I tried to leave, too, but Misha grabbed my hand. "Wait. I must heal you."

The smoldering look Misha gave me told me exactly what he meant. "That's okay—they're only puncture wounds. I'll see Emme tomorrow. She'll fix me right up."

Misha closed the distance between us. "They left deep marks. You should not wait to tend to them."

"Misha . . ."

Chills spread through my body as Misha licked my shoulder to seal the wound. His tongue and breath warmed my skin. Misha had been around for over a hundred and forty years; he'd had plenty of time to learn how to touch a woman. He continued on, even though the bites had closed after the first flick of his taste buds.

I broke his hold and backed away. "Misha, don't." Misha was a thrill ride I didn't want to straddle. My loneliness had become unbearable; every part of me longed to be touched. But it wasn't his hands my body craved.

Misha's heated gaze promised me hours of pleasure. "I'm not done yet, kitten."

My mouth went dry. This was a problem. When it came to fighting, I'd take on anyone, anytime, anywhere. When it came to males, I *changed* into the superhero of dorks—a big ol' "D" blazed across my chest and an army of pocket protector–worshipping fiends bowed at my feet. Any able-bodied female in my situation would have taken control and made Misha beg for pleasure. Where were these able-bodied females when I needed one?

I inched my way back, laughing a little too hysterically for my tastes. "You don't really want to kiss my butt, do you? What will people think?"

A wicked smile spread slowly across his strong masculine face. As if on cue, a gust appeared despite the closed windows and fanned Misha's long blond mane in perfect supermodel fashion. "Do I strike you as someone who cares what others think?"

I darted around, searching for the source of the breeze. My brows knitted tight. "Did you just do that on purpose?" The gleam in his "come hither and do naughty things to me" expression confirmed my suspicions. My gulp dissolved my frown. I'd already backed into the bamboo walls.

Misha continued to stalk toward me. His smoldering gray eyes accelerated my pulse, my forlorn female parts screamed to give in, and my hands itched to take my clothes off. Thank God, my mind still functioned reasonably. "Misha, under no circumstances will your tongue *or* lips touch my backside."

He placed his palms on either side of my head and regarded me with growing desire. "As you wish."

My shoulders slumped with relief . . . until I realized I hadn't been specific enough. Misha grabbed the two fingers of my right hand and placed them in his hot mouth, instantly spiking my body temperature ten degrees. I was so distracted that I didn't notice him yank my yoga pants down to my ankles. By some lingerie miracle, my thong remained in place. He pulled my delighted fingers out of his mouth and smoothed them over my remaining marks. I swallowed hard while he held my gaze. My body was literally shaking with need. No man had touched me like that since Aric . . .

Aric.

I jumped out of Misha's grasp, only to land on my face and scramble away like a damn epileptic inchworm.

Misha sighed when I managed to stand and yank up my pants. "Kitten, why must you make things so difficult?"

"Misha, I don't want this. I told you that before I moved in."

Misha leaned against the wall and quirked an eyebrow. "It didn't appear that way a moment ago."

My hands dropped to my sides in frustration. "I know,

and I'm sorry. But I can't stay here if this is what you'll expect of me. You promised you'd keep your hands to yourself."

Misha pushed himself off the wall and, in a blink, faced me. "I promised to make you the perfect weapon, one that could help us defeat the Tribe." He licked his lips and focused on mine. "I also promised not to do more than you would allow between us."

"There is no us, Misha. I can't allow our relationship to go further."

Misha flashed me another wicked grin before he gave me his usual line. "We'll see."

He offered me his arm. I knew then he was backing off, so I let him lead me out of the dojang. "Come. Our reservations are for seven."

Snow crunched beneath my sneakers. Normally the slate walkway to the main house was kept meticulously clean, but a light dusting of snow had blanketed the stone during our time in the scrimmage. The clouds cleared and the trees parted, revealing the sparkle of a thousand stars in the beautiful Tahoe sky.

We moved quickly, passing through the main garden. Come late spring, Misha's caretaker would painstakingly tend to the flowers and the stone waterfalls that emptied into a beautiful carp-filled lagoon. For now, the garden was mostly quiet, only the faint trickle of running water whispering from the melting ice.

The night was lovely, but carried a "your boobies are going to snap off" kind of cold. My inner golden tigress usually kept me warm yet even she couldn't compete with the chill in the air, especially in my skimpy workout clothes.

Misha slipped an arm around my shoulders when I shuddered. Whoever said vampires were ice-cold had it all wrong. Misha was the supernatural equivalent of the Snuggie. "I better snag my coat from the guesthouse."

Misha tightened his hold, preventing me from veering toward my quarters. "Your coat awaits you in my limo." His hands rubbed against my toned arms. "It would please me if you ate more than your fill this evening. You have grown too thin."

Which was the reason he'd consented to taking me to the all-you-can-eat Chinese buffet in South Tahoe. "My weight remains the same, Misha. It's just shifted a little."

"Your tone is too defined. You've lost too much body fat and your breasts are considerably smaller."

I crossed my arms over my chest. "What the hell are you doing looking at my breasts?" I grimaced when Misha chuckled. "Never mind."

Misha was right. My muscles were more pronounced than when I'd merely exercised for fun. But then, sculpting my body to fight for the newly formed Alliance was now my career. I shuddered again, this time not from the cold. I'd never relished destroying anything or anyone . . . until I discovered the monsters that feasted on innocents and basked in cruelty.

The Tribe had emerged without warning, pimp-slapping the supernatural world and demanding we fall at its proverbial and claw-hoofed feet. Led by demon lords, they recruited ostracized *weres*, witches, and vampires—freaks like me, who never quite belonged anywhere.

I could have called the Tribe a group of crazies and wouldn't have been completely off the mark. The problem was, they were an effective group of wack-jobs seeking to give the demons a new world to overtake and loads of unsuspecting females to impregnate.

"What is it?" Misha asked.

My hatred for the Tribe had momentarily distracted me. I pushed away my anger and refocused on my favorite vampire. "Misha, I don't want you to punish Edith and Agnes for biting me."

The corners of Misha's lips curved. He knew very well my thoughts hadn't been on the good Catholics. Still, he didn't push me. "Celia, they bit you after I specifically forbade it. I do not tolerate disobedience."

I shrugged. "They just got carried away. I was pretty rough on them."

"Why do you defend them?"

"They're my friends."

Misha blinked back at me as if I'd pulled a rabbit out of my yoga pants. I laughed. No one could lie to a *were* or a vamp. I had a strong sense of smell, but even I couldn't sniff a lie the way they could. "I just don't want anyone hurt because of me."

"That I can believe, but, my darling, they have left me no choice but to punish them."

Living with a master vampire sucked. Seriously. They had their own sadistic rules, especially when it came to disciplining their family. "How severely?"

"Well, I may not kill them—this time—but I may have to torture them."

I took his hand and squeezed. It was something I'd started doing recently and it made me feel close to him. "There are other methods of punishment besides physical ones. Can't you try being creative and think of something just as effective?"

Misha glanced at our hands. "Perhaps."

"Please, Misha. I'll sleep a lot better if you do."

"You would also sleep better if you joined me in bed tonight."

Every night Misha asked me into his chambers. Every night I refused. And every night someone else would join him. Now and again, it was several someones.

My head lowered. "I can't."

"What stops you?"

I didn't answer and continued toward the circle drive. I desired to be touched and sometimes the gnawing ache of my loneliness sent me into a state of despair. But Misha wasn't Aric. And it wasn't right, especially since I believed Misha had genuine feelings for me. He was my friend, and it would destroy me to hurt him.

I don't know if my expression gave me away or perhaps I waited too long to answer, but Misha became well aware of my thoughts. "My darling, that mongrel will be married soon. There is no future for you with him. You need to move forward with your life."

"I know this, Misha, but I can't." The purr from his Hummer limo filled the awkward pause between us.

Hank, one of Misha's bodyguards and driver, leapt out of his seat to open the door.

Misha motioned with his hand. "After you," he said quietly.

I nodded. The conversation of becoming bedmates was over. At least for the moment.

I placed my foot into the monstrosity of a vehicle. The aroma of dried crushed herbs and magic smacked me in the nose and sent a stabbing pain into my skull. I whipped around and lunged at Misha and Hank, *shifting* us the moment my knee connected with the slate. I dissolved my body and that of the vampires into minute particles, easily and swiftly passing through the frozen soil and in the direction of the garden. The earth rumbled above us. We traveled fast, but I didn't get us far. I hadn't taken a sufficient breath and my lungs demanded air. I surfaced near an old redwood just as a second explosion sent the limo door spiraling toward us like a giant baton.

I *shifted* us down to our waists as the rim embedded into the redwood above us like the blade from an electric saw, missing our heads by less than a second. Chunks of bark and broken glass peppered my scalp. I surfaced enough for us to crawl away from beneath the dented door. We were knocked onto our sides when a third blast pulverized what remained of the vehicle. I stared blankly at the roaring inferno.

Holy crap. Someone just tried to kill me.

CHAPTER 2

The good Catholics practically shoved me out of the way in their urgency to reach Misha. I limped around Agnes Concepción, ignoring her vicious hiss when I accidently stepped in her way. Hank barked orders at the male vamps. "Search the premises. *Now*. Whoever cast the witch fire may still be here. Tim, check the digital recordings on the surveillance cameras!"

The vamps disappeared like a passing breeze. I hobbled toward Hank, who focused with deep loathing at the bright orange flames encasing what remained of the Hummer limo. The heat grew stronger as I drew near. The intensity of the fire irritated my green eyes and sent streams of tears trickling down my heated cheeks. There was no smoke, just odd orange flames and the increasing aroma of drying herbs. Hank had called it witch fire. To me it seemed more like multiple grenades packed with a mystical combustion. But then, he'd know more than I.

"Did you sense anything when you climbed in, Hank?"

"No. Nothing. I didn't feel shit until you approached." He looked me up and down before taking hold of my arm. He pulled me toward the flame. Or, at least, he tried.

I jerked my arm free. "What do you think you're doing?"

Hank rolled his eyes. "Just trust me. Will ya?"

I threw my hands in the air. "Hank, you hate me. Explain to me why I should trust you to lead me toward a blazing magical inferno."

He scoffed. "I don't deny you're a pain in the ass. But you know the master will stake me if I hurt you."

That much was true. Still, that didn't mean I'd allow him to lead me around like a wimp. "What do you need me to do?"

"Just take two steps toward the Hummer."

I took one step forward. The flames intensified. I took another. The flames screamed. Screamed like a premenstrual woman in serious need of chocolate. That's when I took four hurried steps back.

"Shit," Hank muttered. "Just as I thought. You're the goddamn trigger. Take off your shirt."

"Um. No."

"Your pants?"

"No!"

"Fuckin' A, Celia. They're ripped anyway."

I jabbed my finger in his chest. "They're ripped because I banged my knee when I saved your sorry undead ass!" Hank glared at my finger, then at me. I sighed, ripped a section of my pants off, and tossed it to him. "There. Is that good enough?"

Hank snatched the cloth from me and sniffed it, smiling when he caught a whiff of my blood. No, that wasn't creepy or anything. He neared the blaze and flung the cloth like a Frisbee. A static charge of orange light crackled above the fire and the aroma of herbs built until it coated my tongue with a nasty film. Sections of flames raced inward toward the fabric like small fire entities. They leapt on top of one another in their attempt to reach the disintegrating cloth, but instead of growing stronger by uniting, they extinguished one by one.

All that remained of Misha's ride was a warped, ash-covered frame. "Someone tried to kill you, Celia," Hank muttered, his tone one step shy of a hiss. "This witch fire wouldn't have gone out unless it was satisfied its target had been eliminated."

I pushed my long wavy hair away from my face. I didn't want to be right. And Hank had a point: the witch fire mojo seemed satisfied once it tasted my blood. Awesome. Just one more evil critter wanting to take a bite out of me.

The heat rose around me from Hank's rising temper. It would have been sweet if he was angry that some big bad nasty had tried to murder me. But I knew better. Hank was furious that he'd almost been burnt to toast. As a master vampire, Misha would have survived the blaze and the impact. Hank . . . not so much. He would have been the vampire equivalent of a gasoline-soaked matchstick. "How did a witch get in here to cast such a spell? The entire compound is warded against an attack."

"That's what I'd like to know." Misha walked toward me appearing to any human as calm and collected. The way his family spread out to give him ample space and the bitter scent of fury that alerted my tigress suggested that his pissed-off-o-meter had reached a record high.

Hank bowed. "We will find who did this, Master. And when we do, I'll rip his kidneys out and feed them to him."

Knowing Hank, this wasn't a gross exaggeration. Misha crossed his arms and took in my knee. "You're hurt." Behind me a phone rang. Edith Anne quickly silenced it.

"I'm fine, Misha. It's just a scratch."

Another phone rang. Another Catholic schoolgirl turned off the ringer.

"May I heal you?"

I backed away. "No, Misha. It just needs some ice." Maria raced toward the house. Another cell phone rang, then another, and another. Misha and I turned to the group just as someone's "I'm Sexy and I Know It" ringtone filled the cold night. "Who's calling?"

Misha's vamps exchanged glances, appearing afraid to reveal the identity of the caller. Maria hurried back with a sandwich bag stuffed with ice. God knew a vamp could haul serious ass when motivated by her master. Her phone rang next. She hurled the packet of ice at my face. I caught it and almost launched it back at her until I saw her gaping at her phone. She swallowed hard and raised her chin. "It's one of de mongrels from de pack."

My body stiffened. *Okay. Which one?*

"Answer it," Misha snapped.

The moment Maria touched the screen a thunderous growl erupted on the other end of the line. "Put. Celia. On. *Now!*"

Koda. My oh so gentle and loving brother-in-law. I reached for the phone and hissed at Maria when she wouldn't hand it to me. "Give me the damn phone!" Following a nod from Misha, she threw it at me with as much love as she had the ice pack. "Koda, it's me."

His growls silenced. "Are you hurt? We know about the explosion."

Koda was the techno-savvy guy. Either he'd hacked into Misha's security cameras or he'd put someone on watch near the compound. It shouldn't have shocked me, but that didn't mean I liked it. "I'm fine." I took in the wreckage. The engine collapsed with a loud bang. "Nothing to worry about."

Koda paused, obviously having heard the engine's last hurrah. "There was witch fire, Celia."

"So I'm told. Don't fret. The vampires are looking into it."

Another rumble erupted. This time it wasn't Koda. I froze when I recognized it as Aric's growl. He was there, in the room with Koda. "I'm fine," I repeated once more, my voice shaking from surprise. Aric didn't sound satisfied. He hated me living with Misha. But he'd made a choice, and so had I.

Another sharp snarl cut through the phone. I closed my eyes and pictured his light brown eyes, the sexy five o'clock shadow that covered his strong jaw, and the grin that never failed to stop my heart. My raspy voice softened, just as it always had in his presence. "I scraped my knee, but it's nothing. Please don't worry, wolf."

I no longer spoke to Koda, but rather Aric. His protests abruptly stopped. In the quiet that followed, I could hear him taking deep, controlled breaths. "Okay," Aric answered in his deep timbre. "Be safe." A door opened and closed in the background, letting me know he was gone.

Koda's voice brought me back to the moment. "Do you need us to come for you?"

"No . . . thank you. I'll see you at the house tomorrow."

When I disconnected, all eyes were on me. And, go figure, no one seemed thrilled. One by one, Misha's vampires dispersed. I wrapped my arms around myself. Now that the witch fire had vanished, the air grew cold and dense. "Come," Misha finally said. "Dinner awaits."

Misha slipped his arm back around my shoulders and led me to the house. A team of vamps appeared with saws, sledgehammers, and dirty looks. My body trembled. But the vampires weren't the cause of my discomfort. Moving into Château de Misha had never been about becoming chummy with creatures so self-absorbed I had to work not to smack them. In fact, I was almost used to their snide and catty remarks. What I wasn't used to were attempts on my life, even though I'd experienced my share since being "outed" to the mystical community. I also wasn't used to hearing Aric's voice anymore. All it had taken was his familiar deep tone to tug on my heartstrings and send me into a state of misery.

The scent of roasting duck filled my nose. I squinted a little as my eyes adjusted to the brightly lit European-inspired kitchen. Misha must have used his vamp mojo to put Chef on dinner duty. Chef raced between the industrial steel stove and the tan marble counter, slicing, dicing, stirring, and swearing in French. Out of all the vamps in Misha's keep, Chef was by far the moodiest bastard. "*Merde*," he muttered the moment he saw us.

Chef lived—well, in death—to prepare meals almost too pretty to eat. I ignored him and shuffled toward the table, feeling more chilled than I should have in the warm kitchen.

"I shall discover who attempted to kill you, Celia. Do not fear for your safety in my home."

I must have appeared pathetic for Misha's anger to

resurface. "I know, Misha. Don't worry. I'm fine." I was getting tired of repeating myself, mostly because I wasn't "fine." I was merely forging ahead because, damn it all, there was evil afoot.

My new life as the vampire's weapon was probably the most dangerous path I could have selected, and yet it felt right. I'd almost lost a sister to the Tribe and watched countless innocents suffer as I stood helplessly by. But I wasn't helpless, and while I was far from perfect, I could be the perfect weapon . . . at least where Team Dracula was concerned.

My powers were unique and strong, even in a world packed with supernatural muscle. My ability to *shift* underground unscathed made me difficult to track and conquer. My inner beast also made me formidable against anything with fangs or claws. Pure light could sear a demon and detonate an average vamp, but it had no effect on me. Misha's legion of undead couldn't say the same.

Weres matched me in strength, but they'd made it clear they didn't want me. So in my quest to rid the world of the Tribe, I chose to help the vampires, just as Aric had chosen his pack above and beyond me.

Crap. I rubbed my face. In the end, my thoughts always returned to Aric.

Misha watched me closely. The silence between us grew longer and filled with tension. When he spoke, his light Russian accent dripped with frustration. "You must forget about the beast, Celia. Even if that mongrel does love you, he is obligated by blood and pack to breed with his kind. There is nothing you can do. Your relationship with him is over."

Misha had recognized Aric's snarls just as I had. I'd heard them a thousand times out of fear for my safety. Misha had heard them on the receiving end of Aric's wrath. I'd definitely experienced the cuddlier side of that werewolf. I sat slowly. "Do you realize that you only call me Celia when you're being serious or when you're angry with me?" I smiled weakly. "Which is it now?"

He sat across the table from me, frowning in a way

that would have sent his family scurrying in fear. "Perhaps it is a little of both, since you fail to come to your senses. You could be with a more deserving male." He paused. "You could be with me."

His comment hitched my breath. For once, he wasn't merely asking me to bed. "Are you asking me for a commitment?"

Misha's jaw tightened. "Perhaps."

I stood and walked to his side and brushed his long blond hair away from his face. His expression softened when he caught my smile. "I think you're the one who needs to come to his senses. You deserve better than what I can give you."

I meant that. For a vampire, Misha was a tremendous catch. In addition to his incredible masculine beauty, he was smart, funny, and enjoyable company. And, for anyone who cared, he was also obscenely wealthy. I think he owned Canada.

Misha regarded me with complete tenderness. It was a look he gave me frequently since I'd inadvertently returned his soul. His expression was one of kindness and compassion I'd never seen him demonstrate to anyone, and it warmed my heart. He reached out and stroked my face. "Thank you for believing I'm a better man than I am."

I squeezed his large hand with mine in time for Hank to appear. "Did you find the culprit?" Misha asked without looking at him.

Hank shook his head. "No, Master. We've searched the house and the grounds, and the digital recordings taken over the last twenty-four hours have been reviewed. No one but your family and feasts have entered the premises."

Which meant either the limo had been booby-trapped during an excursion . . . or Misha's family hated me more than I thought. My thoughts played across my Latina features like a violin. "None of my family would dare harm you," Misha said. He turned to Hank.

Hank backed out of the room as if Misha was wielding a flamethrower. "No . . . of course not, Master." He jerked his head toward me. "We would never think to hurt our lovely Celia."

It was all I could do not to roll my eyes. *Sure. Yup. Whatever.* "How long can a spell like that stay dormant? I haven't ridden in the limo in over a week."

"At least a month, under the proper conditions. The longer it's inactive, the more dangerous it becomes. Its hunger for its destined prey fuels the accelerant."

My inner tigress sat up and pawed at me irritably. We didn't like being referred to as prey; it enticed our need to hunt and made our claws itch to fight. "So either a witch is after me or someone hired one to cast a spell."

"It would appear. Such magic is ancient. It continues to be created in a cauldron and poured into a vial upon its completion. Since the magic targets a specific subject, anyone may carry the specimen without risking injury and dispense it wherever he pleases."

My tigress grew restless and paced within me. "I'm picturing witch fire lying around the compound like land mines. Please tell me I'm wrong."

Misha shook his head. "Witch fire is potent, yet easily destroyed when exposed to the elements. Those few who can cast such a spell rarely choose to. Their magic is squelched to give the spell its strength, and often it fails to return." His hand covered mine when he sensed my doubt. "Trust me, my dearest. Witches hoard their power—they're not ones to gamble something considered so precious."

"Unless the witch was desperate enough to take me out, or someone forced her."

"Or filled her pockets. Such magic costs more than most American homes."

Whoa.

Another apprehensive vamp entered the kitchen with her head lowered. "Master, your dinner is ready."

Misha sighed, annoyed. "She can wait. I will be with her when I finish my meal with Celia."

I couldn't help but chuckle. The supernatural world

was a twisted laugh riot, doubly dipped in a gravy boat full of crazy. Where else would *anyone* refer to dinner as "he" or "she"?

"What's on the menu tonight, Misha? Blonde, redhead, or brunette?" I asked.

I wouldn't have joked if I thought any of the vamps were going to harm their dinner guests. Vampires kept their beauty, their youth, and their bodies functioning by taking small amounts of blood from humans throughout the day. Between their supermodel good looks and the seductive pheromones they emanated, humans flocked to them. It also didn't hurt that the blood consumption process was the equivalent of multiple emotional orgasms. Misha especially seemed to be a remarkably great eater. I could usually hear his meal screaming for Jesus and all his disciples clear to the guesthouse. Oh, yes, being a so-called creature of the night didn't suck; most spent their days tanning.

But even though I knew vampires weren't as scary as Bram Stoker claimed, their "feasting" was not something I could comfortably observe. The vamps ate away from me. Since my arrival, Misha usually ate his non-stiletto-accessorized meals with me first. I suspected it was his way of bonding with me, especially since he consumed food because he could, not because he needed to. Only blood could keep him alive and young.

Misha smiled. "Do you truly desire to know the specifics of my entrée?"

I grimaced a little. "No. Not really."

Chef interrupted by placing a beet salad with mandarin oranges in front of me. The wine-colored liquid from the beets pooled at the bottom, smearing the elegant white china and robbing it of its purity. It reminded me of blood. My blood.

I moved the slices around, wondering if I'd be able to stomach it now that I'd made the comparison. "Misha, why would anyone try kill me? My assignments have been carefully concealed and the vamps and I haven't left any witnesses following our battles."

Misha placed his fork down and leaned back in his

chair. His gray eyes flickered with something I couldn't quite interpret and his voice lowered to an ominous tone that sent goose bumps racing across my flesh. "I've told you, the lake whispers to me the secrets carried in the wind. The dark ones see you as a threat. But one in particular perceives you as the key to its destruction. I caution you, Celia: it won't stop until your death."

CHAPTER 3

Virginia stood in the hall, watching as Misha and I ate our red velvet cake. She was possibly the most striking redhead I'd ever met. Her skin was flawless and milky white. Her eyes were a beautiful blue and always lustful when fixed on Misha. She was human, but she made me strangely uncomfortable.

At one point in her life, she'd been an extremely successful attorney. She'd originally met Misha at a charity ball, where they had snuck off together and had a moment. According to what Hank told me, Virginia had been obsessed with Misha ever since. She was now a "regular," allowing Misha to frequently feed and have sex with her.

Every now and then, a master of vampires chose to let a human become aware of the vampire society. This was allowed only because humans could be hypnotized into keeping their secrets. In this case, Misha chose Virginia. She no longer practiced law; pleasing and seducing Misha became her full-time job.

I leaned forward and spoke softly. "Virginia is standing in the hall."

Misha didn't bother to glance up from his plate. "I am aware of her presence."

"Would you like her to join us?"

"No."

I dipped my fork into the thick cream cheese icing and dabbed Misha's nose with it. "Why?"

Misha paused and attempted to glare at me, but he couldn't hide the sparkle in his gray eyes or his wicked grin. He wiped his nose with his white silk napkin before placing it back on his lap. "My darling, this is our time together and she will only prove distracting."

Virginia slid her outrageously long tongue across her collagen-injected lips. I felt sorry for her in a way. She didn't have friends. Misha was her universe. "Um. Maybe she'll tone it down some if you ask her nicely."

Misha let out a frustrated breath before turning to address Virginia. "Virginia, come in here, please, and do try to restrain yourself."

Virginia glided in, panting in anticipation. By the time she straddled Misha, her blouse was completely undone and she'd forgone wearing a bra. She licked Misha's ear and gyrated on his lap. I sat there gawking at them, a fork still poised in my hand. Misha rolled his eyes and gave me an "I told you so" glare.

I pushed back my chair. "All righty. I think I'll head back to my place."

"That's not necessary, kitten. Virginia was just leaving. Weren't you, Virginia?"

Virginia stuck out her bottom lip and pouted. She stamped her foot, then made a dramatic and riveting exit. I continued to watch the doorway even after she'd left.

"I thought for sure she'd obey you when you told her to behave herself."

"She did behave, kitten. Did you fail to notice I'm still wearing my trousers?"

I glanced under the table just to make sure. Virginia struck me as the kind of gal who could remove pants with her toes. "Has she always been this . . . obvious?"

"She has become worse as of late, since insisting I *turn* her vampire."

I straightened a little, surprised by the news. "Do you think you will?"

"I very much doubt it. Should I succeed, I will never rid myself of her. Moreover, I could never completely trust her."

"I thought your vampires are under your control and must follow your orders . . . or else."

"They are. However, once in a while some are able to resist, especially if they are reborn as masters. I believe Virginia would be among those if *turned*."

"I can see why you'd be apprehensive about it." I waited, debating whether I should ask what I'd wondered about for so long.

Misha quirked a brow. "Is there something you would like to know, my darling?"

"Hmph," Virginia moped from the doorway. She'd accepted Misha's command to leave the kitchen, but refused to go far. She scowled, angered by his dismissal, and clearly ticked he'd called me his "darling."

"Virginia, if you wish to receive any pleasure from me this evening, you will cease your childish behavior." Misha didn't bother to turn toward her; instead he swept my long waves behind my shoulder. "Now, if you will excuse us, Celia and I would like to be alone."

Virginia smiled at me before she left. It wasn't a friendly smile. It was more like a crazy "one day I'll eat your liver with fava beans" kind of grin. Like I said, she gave me the willies.

"You were saying?" Misha asked.

I shrugged. "I was just wondering how a master creates a vampire."

Misha leaned forward. "Why? Are you interested in becoming one?"

I rested my chin on my hand. He didn't intimidate me in the least. "No, I'm just curious. It's okay if you don't want to tell me."

Misha walked around the table and knelt in front of me. He took my hands, placing my fingertips over his crown line and rubbing them gently. I felt two indentations. He then slid them down a little to his forehead and I traced two more grooves. At first, I didn't understand, but then it hit me. "You pierce the brain . . . with your *fangs*?"

He nodded and smiled, but his grin lacked any trace of genuine humor.

"But wouldn't that kill a human?"

"Yes, usually, but that is why it proves difficult to make a vampire."

"But why the brain? *Weres* pierce the hearts."

"I think it is simply because vampires have traditionally valued the brain as the most important organ. We are intelligent and analytical. The *weres* believe the heart to be all-encompassing."

In that simple statement, Misha had spoken volumes about the differences between himself and Aric. I continued to gape at him. "So then, like the *weres*, you transfer your power into the person you're *turning*?"

"Yes, but unlike the *weres*, vampires do not risk death, should we fail. It either works or it doesn't."

"And this is how Uri *turned* you?"

"Yes."

I couldn't stop my cringe. "Did it hurt?"

Misha quieted, as if remembering. "It happened over a hundred and twenty years ago and . . . I still remember the pain."

The thought of him suffering made me inexplicably sad, perhaps because, like him, I'd experienced my own share of pain. I placed my hands on Misha's head and swept my lips over the fang sites. He grabbed my wrists, locking eyes with me as he stood. "Do not pity me, my darling. Look around. As you can see, it was all worth it."

I didn't bother to do what he asked. In my attempt to show him compassion, I'd inadvertently insulted him. Master vampires believed themselves gods who ruled the earth and there I'd treated him as my equal—or, as he saw it, someone beneath me. His dark expression brought me a sense of unease. "If you say so, Misha. Look, I'm tired, and Virginia is probably waiting for you. I think it's time for bed."

He didn't release me right away. Just when I thought

I might have to break his hold, he dropped my hands and nodded curtly. "Good night, Celia."

It wasn't a good thing that he reverted to calling me by my name—especially at such a volatile moment. "Good night, Misha."

I abandoned the kitchen and hurried out the back door and onto the terrace, hugging my body tightly when I felt the first sting of the bitter night. Misha usually accompanied me or had someone escort me to the guesthouse. He didn't tonight and in a way I preferred it. My mind tried to make sense of his actions and the sudden change in his mood. The more I analyzed the situation, the more I decided I was better off not knowing.

My sneakers crunched against the thickening snow in the garden, but the sudden alertness of my tigress slowed my steps. She veered right and left, searching for a way out of me and thrilled by the sudden aroma breaking its way through the flurries. I lifted my head to the sweeping sugar pine to my right, my lips parting at the sight of the dark figure crouching on the branches. He leapt and landed with the controlled grace of a predator, watching me as he rose.

Aric.

"You caught me," he said quietly. I nodded, my breath lodged deep in my lungs. "I know I shouldn't have come. But I needed to be sure you were safe."

Five vampires emerged from behind the trees, their sharp hisses forcing Aric's deep voice to morph into a challenging growl. They circled us, their vicious gazes fixed on Aric. "Try it," he rumbled.

I stepped away from Aric and faced the lead vamp. "Go back to your posts."

"The dog doesn't belong on our master's land, Celia," he hissed, his incisors lengthening.

"He does as my guest." My voice remained calm. My protruding claws revealed I'd skewer hearts like chicken if anyone laid a fang on my wolf.

The vampires advanced. "Move, Celia—"

"I'm not asking!" I snapped. "I'm ordering you to go back to your damn posts!" Misha had bequeathed me the title of Mistress of the House of Aleksandr when I first moved in. For the most part, his family and I ignored the so-called promotion. I rarely pulled rank, but I did then. Slowly the vamps withdrew, easing back into their hiding spots with audible swears and grumbles.

My breath released in a shudder only to catch when Aric's heavy black leather jacket fell against my shoulders. The same jacket I'd given him on his birthday so long ago. I lowered my lids to beat back the raw emotions of our breakup. Months had passed from that awful night and still I hurt so much.

Aric's brown irises flared as he gathered the soft leather against my chest. "You're cold," he said.

I backed away from him. "I—I don't understand why you're here." He straightened, falling silent. Snow fell in thickening clumps, coating his dark brown hair and plastering the ends over his thick brows. I focused on the exhaustion creeping from his five o'clock shadow to the creases in his eyes. The silence and tension stretched between us. Eventually words found their way through my lips. "Come inside."

Aric followed me through the garden and into the guesthouse. The lights flickered on, illuminating the green granite counter and stainless steel appliances. I kicked off my soggy sneakers and tossed my socks into the empty hamper in the laundry room. Without looking at him, I draped his jacket over one of the wrought-iron barstools and flopped onto the chocolate suede couch in front of the gas fireplace. I focused on the flames, the same flames I'd flung Barbara's wedding invitation into. Traces of the jab she'd sent via courier were no longer evident. But the insult and the slap to the face lived on. I tucked my bare legs beneath me, ignoring the throb to my injured knee, and waited while Aric kicked the snow from his heavy boots.

He sat beside me, resting his forearms over his muscular thighs. The warmth from his body trumped the heat from the fire. "You shouldn't be here, Aric," I said quietly.

Aric pushed his wet hair from his eyes, taking in my visage. "I don't mean to upset you, Celia. It's the last thing I want. But I needed to see for myself that you weren't harmed." He swallowed hard. "It's killing me that I can't be around to protect you."

"You'll soon have a wife to protect and look after. Don't worry about me."

Aric dropped his head into his large hands. "Don't."

My eyes burned. I bit my bottom lip to hold back my sorrow. "Don't what? It's the truth."

He angled his chin toward me. "Don't remind me of what I have to do. If this goddamn war hadn't broken out I never would have left you." He paused as the first of my tears trickled down my cheeks. He never could stand to see me cry. I wiped my tears irritably with my hand. He reached for it and linked our fingers. We both stiffened as a surge of heat spread across my body.

Instead of loosening his grasp, he squeezed my hand tighter. The haunting pain hardening his expression seeped into his hoarse tone. "I meant what I told you at Koda and Shayna's wedding, sweetness. You're the one I want to spend my life with."

My other hand covered the back of his. "Do you have any idea how much it hurts me to hear your words, knowing you'll soon spend your life with another?" He wouldn't answer. I slowly slipped away from him and moved closer to the fireplace, crossing my arms over my chest. His silence and the bitter aroma of his sadness made me think he easily sensed my pain. Still, I continued, releasing the dam on everything I'd wanted to tell him. "I get that a union of two purebloods guarantees a *were* child. I get that your kind has been decimated and needs to reproduce in order to stop the Tribe and any other superevil that threatens our world. I get all that, Aric—I do. But it doesn't comfort me when I'm alone at night without you." I turned to him then. "Nor will it comfort me the remainder of my days. You shouldn't be here, wolf."

Aric rose from the couch, his jaw clenched. "I'm forced into a corner, Celia. My animal instincts roar to me to come out fighting, but my commitment to my pack keeps me in place." He lowered his head. "I don't sleep anymore. And I haven't known happiness since the day I left your arms. I don't expect your forgiveness nor do I deserve it for what I've done to you and to us. Just know that I hurt along with you, that I suffer without you, and that I'll love you forever."

Aric's thick boots marched across my small living room and into the kitchen. He grabbed his jacket without bothering to put it on, then walked out of the house, disappearing into the darkness.

CHAPTER 4

The next morning greeted me with bright sunlight streaming through my large kitchen window and naughty Catholic schoolgirls pounding on my door.

"Are you going to let us in or what?" Liz wailed, following more obnoxious knocking.

It was their way of saying, "Good morning, Celia. My, don't you look beautiful today. May we come in and shower you with our cheery dispositions and love so that you may forget your hideous and sleepless night?" I placed my mixing bowl on the counter and padded to the door. I let them in only because if I ignored them, they had an annoying habit of watching me through the windows like a bunch of Peeping Toms.

I returned to the kitchen and removed a tray of sticky buns from the oven. They were sweet and stuffed with cream cheese—and they were Aric's favorite. We used to eat them together in bed.

Maria sat on the kitchen counter, watching me with her dark eyes narrowed. Supposedly, she was quite a skilled businesswoman. When she wasn't entertaining Misha with her leather whip and her collection of masks, she attended company meetings and advised him on his financial affairs. I wasn't familiar with her savvy side— only her sadistic bitchy one. She wrinkled her nose at me before speaking in her thick Brazilian accent. "What are dose?"

"Sticky buns."

Maria scoffed, tossing back her waist-length cinnamon hair. She had the same golden skin tone I did and similar-colored eyes. That's where our resemblance ended. I barely hit five feet three. She was at least five-nine without the kinky go-go boots she wore. "I can't believe you eat dat garbage. Consider de vampire route. Believe me, you'll be more satisfied."

"Just because they don't contain AB-negative filling doesn't mean they're not delicious."

Edith Anne strutted around the counter and glared down at me. "They look disgusting."

I really wasn't in a mood for her attitude. I smiled and rammed one in her mouth. The others laughed as she choked it down. I could tell she liked it, but Edith wasn't the type to admit it. She was the type, however, to put me down every chance she got.

I picked up a bun to munch on. "You're just ticked because Misha made you give up your presents." I'd dragged myself out of bed to find a key tied with a bow and a flat velvet case lying on my kitchen table. The case held a stunning diamond and platinum necklace Misha had given Edith for Christmas, and the key just so happened to start Agnes's brand-new Shelby Mustang. I had to give it to Misha—he knew how to hit the naughty Catholics below the gold-digging belts. I couldn't have come up with a more creative punishment and, whether the ingrates knew it or not, it had spared their undead asses.

Edith wiped the dripping filling on her chin with the back of her hand and hissed, "I don't care what anyone says. You'll make a shitty vampire."

I crossed my arms. "What's with all the vampire talk?"

Agnes Concepción draped her long pigtails over her breasts and adjusted her tiny librarian-looking glasses. It was something I'd noticed she did when her patience was wearing thin. She had supernatural eyesight; she didn't need the stupid glasses. Hank told me she'd started wearing them to enhance her naughty schoolgirl persona. And yet as ridiculous as I thought her entire getup was, I had to admit she was pretty brilliant. Agnes was the expert on, well, everything, be it rare species of monkeys or even rarer species of demons. "Come on, Celia," she griped. "With everything that's happened between you and the master, it's the obvious next step."

"Ah, no, it's not." I finished my bun and wiped my hands with a kitchen towel. "I hate to break it to you, girlfriends, but there's nothing between Misha and me."

Liz stopped filing her nails, at first I thought to ram her file in my eye. The fact that I didn't bang Misha like a pair of cymbals bugged the bejeezus out of her. Unlike Maria and Agnes, Liz didn't do business or academia. Liz just did Liz. She'd become their little leader after she'd won the fight for dominance. She sneered, mostly to show off her new set of choppers. "You may not be bedding the master, but you're a fool to think there's nothing between you."

"I'm serious."

Edith circled me with an evil gleam in her stare. Like the rest of them, she was very tall, thin, and beautiful. The good Catholics were often mistaken for runway models and used their charms to get anything they desired. For some reason, they didn't feel the need to be charming around me. Edith bent forward. Her gaze raked down my neck to my breasts. She licked her lips and her pupils dilated. It was similar to the way I reacted at the sight of a cheeseburger. "I see the marks we left on you have disappeared." She lengthened her incisors as she smiled. "Would you like more, so the master can tend to them as well?"

I smiled back. She didn't scare me in the least. "Go ahead. Emme would love that new Porsche Boxster Misha gave you for your birthday."

Edith's olive skin paled. The others cracked up. Besides prom night, there was nothing they enjoyed more than laughing at someone else's expense.

"Faster."

I groaned. "*Misha.*"

"Faster, my love, faster." He laughed when I snarled. "If it pleases you, I can push harder from behind."

I smacked his arm. "Knock it off before I throw you out of the damn car!"

Vampires were ridiculously oversexed creatures. Mostly, it got on my nerves. But when Misha interjected comments best said in a dark room filled with the scent of sex and sweat, it made me uncomfortable. Although it was his manner of teasing me, in part his propositions carried a serious offer. All it would have taken was a yes from me and we'd end up parked on the side of the road bouncing harder than a mob of horny kangaroos. That knowledge in itself scared the hell out of me.

"Behave, Misha." I'd been scolding him the entire way to Dollar Point, where my sisters and I had shared a home. As much as he'd bugged me, he kept me distracted from dwelling on my brief time with Aric.

Aric had told me he loved me. This was only the second time he'd shared the depths of his feelings. And just like the first time he'd told me, it wrenched my heart. Against my better judgment, I'd spent the night clinging to his words, knowing it was likely the last time I'd hear them and lamenting that our time together had ended so soon. I wished our interlude had been different. When I peeled off my socks, I wished that the rest of my clothes had followed, and that we'd made love. But as much as I wanted him, it was wrong. Forced marriage or not, he was engaged to someone else.

"I said, *faster*." Misha's lips tickled my ear, making me squirm and hauling me back to the moment at hand. I rubbed my ear against my shoulder. I'd insisted he come along, so Taran could thank him for the gifts. Hank followed us in the new limo, since we also recognized it was best that Misha not stay.

Misha wasn't happy with my sluggish speed, which even made an elderly couple pass us, but the last thing I wanted was to hit a patch of ice and damage the car. So Grandma and Grandpa could go ahead and flip me off; I didn't care. It was another cold January day in Tahoe and flurries spun from the sky, slicking the already precarious asphalt.

"If you wish to attend the brunch, I advise you, *go faster*," Misha complained.

"If you wanted a fast driver, you picked the wrong sister. That's Shayna's territory."

"You have told me stories about her spirited driving techniques . . . how did you put it? Oh, yes—she has a need for speed."

"More like a need to drive us along the highway to hell."

The flurries stopped before I turned onto our cul-de-sac. I honked the horn a few times, but that only brought me the wrath of our evil neighbor, Mrs. Mancuso. She stormed out of her house. She must have had her hearing aid at its highest setting. "Celia Wird! What are you doing here? I thought the neighborhood was finally rid of you."

My sisters might not have heard the car horn, but they heard that mean hag loud and clear. Taran threw the front door open and stomped onto the wooden porch of our custom colonial. Of all my sisters, Taran was the most striking and carried the exotic beauty of our mother. With her long black hair, deep golden skin, killer curves, and striking blue eyes, she was the walking cure for erectile dysfunction. Still, even without her loveliness, her mouth would have brought her attention. "For shit's sake. Leave her alone, you old fart!"

"Stay out of this, tramp," Mrs. Mancuso shot back.

"Die, lady. Grant me a happy birthday and just die already."

Gemini stepped forward and turned Taran to face him. His dark almond eyes stared at her with adoration before he kissed the top of her head. "Taran, honey, she's just trying to upset you. Don't let her ruin your day." His gentle words would probably have been enough to calm Taran, but Mrs. Mancuso wasn't done.

"Gemini, leave her at once before you get syphilis!"

Taran launched herself across our snow-covered lawn right at Mrs. Mancuso. It's a good thing for Mrs. Mancuso that Gemini's werewolf ability gave him superhero-like strength. No human alive would have been able to hold Taran back.

Mrs. Mancuso, finally satisfied that she had done enough damage, shuffled merrily back to her house. "Trust me, Gemini, you'll go blind," she sang before shutting her door.

Misha and I stepped out of the car just as Taran let loose some of her more colorful invectives. Everyone else, including Bren and Danny, our extended family members, now stood on our front walkway. Hank cackled from inside the Hummer. He obviously thought the confrontation was funny—I didn't, and neither did Koda. He growled at him and glared at Misha. "Anyone giving you trouble, Celia?" he asked.

Koda's long black hair did nothing to soften the strong planes of his Native American face. At six feet five, he intimidated without even trying. "No, Koda. Everything is fine."

My sisters and their wolves welcomed me warmly. Shayna skipped to me, with her long dark ponytail bouncing happily behind her and her blue eyes sparkling. Her perky personality had always put cheerleaders to shame. But it was her recent marriage to Koda that gave her an extra special spring to her step. She hugged me tight. "I've missed you, Ceel," she said. She released me slowly, the gleam in her smile fading as worry spread across her pixie face. "The witch fire . . ." she began.

I pursed my lips. "Let's talk about it when we go inside."

She nodded while our youngest sister, Emme, walked timidly to Misha.

"Hello, Misha," she said. Emme's blond wavy hair had grown longer since the last time I'd seen her. I chuckled as her fair and freckled skin blushed when Misha returned her smile. She and Misha were dead opposites. Emme reminded me of an angel, sweet, quiet, innocent. Misha reminded me of sin. He radiated sexual attraction and temptation like a brothel sign. He was well aware of his allure and so was everyone else. Liam, Emme's rock star–looking boyfriend, gathered her in his arms protectively and pulled her away.

Misha was about as popular with the wolves as *E. coli*. With the exception of Danny, who stepped over to shake his hand, the rest scowled at Misha when my remaining sisters greeted him.

Taran remained on edge. Emme clasped her arm and surrounded Taran with a soft yellow light, using the power of her healing to soothe her. It worked up until Liam opened his mouth. "Sorry about the syphilis, Taran."

Shayna threw her hands in the air. "Dude—She doesn't have syphilis!"

I grabbed Taran's hand and motioned to the Mustang before she could gather her magic and set both Mrs. Mancuso's house and Liam on fire. "Check out the new wheels."

The car was a big hit. The guys examined it inside and out, and Bren even asked me to pop the hood. Taran actually fanned herself. "Damn, Celia. That's one hot car."

"I'm glad you like it." I placed the keys in her hand. "Happy birthday, Taran."

Taran grabbed my shoulders and shook me lightly. "Are you serious? How the hell can you afford this?"

"It's actually from Misha."

Misha slipped his arm around my waist and smiled. "It's from both of us."

Taran jumped up and down screaming, pretty damn impressive in her sleek high-heeled boots.

Koda frowned at Misha. "What's the catch?"

The tension rose like a tidal wave. I inched my way between Misha and the wolves. "There's no catch. It's just a gift."

Gemini, who was ordinarily quiet and passive, slipped between me and Misha to bellow a bladder-releasing growl in Misha's face. "Taran is my mate. And she is *not* for sale."

"I am not trying to purchase her, Gemini. I gave the car to Celia. She chose to gift it to Taran." Misha's voice sounded calm, but it often did before he struck. Hank appeared beside his master, cracking his knuckles when he balled his hands into tight and ready fists.

I pushed myself between Misha and Gemini while Taran pulled at Gem's arm. "Damn it, baby. Please don't do this. It's my birthday," she urged.

Gemini rubbed at his goatee, clearly agitated, stopping his onslaught at the sight of Taran's plea-riddled face. He took one of those deep, controlled breaths that helped settle a *were*'s beast, then another before finally speaking. "If this is what you want, Taran, I won't deny you."

Gem regained his calmer disposition, but being *were*, it wouldn't last. I could have kicked my own ass for bringing Misha, especially knowing the wolves would be present, and especially on Taran's birthday. I turned to him. "Maybe you should go. I'll see you tomorrow, okay?" I hated asking him to leave. He hadn't done anything wrong, but I didn't want any more drama.

"As you wish, my darling."

Koda and Liam growled. When I'd been with Aric, they'd always teased us when he showed me affection. They didn't seem to appreciate Misha's term of endearment or the peck on the cheek he gave me before climbing into the Hummer. Of course, Misha wouldn't be Misha without leaving with a bang. He rolled down the window and flashed me a wicked grin with a little added fang. "Don't forget to present Taran with her other gift, kitten. I'm sure she'll enjoy it as much as her new car."

Taran's lids peeled back. "What other gift?" She likely wondered what could top the car.

I hurried to pop the trunk to retrieve the sticky buns. "Umm . . . we'll talk about it inside." *Oh, geez.* Between the attempt on my life and Misha's ideas of gift giving, there were loads to talk about.

There were several containers of sticky buns. Shayna hefted the one on top into her arms, and Koda carried the remaining five. He blocked my path before I could follow Shayna. "Celia, Aric has been depressed as shit lately. He disappeared last night, furious that someone tried to kill you. When he returned he looked more beat down than ever. I'm worried about him." He motioned to the stack in his hands. "If there're extras, would you mind if I take them back to him? It might remind him of better times."

They reminded me of better times, too. "You can, but I don't want to cause problems between him and Barbara."

Koda gave me a hard stare. "There is no him and Barbara. He's only marrying that egotistical princess because the Elders are forcing him to. Anara especially has come down hard on him—believing another pureblood is just what Aric needs." He lowered his head when he caught a whiff of my sadness. "Sorry. I shouldn't have brought up the wedding."

I looked toward the lake. "I know it's coming. Barbara sent me an invitation to her bridal shower." I failed to mention she'd also stuffed a photo of herself dressed in the lingerie she planned to wear on their wedding night with the caption JEALOUS? written in black marker across the bottom. The picture had made me ill. Between that and the wedding invite, I was sure the baby announcements were next. My fists clenched and unclenched. I couldn't imagine ever being so mean to someone.

Koda lifted his chin. "She did?" I nodded. "I wouldn't put it past her. She's always had a vicious streak." He watched me for several beats. "Aric can barely stomach her. He knows she only wants him for his status among our kind and that she doesn't care that he's miserable. If it weren't for his pack obligations, he'd have nothing to do with her."

The future that awaited Aric broke my heart. Whether we were together or not, I wanted him to be happy. "I wish the Elders would have chosen someone more to his liking."

Koda huffed. "Anara didn't choose Barbara for Aric. He chose her because she comes from a long line of fertile purebloods. Anara's focus is to help reestablish the *were* race at all costs. If he or the other Elders gave a damn what Aric wanted, they'd allow him to be with you. You're who he wants. And you're who he needs."

I closed my lids tight, not wanting to release more tears. My tigress rose to the surface, giving me much needed courage, despite how much she missed Aric's wolf. "We both know that's not going to happen." I walked slowly around Koda and into the house. He mumbled a curse and followed me.

My sisters were taking the food out of the oven and placing it along the black and tan granite counter when we entered the kitchen. Bren and Liam met me with smirks and implicit challenges. It was a game my fellow ravenous beasts and I frequently played at chow time. I smiled despite myself. It was great to be around those I loved and who loved me back. The Catholic schoolgirls weren't cutting it.

My sisters hurried out of the way. Shayna lifted a dish towel from the safety of the family room. "Get on your mark," she said. The wolves and I crouched. "Get set." My tigress flicked her tail in anticipation. "*Go!*"

The wolves and I raced to the stacked plates, playfully elbowing each other in an effort to be first in line. Never get between beasts and their meals. I made it first, my small frame and quick speed allowing me to slip around the snarling pack of "big bads."

Bren's growls were especially loud—after all, there were blueberry-stuffed crepes and sausages at stake. Taran shoved us into the family room as we finished filling our plates and then grabbed a few things for herself. I sat on the cream-colored sofa with Danny and Bren and dug in.

"So, witch fire, huh?" Liam said through a mouthful of bacon.

I sipped my milk, then placed it back on the coffee table. "Apparently. There are no signs of anyone entering Misha's home—"

"Which means one of the unholy bastards tried to snuff you."

Gee, Koda was pissed. There was a shocker-roo.

"Misha says the lake has been whispering sweet nothings in his ear again," I said. "Apparently some dark critter sees me as the end to its existence. Did you happen to pick up on any would-be psycho wearing a 'Celia Wird Marks My Doom' button when you reviewed the recordings from the surveillance cameras?"

"Nope. I went back a week—nothing unusual near the Hummer." Koda's tumultuous brown eyes cut to me and narrowed. He continued making his eggs Benedict his bitch without much comment. I'd tricked him into admitting he'd hacked into the vamps' surveillance system. And he hadn't liked it one bit.

"Aric wants you home," Gemini said. "Once he hears what the vampire has discovered, he's not going to be happy."

Without Aric there, home wasn't exactly the same, even though my sisters remained and the wolves frequently stayed with them. "As an Alliance member, I'm trying to bring down the Tribe just like the other remaining *weres*, witches, and masters in the coalition. It's not any less noble because I happen to fight alongside the vampires."

"The same dead assholes who are trying to kill you," Koda snapped. Shayna cupped his knee with her long slender fingers, instantly calming him.

"You don't know that." My gaze swept the room. "And what's to say I would be any safer here? Our days of flying under the radar and avoiding the supernatural are long gone, peeps."

Taran placed her half-eaten plate on our heavy wooden end table, between the picture of our parents and foster mother. "But at least then you'd be with your kind *and* with your family—where you belong, Ceel." I could taste an inkling of her bitterness. She hadn't liked it when I informed them I'd be leaving home to work for Misha, but as the months went by, her dislike had turned to resentment and now loathing.

"I'm not moving back. If someone or something is trying to kill me, I want to keep it as far away from you as possible." I tried taking a bite of my waffle. It was cold and suddenly didn't taste as sweet. "Misha wouldn't be investing so much time in me just to off me later."

"No, but he would to bang you." Bren didn't mince words nor did he apologize. He continued to dig into his plate. "Keep your eyes open, kid. Murderous psychos aren't the only thing you need to worry about in vamp camp."

"Son of a bitch. Is this shit real?" Taran opened her presents the moment Bren swallowed his last bite of food. She'd gone insane over the car. The shopping spree from all of us had floored her, and you could have heard a pin drop when she pulled the necklace from its velvet case.

Emme shook her head. "Maybe they're Austrian crystals."

I played with my hair. "Knowing Misha, they're real diamonds." I explained about Agnes and Edith's naughty ways and how Misha had chosen to punish them. That made everyone else, with the exception of Gemini, more accepting of the gifts. Taran immediately clasped it around her neck. As with everything else, it looked stunning on her.

Shayna shielded her eyes as if blinded by the dazzling necklace. "Holy sparkling rocks, Batman," she said.

Taran admired her reflection in the hall mirror. "Damn. You can say that again." Another small velvet box remained. Gemini snatched it off the table and shoved it into his pocket. I noticed, and so did Taran. "Babe, what are you doing?"

"It's nothing. I'll take it back."

Taran frowned and strutted to his side. "Let me see it."

Gemini reluctantly gave the little red box to her and we watched as she opened it. Taran pulled out a beautiful silver cross with a single diamond set in the center. Emme and Shayna stepped closer, smiling. The silver necklace sparkled despite the dim lighting in our family room.

"It's so pretty," Emme said quietly.

I leaned forward to get a better look. "It's engraved." I grinned when I saw the lettering. "Taran, read what it says."

Taran's eyes brimmed with tears. "It says . . . '*Mi Bella* Taran,'" she whispered softly.

Gemini had engraved it in Spanish, a tribute to our mother's Latin heritage.

"What does that mean?" Koda asked.

Gemini's face mimicked the color of his burgundy sweater. "My beautiful Taran." His gaze swept to her. "I wanted to get you a ring . . . but I know you're not ready for that."

Taran's actions spoke louder than any words she could have uttered. She removed Misha's necklace and tossed it to Shayna. Tears streamed down her face as she placed the cross around her neck and threw her arms around Gemini. "It's the most beautiful gift anyone has ever given me," she whispered. Taran had dated many men. But she had never found true kindness or love until she met Tomo "Gemini" Hamamatsu.

Gem murmured in her ear, "Happy birthday."

The rest of us returned to our seats in an effort to ignore the heat from Taran's thank-you.

"Do you mind if I try on your other necklace?" Shayna asked.

Taran snuggled against Gemini. "I don't care—"

She jerked away from Gemini, stumbling back against the wall. Gem grabbed her to keep from falling as her irises bleached to white. Everyone tensed. The wolves and I jumped to our feet, straining to detect something with our preternatural senses. Nothing registered except the frantic efforts of my tigress, struggling to free herself from within.

Emme clutched Liam's arm. "What is it, Taran? What's here?"

Taran's voice lowered to a deep, unrecognizable rasp. "*Tribemaster.*"

CHAPTER 5

If *Webster's* published a supernatural equivalent of a dictionary it would define Tribemasters as "the deadly and highly intelligent offspring of a demon father and a powerful witch mother, capable of producing spawn with predatory instincts who feed on human flesh" or "supernatural evildoers in charge of a large group of Tribesmen." They might even include an illustration of Noah Webster himself screaming and sprinting away from said evildoer.

I had the nightmarish displeasure of meeting a Tribemaster when the Tribe emerged several months back. He thought my sisters and I had the perfect wombs to bear his children. He also pummeled three pack Elders and Misha's maker, Uri, and he beat the unholy snot out of me and tore off Misha's arms. I managed to punch a hole in his head and rip out his brain, only because his claws were busy skewering Aric.

We didn't sense anything at first, until the ground began to tremble. There was a loud squishing sound, similar to someone pulling his or her galoshes out of the mud.

"Oh, shit. That can't be good," Bren said.

"Celia, get your sisters and— Where the hell is Shayna?" Koda's head whipped around, searching for his mate.

Shayna barreled down the stairs, holding the sapphire-encrusted daggers Misha had once gifted her and Taran's necklace fastened around her neck. Silver light streaked from platinum facets and into her arms. The diamonds glimmered in a burst of light as Shayna's power transformed the daggers into long and deadly swords.

Squish, squash, squish.

Gemini stalked toward the door. "It's getting closer. Everyone outside—*now!*"

"I don't want Shayna involved," Koda growled.

Gemini furrowed his brows. "There's no choice, Koda. It's too late to get them to safety."

Shayna jetted past me, her determination tensing her slender frame while fear blanched her face. She was spooked. And yet there she was the first one out the door. Koda and I bolted after her. I didn't understand her need to race ahead of us, especially given her blatant terror. I stopped short of plowing into her when she stumbled to a halt on the snowy front lawn. She froze, her focus glued toward the sloping entrance of our neighborhood.

I froze, too, when I saw what had crashed the party. *Oh, hell no.*

What appeared to be a giant maggot, the size of a city bus, slithered and crept its way along our cul-de-sac in wet and small slimy bounces.

Gemini rushed to my side. "Taran," he growled, "put the neighbors to sleep—as many as you can. No one else needs to see this."

I wished she could have done the same for me. The thing looked nasty. I didn't remember Buffy having to deal with this shit.

Taran stepped forward, releasing ribbons of blue and white mist from her core. They spread like widening translucent streamers encasing the neighborhood in a light fog. Unfortunately for Mrs. Mancuso, that was the moment she chose to storm out of her house to harass us. "*Taran Wird!* What in the name of sin are you up to?" Mrs. Mancuso's eyes crossed the moment she inhaled

Taran's mist. She flipped over the porch railing and landed in her hedges, snoring the moment her orthopedic shoes hit the lawn. It was a tense moment, yet one that couldn't stifle Taran's chuckle.

The wolves *changed* and prowled toward the Tribemaster. Danny, the pack's newest werewolf, awkwardly followed suit. Poor guy, he hadn't signed up to go furry. Bren had *turned* him following a near-death battle a few months back. The others moved with predatory grace, their heads lowered and their ears pinned back. Their actions promised a vicious assault and a battle to the death. Poor Danny just concentrated hard to put one paw in front of the other. The giant larva lifted his wobbly head when he saw them approach, though his eyes weren't visible through the rolls of pale gray flesh. His voice sounded wet, garbled, and sinister as his giant lips peeled back to reveal a mouthful of serrated fangs. "*Bring me Celia Wird and I might let you live.*"

Emme's breath caught. "Could he be the one who tried to kill you last night, Celia?" she whispered.

Maggots weren't known for their hearing. This one did just fine. His wrinkled face shot in my direction. He didn't know me when he'd first arrived, but now he did. He roared, furious and loud, his black tongue shooting out past his daggerlike choppers. "*Mine!*"

"Sorry, Celia," Emme squeaked.

I answered my attacker with a roar of my own, my anger and fear calling forth my protector. I took the offensive and ran toward him, yelling at the wolves to destroy the brain. My sweater and jeans ripped like Velcro from my almost four-hundred-pound tigress form as my claws broke through the frozen surface of the snow.

The wolves and I attacked as one. I leapt and dug my claws and fangs into where I thought his skull might be. His skin bounced like thick, rubbery gelatin—really nasty, slimy gelatin. I raked his flesh; it felt like I was scratching an oversized bouncy ball with human nails. He shook his head sharply, more to buck me off, and definitely not because I was inflicting much damage. I flipped back and sprinted around him the moment my paws touched the freezing asphalt. I circled him, searching for a weak spot. Strange rounded spikes protruded along the length of his back. I didn't think they were meant to enhance his beauty and hoped we'd kill him before we discovered their true purpose.

A wolf howled in pain as I leapt onto the Tribemaster's back. The maggot struck Danny hard with his monstrous head. Danny staggered back, trying to escape.

The Tribemaster flung his giant tongue out his mouth and spiraled it around Danny. He lifted him high into the air and slammed him repeatedly against the road. I drove my claws into two pink spots on the Tribemaster's head, mistaking them for eyes precisely the moment my sword-wielding sister stepped in.

Shayna sliced off the Tribemaster's tongue with an expert flick of her wrist. He roared in pain and spewed Shayna with black-colored fluid. The inky mess knocked her back, blanketing her completely. She rolled to her feet, narrowly dodging his snapping fangs.

I yanked my claws free, pulling out what resembled long, wrinkled, fluid-filled earlobes. I realized too late they were his testes. *Oh, gawd.* I shook my paws like a madwoman—or, rather, an extremely skeeved-out tigress. One of them landed on the hood of Taran's new car, splattering the windshield with thick pink foam; the other exploded all over Danny's back. He yipped excitedly over the Tribemaster's roars, knowing I'd caused some damage, but sadly oblivious to the amount of supernatural semen coating his bluish fur. Perhaps that was a good thing.

I shook off the disturbing chills buzzing down my spine. I didn't like how close the maggot's fangs were to Shayna, and neither did Koda. We landed at her side. Koda caught one of the larger fangs between his jowls and pulled with the force of his entire body. He extracted the tooth, causing the creature to writhe in agony. I tackled Shayna out of the way just before his head whipped back, barely missing us. His skull landed so hard it rattled the neighborhood and cracked the road. Danny wasn't so lucky. The Tribemaster nailed him in the ribs and sent him flying into our neighbor's yard. He landed with a loud crack and his head twisted in the opposite direction. I shoved Shayna back toward the house with my body and growled at her to stay put. Her fear was making her reckless. I worried she'd get hurt. When she didn't make an effort to return, I raced back to check on the others.

Emme knelt over Danny, trying to heal his broken neck. Liam perched at the top of the screaming creature's head. All I could see were his back legs and his wagging tail as he burrowed his way through the thick gray flesh and toward the creature's brain. Black blood and chunks of flesh splattered his brown fur. He'd caused major damage. In a few more feet he'd cast the blow to end the Tribemaster's life. Koda distracted the creature from attacking Liam by continuing his role as the periodontist from hell. Extracted fangs littered the street like piles of bones.

Taran stood in the middle of the road, generating wicked blue and white fire and waiting to strike should Liam fail. She was in a good spot—safe, and ready to sear the Tribemaster's hide. I joined Gemini and Bren, who gnawed at the creature's side trying to reach the vulnerable underbelly. I raked with my claws and pierced the flesh until I caught something long and slick reaching for my throat. I veered out of the way, narrowly missing the long wet tongues that ensnared my friends. The tongues had emerged from the spikes lining the Tribemaster's back. They squeezed, cutting through the wolves' fur and into their flesh.

I sliced through the tongue, tightening around Bren's large neck, only to have another whip me across the face and pull Bren tighter. Gemini howled, *calling* the pack. Another tongue encircled his muzzle, sealing it tight and silencing him. Usually another *were* would answer his howl. My ears strained to hear a reply. None came. The pack wasn't coming, and we needed help.

Having a master vampire for a guardian angel had its advantages. I concentrated on Misha and *called* him through the connection he'd passed to me long ago. *Misha, I'm under attack. Get your Armani-clad butt over here.*

I fought the other tongues trying to snatch me while I clawed my way up the creature's back. I sliced Bren free and charged toward Gemini. Gemini's oil-black wolf snarled and something cracked. A second identical wolf punched through his back, severing the tongues with a powerful snap of his fangs. My tail flicked with excitement. Watching Gemini split into two wolves never got old.

I helped Gemini's twin wolf free his other half and then trudged through the jungle of tongues toward Liam, slicing at anything that attempted to rope me.

Liam scrambled out of the hole he'd made before we reached him. He *changed* back to human, panting and covered with black ooze. "It's not there! The brain is somewhere else in his body."

Which made sense, considering I'd cut his male parts from his forehead.

Shayna's screams cut through the mist. "Danny, look out!"

Danny had attempted to rejoin the battle. He should have stayed down. The Tribemaster batted him with his tail and launched him into the side of Taran's new Mustang, leaving a huge dent. Emme lifted Danny with her telekinetic *force* and pulled him to the side of the house and away from the fight.

Taran, encased in an inferno of blue and white flames, gaped at the enormous dent before fixing her royally pissed-off face back on the Tribemaster. "For shit's sake, get away—*now!*"

We landed on the ground in time to see a fireball the size of an elephant slam into the giant maggot's side. It bounced off his rubbery skin and into Taran's new car, engulfing it in a sea of flames.

"*Son* of a *bitch!*"

So maybe the fireball was more the size of a Mustang.

Shayna sprinted across the lawn and attacked. She lifted her swords and rammed them into the two small holes above the maggot's mouth. She was now unarmed and helpless. The wolves and I rushed to protect her when the remaining tongues enmeshed us in a wriggling net.

Taran struck the Tribemaster with vicious blue lightning bolts. She sizzled the creature's flesh, but failed to cause much harm. Danny staggered to his feet only to stumble back into the snow. His wolf was exhausted from healing; it would take him time to recover. The pack wasn't coming and Misha didn't appear. We were seriously screwed until Emme got creative. She raised Taran's flaming car with her *force* and smashed it into the Tribemaster. The creature wailed in pain and the tongues loosened enough to allow us to breathe.

Shayna ripped the borrowed diamond necklace from her neck, ignoring Taran's loud and descriptive protests, and converted it into a giant translucent sword. Emme hoisted Shayna with her gift and onto the Tribemaster's back. Her face remained fearful yet resolute. She hacked through tongues and sliced us free. We fell to the ground. Shayna remained on his back, spinning with a dancer's elegance as she cut through writhing appendages. The wolves and I gathered for an offensive assault and rammed our prey with our claws extended.

"Taran!"

I jerked my head toward Emme's screams in time to see the Tribemaster lurch forward and swallow Taran whole.

No!

The Geminis roared and dove at the Tribemaster's face. One latched to the mandible and snapped the bone while the other gripped the lower jaw and yanked. The Tribemaster squalled as his mouth crashed to the ground.

The rest of us attacked the underbelly, determined to kill him and free Taran. Thick and sticky chunks of flesh embedded into my claws and black ooze dripped into my right eye, but I couldn't stop—I *wouldn't* stop. He had my sister.

We tore open the belly just as a horrible gurgle rumbled my front paws. Horror slapped my face like a tangible force. In my mind I believed he was digesting Taran, until a scorching heat built beneath me. I *changed* back to human, sensing her fire build. "*Pull back—now!*"

Shayna jumped off the Tribemaster's back and into my arms. I shoved her ahead of me and tried to scramble away, but I wasn't fast enough. The Tribemaster exploded. Tarlike innards splattered against our backs and propelled us forward. I landed face-first in a bank of snow on Mrs. Mancuso's front lawn. I pushed myself up with my arms and gagged. Everything smelled like rotting fish and my exposed skin stung from my belly flop into the frozen snow.

A pile of leftover flesh the size of a mattress stirred to my right. I stumbled to my feet and lifted the edge of the nasty slippery skin. Taran crawled from beneath, spitting vile liquid. "I found the brain," she sputtered, before she proceeded to projectile vomit.

Gemini's wolves merged into one and *changed* to human. He tore across the lawn and hauled Taran into his arms, gallantly stroking back her slimy hair while she continued to hurl.

It must have been love.

Danny, also now human, had finally regained consciousness. He staggered over to me. "What happened?"

Snarling echoed behind me. Koda's wolf form growled at Shayna. I wasn't sure what he said, since I didn't speak wolf, but it didn't sound pretty. Shayna put her hands on her hips and frowned. "Miakoda Lightfoot, don't you dare take that tone with me!"

I looked around the neighborhood. The universe had a sense of humor. Seven cars were parked on our street. They remained unscathed, while Taran's Mustang continued to smolder.

Liam and Bren tended to Emme, who threw up violently into Mrs. Mancuso's snow-covered rhododendron bush.

"Is she okay?" Danny asked.

Bren sauntered over to us, covered in maggot slop, naked, and obviously not giving a damn. "She's fine, Dan. She just got hit with a chunk of spleen." He sniffed the air and backed away from him. "But forget that. Why the hell do you smell like evil's nut sack?"

CHAPTER 6

For years, the local witch clan had gathered during the winter months and practiced making it rain. My sisters and I generally avoided witches, and they kept their distance from us. The supernatural catfight we'd had with them ensured we'd never be BFFs. "Weird" and witch just didn't mix.

I must admit, I enjoyed how the fragrant scent of their magic mixed with the bewitching power of Lake Tahoe when they called upon the rule of nature. And while I'd been drenched in too many unexpected downpours, today their ability to manipulate the elements proved useful. All it had taken was a call from Gemini for the coven to command a rainstorm strong enough to wash away the putrid remains of the Tribemaster. I may have aligned with the vampires, but the witches had managed to get awfully cozy with the *weres*.

By the time Misha arrived—pissed as all hell that I'd nearly died again, and fired up from his own smackdown in Incline Village—the disgusting mess had almost completely dissolved. Misha's vampires altered the memories of the firefighters who'd sped into our neighborhood with blaring sirens to extinguish Taran's car and arranged for a tow truck to haul away the warped piece of metal and chrome. Two demolished vehicles in less than twenty-four hours. That had to be some kind of record.

I glanced to where Mrs. Mancuso continued to snore loudly from her position in the bushes. Taran had tried to revive her while the vamps did their Jedi mind-altering thing so the rescue team wouldn't notice her. But when the lovely Mrs. M woke up in a pissy mood, Taran knocked her out again.

"Taran, I know you don't like her, but you can't leave her out there. She'll catch pneumonia."

Taran huffed. "She called me the Judas's whore child, Emme. I'm not waking the old battle-ax again."

Emme shook her head and asked Liam to carry Mrs. Mancuso back into her house. When they walked out, Emme was blushing and Liam was laughing. He jerked his thumb toward Mrs. Mancuso's house. "Hey, there're pictures of us shirtless framed on her wall."

Emme tugged on the sleeve of my bathrobe. "There were also stacks of J. R. Ward novels piled everywhere," she whispered. Her blush deepened when she caught Misha's wink. "I—I'll see if Shayna and Koda are done in the shower."

Misha moved to my side when Emme hurried upstairs. His more sober tone returned when he once more took in my haggard state. "I may have to assign you permanent guards. Danger continues to stalk you like a deranged ex-lover."

I pictured myself flanked by an angry mob of Catholic schoolgirls at the grocery store, hissing at the produce guy for getting too close. "That won't be necessary, Misha."

"I disagree. You are my most valued weapon, and one I must protect." He swept my matted hair behind me and stroked my jawline with his finger.

I cleared my throat and stepped away from his caress. "How's your family? Is everyone safe?" The vamps had fought the Tribemaster's army in Incline Village. According to Koda, the *weres* Gemini had *called* battled it out with the remaining Tribesmen near Squaw Valley. I found it bizarre the Tribe had arrived in Tahoe of all places, especially given the strong presence of Alliance members in the area.

"My family is well and rather enjoyed the combat." Misha frowned. "But you are my primary concern at the moment. The invasion was not well planned and rather foolish. The Tribemaster abandoned his subordinates to come here. Why? And why divide them into smaller, more vulnerable groups?"

Danny appeared from the downstairs bathroom. Considering what he'd been splattered with, we'd allowed him to have dibs on the shower. He rubbed his hand through his mop of black curly hair, glancing at me before addressing Misha. "He came looking for Celia. He asked for her specifically."

Misha raised his chin, the heat from his rising anger bristling against my skin. "To ignore his army and hunt Celia by himself suggests either extreme arrogance or foolishness. It also raises questions as to why he would want her specifically."

I tapped my fingers against my arm, remembering what Misha had told me. "You said the lake tells you the secrets carried in the wind. Did it happen to mention whether the Tribemaster we hacked to pieces was the dark one after me?"

Misha lowered his lids. Through the open front door I sensed a change in the wind. The vampires lolling on the porch tensed and looked toward the lake. The breeze intensified and swept into the house, and right into Misha's back. Harnessing Tahoe's power was a hell of a talent, one I didn't have a knack for. Misha shook his head and opened his eyes. "What seeks you remains among us."

Awesome. "Well, considering one of their supervillains just ran amuck in the neighborhood, I get the feeling the Tribe is what's after me." I shrugged. "Maybe they do know I'm your ammunition against them."

Misha waited before answering. "The Tribe appears to be the most plausible enemy."

Danny leaned back against the wall. He hadn't been

a werewolf long, so his lanky frame had only just begun to develop some bulk. "I'm wondering if the Tribemaster's invasion could have been a distraction of some sort. Just like when that witch raised all those spirits a couple of months back."

Gemini edged his way to stand next to me, his eyes never leaving Misha. "A distraction from what? We've dealt with every last disturbance reported."

Danny focused on the floor as he often did when his brilliant mind was at work. "It just doesn't make sense for him to go after Celia. Sure, she killed the last Tribemaster. And, yes, she's powerful. But why would the Tribe target her specifically?"

"Celia may be powerful, but in a way she's also the most vulnerable." Gemini raised his hand when I attempted to protest. "Your predator instincts and the physical combat you engage in put you at greater risk. Emme can assault from afar; so can Taran. Even Shayna doesn't have to face an opponent with her sword. Between her bow and arrows and her throwing knives she can keep others at bay. You have to engage in physical contact in order to kill. If the Tribe does recognize you as a threat — one worth eliminating and one who couldn't survive a mortal wound — it would make sense to take you out first, especially given you're your family's protector."

I sighed. "I guess. But am I worth the loss of — what, thirty Tribesmen and a Tribemaster? The Alliance as a whole is crippling them, slowly but surely. They don't exactly have numbers to spare."

"I realize my theory is very flawed, Celia. But you were targeted last night, and now today." He rubbed his goatee. "If I were to hunt deer, I would seek out the most vulnerable in the herd. Despite her speed and strength, I would catch her. I'm afraid someone is trying to catch you."

Danny tapped his hands against the wall. "You think a Tribe witch planted the witch fire. And when that didn't work, a Tribemaster was sent for her?"

Gemini shook his head. "I don't know. But it's too much of a coincidence to ignore the connection."

My heart pounded with a dull and determined thud. I looked to Misha. "I think it's time for me to go on another assignment. I want these assholes to know they can't mess with me." My jaw tightened. "And that I'm not their damn deer to hunt down."

Misha nodded. "There's much to be done. I'll see what I can arrange."

Gemini's phone rang. I stilled when I heard Aric's voice on the other end. "I just hung up with Koda. He told me what happened."

Gemini's voice lowered. "It was an all-out brawl, but we managed. How was the battle at Squaw?"

"We wiped them out. There were skiers who witnessed the attack. We rounded them up and had Genevieve's witches change their memories. I tried to get to you when I heard your *call*, but we were in the middle of the fight." Aric paused. "This is the second attempt on Celia's life."

Gem's dark almond eyes cut to me. "I know. Something's up. We just don't know what it is yet."

"If those Tribe assholes are after her, I'll kill every last one of them myself." In the silence that followed, I could hear Aric breathing hard, trying to calm his wolf. "If she's still there, I'd like to talk to her. My beast will settle easier if he hears her voice."

Worry creased Gemini's brow. It wasn't like Aric to have to work to wrangle his beast. And yet I understood. I doubt I could control my tigress if something threatened him. I reached for the phone—it felt heavy in my hands—and walked into the kitchen, careful to keep my voice low and soothing. "Please calm down, Aric. I'm safe."

I instinctively pictured my tigress rubbing against his wolf and my arms embracing his human half. I concentrated so fully, I could practically feel the deep thrum of his heart beating against my breasts. I'm not sure if he could see or feel me, or if it was merely my gentle tone that relaxed him as I continued to reassure him, but the harsh breathing on the other end receded. "Thank you," he finally said.

Misha called from the doorway. "My darling, may I speak with you a moment?" I hadn't even noticed him step outside.

"I'd better let you go," Aric said quietly.

"I guess you should," I answered back. I stared at the screen when he disconnected before tightening the robe around me and walking to the porch, where Misha, Gemini, Koda, and Shayna waited. The tow truck and Taran's birthday gift were gone; only a line of vampires standing at parade rest remained along the street.

Misha clasped his hand over mine. "Celia, neither you nor your family will be staying on the premises this evening," he said. "We can't be certain more Tribesmen won't return."

Liam spoke to my sisters. "The Elders want us to come back to the Den and bring you so you'll be safe. You'll need to pack for at least a few days."

Shayna crinkled her nose at him. "What about Celia?"

The wolves exchanged glances, probably trying to find the right words to tell me I wasn't welcome. I saved them the trouble. "Shayna, the Elders don't want me anywhere near the Den." *Or Aric.*

"Celia, it's not Makawee or Martin. It's Anara who's opposed to your presence," Gemini said quietly.

That was a hell of an understatement. Anara despised me from the first moment we'd met and had made it clear I needed to stay far away from Aric. As a pureblood werewolf he believed himself of superior status. Pures and whatever I was shouldn't mix, in his almighty opinion.

Koda glared at Misha. It wasn't until he glanced down at our hands that I realized his anger stemmed from Misha's contact. Aric and I were no longer a couple. The scrutiny from the wolves made me uncomfortable. I was about to release Misha's hand when I stubbornly decided against it. I found it hard to believe one of them would ever tell Aric's fiancée, Barbara, that she shouldn't touch Aric. Misha and I were friends, and considering the day I'd had, I welcomed his comfort. I wanted to call the wolves out until Taran interrupted.

"What the hell? It's my goddamn birthday. I want Celia with me."

"I know, sweetheart," Gemini said. "And I apologize, but try to see the invitation as a compliment. They consider you valued members of the Alliance and wish to keep you under their protection."

Taran scoffed. "It's more like they want to keep us on a leash, Gem. The only reason they want us there is because they're worried we'll join Team Misha."

Shayna's long black ponytail swung when she shook her head. "And how can we take it as a compliment when they insult Celia by excluding her?"

I didn't want my family upset, especially on Taran's birthday. The Tribemaster had seen pony rides and lollipops enough. "It's okay, peeps. That's what I get for throwing demon brains in Anara's face." I tried to laugh. No one laughed with me.

Misha tightened his grip on my hand and moved me closer to him and away from Shayna. "You will stay with me, as always."

The way Aric's Warriors glared, you'd think they had caught us in bed. My eyes narrowed, despite the flush to my face. I didn't have anything to be embarrassed about, and they very well knew it. "Thank you, Misha. I'll be ready as soon as I wash up."

I stormed to my suite, wanting to scrub the maggot juice off me and to distance myself from the wolves. *Shit.* Didn't they realize that, if Aric hadn't left me, I'd never have chosen the vampire road to Nutsville? Yes, I would have continued to hunt the Tribe. But it would have been at Aric's side. He fortified my strength and bolstered my courage. Only in his arms had I ever felt truly safe.

I washed my hair, pausing when I thought about how his fingers used to bury deep into my long waves when he kissed me. When I swept the sponge over my biceps, it was easy to envision those muscular arms that held me close and silently promised to protect me. I pictured Aric's large hands as my own slid down my body. I loved him, needed him, and desired him. My hands idly traced my curves as

I continued to think of his caress. I wanted him to touch me, to feel his strong hands grip my—

"Hey, Celia. We're out of soap. Can we borrow yours?"

"*Liam!*" I tried to cover my girl parts. *"What are you doing here?"*

Liam seemed confused. He scratched his spiky blond hair. "I told you, we're out of soap and I was wondering if—"

"*Get the hell out of my bathroom!*"

Liam sighed dramatically and shook his head. "Celia, you need to get over your shyness. I told you, the body is a marvelous wonderland—"

I hit him in the face with a bottle of conditioner. Emme appeared as I reached for the liter of shampoo. "Liam, honey, not everyone wants you to see them naked. We've discussed this, sweetie . . ."

Emme guided Liam out of the bathroom while he continued to hold his bleeding nose. *I'm sorry*, she mouthed to me over her shoulder.

I fell back against the tile. The water grew cold the longer I stood there alone, a painful reminder that nothing would change when I stepped out. Aric wasn't there to fight beside me. I was on my own. And monsters had already begun to hunt.

CHAPTER 7

"There is something I believe we should do."

I quirked a brow at Misha. He leaned across the kitchen table. Most of the things he "believed we should do" involved fur cuffs and frosting. I paused in the middle of pouring my juice. Behind me Chef swore as he cut watermelon to resemble a blooming flower. "What might that be, Misha?"

"We've been focusing on training your physical abilities, but have neglected your other talents."

I didn't like the direction of this conversation and put the pitcher of OJ down. "I'd rather you concentrate on landing me a new mission so I can kill the big creepy bastards hunting me before they strike again. My beast has grown restless with the need to protect me, Misha. If I don't sink my fangs into evil soon, I'll go nuts."

Misha continued unaffected. "If what seeks to kill you recognizes you as the key to its annihilation, perhaps you need an additional weapon." He smiled at my unyielding stare. "Your dormant magical abilities need to be awakened, dearest one. And I believe I know how."

"My magical abilities are just fine and dandy. Leave them the hell alone."

Misha met my scowl with a sigh. "I disagree. From

what you describe, you cannot control your *change* when exposed to animals."

"Yes, I can. If I know they're there, I can block their spirit and not accidently *change* into them."

"That's not what I mean, my darling. You need to train yourself to absorb their spirits and control the *change*, as opposed to trying to prevent it. It would please me if you could transform into any animal at will."

"I don't want to be considered a shape-shifter; those things are freaky."

"Shape-shifters spend decades making blood offerings in order to command their forms. I assure you no lives will be taken or virgins sacrificed. I'm merely suggesting an experimentation of sorts." A vampire entered the room. Misha sent him scurrying with a subtle wave of his hand.

I slammed my palm on the table and grinned. "Good to know virgins are safe in your hands, but I'm still not doing it."

Chef placed more food in front of me and glowered at my plate. "*Merde!* Eez zat all you are eating?"

Misha ignored my protests. And we both ignored Chef. "My love, developing your gift would give you an advantage no one else on earth possesses and would further add to your uniqueness."

"Don't you mean my weirdness? Misha, I think you believe I'm capable of more than I am. Aside from my tigress, all other forms I've managed have been temporary. Besides, it's not pretty when I come in contact with an animal—I have seizures during which I'm vulnerable. I drool, and my skin turns so raw I feel like I'm being raked by broken glass." I threw my hands in the air. "I can't even return to human or tigress until I completely relax."

"My darling, I believe that is related to lack of practice with your abilities. Which is why I am suggesting we start strengthening your power."

"No. Sorry. It's not going to happen."

Misha's gray eyes brightened when he flashed me his typical wicked grin. "We'll see."

"Where the hell are you going?"

Vampires weren't the friendliest of creatures. I muttered a curse and veered toward where Hank stood in the driveway. His black hair was mussed and his white collared shirt spread open from the cold breeze. All the buttons were missing and lipstick marks ran the length of his excessively tanned torso. I raised my chin and adjusted my cream-colored sweater over my skinny jeans. "Go back to your room, finish deflowering whatever coed you managed to dupe into thinking you know Rob Pattinson, and leave me alone."

I'd taken the day off to spend with my family. The giant maggot fiasco and my sisters' prompt escort to the Den made sure that wasn't possible. My tigress was restless and feeling claustrophobic. I needed to get off the premises before I killed someone—starting with Hank—and to avoid any of Misha's magic "lessons." Of course, Hank caught me. And of course, he told Misha.

"Master," he called over his shoulder. "Celia is trying to leave."

Misha stepped out onto the terrace that ran the length of his suite, with the half-naked Virginia fastened to his neck. The sexcapades just never ended in the land of the undead. "Do you feel that's wise, my darling?"

Virginia's hands slipped from Misha. If scathing looks could strip, I'd have been standing there in my thong. I ignored her and spoke to Misha. "Ying-Ying is checking for any magical murdering devices. Aren't you, Ying-Ying?"

Ying-Ying levitated in a lotus pose over and around the silver Lexus LFA Misha had assigned to me, yodeling in Mandarin. My sadistic yoga instructor specialized in extreme contortion and torture devices she claimed would help my flexibility. Mostly they just scared me. Her body circled around the car twice more before she glided down the hood and onto her feet. She said something in Mandarin before laughing psychotically and patting my back, something she often did during our sessions.

Misha nodded. "Very well. Your vehicle appears to be secured and the wards have just been reinforced against any magical assaults. You may leave."

I gave Hank a little pinkie wave before sashaying toward the Lexus, only to have Hank *and* Tim block my way. "Of course," Misha continued. "Not without escorts."

Misha insisted I take Hank and Tim with me. I insisted that I not. We argued for a bit and I ended up winning—sort of. Having picked up some of Shayna's driving techniques, I took off on my own and lost his vampires when they tried to follow.

On my way to Incline Village, I called Taran to tell her where I was headed in the hopes she and our sisters would join me. I left a message on her voice mail when she didn't answer.

I pulled into the trendy town of young hip professionals just to have lunch, only to be greeted by outdoor tents set up by vendors. Ski season remained in full swing and business owners were taking advantage of the tourist rush. I found one of the last spots on the street and slipped out of the supercar. Couples meandered on the streets in thick sweaters and with steaming lattes in their hands. Across the street a Japanese chef handed out kabobs of sizzling steak, chicken, and vegetables with a happy grin. He could so teach Misha's chef a thing or two.

My tigress craved sushi. I obliged her and crossed the street. After lunch, I strolled along the rows of tents and checked out the merchandise. Most consisted of touristy type T-shirts and apparel I didn't care for. I did find a stand that sold jewelry, and picked up a few earrings for my sisters. As the sidewalks grew more crowded, I decided it was time to head back to the land of the living dead and horny.

I took a shortcut through the rows and discovered a

merchant selling large bouquets of flowers. When we lived together, Aric bought me fresh flowers every week. I thought of him as I selected the perfect arrangement of white lilies and orange roses. I'd just paid for them when I scented a werewolf standing next to me.

She was a few inches taller and wore a dark red sweater and tan slacks. Her skin was fair and her pure white hair cut into a stylish bob. I thought she was pretty and carried a certain elegance. There was also something familiar about her eyes, but I couldn't determine what without staring. I assumed she caught my scent, because she turned to me.

She smiled kindly. "Good afternoon, dear."

Wow. Talk about polite. Usually, I received challenging or strange looks from *weres* when they caught my scent. I smiled. "Good afternoon."

"Those are pretty flowers you have there."

"Thank you. I like the orange—" I stopped speaking when the strong clean scent of water crashing over stones cut through the aroma of ferns and exotic arrangements. As Aric approached, I realized why the other wolf's eyes had looked so familiar. They were the same eyes she'd passed on to her son.

His expression softened when he saw me. I hadn't expected to see him again so soon, and despite the problems between us, an overwhelming sense of joy stirred inside me. Aric's steps slowed as he neared and as he took me in from the top of my loose flowing locks to my chocolate boots. A warm smile spread across his face, minimizing the signs of his sleeplessness. "Hello, Celia," he said.

At the sound of my name, the other werewolf's eyes widened. My heart drummed frantically against my chest and my tigress leapt to attention. "Hi, Aric."

Aric's long hair slightly darkened his beautiful light brown eyes, and his ever present five o'clock shadow was thicker; he'd probably skipped a day without shaving. But despite the small traces of fatigue that lingered, his facial features remained just as strong, just as handsome, just as sexy. I cocked my head to the side. The tension and the circumstances from the other night hadn't allowed me the luxury of admiring my wolf. But I did then, and drank every inch of him in. Aric in turn stepped closer, staring at me in the way that made my toes curl.

If the other wolf hadn't elbowed Aric subtly, I'm certain we would have stood there much longer. He cleared his throat. "Celia, this is my mother, Eliza Connor."

All of a sudden, I was eight again. My cheeks blushed feverishly while I shuffled my feet. "Hi, Mrs. Connor," I mumbled.

When they both grinned at me, I realized Aric had also inherited her smile. Eliza placed her hand on my shoulder and gave me a gentle squeeze. "It's so nice to finally meet you, Celia."

We'd spoken a few times on the phone, but I hadn't recognized her voice. I should have. It was just as kind and lovely as it had always been. "It's nice to meet you, too. Will you be in Tahoe long?"

The cheer faded from their faces. "No," Eliza said quietly. "I don't plan to stay more than a few days."

A horrible emptiness threatened to tear my chest wide open. I realized why she was there. "You're here for the wedding."

A sense of foreboding swept around us, reminding Aric of the albatross that awaited him and robbing him of the pleasure that had so briefly enlivened his striking face. Eliza watched him, her expression void of the happiness she'd initially demonstrated. She reached out to touch his arm and glanced back at me.

I peered at the flowers clutched tightly in my hands. The sudden meeting had briefly pushed aside our troubles and circumstances—enough that I'd forgotten about the Tribe, the attempts on my life, and the end of my and Aric's relationship. For those brief minutes I was happy again, beside my love, meeting his mother for the first time. Funny how reality could clobber dreams like a fist.

I didn't know what gamut of emotions played across

my features. I only knew I couldn't stay there any longer. I handed Eliza my flowers. "I'd like you to have these." I swore in my head when I realized my voice had cracked.

She took the bouquet, not bothering to look at it. Instead she searched my face, grasping, I imagined, for something to say. My eyes stung. I needed to get away. "I'm glad I had the opportunity to see you. Please forgive me, but I have to go."

I hurried away. Behind me I heard Eliza's insistent voice. "Let her be, son. She's been hurt enough."

I collapsed into the driver's seat and wiped my eyes with my sleeve, frustrated with how I'd reacted. It took me a few minutes to calm down enough to drive. I arrived back at Misha's so upset I barely remembered the ride. Resentment, sadness, and anger churned my stomach. All I wanted was to go back to the guesthouse and lock myself in. Yet, when I saw Misha waiting for me in the garden, I knew I wouldn't be able to make my escape.

Misha stood along the freshly swept stone path like a man who could crush the pyramids to dust, despite holding a Cavalier King Charles spaniel in his arms. The dog was completely enamored with Misha. *It must be a girl. The bitches love Misha.*

"Hello, kitten. It pleases me that you made it back safely—despite your lack of escorts." He pointedly glared at his bodyguards. Rivers of sweat ran down Hank and Tim's faces and fear of Misha's rage made them quiver. The Catholic schoolgirls wore smiles, obviously delighted they weren't the ones in trouble for once.

My hands fell to my sides. I didn't want to deal with any of this crap. "Misha, don't be mad at Hank and Tim. I'm the one who ditched them. And what the hell's up with the dog? I told you I don't want to participate in your freaky science experiments."

Mish sped to my side me before I could blink. "Come now, my darling. How bad can it be?" He swatted my shoulder with the dog's tail. I already had my guard up in an attempt to block the dog's essence. It didn't help. Either I was too upset or too distracted. Whatever the reason, I crashed to the ground in a violent seizure.

Hank swore. Maria said something like, "If she dies, I call dibs on de master." A huge commotion ensued and everything became a dizzying blur of images and noise.

As my world and teeth rattled, someone lifted me from the ground. I screamed from the torturous agony the contact inflicted. In mere moments, I found myself on a very large bed. My body shrank and my ears elongated. I panted profusely, tasting merino wool as my lolling tongue scraped against the expensive fabric.

My vision cleared slowly. When I finally focused, I didn't like what I saw. Misha and his vampires had me surrounded. Most had big grins and some were shaking, trying to hold in their laughter. Misha leaned over the bed, his fists digging into the mattress, his shoulders rigid. A sinister shadow darkened his stone-cold features. "Whoever laughs first shall die by my hands," he said in a deadly whisper.

There was such an immediate silence, I feared I'd gone deaf. I tried to sit up. Big mistake. The supersized room spun in a stomach-lurching whirl. I quickly flopped back down and shook my head to clear it. My long ears slapped against my fuzzy face. The shake had helped some, but by then I was royally pissed off.

What the hell, Misha? I told you this was a bad idea. I can't believe you freaking did this to me. Just when I thought we were friends you had to pull a prick move like this!

That's what I was thinking. What came out was, "Woof, woof. Yip, yip, bark, growl, bark!"

Liz leaned in close to my face, her ice blond hair hitting my little wet nose. "I think she's trying to tell us something. Do you need to go for a walk, Celia?"

Agnes Concepción adjusted her glasses and peered down her nose at me. "No, she wants a biscuit. Celia's always hungry."

I growled at both of them.

"She does not want a damn biscuit," Maria spat in her thick accent. "She wants ah steak."

"Is that it, Celia?" Edith asked. "Do you want a steak?"

No, I don't want a steak! I just want my body back! You all suck! Once again, "Yip, bark, bark, bark, woof," was what they heard.

Someone wanted to kill me, Aric was getting married, and I was a damn dog. I wanted to pee on the fire hydrant I called life. What I didn't know was that things were about to get much, much worse.

CHAPTER 8

"Bad, Celia. Off the couch!"

Liz swatted my butt with a rolled-up newspaper and had the ovaries to flip out when I bit her hand. "You're getting hair all over the furniture, you little bitch!"

Aside from the time I was awaiting my Nursing Board results and accidently came in contact with a skunk, this was the longest I'd gone without *changing* back to human. The entire day was miserable. Everyone took turns walking me and trying to force steak down my throat. I gave in after a while and ate the steak—but only because I was hungry. I refused to pee on the lawn, though. After escaping Edith Annes and Agnes Concepción's clutches, I found a bathroom and used it privately. It took some maneuvering, but I managed to use the toilet without falling in.

Misha spent the day pacing and muttering to himself. He barely glanced at me. When he did, guilt darkened the strong angles of his face. His eyebrows remained furrowed and that damn arrogant grin of his was noticeably absent. I repeatedly bared my teeth at him. *You should feel bad, you jackass. I'm drinking from a damn bowl!*

When nighttime arrived, I tried to make my way back to the guesthouse, figuring I could *shift* underneath the ground and come up inside my quarters. I was almost to the back door when strong arms grabbed me and scooped me up. "No, Celia. You *will* stay with me this night." Misha's voice sounded stiff and unyielding. I barked in protest. He ignored me, carried me to his room, and shut the door.

The minute he released me, I tried to escape. "Growling and scratching at the door will accomplish nothing," he said. "I need to ensure your safety this night."

I tried not to eye Misha. He wore silky black pajama bottoms and nothing else. His long blond hair hung loosely against his strong, muscular shoulders, and his chiseled abs and chest resembled stone. Any other bitch would've humped his leg.

Misha picked me up again. I fought against his hold. It was a pointless effort. I may have been stronger and at least twice as big as the average spaniel, but I would never have been a match against a vampire. Even still, I was an extremely stubborn spaniel, and I let out a warning growl when he placed me on the bed. He threw back his head and laughed. In a way, I couldn't blame him. How ferocious could I have possibly been? Nevertheless, I meant business, and I was going to bite him to prove it, but then he played dirty and rubbed my belly.

I hate to admit it, but it felt pretty damn good. My back leg started twitching and I melted in his hands. I relaxed, not enough to *change* back, but enough so I wasn't so ornery. Misha took advantage of my momentary lapse of anger to get ready for bed. When he emerged from the bathroom a few minutes later, I couldn't help but gawk at him. If Greek gods walked the earth, Misha was Adonis. But when he slipped off the pajamas before climbing into bed, he was more reminiscent of Thor.

I jumped off the bed and grabbed his pants with my fangs, growling and shaking them at him. A big sly grin spread across his face. "Do you need to go for another walk?"

You're just a funny, ha-ha comedian, aren't you? Get the damn pants back on, Misha! I've had a rough day and I'm feeling really vulnerable.

"Bark, yip, yip, bark, growl, woof, woof!"

He knew I didn't approve of his behavior and yet he picked me up and laid me against his chest. "My darling, I have not worn clothes in my bed for well over a hundred years."

Misha's chest was warm and comforting. He stroked my head in rhythmic and hypnotic movements. I struggled to resist his charms, but I was fading fast. Somehow, I managed to jump down and retrieve his pants. He sighed as if he'd caught me rummaging through the garbage. "Very well. I will do as you ask. But no more barking, agreed?"

I turned my back to wait while he dressed. When he was done, he pulled me under the covers with him. After a few minutes of Misha stroking my head, I drifted off to sleep. I dreamed of Aric's soft lips. How they swept across my skin the mornings he'd woken beside me, his body alert and craving my touch. My eyes blinked open. I was human again. And naked. I felt relaxed, warm . . . sexy. But the lips that sought me weren't Aric's. And this wasn't our bed.

Misha's tongue slid along my shoulder and to my neck in teasing strokes. His arm wrapped around my belly while his fingers tickled my skin. I turned to face him. "Misha—"

His lips immediately pressed against mine and he pulled me on top of him. My nipples became erect upon meeting his bare chest. I jerked away from him and leapt out of bed, yanking a sheet with me to cover my body.

"Kitten, wait."

"No, Misha. I can't do this to me or to you. I'm going back to the guesthouse." I moved like lightning, but it wasn't fast enough. He blocked the door with his body.

"Why will you not surrender yourself to me?" he demanded.

Humiliation heated my skin. My body, desperate for touch, had responded to his. I couldn't meet his eyes. "Because I can never be what you want."

"That should be my response. If I stank of beast and howled at the moon, would I then be your match?"

Misha was bitter, hurt, and completely furious with me. At first, I expected him to lash out, either with more words or the violence he was capable of. He didn't. Instead, he surprised me by stepping away from the door. He needed and deserved an explanation for my actions, but what could I have said? Anything would have been cruel. So I left, passing several vampires on my way out. They glowered at me, no doubt having heard our words. But their opinion of me didn't matter; only Misha's did. When I returned to the guesthouse, I slammed the door behind me. I slumped on the bed and reached for the phone.

Taran answered on the first ring. I spilled my guts like a disemboweled fish.

"*Damn.* I can't believe you kissed Misha!"

Taran's outburst wasn't exactly a ray of sunshine I needed. "I didn't exactly kiss him back, Taran. Like I said, he caught me off guard."

"And you miss Aric," Emme added softly. I wasn't surprised to hear her gentle voice on the other end. Taran always put me on speaker when our other sisters were around.

"Yeah. I miss him. I saw him today, and his mother."

"We know, Ceel," Shayna said. Her voice lacked its typical liveliness. "He'd gone to the airport to pick her up and called us on the way back wondering if we knew where you were. He wanted you to meet Eliza ... before she met Barbara."

"She was naked in bed making out with Misha," Liam said from some distance away.

I sat up in bed. "Oh, my God. Liam is listening in!"

"Are you sure, sweetie?" Emme asked.

"Yes, I'm sure! He just announced that I was naked and kissing Misha." A thunderous roar erupted farther away. Aric's thunderous roar. *Oh. God.*

I heard someone hurry away and throw open the door. "Liam!" Emme shouted. "Oh, no. What did you do?"

Taran yelled at Liam over Aric's increasing growls. "For shit's sake, Liam! Did you happen to tell Aric it was an accident and she left right away? Did you tell him *that*, Liam?"

Koda's deep voice boomed in the background. "How do you accidently get naked and start kissing someone?"

"It's not all that uncommon," Bren interrupted. "It's happened to me more than once."

"There's a shock," Danny muttered.

My jaw unhinged. *Good Lord.* Did everyone know?

"I need you guys outside now!" Gemini yelled from farther away. "Aric is completely losing it."

"Taran, please go to the window and see if you can put Aric to sleep," Emme pleaded. "Someone's going to get hurt."

I heard Taran's quick footsteps, presumably running toward the window. I grabbed some clothes and frantically began to dress. "Emme, tell Aric I'm coming. I need to explain—"

Taran interrupted. "Don't, Celia. It's over."

I stopped in the middle of putting my pants on. "Did you put him to sleep already?" I was begging her to tell me yes.

"No. He went wolf and took off." I heard her tap her nails against something hard. "I shouldn't tell you this, but I think you have a right to know. Gemini says the burden of continuing his species and being without you has taken a toll on Aric's animal and human forms. Gem is . . . worried Aric's beast is rising to the surface and taking over the man."

I straightened and let the hem of my jeans fall from my grasp. "What does that mean exactly?"

"It's his wolf's way of trying to keep him strong and protect him from his pain, Ceel," Shayna answered hesitantly. "The problem is, his beast isn't as reasonable or patient—and if his present condition worsens he'll eventually just stay wolf. Koda says it happens sometimes . . . when *weres* are deprived of their mates."

I closed my eyes and tightened my jaw. "The Elders must obviously know this. Why—I can't comprehend why they would allow him to lose his humanity!"

Taran chimed in. "Anara doesn't care, Ceel. He can

still order Aric to make pups with Barbara. All she has to do is take on her wolf form." She scoffed. "I think that bridezilla from hell knows it and is trying to work the animal angle. When Aric *changed* just now, she did, too, and went after him."

I missed my bed when I attempted to sit and ended up sprawled on the floor. I kicked off my jeans and rose on wobbly legs just when the door slammed open on the other end of the line and several pairs of feet trotted in.

"Hey, do you think Aric is finally going to mount Barbara?" Liam asked from somewhere in the room.

Emme gasped. I didn't make a sound. I was too busy begging God to kill me.

"If he does, maybe he'll stop being such a tight-ass bastard," Bren said. He stomped away. His voice echoed as if he were yelling out the window. "Hey, Lorraine!"

"Her name is Barbara, moron," Koda muttered.

"Like I give a shit. Hey, you! While you're at it, take out that cougar Aric has rammed up his ass."

"Bren, shut your snout. Celia is still on the phone!" Danny yelled.

"She is?" There were some rustling sounds and then Bren came on the line. "Hey, Ceel, how's it going? Look, don't worry about what I said. No one can make Aric scream like you can. One time I was hungry and stopped at your house for a bite. You probably didn't know I was there since you guys were going at it like gorillas in heat—"

"*Dude.* Shut up!"

"Back off, Shayna. I'm trying to make her feel better about Aric bumping uglies with what's her face."

"Oh, my goodness, Bren," Emme whispered. Like me, she probably couldn't believe the words pouring out of his mouth.

"Anyway, you guys were inspirational. After I ate the sandwich and had some dessert—by the way, your blueberry pie rocks—I picked up a girl at a gas station and had one of the best lays of my life. Seriously, you guys should tour or some— *Ow!* What the *hell*?"

The sizzling sound alerted me that Taran had zapped

him. She flipped out. "Everyone out before I jolt the shit out of you!"

There was a collective groan from the wolves in the room before I heard the shuffle of feet exiting. "Are you all right, Ceel?" Shayna asked.

"No. But I will be," I answered, though I knew it was a total lie.

"Good morning, Misha."

He was wearing his black silk pajama bottoms. And judging by the four exhausted and extremely pleased-looking women caressing him, he probably hadn't slept a wink.

"The Elder Anara contacted me this morning. You have the assignment you claim your beast so desperately needs." He paused to chuckle at the cringe-worthy suggestion Tramp Numero Uno whispered in his ear. "You will fly with a group of my vampires to Nicaragua today. A Tribe nest has been discovered. We need you to destroy it and the Tribemaster."

A Tribe nest was where a Tribemaster bred with human women to make demon children for his army. I still had nightmares from my first encounter. These poor women were forced to carry the monsters to term and then died à la *Alien*-esque delivery. It wasn't going to be an easy assignment, yet I was more than willing to take it. The supernatural war had claimed many innocents, and I'd grown sick of it. Even if Misha hadn't recruited me and the Tribe hadn't targeted me specifically, I still would have fought to take those assholes down.

The task itself wasn't what bothered me. I'd trained for it. What upset me was Misha's callousness. His cold, dismissive tone coupled with kissing that leggy blonde . . . He had some nerve. It's not like I'd expected he'd join me on assignments. After all, masters and Elders, like military generals, fought only when there was no other choice. Still, Misha didn't have to behave like an idiot.

"Misha, I'd like to talk to you about last night—in private."

Misha didn't acknowledge me, but the brunette licking his chest stopped long enough to glare and speak for him. "Misha doesn't have time for a little girl when he has women to keep him occupied."

Okay, sister, you're pissing me off. "What kind of women are you if he needs four of you to replace one of me?"

Misha tensed but still wouldn't look at me. And except for the one kissing his lips, the remaining "women" scowled at me. Knocking them into oblivion would have accomplished nothing. They were only human—stupid, slutty, and probably diseased, but human nonetheless. Besides, Misha was just as responsible for their actions.

"Fine, Misha. If you don't want to talk about last night, we won't. Just tell me, is there anything else I need to know about the mission?" He finished his kiss and then began another one with a different groupie. The little patience I had left quickly disappeared. "I *asked* you if there was anything *else*," I hissed.

"No. You will receive further instructions half past the hour. Go pack. Breakfast will be brought to the guesthouse. You are excused now." He motioned me toward the door and returned to his entourage.

My rage forced my claws out. I turned and stormed out. Between Misha and everything going on with Aric, I had a lot of anger to unleash. The Tribesmen wouldn't know what hit them.

Screw Misha, screw Barbara, and screw this whole stupid mess. I called my sisters to inform them of my absence, but couldn't reach them. I did finally end up talking to them—on the plane.

I jumped out of my seat when they boarded Misha's private jet. They smiled and waved, and apparently had been shopping. They slipped off their long coats to reveal matching camouflage tanks and cargo pants. They even wore army boots. I think they were trying for military chic, but the results were more like Special Forces Barbie. Taran sat down as if she owned the plane, tossed back her dark hair, and began applying another coat of lip gloss. God forbid we take on demons with chapped lips.

Emme tried to give me a small smile, but when she caught my not so cheery expression, she quickly sat next to Taran and shrank back into her seat.

"What the *hell* are you three doing here?"

Shayna finished adjusting her ponytail and grinned like I was the flight attendant welcoming her on board. "Misha called and told us you were going on another assignment. We've missed your last few so we asked him if we could come along." She tugged on the strap of her tank top as it fell off her right shoulder. Unlike Taran, she didn't have the goods to fill out her stretchy shirt.

If Misha had arrived I would've staked him in the ass. "It's more like he manipulated you into coming along!"

Taran closed her compact and huffed. "No shit, Celia. But that doesn't mean we don't want to help." She eyed me up and down. "Why the hell are you dressed like that? Aren't we headed for a jungle?"

The vamps and I wore shorts and T-shirts. I rubbed my temples to fight off the headache pummeling my brain with each passing second. "The plane is not going to drop us *in* the jungle. We still have to drive by jeep to the Bosawás Reserve. We're trying not to stand out. But forget how I'm dressed. Are you out of your minds? There's no way you're coming!"

Taran jutted out her chin and narrowed her blue eyes. "Look, Ceel. We're going with you whether you like it or not. Those assholes tortured you guys and pissed on my birthday brunch. Now they're trying to kill you." She pointed an irate finger. "That's just goddamn rude."

I reached for my cell phone. "Oh, really? Well, I think your wolves may have something to say about that." I hit Koda's number on speed dial, knowing he'd be the most furious.

My sisters exchanged panicked glances. Emme ripped the phone away from me with her *force* and held me in place when I lunged for her. I opened my mouth to tell Koda everything the moment he answered the phone, but my voice was immediately silenced. Taran's irises blanched and I felt my vocal cords constrict. I couldn't speak. I couldn't scream. I couldn't even whistle.

The vamps watched the drama with quiet and wide-eyed enthusiasm. The bastards didn't even lift a finger to help.

"Celia?" Koda's deep voice reverberated through the cell. "What's wrong?"

"No, puppy. It's me," Shayna answered.

He paused, already suspicious. "Why are you calling me on Celia's phone, baby?"

"Um . . ."

Emme's eyes widened and sweat beaded on her forehead. Her head smacked against the cushioned chair as I pushed against her power. "Hurry up and tell him something. She's too strong. I can't hold her."

I smiled to myself and stopped thrashing. My sisters never could grasp how great our hearing was.

"What's going on?" Koda growled. "Who is Emme holding back?"

"Oh, puppy . . . what could possibly be going on?" Shayna answered, laughing a little too hysterically.

"Put Celia on now!"

Taran covered her throat with one hand and motioned for the phone with the other. Shayna gave her the phone and Taran began speaking, using my voice. The words she used and the way she spoke screamed loud and clear that it wasn't me. "Relax, man. We're just out shopping for tampons and stuff."

I laughed silently. I could almost hear the vein on Koda's forehead pop. "What the hell is happening? This isn't Celia!"

"*Pssst. Pssst.* Sorry, puppy . . . *psst* . . . The phone is breaking . . . *psst* . . . up. Don't wait . . . *psst* . . . up . . . *psst*." She disconnected and gaped at the screen.

The vamps roared with laughter. Emme blushed two shades deeper than usual. "*Taran!* Did you have to tell him we were buying feminine products?"

"Emme, why do you have a goddamn problem saying the word 'tampon'? Just say it. It would be so liberating."

"Taran, the *vampires* are listening—"

"Tampon, tampon, tampon!" Taran sang.

Shayna's head whipped from the phone to us. "Forget the tampons! I think puppy knows I lied to him."

Taran rolled her eyes. "No shit, Shayna." She scooted to my side. Her irises blanched to crystal; as they deepened to their blue color, my vocal cords relaxed.

I touched my throat with the tips of my fingers. "How did you do that?"

"I've been practicing harnessing Tahoe's magic." Taran shrugged. "Sometimes it works; most of the time it doesn't."

I nodded. "Interesting— Oh! But guess what. You're still not coming." I grabbed hold of the plane door just as it was about to shut.

"Oh, yes, we are," Taran shot back, right before she put me to sleep.

CHAPTER 9

The villager called the nest *El Hogar del Diablo*. The devil's home.

Taran's spell had knocked me out for the entire trip. I woke cranky as hell and ready to make evil my bitch. And yet the young woman's fear gave me pause. I may have been residing with vampires, but she was living among monsters.

Emme's face blanched at the name despite the choking heat and humidity. I tried asking the young woman more, but she shook her head and hurried away. The residents of the small Nicaraguan town knew of the evil lurking in their forest, but they were too frightened to speak of it. I pulled my out-of-control curls into a ponytail and nodded my head toward an approaching male. Maria smiled and licked her lips. You didn't need a GPS with a vampire around.

"Can I eat him? He looks so tasty."

I held up a finger. "One bite. That's all you get."

The man led us to the nest with a big grin on his face and his eyes swirling from Maria's hypnosis. We had formed a plan, one I wasn't happy with. The vamps thought it best to split us up, but I refused to leave my sisters alone. My sisters sided with the vamps, feeling we needed to attack strong from all sides in order to emerge victorious. I suspected they didn't trust them and felt they needed to be kept in check. Regardless of the reason, we needed to act fast. My group would be the first to go in and the others would commence an assault from different sides.

Shayna especially made me anxious. She tossed the hilt of her new sword back and forth between her hands as we bustled through the dense vegetation in the back of a pickup. She wasn't able to return Taran's necklace to its original form. Taran told her to consider it her birthday gift for the next thirty years.

"I want to be the one to make the kill," Shayna told us. "I want to be the one to kill the Tribemaster."

Taran and I exchanged glances. "Son of a bitch," Taran snapped. "Are you out of your mind?"

"You and Celia have both done it," Shayna protested.

"Yeah, and almost died in the goddamn process!" Mini bolts of blue and white sizzled from Taran's fingertips.

Shayna veered on Taran. "Did you get eaten alive by demons?"

Taran answered her with a scowl.

"Did *you*, Celia?" Shayna asked, turning back to me.

I stopped drumming my fingers against the rim of the truck bed. No. I'd been bitten and I'd been tortured, but my injuries paled compared to what those damn Tribesmen had done to Shayna. If it hadn't been for Koda's attempt to *turn* her wolf, we would have lost her. She couldn't *change*, yet she'd received enough of Koda's essence to heal her ravaged body.

I leaned forward. "What's going on?" Her hands shook and that terrified look returned to her face, just as it had the day we'd fought the giant maggot. "Shayna?"

Shayna released a shaky breath. Then another. And another. She spoke very softly, likely so Emme couldn't hear her in the cab of the truck. "I dream every night that I'm being devoured by demons. I wake up screaming. Koda's freaking out." She glanced back to where

Emme was sitting up front. "I've asked Emme to use her healing touch to tend to my emotional wounds, but it's not working. I think I'm losing it, Ceel."

Blue and white sparks sizzled above Taran's head. "Celia, tell the vamps to turn around. She shouldn't freaking be here."

"I'm better since the fight with the last Tribemaster," Shayna insisted. "It's like it helped knowing I could still fight and protect myself. I think . . ." She swallowed hard. "I think killing one of these things will be the ultimate therapy."

I watched her closely. I knew revenge. We were the best of friends and the worst of enemies. But Shayna wasn't asking for a chance at vengeance. She wanted to feel safe. It's not something I could grant myself. Yet maybe I could gift it to her. "We'll see what happens. Just don't do anything stupid."

My sisters and I prayed before leaving the pickup. The Catholic schoolgirls kept their distance from us. Unlike some vampires who were devout Catholics—bizarre, considering they didn't possess a soul—these she-vamps embraced the uniform and very little else. It's not that a Hail Mary would have killed them; it's just that it probably made them nervous. In becoming vampires, they'd ceded the opportunity for heaven or hell. An eternity on earth was the only thereafter they'd know. If ever killed, they'd simply cease to exist. After all, you can't move on without a soul. That's what made Misha so powerful. He simultaneously balanced life and death.

We separated into our groups. My team and I moved silently through the area and stopped when we spotted the main entrance to the compound. A gangly man hauled a whimpering young girl to the gate. The gate opened and a vampire stepped out. I could scent his aroma of sex and chocolate from where we huddled.

"*Aquí está mi hija*," the man said. "*Dame el dinero que me prometiste.*"

I swore as the vamp tossed him a crumpled twenty-dollar bill.

"What happened?" Edith Anne whispered.

"He just demanded money in exchange for the sale of his daughter."

"Well, that sucks."

I raised my eyebrows at her. "You think?"

"Oh, calm down, Celia," Liz complained. "If you'd like, I'll eat him for you after we're done."

The girl trembled with fear as the vampire scrutinized her. He laughed when her cries turned into choked sobs as he dragged her screaming into the camp. Her father picked up the bill from the worn path and dashed off in a mad run. "I don't think you could catch him if you tried," I added bitterly.

The closer we drew to the compound, the cooler the air. A horrible sense of death and wrongness shadowed the nest like a cloak fashioned from iniquity and suffering. I nodded toward the demon children in the nearby trees. There were fifteen, sleeping upside down like bats. Fangs protruded out of their reptilian mouths and their long leathery wings encased their scaled legs and arms. Taran once described them as "the flying monkeys from the *Wizard of Oz*." I disagreed; the flying monkeys were way cuddlier.

The demons varied in size; some were only about two feet tall, others a hell of a lot bigger than my five-foot, three-inch frame. The leftover bones and skulls from their dinner had been licked clean and cluttered the ground beneath them. The bones were human. I was sure the Tribesmen had also paid about twenty dollars for them. *Bastards*.

"They're sleeping off their dinner. Let's keep this quiet."

The Catholic schoolgirls and I worked fast. The little buggers didn't know what hit them. Tearing into demon children released their innards, which resembled pulsating worms that slithered away until the air dried them into shriveled clumps. The hardest part about the whole thing was trying not to hurl. We almost lost it a couple of times and I really didn't want to see the schoolgirls vomit. Unlike Misha, they didn't eat food.

"Hold your positions and stay together. We're moving

now." We disappeared into the shadows, embracing our predator instincts. We stalked in silence. My goal was to sweep in and obliterate the biggest threat before my sisters' teams advanced.

I think it would have worked if Taran hadn't lit up the vamp at the gate like a Fourth of July Roman candle.

The vamp shrieked and swatted the blue and white flames burrowing through his back and engulfing his face. He exploded in a mountain of ash, coating the wood fencing surrounding the compound. If Taran had taken the offensive without us present, there must've been a reason for it.

"Attack!"

We ran full out. Werebears belonging to the Tribe leapt over the high wooden walls, easily clearing the barbed-wire fencing that wound along on top. They landed with a hard pound, indenting the moist forest floor and blocking our paths to the gate. I kicked my opponent in his temple and severed his head with my claws as he spun. I grabbed the one on top of Liz and yanked him into a headlock. She leapt to her feet and broke through his chest, ripping out his heart in one pull.

The heart finished beating in her hand. "Do you want a bite?" she offered.

Was she trying to make me sick? I ripped the arms off the bear that was trying to decapitate Maria. "Er, no, thanks."

"Are you sure? He's a sun bear. They're considered a delicacy in—"

Rather than listening to what vamps considered yummy morsels, I raced to find my sisters. I ran into Emme first. She'd quickly freed a bunch of villagers from a large cage using her power. They huddled against one another, too terrified to move.

"*Corran, corran. Escapen de aquí.*" Emme's small stature and soft features made her appear more friend than foe. The shaking villagers exchanged brief panicked glances before jetting out of the cell at her urging.

Anger fueled my onslaught *and* Emme's. Once the

villagers cleared the gate, she flung shards of firewood stacked in a corner and impaled the Tribesmen sprinting toward us. Those whose hearts she missed were quickly beheaded by me or by Misha's vampires.

Taran was literally rolling in the mud with another witch. They screamed, slapped, and tore each other's hair. They may have lacked a true fighter's grace, yet the sparks from their clashing magic collided hard enough to charge the air. It was the ultimate catfight, one Bren would have paid to see, and one I couldn't tolerate. I grabbed the witch by her neck and flung her away from Taran. Edith finished her off, but not before tasting the merchandise.

"Come on, Edith. We don't have time for this."

"Celia, it's hotter than blazes out here. I'm thirsty."

Taran's screaming interrupted my reprimand. "*Celia!*"

More than twenty cages lined the wall. In one of them, a poor village girl had just given birth to a demon child. The thing had busted through her stomach and splattered her organs against the metal bars. I'd witnessed this too many times, but it didn't make the moment any less horrifying. The newborn jumped through the cage toward Taran. I snatched him out of the air with my claws. His leathery wings slapped against my knuckles and his incensed screeches pained my sensitive ears. The warm slick blood slathering his reptilian body made him hard to hold. He bit into my wrist and licked my skin eagerly. I slammed him into the muddy ground and stomped on him. Bones snapped beneath my sneaker and yet the little bugger still wouldn't die. Worst of all, he spoke in a dark psycho voice, "*Celia Wird.*"

I immediately cracked his head off like a Kewpie doll, not wanting to hear him say my name again. Maria approached me as his insides scurried away to dry beneath a rusted wheelbarrow filled with bones. "Hmm, you must have left quite an impression in hell if dey know you already."

Perhaps she'd meant it as a compliment. I'd never

been popular in high school, but knowing I was up for homecoming queen in Hades did nothing to lift my self-esteem.

More demons charged us. I turned my fear and trepidation inward and morphed them into anger and hate. My claws dug into chests to stab hearts, and punctured through eyes and into brains. If I let my human side think through my actions, I'd hurl from the brutality. So I called forth my beast to guide my hands. She could hunt, she could maim, she could protect, and she could push me forward. Her eyes replaced mine as I stalked through the mounds of slithering innards, ignoring the reeking scent of old blood, rotting flesh, and the mingling of defecation and sweat. Taran didn't have a tigress to strengthen her and the gore became too much. She collapsed on her hands and knees, puking.

My tigress compelled me to the cages, to those we couldn't allow to escape. The naked women inside cackled hysterically or drooped on their sides, staring expressionless ahead. All of them were pregnant. Some twitched with prebirth seizures.

My tigress drove me to kill them, knowing what slithered beneath their protruding bellies. My human side couldn't, and wrestled to find a more merciful solution. I yanked Taran to her feet. Black strands of her hair stuck to her pale, sweat-soaked face.

"Taran, you have to draw up some magic-born sunlight." Her lids peeled back and she wrenched herself loose from my grasp.

"Hell. *No!* It's a pure light. It'll kill the vamps and demons, but it will also toast these women like bread!"

I gave her a hard stare. "I know, Taran."

"Goddamn it, Celia—I'm not killing innocents!"

"Taran, they're only vessels for the creatures. They're suffering. The only way to help them is to free their souls." She seemed torn. "Do it, Taran." More women fell to the filthy floor, seizing, their bellies vibrating from the demon children restless to get out. "Do it now!"

Emme stumbled to my side, her face the color of

chalk. She wiped the perspiration from her eyes. "Wh-what about Misha's family?"

"I'll take care of them. Taran, go. Emme, you protect her." The air charged and cracked around us as Taran drew from the magic surrounding the forest. I tore the head off a weremonkey trying to stumble to his feet and tossed it loudly against a steel drum used for fire. "SPF fifty!" I screamed.

At the sound of my oh *so* clever secret code words, Misha's vamps abandoned their targets and scrambled for cover. Their adversaries paused. One lifted his fist in the air and screamed in victory. Boy, was he in for a letdown.

A sapphire and twirling white mist permeated into the cages and put the women to sleep just as Taran levitated in the air. Her irises blanched to clear and scorching heat built around her small figure. I shielded my eyes against the giant explosion of light that cut through the air like the snap of a whip.

I blinked my eyes to clear the spots as the torrent of light faded. What remained of the women, opposing vamps, and demon children were mere ashes. I caught Taran as she fell. She would no longer be able to fight. The magic she had performed had drained her completely. I cradled her in my arms. "Look, Taran," I said as I held her up. "You did it."

From the cages, glittering wisps of light bounded up to the sky. I prayed Saint Peter was welcoming the battered and tortured souls into heaven. Taran smiled and tears brimmed in her eyes briefly before she wiped them away and swore under her breath. I helped her to her feet and released her when Emme grasped her arm.

Misha's vampires trailed the remaining *weres*, which were busting through the wooden fencing in an effort to escape. I thought to give chase and force a Tribesman to reveal the whereabouts of his master. It seemed I didn't need to. A horrible roaring erupted from a large structure composed of a tin roof and cinder-block walls.

"Liz, Maria, get over here!" They scrambled to my side as if jolted by live wire.

Liz glanced nervously toward the building. "What, Celia?"

"Take Taran and Emme back to that hotel we spotted on our way into the village. If we're not back within the hour, get on the plane and back to Tahoe."

"No," Maria protested. "De master says we are to stay by your side and keep you safe."

"Misha is safe at home getting it on with his harem of hussies. *I'm* in charge, and I'm ordering you to keep my sisters safe!"

"I don't want to leave you, Celia," Emme said.

"Emme, Taran is vulnerable and I need you to protect her. Maria and Liz will see to your safety." I growled at my good Catholics. "Won't you, girls?"

Glass shattered and Hank flew past us like an irate, battered missile. Blood spurted from a deep gash on his head and onto his face. It sealed from one blink to the next. His shirt was missing and his shorts appeared to have been used as a tissue by something with a nasty cold. He leapt to his feet with a hiss and bolted back into the building. That was all the convincing Maria and Liz needed. They hauled my sisters into their arms and disappeared into the darkening forest. Night was quickly approaching. My tigress eyes could help me see in the darkness. Emme and Taran didn't have that advantage. I needed them to be safe. And I needed to find Shayna. I chased after Hank and into the chaos that awaited.

The best way to describe what I saw was a bar brawl. Lynyrd Skynyrd even blasted from an old boom box in the corner. Fists and chairs flew harder than at last call at a biker bar. I ducked as a bottle of Victoria beer flew over my head and smashed into the crumbling cinder block wall.

Misha's vampires held their own against the remaining Tribesmen. Agnes and Edith stumbled to my side, half naked, but that was nothing new. "Let's finish this," I told them.

They launched into the foray, shrieking like a band of angry streetwalkers in serious need of penicillin. Since blood already coated my skin, I had no problem attracting attention. A flock of skinny, winged newborns flew toward me, their tongue slithering like leeches through their fangs. As a sick joke, some idiot had tied baby bonnets on them. I decapitated two and crushed a third just as a witch set her sights on Tim. He hollered when a dark cloud of green swallowed him whole. I seized a demon child leaping toward the ceiling, snapped off his head, and nailed the witch in her face with it. She released Tim from her spell and veered toward me. "*Celia*," she said, blood oozing from her nose.

Witches were funny. Not in a ha-ha kind of way, more like insanely twisted. They lacked in strength and speed, but compensated with spell work and personality. She spat at me from a distance. "*Puta sucia. Te mato, puta—te mato!*"

I didn't like being threatened, *or* insulted. "*You're* the dirty bitch!" I growled. *Hoo-rah! Take that.*

She'd started it, but she didn't seem to appreciate the name-calling. Her magic assembled in a nauseating bouquet of molding herbs and rotting leaves. With every step, she barraged me with fireballs swirling with green and black smoke. But she was too slow and no match for my speed. I swiped demon children from the air and pitched them into her fireballs, using them to shield me from her flames. They exploded like mini fireworks stuffed with guts. Well, *shit*, didn't that make her mad?

"*Hija de la gran chingada!*"

I didn't catch what that meant. But I knew it wasn't a good sign when her eyes rolled behind her head and disappeared into her skull. A giant swamp-colored ball rolled out of her mouth and spun toward me. It wasn't anything I thought I could or should fight. Nor did I want it anywhere near me. I lifted what remained of a large table and fanned it back at her. I wasn't sure it had worked since I was batting the table like the dickens, but I snuck a peek at the sound of her screeches.

Bile rose to my throat. She wasn't a cute girl to start with, but even the most beautiful of starlets could not have pulled off her new look. Snakes spun free from her eye sockets—and every other orifice in her body—like pulled Slinkies. The serpents coiled around her limbs and torso, feasting on her flesh as they twirled and squeezed. My stomach roiled with disgust and terror. Her fate was meant for me. I needed to find Shayna, and we needed to finish this mission—now.

The harsh clinking of metal signaled her arrival. With Jedi grace and speed, she beheaded four machete-wielding vampires. I fought my way to her, killing every Tribesmen in my way. "*Shayna!*"

I ducked when she flung knives over my head. Her reflexes and skill were startling. She hit a *were* in the throat and a vamp through the eye, allowing Misha's vampires to kill them with ease.

Shayna grunted and whirled until the fighting around us gradually ceased. Her eyes darted wildly, seeking more targets. I approached her slowly, pulling my tigress back and speaking softly. "It's okay, Shayna. They're dead. Take a breath, babe."

The floor was littered with the remains of dead Tribesmen. I had to step over several limbs to reach my sister. Our group stood triumphantly. Hank pointed to the decapitated torso on the floor. "Yeahhh! Take that, fuckers!"

I lifted the edge of my tank to wipe the blood trickling from my chin. "It's not over yet, Hank. We need to find the Tribemaster."

You'd have thought I'd sent the villainous bastard an Evite. The scent of pure evil filled the room, sharp and sour all at once, announcing the Tribemaster's arrival. I swore when my tigress fixed on the rear entrance. The good news was, there wasn't a Tribemaster. The really bad news was, there were two.

Twins. Fantastic. Just what we needed. Our mission had just doubled in size, viciousness, and ugly. Their faces were similar to that of rhinos. Tusks protruded over their drawer-sized snouts. Silvery reptilian scales covered their skin like body armor. And, funny thing, the last rhino I saw didn't have long leathery wings, glowing yellow eyes, or fangs the size of yardsticks.

We charged on pure instinct. There was no command, no hesitation. I dodged a barrage of swings from arms as thick as tree limbs and grabs from meaty fingers tipped with six-inch nails. Five of Misha's vamps weren't so lucky. Blood splattered my face when the Tribemaster I fought ripped them in half. I fell to a crouch and dug my claws into his stomach, attempting to tear it open. They stuck in his thick belly and I couldn't break free . . . until he hauled me up by my hair. He jerked me with such force my head snapped painfully back and two of my nails stayed embedded in his stomach.

He lifted me to his face. "*Vení, muñeca, te quiero besar.*"

It was bad enough that he called me "doll" and I wasn't lovin' the fact that he wanted to make out with me, but it was his dark demonic voice that made my skin crawl.

His tongue reached out to kiss me. I brought both my fists down to his snout. My claws raked down his chest when he dropped me, allowing me to *shift* him through the cement floor.

I plunged him deep into the earth, so only his neck and head were exposed. "*Shayna!*"

Shayna's head whipped toward me. She sprinted from the fight with the other twin. Her opportunity had arrived. And damn it if I wasn't going to let her take it.

Chunks of concrete burst upward as the Tribemaster punched through the floor. I dove on his free arm and ducked, allowing Shayna to sever his head in one clean swoop. His insides spewed like a volcano and sprayed my back in quivering chunks. I lurched to my feet, ignoring the remains crawling down my legs, and bounded toward the other twin.

Shayna chased the head she'd disjoined to finish off the brain. I heard her hacking through the skull behind me as I reached the remaining Tribemaster. The last of Misha's vamps covered him like a swarm of insects. The

Tribemaster roared with pain. But Misha's family wasn't enough to cripple him. He ripped them off and tore their limbs as if shucking corn. I propelled myself into the air and into a jumping spinning kick. He caught my leg and crushed my ankle.

My screams turned to roars. I *changed*, knowing my human body wasn't enough to make the kill. I maneuvered my body and went for his throat. My fangs accomplished what my claws could not; I tasted his blood as I ruptured his larynx and pulled it apart. He heaved my body and threw me into the wall. It was like a Bugs Bunny cartoon. I crashed to the floor and looked up to see the perfect outline of my body dented into the cinder block. Too bad we never made it to a commercial break. I could have used the opportunity to remember how to breathe and to stop my bleeding.

I struggled to get up. Shayna appeared, twirling her sword with dizzying speed. She cut the Tribemaster's legs off at the knees. Hank jumped onto his shoulders and wrenched his jaw back while four vampires buried their fangs into his arms. "*Kill him!*" Hank hollered.

I stumbled to my four paws, gaining momentum with each step I took. My claws scythed through his neck as I tackled him to the ground. His scale-skinned neck split near the torso. I thought we had him until what felt like a bomb exploded beneath me.

I remembered flying, then falling . . . rather ungracefully and painfully against a pile of rubble. The shock of the impact forced me to *change* back. When the black smoke and dust had cleared, the Tribemaster was gone. Shayna lay sprawled a few feet away, a giant shard of glass embedded in her chest. I crawled to her side, coughing from the dust layering the air.

Her breathing was fast and ragged, and a delighted smile lit her dirty face. It freaked me out. I thought she was going into hysterics. I tugged out the glass and quickly covered the site, but there was no blood. There was no oozing. There was . . . nothing. I removed my hand to examine the wound closely. My lips parted with shock. It had already sealed. She sat up by herself and grinned even wider. "I may not be able to howl at the moon, Ceel, but lookie what I can do."

Despite the agony vibrating through my organs in painful rushes, I smiled back. Koda wasn't able to *turn* her into a wolf, but he'd given her the perfect gift: the ability to heal.

CHAPTER 10

Maria held someone's severed leg and waved it as she spoke. "Whose foot is dis? Oops—sorry, Celia," she said when blood from the limb splashed me in the face. "Hello, I'm trying to sort here."

"I think it's mine," a vamp mumbled. He lay draped in one of the truck beds, on top of two other vamps.

Maria huffed. "It cannot be. You are already holding two."

He lifted one leg in each hand. "Yeah, but these are both lefties. And see, now I have an extra knee."

The rest of Misha's vampires had returned after tracking the enemy *weres* who'd tried to escape. The Tribemaster we'd fought remained at large. The vamps had found only more caged villagers. They'd released them following a light snack. I wasn't pleased, but what could I say? Saving the world worked up an appetite.

Agnes Concepción, Edith Anne, Hank, and Tim were among the few in our group still completely functioning. Most of Misha's other vamps were in bad shape and needed blood to regenerate.

"I guess you should get to the village so you can find something to . . . eat." My suggestion bothered me, but if the injured vampires didn't feed soon they'd develop bloodlust, making their appetites voracious and uncontrollable. The last thing Nicaragua needed was a bunch of blood-ravaging limbless vampires crawling around.

Shayna and I inched away from the vamps. We were team players and all, but no way in hell were we offering our blood. I left the healthy vamps to tend to the others. Vampires weren't known for their patience. They gave up trying to arrange the various missing appendages and piled the injured and all their body parts into three trucks and left for the village.

Edith carried me to a Tribe jeep and drove us to the hotel, where my sisters and the remaining Catholic schoolgirls anxiously waited. "Later," Liz said the moment she saw us. She and Maria flounced by us without so much as a "Thank God nothing with horns munched on you, Celia."

"What?" Maria asked when she caught my glare. "We are hungry."

I waved them off, although I could already hear them runway-strutting the length of the dilapidated hall. Emme rushed to my side. "Oh, my goodness, Celia. Your face is cut open."

I rubbed my face. My tigress made my hide and limbs extra sturdy, but we had our limits. Everything hurt so much it was difficult to tell the extent of my injuries. Edith tried to help. She grabbed my face in her hands and took a lick. "No, that's from a wereraccoon. Hmm . . . or maybe it's werepossum. Let me have another taste."

I had to physically restrain her. "Will you cut it out? I didn't like you licking me the first time."

Edith had the nerve to act insulted. She tossed her hair and scowled. "I've never had any complaints before."

"Just go and find someone nice to nibble on." She smacked her gums and took off. That was my favorite thing about Edith: all it took was something shiny or the offer of food to distract her.

I winced and squirmed as Emme's healing light surrounded me. The moment she released me I bolted into the shower, eager to rid my body of whatever was making my hair stick to my flesh like glue. I'd survived my latest assignment and picked up a few new admirers along the way. I hated that I'd become so popular among the supercreepy. I'd accepted I'd eventually be well known, but why so soon? Could someone be informing the bad guys of my presence? I tried not to be so paranoid, but my sisters reinforced my fears on our way back to the plane.

Old rusted streetlamps lit our path, the low wattage barely enough to cut through the darkness. "The Tribe assholes keep calling you by name, Ceel," Taran said. She leaned into me. I helped her walk—hell, I helped her stand. The magic-born sunlight had wiped her out. "It's like the whole lot of them want you dead. Even those gruesome newborns."

"I've noticed," I answered her over the hoots and hollers. People lined the cobblestone streets, dancing and celebrating despite the arrival of the midnight hour. The dread surrounding the village had lifted, permitting the crisp pure air to fill the night. Hope tickled and enlivened my skin. I suspected the villagers sensed it, too. They didn't need supernatural perception to realize the monsters were gone. At least for the moment.

"Son of a bitch. Is that all you have to say?" Taran muttered.

"There's not much to say. The Tribe's put a hit on me, but so what?"

Taran swore again. "What do you mean 'so what'? This shit isn't funny, Ceel!"

"I'm not laughing, Taran. Do you think I like being stalked? Bottom line, this doesn't change anything. It's not the first time something terrifying has come after me." I sighed. "And it's likely not going to be the last. The difference is that if it is just the Tribe, at least this time I know my enemy and I can prepare myself to fight."

Shayna jerked her head toward me. "You think it could be someone else?"

I tried to sound indifferent—a nearly impossible task considering the subject. "It just seems strange to hear my name called. It's like they know something about me I don't, or someone has sent them after me."

Emme nodded, her soft voice trembling slightly. "I can see that, but who? Those you've faced are all dead . . . aren't they?"

I shuddered involuntarily, thinking back to the line of psychos I'd fought and supposedly conquered. "I hope so, Emme."

We walked down another block to where Edith planned to meet us. A crowd of men hurrying toward us separated and rushed into the street when they sensed my predatory side. My beast remained on high alert, ignoring the celebration and seeking out those who dwelled in the shadows.

"I wish you could come home, Ceel," Shayna added quietly. "At least we're there to watch over you."

I shook my head. "All that would do is bring the danger to you. Look, the Tribe has obviously targeted me, and maybe something else has, too. But at least it's only me, and not any of you. If we're lucky, it will stay that way." Or so I hoped. If my sisters didn't have their wolves, Misha would be housing three more Wird girls.

A jeep skidded to a halt to us. Two sexy males stumbled out in their tighty-whities. Their dark skin glistened with perspiration despite the cool night air and they panted like they'd run with the bulls. Edith pulled the emergency brake, crawled across the front seat, and yanked each to her. She kissed them as if her diamond earrings had fallen down their throats and only her tongue could retrieve them. The men staggered back when she released them. "Adios, Edeeth," they both chimed.

Edith waved to her fans. "Addy ose!" She adjusted her thong beneath her tiny plaid skirt, snapping the back against her butt cheeks. "You freaks coming?" She asked without bothering to look up.

This was the vamp assigned to keep me safe from death. I pinched the bridge of my nose. "Yup. We're coming."

By the time we reached the plane, most of the injured vampires' limbs had reattached or regenerated. I shuddered. They must have taken a lot of blood to heal that quickly. Tim rolled his eyes. "Celia, our dinners are partying and having a good time. I swear on our master they're alive and well"—he grinned—"and very, *very* satisfied. I have to tell you, your people are flexible."

"My people?" I held my hand up before he could make another asinine remark. "Good to know, Tim. Let's get back to the States."

We piled onto the plane and collapsed into sleep. I remember waking up briefly in Texas when we stopped to refuel, but then quickly dozed off again. The entire flight was about seven hours. Shayna nudged me awake when the plane began its descent into Tahoe.

"I didn't wake up screaming," she whispered excitedly. "That's a good sign, don't you think?"

I rubbed my eyes and tried to slap myself awake. "It sure is. Maybe getting some revenge was what you needed after all." Rain splattered against the windows. "What time is it?"

Shayna nibbled on her bottom lip. "Almost noon."

The gray sky made me believe it was closer to twilight. I peered out the window as we landed smoothly on the runway. The plane glided to a halt, veering ever so slightly where a row of cars waited. I stiffened when I caught a pack of angry wolves emerging from the cars. Koda, Liam, and Gemini stalked to where the plane had taxied. My sisters cringed.

"Uh-oh," Emme whimpered. "Liam looks angry."

No. Liam looked ready to devour a T. rex.

My shoulders drooped. I wished my pissed-off werewolf was waiting for me. Especially after learning of his potential to go beast for life, I was eager to make sure he was safe.

Bren and Danny ambled next to the wolves and waited. Bren rubbed his scruffy beard, the way he often did when he was worried. Danny fidgeted back and forth, eyeing the other wolves while they continued to prowl. Behind them idled the Hummer limo with the familiar BYTEME plates. Either Misha hadn't stepped out yet or he was still mad at me and hadn't bothered coming.

"Shit, Ceel. Gem's super pissed. Do you think you can carry me off the plane so I can appeal to his sympathetic side?" Taran asked.

Shayna glanced nervously toward Koda. "Yeah, dude. Carry us, too, while you're at it."

What made things worse was that the recovering vamps were hauled out on stretchers first. By the time it was our turn to exit, the wolves were out of their minds. I carried Taran just as she had requested and her little plan worked. Gemini rushed to us. The anger vanished from his face and he immediately lifted her from my arms. "Taran, honey, are you okay?"

"She's just tired," I answered, calmly. "There were several women at the nest. She had to gather sunlight born of magic to free them."

Gemini shook his head and stepped away from me. "You shouldn't have gone without me," he said quietly.

Taran wrapped her arms around his neck. "I'm sorry, love."

One down, two to go.

Emme poked her head out of the plane. Liam scowled, but his ferocity was no match for her cuteness. She gave him one of the sweetest smiles in her arsenal and threw in a blush for good measure. If that wasn't bad enough, she wrinkled her nose at him in that way that drove him wild. Liam watched her as she timidly made her way down the steps until the wait became too much for him. He raced up to meet her when she was halfway down and greeted her with a kiss. "Angel, I was so worried about you. Don't ever do that to me again!"

Liam slipped his arm around her and escorted her down the steps. "I'm so sorry I scared you, Lee. I hope you can forgive me."

It was pretty damn obvious she was already forgiven and I tried not to smile. Koda wouldn't be so easily swayed. Shayna moved down the steps slowly. When she stood before him, he was red with fury.

"Puppy, I—"

"Don't you 'puppy' me! Do you have any idea what you've put me through? What you put all of us through?"

Shayna didn't say anything. Anyone with half a brain could tell Koda hated yelling at her, but his fear had turned to fury. He then turned to me and growled. "And where were you? You're the responsible one. Why the *hell* did you let them tag along? It's bad enough you're involved in all this shit—now we have to worry about the rest of them, too?"

Gemini and Liam both turned on me and glowered, completely taking Koda's side. *What the hell?* I shoved my hands on my hips and glared back at them. "Do you guys honestly think I didn't try to talk them out of it? I even tried calling you, but *your* girlfriend snatched the phone out of my hands and froze me in place, Liam." I pointed at Gemini. "And *your* girlfriend gagged me with some kind of spell, used my voice as her own, and then knocked me out."

I paced back and forth where the wolves had lined up. Their scowls had softened. That didn't mean I'd forgiven them. In fact, I let them have it. "All I know is you guys better grow a few pairs and take back some control before I revoke your man cards. What kind of lupines are you anyway? You let these tiny girls walk all over you." Okay, maybe that was a little much. But it was kind of hilarious to see their reactions. Their faces flushed slightly and they failed to meet my gaze. *Take that, Guardians of the Earth.*

Bren laughed out loud. "Celia's got a point. Damn. You poor, dumb pricks are whipped!"

My stupid rant eased some of the tension, but not enough. Koda remained upset. He pulled away when Shayna tried to touch his arm.

"Puppy, don't—don't push me away like that," she said.

Koda relented at the sight of her glistening tears. "Shayna, you are my mate. Running off like that is not okay. I almost lost you once. I can't go through that again."

"Koda, I go through the same thing every time you and the others leave to hunt the Tribe. I want to help, too." She glanced back at me. "And I wanted to help my sister. The Tribe's after her. A witch and a newly born demon child knew her by name."

I suddenly had more attention than I could handle. Danny turned to Gemini. "If a newborn knows Celia by name, that means hell's familiar with her, too."

Gemini didn't blink. "I'm not surprised. The Tribemasters themselves are linked to damnation." He nodded slowly as he thought matters through. "Which further verifies they're the ones who seek to kill her."

Emme clasped Liam's wrist. "Could someone also be sending them her way? That's what Celia thinks."

Liam's boyish features darkened with a pinch of fear and a cupful of pissed-off. "Hell itself could be commanding the Tribe to annihilate her, Emme."

My tigress poked at me irritably, to make sure I was listening. *Yup. No worries. Heard that one loud and clear.*

Koda's jaw crunched. His tumultuous brown eyes met mine briefly before returning to Shayna. "The Alliance knows Celia's been under fire. As Aric's mate, we owe it to him to keep her safe, and we will. No matter what seeks to harm her."

Koda's reference to me as Aric's mate hurt like a punch to my chest. I still refused to believe. After all, *weres* didn't abandon their mates. The bond was supposedly too strong. I stared hard at the ground when the wolves collectively murmured their vows to protect me. The next moment or two of silence seemed like a lifetime as I worked through my drove of emotions—pain at Aric's mention, worry for my future, fury at those who sought me. I was grateful when Koda shifted his attention back to Shayna.

He lifted her chin with his fingertip. "As for you, you know I leave you only because I have to. I have abilities you don't. I've been trained to kill. You haven't. I can risk more and still be okay. You can't." His thick brows furrowed upon catching the grin spreading across her pixie face. "Why are you smiling?"

"I killed a Tribemaster."

Okay, *so* not the way to calm a raging wolf.

Except for Shayna, we all took a few collective steps

back. *Way* back. Growls belted out from Koda's throat—loud enough to smack against my face. I didn't know what he said, but I had a keen sense of swearwords in any language. And still Shayna grinned. Hands down the perfect example of beauty taking on the rabid, psycho, severely homicidal beast.

She clasped his arm. "It's taking the nightmares away." Koda froze, his eyes widening. Her slender fingers slipped from his bulging arms. "For the first time, I'm starting to deal with . . . what happened to me. I'm not completely over it, but I feel like I could get there."

Koda's large hands cupped her face carefully, his dark eyes filling with sorrow. "I just wish it hadn't come at the expense of your safety. I wish I could've helped."

"You did, Koda," Shayna said softly. "I can heal now. By giving me some of your wolf's essence, I'm able to mend my injuries . . . And now that I'm gaining my confidence back, I think it will also help my trauma." Her grin widened. "Cool, huh?" Koda swept her into his arms and held her close. She nuzzled his neck. "Thank you . . . for loving me, and for saving me."

I almost bumped into Bren's wide chest when I stepped farther away from Shayna and Koda. He picked me up and planted a smooch on my cheek. "Did you get hurt, kid?"

I shrugged. "Crushed ankle—and I lost a few nails trying to gut the Tribemaster."

Bren chuckled and scratched his scruffy beard. "Hey, that's not so bad. It's better than last time."

"Yeah, tell me about it." I flashed him a small smirk. "We eliminated the nest and killed one of the Tribemasters."

Danny squeezed my shoulder. "There were two?"

I nodded.

"Whoa. Congratulations. You did an incredible job."

"I disagree. Celia allowed the other Tribemaster to escape, thereby ensuring he will continue to breed and carry on with his onslaught." His Royal Prince of All Things Batty aka the Deflowerer of Prom Queens finally decided to emerge from the limo. His gray eyes flickered with annoyance.

Oh. Hell no.

The look on my face must have been classic—everyone gave us ample space. "Well, maybe if you'd gotten off your lazy, bloodsucking, womanizing ass and helped, he wouldn't have gotten away!"

Misha's vampires all gasped, right before they scattered like flies. No one had probably ever spoken to him that way. "*What did you say?*"

Bren and Danny stepped in front of me. I moved around them and stormed up to Misha. "You heard me, you Hugh Hefner wannabe. I'm in no mood for your crap. So unless you have something good to say, keep your fangs shut!" I turned back to my shell-shocked sisters and their laughing wolves. "I'll call you later."

I stomped toward his limo, making a hell of a lot of noise considering I wore UGGs. "There better be food in there!"

I wrenched the door opened. The sound of familiar laughter stopped me before I slipped inside. Aric waited near the road leading to the highway, leaning against his black Escalade. I hadn't noticed his car in the darkness of the miserable morning. Yet I couldn't help but notice how his tight washed-out jeans hugged his strong legs or how his black leather jacket broadened his wide chest. He'd been there the whole time. The misting rain had likely dulled his scent. He stopped laughing when he caught me staring. I smiled and gave him a small wave. If his wolf was struggling for dominance, I couldn't sense any trace of it. He was still Aric, at least in my presence . . .

His wink instantly made my heart race. All it had taken was that minute gesture to make me want to melt against him and distract me from all the problems between us. "I love you," I squeaked out in a whisper. *Shit.* I wanted to punch myself for being so weak and foolish. Barbara was a gold-digging wench who didn't give a damn about Aric. I knew it. He knew it. But, bottom line, she was still his fiancée. I had no right to say that to him. "I—I'm sorry—"

Aric's light brown eyes fixed on mine with such intensity, I almost stumbled back. "I love you, too, Celia," he answered, loud and clear. He took a step toward me, only to freeze. All at once, his expression hardened. So instead of moving closer, he turned back to his SUV and placed his palms on the hood. His back rose and fell with each hard intake of breath. What I saw wasn't his wolf taking over. It was a *were* struggling to commit to the obligations his pack had thrust upon him, a man fighting to do what was right. No wonder his beast felt the need to protect him.

I watched and waited as the strain of his burden continued to divide him. For just a moment, I thought he would rush to me as I so needed him to. Instead he climbed into his car and sped aggressively away.

I lurched forward. My tigress insisted we chase after him. I dug in my heels, denying her. *Chase after the speeding SUV? No, that wouldn't seem desperate or anything.*

I ran my fingers through my hair, damp from the drizzling rain, and resolved to return to my new life, where superbaddies couldn't wait to sink their claws into me. I couldn't be with Aric, and that's all there was to it. Problem was, my heart would never completely abandon him.

Stupid heart.

I stepped into the limo and was greeted with glares from the four bimbos who'd fondled Misha the other morning. This was *so* not the moment to piss me off. I yanked them by their smut-wear and threw them out on their asses. One by one they landed on the asphalt screaming and launching into tremendous fits, but none of them dared to climb back in.

Lucky for Misha, there were two large milk shakes and a tremendous bag full of burgers waiting for me. It was the only thing that saved his hide. He climbed in a moment later, leaving his hostile mistresses behind. If he was trying to pretend he was mad at me, he did a shitty job. A satisfied smirk played across his face. "Why did you toss the girls out?"

I spoke through a mouthful of food. "Because they're nasty, spoiled, sleazy hoochies." My eyes narrowed further. "And where the hell are the fries?"

CHAPTER 11

"Oral sex."

I gawked at Maria. "Ah, no, thanks."

She rolled her eyes. "I was not offering."

I held out my open palm. "Then . . . ?"

"Celia." Liz said my name like I was some kind of simpleton. "Maria is suggesting a way to make amends with the master."

I crossed my arms. "So an apology would just be out of the question?"

Edith Anne threw her hands in the air. "Oh, hell, Celia. Nothing says I'm sorry like a little—"

"Stop right there, Edith."

"I'm just saying—"

"I don't want you to finish your thought. Trust me, nothing you say will make what you're asking of me more tempting."

Misha hadn't apologized for being so cold to me. Then again, I hadn't apologized for ripping him a new one in front of everyone. I considered us even. He obviously didn't. The underlying tension between us continued over the next week. When we'd met for breakfast, neither of us spoke or made eye contact. I couldn't stand the awkwardness. I ate quickly and left without a word. On my way to the dojang, the Catholic schoolgirls stopped me in the garden.

"Come now, Celia. You have to do something," Agnes Concepción demanded. "At least walk around naked for a while."

"You really expect me to walk around naked for him?"

Agnes scowled. "Fine. You can wear shoes if you'd like."

I rubbed my eyes and begged God for patience and guidance. In my mind, I envisioned Him dropping a stake from the sky. He had His limits, too.

Liz tugged on the sleeve of my sweatshirt. "I have a cute pair of Cinderella shoes you can borrow," she offered.

Edith nodded with determination. "I think we should all do it. It will please the master." She raised a fist in the air. "For the master."

They continued to excitedly discuss the matter as I continued on the path. Misha's estate was beautiful, elegant, and decorated with hand-carved mission furniture, expensive leathers, and magnificent sculptures and paintings. It was the vision of a gifted architect who would probably keel over if she knew it housed a bunch of horny nutcases.

I'd reached the fork in the slate walkway. The right branched out toward the guesthouse overlooking the lake. The other took me deep into Misha's wooded property where the dojang lay hidden amid an Asian garden surrounded by dense fir trees. I'd just veered left when something shattered a third-floor window and crashed onto the snow-covered lawn near my feet.

I leapt aside with my claws out. A vampire landed and rolled like a giant baseball. I gathered Misha was the "bat" who'd swung. The vampire groaned and tipped onto his back. I tried not to react as his dangling eye slowly crept back into his skull. It didn't work. *Ew.*

The vamp poked his eye a few times—I presumed to make sure it was all the way back home. "The master is not in a good mood," he said.

"I can tell." I tried to haul him up by his arm. It would have worked if it was still attached to his body. He scrambled upright and accepted the appendage. "Thanks." He stepped toward the front of the house, pausing to glance over his shoulder. "Try not to piss him off, Celia."

First the schoolgirls and their Oral Pep Talk, and now this swing and miss.

A growl rumbled deep in my chest. If Misha's attempt was to intimidate, he picked the wrong gal. I stormed down the path and up the stairs to the dojang. I abandoned my sneakers in the foyer and slid back the woven bamboo wall. The soothing warmth of the brightly lit room greeted me like a friend. A friend who liked to nut-punch when you'd least expected. The light wood flooring and soothing aromas of the shelved orchids, jasmine, and dahlias suggested this was a place where one could find inner peace and tranquillity. I'd quickly learned it doubled as a torture facility.

When Misha first told me I would spend several hours a week doing yoga as part of my training sessions, I thought he was nuts. Martial arts I understood, cardio was a given, weight training, ditto, but yoga? I hated to admit how right he had been. My flexibility had improved and I'd become more aware of my body. Yoga had taught me and my tigress to move more like the preternatural creature we were. I could flip, land, and pounce better than ever. That being said, I hated the training. Ying-Ying, my yoga master from planet Whoop Yo Ass, often subjected me to hours of grueling stretches. Today, I managed to bypass the Gumby routine for a day of martial arts training aka a trip to the emergency room.

I bowed to Kuan Jang Nim Chang. A white gi covered his rotund figure and a wide grin took up most of his round face. The five-foot-tall barbaric bastard returned my bow, then rubbed his hands the way villains did in movies. If he had a mustache, he'd twirl that, too. Seriously, he scared the shit out of me.

He ranted about something and gestured frantically. But Chang wouldn't let something like a little language barrier stop him from brightening my day. His specialty was tae kwon do, but he was also a hapkido and a muay thai master. He directed me to the rear of the dojang. Spurts of his mysticism flickered from the soles of his feet as he hurried to where my stoning—I mean, training exercise—awaited.

The pile of bricks in the center of the room should've tipped me off. The day's fun consisted of repeatedly breaking bricks with my ridge hand and instep. It wasn't enough to hold them in place and break them. Oh, no. He thought it would be more effective to throw them at me. The little bitch had lousy aim. I kept leaping out of the way to keep my toes from being crushed. I didn't speak Korean and screaming at him in English didn't get me anywhere. He just gibbered on with a big smile on his face. He could've been reciting the Korean version of the Sesame Street theme song for all I knew.

I'd been born "weird," but I never thought my life would turn as whacked-out as this. "There's something wrong with you," I snapped.

He paused and pointed to the extra-large brick in his hand. "Tribe coming for you," he said in broken English. He gave me a stiff nod for emphasis, then pitched the brick at my face with a jolly grin.

I had just showered and was soaking my brick-bashed hands in ice when someone knocked on my door. I was surprised to find Misha there with a little elderly woman. She was dressed from head to toe in black and carried a giant wicker basket covered in red cloth.

He smiled. "May we come in?"

Although vampires needed to ask permission before entering another person's dwelling, technically he didn't have to ask since the guesthouse was part of his domain. Regardless, I appreciated his attempt at being polite. Maybe he'd started to come around. "Sure. Make yourselves at home."

Misha stopped smiling when he saw my hands. He frowned as he examined them. I didn't protest. It was the first time he'd shown any concern. "Would you like me to send for Emme?"

I was surprised he didn't offer to heal me himself. Maybe it was because of the old woman's presence. No, never mind—her watching would've probably turned him on. "No, I'm okay. I'll be seeing Emme the day after tomorrow. If they're still bothering me then, I'll have her mend them."

"You should still have them tended to whether they feel better or not." He met my eyes. "If it pleases you, I would like to spend the day with you tomorrow."

My hands slipped from his. I waited for him to say more, surprised by his kindness, considering his mood lately. "Okay. What did you have in mind?"

"Anything of your choosing."

The tiny woman interrupted us by speaking quickly in Russian. Misha answered her and she extracted a tape measure from her basket. She looked at me and scowled. She pointed to my stomach and then my breasts and said something that made Misha laugh. Whatever it was I doubted I'd find it as funny. She grabbed me and turned me in a slow pirouette. For someone who looked ready to shatter a hip, she was a strong little thing.

She forced my arms up and measured my bust. "Misha, what's going on?"

Misha didn't answer me right away. He was too busy laughing as Little Miss Personality waved the tape measure in his face and babbled on about something. I don't know what the hell she was so mad at, but she seemed to reach her breaking point when she measured my waist. The little twerp threw her hands in the air and yelled, her deeply wrinkled face contorting with rage. She took more measurements before screaming yet again.

Misha said something else to her that made her shake her finger at him. He flashed me a wicked smile as she placed the tape measure against my hip and let it fall.

She pointed right above my knee. Misha shook his head and said something else. She moved her hand higher and again he shook his head. This went on until she almost aligned with my happy place. When Misha finally nodded, she lost her mind and started shouting at *me* in Russian. Although I couldn't understand her, I just knew she was swearing. The hand gestures and snarls gave her away. She threw her measuring tape in her basket and started to stomp away. Misha grabbed her by her long knobby fingers and whispered something softly in her ear. The woman turned from bitter old maid to lovestruck maiden. She actually blushed and smiled toothlessly at him before skipping away.

I scoffed, annoyed at how easily Misha had won her over. "What the hell was that about?"

"She wonders what a nice girl like you is doing with me."

"I'm beginning to wonder that, too," I said, though I didn't believe a damn word he said.

Out of nowhere, a scrawny little old man scurried into the guesthouse with a piece of paper and a pencil. His wiry white hair stuck out in a tuff, contrasting his dark skin. He gave me a warm smile before motioning me to a chair. As soon as I sat, he gently lifted my bare feet and traced them onto the paper. He then waved before leaving as quickly as he came.

"Will you please tell me what's going on?"

"Kitten, there will be a gala at the Den in two weeks to honor Alliance members who have had the greatest impact on the war. Representatives from *were* packs, vampire clans, and witch covens worldwide will be there. Our combined efforts have helped cripple the Tribe. Your capture, attempted escape, and our rescue of you alone resulted in the destruction of over four hundred Tribesmen. Not to mention that in the few hours you spent in Nicaragua, you helped destroy over a hundred of the enemy and prevented the birth of over twenty demon children. You have also aided in killing three Tribemasters that otherwise would have continued breeding. We are winning the war and it is time to celebrate."

"So all this . . . *stuff* was to fit me for a dress for the gala?"

"Yes."

I smoothed my finger over the sore knuckles of my opposite hand. "Misha, the Elders don't want me at the Den. Anara especially hates me."

"Whether the Elders like it or not, you are an Alliance member — just like the vampires, witches, and were-beasts. And you are respected. Anara was the one who recommended I send you to the nest. He knew your skills would be needed to ensure victory."

I pursed my lips. "Sending me somewhere where I might be killed is different than welcoming me into a sacred place among *weres*."

Misha stiffened. "You fight with us and therefore have earned a place among those invited. It would be a tremendous insult to the vampires to show you anything but hospitality."

Aric would be there, married by then. The thought of Barbara standing alongside him as his wife drove the last knife into my heart. "I'm not going, Misha. I can't."

"You can, and you will, Celia. You and your sisters will be recognized among the honored guests. Don't allow that mongrel to rob that from you." He turned on his heel. I didn't know whether his derogatory comment was meant for Aric or for Anara. I was resigned to believe it was directed at Aric. After all, Misha had caught my broken expression, the one that overtook my visage every time I thought about my wolf.

I returned to my small living room and slumped on the chocolate-colored couch. Moisture dripped from the green ceramic bowl I'd soaked my hands in and the chunks of ice had almost melted. I knew I should continue my therapy, but thoughts of seeing Aric raced through my head. If I decided against attending the gala, Misha wouldn't force me. While I recognized our friendship remained strained, I knew he'd never intentionally hurt me. And seeing Aric married would destroy me.

CHAPTER 12

A sonic boom followed more yodeling in Mandarin. I peered through the thick glass of the library window. Ying-Ying had the naughty Catholic schoolgirls dancing with their arms up as she hovered around my assigned Lexus. The good Catholics didn't appear happy as they twirled around the car to the beat of something Ying-Ying. Like me, they knew better than to risk riling my yogi. She was kind of like the Hulk—but not green and not as charming. Ying-Ying was psycho in a good mood. Nobody wished to see her angry.

Every time she drifted over the hood, lightning crashed over Tahoe and sparks of peach and pink swirled from the water and onto the car. I turned back to Misha. "Are you sure this is necessary?"

He didn't look up from the chessboard. "Considering beings spawned from hell itself wish to annihilate you, I believe magical reinforcements are in order." He lifted a knight. "Especially given that your beast grows restless if restricted and you find my bodyguards . . ."

"Annoying? Obnoxious? Rude?" I offered.

The edges of Misha's mouth lifted, but he ignored my jabs at Hank and Tim. "The shields will help block any magical attacks while you're off premises and keep you secure until help arrives."

Misha placed the knight in front of one of my pawns. I knew the little guy was screwed, but not sure why. I couldn't play chess; I barely managed checkers. Misha considered it an important skill, so I let him try to teach me. "I don't get why you want me to learn this stuff."

That earned me a full smile. "This *stuff* has helped leaders like Napoléon conquer Europe."

"I just feel bad for the little guy."

"Napoléon?"

"No, the pawn."

"Kitten, the pawns are necessary sacrifices to win the game."

"It's just so unfair. Why doesn't the knight or the king ever try to protect them?"

"They are more important and need to be spared. Do you not consider the president worth protecting, say, over a vagrant?"

"A vagrant would feel just as much pain if he were shot."

Misha scrutinized me carefully. His hair cascaded over a silver-colored sweater that accentuated his powerful gray eyes and swathed his strong physique. He hadn't said much since he'd left the guesthouse earlier. When he asked me to join him for a round of chess after dinner, I thought it was to finally iron out our differences. He'd spoken only a few words. I tilted my head, trying to figure him out.

Misha could be so very hard, like his body. I sometimes wished his master status would allow the gentleness of his soul to rise to the surface. But that wasn't possible. Any sign of weakness invited an attack from another master. That meant bloodshed until only one master stood victorious.

I watched him take my pawn following my oh-so-strategic move and tucked my legs beneath me. "What's up with the queen?"

"She is the most versatile."

"She also seems to be the one in charge, even more so than the king."

"A strong woman is capable of bringing even the most powerful male to his knees."

I blinked back at him. "Are we still talking about chess?"

Misha ignored my question and instead he brushed his hair away from his face. "Tell me about your parents," he said.

My legs slipped back to the floor. "What do you want to know?"

"How they came to be as one."

I gripped the chair arms and forced myself to relax when I felt my claws protrude and dig into the heavy mahogany. "My mother was born in El Salvador. She was the youngest of seven children and moved to the States when she was about four."

"An immigrant?"

I nodded.

"Like me?"

I smiled without humor. "No. Not like you. Being the youngest, and educated here, she became the most Americanized. She embraced the culture, fell in love with the music, and lost her accent completely. Her skin and eyes were lighter than the rest of her family and she was often mistaken for a Caucasian American. She was kind and funny." A hint of anger found its way into my husky voice. "But her family didn't like her much. I think they were jealous she managed to fit in so well while they continued to struggle."

Misha abandoned the game and leaned back in his chair. "Success often breeds envy."

"So it seems." The subject of my parents was a touchy one at best. I forced myself to continue, reasoning that it was okay to tell Misha. He was a friend, right? "My mother met my father at Rutgers University their freshman year. My father was prelaw and my mother was a criminal justice major. They started talking and realized they had a lot in common. It wasn't long before they began dating."

"How did the families react to their union?"

"Not well. My father was of German descent and grew up in a small town near Lancaster, Pennsylvania. His family didn't know what to think of my mother. They were all light skinned and fair haired like Emme. My mother had wavy brown hair, olive skin, and green eyes."

Misha smiled. "Like you."

I bowed my head. "Yes. Taran remembers us looking a lot alike. But despite how my father's family reacted, my mother's was much worse."

"In what manner?"

I didn't answer. My nails had slowly punctured through the wooden chair. I splintered the wood trying to extract them. "God, I'm sorry. I'll pay for it—"

Misha's tone softened. "Do not worry about something so expendable. Please, finish your story."

Tears burned across my irises despite my feeble attempts to halt them. "Th-they thought she had betrayed her race and disowned her. Shortly after my parents graduated, they married. My mother became pregnant with me right away. When my mother's family found out, one of her crazy aunts showed up at her door and cursed my parents with short lives." I stared at the pawns that were cast aside. "They died when I was nine." I wanted to stop talking then, but I just couldn't. Everything spilled from my lips in one breath. "She also hexed all of my mother's unborn children. But the curse somehow backfired and . . . and made us what we are."

Misha studied me closely. "Do you know the words your aunt used when she cast the spell?"

I considered his question. No one had ever asked me that before. "My mother said it was something like 'Your children will devour blades and weep like weak and sickly runts. Animals will hunt them and pierce their flesh with fang and claw. They will burn with fire and hide from shame for nowhere will they find strength or love or kindness.' There was more—" I brushed away my last tear. "But I forgot the rest."

Misha frowned. "I'm surprised your mother shared the severity of the words with you."

My head snapped up. "She wanted us to know. She felt we should always believe in ourselves regardless of what others might say or do." I stood abruptly. "I'm glad she instilled that hope in us. It got us through the cruelty we were showered with all through school and helped us survive after they died." I didn't like how Misha regarded me with pity, and my harshening tone made it clear. "Don't look at me like that, Misha—none of it matters now." Still, the recollection had burned a hole through my chest.

Misha stood. "If something has caused you pain, I cannot merely dismiss it because you ask it of me."

I hadn't realized how much discussing my parents had upset me until my throat developed an ache I couldn't swallow. I needed to leave. "I'm really tired. I'm going to bed."

Misha placed his hands against my shoulders and slowly pulled me to him. His expression wasn't one of lust, but of something entirely different. He opened his mouth to say something, only to close it tight. I thought he was about to ask me to join him in bed. Instead he released me and linked our hands. He continued to watch me as he escorted me back to the guesthouse. The moment we arrived on my doorstep, he kissed my forehead and returned to the main house.

Even though we'd both lived in Tahoe a few years, the next day Misha and I did the tourist thing. It would have been a relaxing day if not for the vampire snipers looming at the top of every building we entered, or the hit squad shadowing us. We had just stepped onto the dock on our way to Fannette Island when a young woman frantically waved her arms just a few yards away. "Celia! Celia! Over here." I recognized her as one of my former labor patients. I rushed to greet her and her little family, but not before I elbowed the vamp reaching for his holster. Thankfully, the family didn't seem to notice.

The father tried futilely to wipe some food off his screaming toddler's face, while Mommy held the outrageously bundled baby. "Oh, it's so good to see you," she said. She hugged me with her free arm while her eyes fixed on Misha.

"Hi, Celia." The dad shook my hand.

I smiled. "Hello, Amy, Les. It's so nice to see you again."

Amy pushed out her cleavage just a little bit. Misha had that effect on females. "And who's this?"

"This is my friend Misha."

Amy raised her eyebrows. "Just a friend?"

Misha offered a thong-dropping smile. "We live together."

My cheeks burned at Amy's giggle. "Can I hold the baby?" I asked.

Amy placed the chubby-cheeked infant in my arms and explained how we knew each other. "Celia is just the best nurse! She delivered both my children."

"Celia has many, many talents," Misha added with a wink. He extended his arms to the toddler. "May I?"

"Of course," Les said. "But watch out—Cindy bites."

"So do I," Misha answered. I would have killed him if there hadn't been so many witnesses. The parents just laughed. Oh, wasn't Misha quite the funny man!

Misha picked up Cindy and instantly captivated the toddler. She stopped screaming and touched her small fingers to Misha's face. The baby didn't need charming. He smiled and cooed as I rocked him. I thought back to a time when Aric and I were still together. It had been a similar situation; we'd run into another couple whose child I'd delivered. Aric had watched me as I held the baby. When she reached out to him, he'd taken her like an old pro. It had been such a beautiful moment between us. Now it just made me sad.

Little Cindy hollered when Misha returned her to her parents. We said good-bye and stepped onto one of Misha's smaller yachts. I was still thinking of that moment with Aric as we took our seats at the elegantly set table.

"Would you like a child?" Misha asked.

Misha had asked me a great deal of personal questions in the past. This one bothered me more than the others. I didn't want to answer, but I did, figuring it could do no harm. "Yes . . . Someday I'd really like one."

"I could do that for you."

I froze in the middle of placing my napkin on my lap.

It was a subtle response but one that had our security detail springing into action. The bodyguards surrounded us. On the deck above, a sniper appeared and scanned the area for a possible threat. Misha waved them off. They disappeared with their heads lowered, likely disappointed they didn't get to lacerate some immortal assailant's liver.

My attention returned to Misha. "I thought only the most powerful vampires in the world could conceive a child."

"What do you expect after returning my soul and helping me to acquire the power of several ancient masters?"

"You're right. I guess I just hadn't realized the extent of your supernatural muscle." I moved my utensils around, despite their perfect placement. I'd always wanted children. I considered them cute, wonderful little miracles who needed to be loved and protected. Once I met Aric, my maternal desires became so strong I could taste them. But as much as I still wanted a family, I could no longer foresee one in my future. The dreamworld I'd envisioned in which Aric and I would be married and have a brood of babies was no longer plausible. And yet I continued to desire it.

"What are you thinking, my darling?" Misha asked.

I ran my fingers through my hair and leaned my chin against my palm. My other arm rested against the soft linen of the tablecloth. "Misha, what kind of child could come from a preternatural and someone like me?"

Misha smiled. "I don't know. Nothing like you or your sisters has ever existed."

"So a baby born of a union like that could be scary and have, like . . . eighteen legs or something?"

Misha choked on his wine. I'd never seen him laugh so hard. He wiped his eyes. "Kitten, we could not conceive a monster because neither of us resembles one. The only guarantee is that the child would be extremely powerful, seeing as we both are."

A deep blush found its way to my cheeks. I hadn't meant for Misha to think I was soliciting him to be my baby daddy. I should have said something, but didn't want to embarrass or hurt him, especially in the presence of his hit squad. Instead I munched on the goat cheese salad placed in front of me. Misha took a bite, too. I watched how he neatly chewed on the greens. "Why do you still eat food if you don't have to?"

Chef swore as he banged pots and pans from the galley. The guy was just loads of fun.

"I still enjoy the taste, and I suppose . . . Well, never mind."

"What?"

Misha leaned back in his seat. "It's nothing of importance."

"Tell me."

The waves splashed harshly against the boat as I waited.

"No," he finally answered.

I flicked a crouton and nailed him in the nose with it. By the look on his face, you would've thought I tossed him a severed toe.

"Celia, your table manners are—"

"*Tell me.*" I growled, but couldn't manage a straight face.

He chuckled before speaking. "I suppose it makes me feel human."

My lips parted. Most of the time I forgot Misha was a vampire. If it wasn't for his necessary diet, he could have passed for any average supermodel on the street. "Ever wish you were human again?"

His eyes never left mine and he took his time answering. "No," he said finally.

I realized I had caught Misha in a lie. I didn't push it, though; some things were better left unsaid. And some vampires shouldn't be messed with.

CHAPTER 13

I didn't want to move.

The day of Aric's wedding had finally arrived. I didn't get up for breakfast, preferring to lie in bed and wallow in my misery. It was the ultimate jilted ex-girlfriend moment. Empty boxes and wrappers of Tastykakes littered the bedroom floor while Celine Dion's "All by Myself" blasted away for the hundredth time. Tears streamed down my face as I devoured the last cupcake. There was no point in getting out of bed. I had Celine, a box of tissues, and was moving on to the Butterscotch Krimpets next.

My phone rang all morning. My sisters left several messages, claiming their calls were just to say hi. I knew better. Eventually I just shut it off and prayed the Tribe would invade Tahoe City so I could have something to kill. Around dinnertime, there was a knock on my door. When I opened it, a tremendous brown wolf tackled me to the floor. The wolf slobbered all over my face. "Bren, get the hell off me." He didn't move; he just wagged his tail and bombarded me with sloppy kisses. I adjusted my hips and tossed him across the kitchen floor and into my living room. I wiped my face with the sleeve of my night-shirt. He grinned at me with his giant fangs. When he bounded to my side, I knelt down and patted his head. "What are you doing here?"

Liam and Danny raced in; my sisters stumbled in behind them. Everyone babbled in loud, excited, breathless voices all at once. I couldn't hear or understand a thing. Especially once Liam pulled me to him and spun me in the air, howling like a crazed beast.

I pressed my hands into Liam's chest until he put me down. Everyone stared at me, smiling, their cheeks flushed with excitement. "Aric couldn't go through with it," Liam said.

I gawked at him, unsure I'd heard correctly. It felt as if my brain had abandoned my skull and my body was hovering above the wood floor.

He grabbed my shoulders and shook me lightly. "Did you hear me, Celia? Aric didn't marry Barbara. He bailed at the last minute."

I clasped my hands over my mouth. "Oh, my God," I whispered. "What happened?"

Liam wore a navy suit and red tie, but his brown eyes shimmered with the excitement of a three-year-old and his blond hair spiked out of control. "Well, we knew all hell was going to break loose when Aric showed up at the civil ceremony dressed in the jeans and T-shirt he'd obviously slept in and lookin' ready to maul. Barbara ignored him and said her vows like there was no way he'd ever have the stones to back out." He chuckled. "Aric couldn't or wouldn't say shit. Barbara threw a major fit and called Anara. Anara ripped Aric a new asshole over the phone and ordered him to marry Barbara. Aric flat-out refused and hung up on him. Well, then the shit hit the fan. Barbara marched up to Miss Eliza and told her she's been throwing herself at Aric and since he's failed to respond she must have birthed the gayest wolf on the planet."

My lids peeled back and I had to grip the counter to keep from falling over. "What happened after that?" Good Lord. I could barely spit the words out.

"You're going to love this. Miss Eliza was all calm. She smiled real sweet like and said, 'That's so strange, dear. I don't recall Aric ever having problems showing Celia affection.'"

Oh, snap!

My heart pounded in my chest. I couldn't believe it. I was almost out of my mind with joy. I tried to hide my brimming tears. Liam stopped me by clasping my hands. "I think Aric was able to resist Anara because he doesn't want to be with anyone . . . unless it's you."

The tears leaking from my eyes earned me a much-needed hug from Emme. "Thanks, Liam. I needed to hear that." I wiped my cheeks. "Where is Aric? I have to call him."

"You can't do that, Celia," Liam answered.

I nodded. "You're right. I don't want to get him into more trouble with Anara."

"Oh, no—I don't mean you shouldn't. I mean you can't. Barbara smashed his phone into his face and broke it." We all gasped. "Anyway, Aric went wolf and took off. We don't know where he is." He shrugged. "I'm supposed to help the Warriors search for him. The Elders are worried he's gone off the deep end and they want us to find him before he eats a mailman or something." He bent to kiss Emme before jogging off.

My sisters threw their arms around me, thankfully shielding me from Bren's naked form. He yanked on the jeans Danny tossed him. Taran shoved me into my bedroom. "Get dressed, Ceel. We're taking you to Hairy Bastard's to celebrate."

Hairy Bastard's was the premier steakhouse in Carson City, famous for booze, big servings, and catering to *weres*.

"There's that vamp tramp, Celia Wird," some were-hyena said in a barely audible whisper.

The patrons were famous for hating vampires and, apparently, anyone associated with them. I ignored her and slipped into our booth. Bren and Danny kept their sights on her, but it was Shayna who spoke up. "Don't talk about my sister that way!"

We angled our heads slowly toward Shayna. "You heard her?" Bren asked.

Shayna continued to narrow her eyes. "Well, duh—she said it loud and clear." Usually such a response fell under Taran's list of personality traits.

"No, she didn't, Shayna." I took a sniff to see whether I could detect any underlying lupine aroma. I couldn't sense anything. She was still Shayna, but something about her had changed. "It looks like Koda gave you more than just healing abilities."

Shayna placed both palms on the table. "Dude! Are you serious?"

Taran shut her compact closed. "What the hell's going on?"

We told Taran and Emme what happened and they began to question Shayna on other new abilities she might have noticed. Shayna jumped in her seat, her pixie face beaming. "I am a lot hungrier now. And Koda did say I'm more aggressive . . . um, in certain situations."

Bren danced his eyebrows. "Do you mean in bed, Shayna?"

Shayna laughed despite her pink cheeks. "Yeah, but he doesn't seem to mind."

"You were also aggressive in how you responded to that werehyena," Danny said. "It's not like you to snap at someone—you're usually the one who keeps the peace."

Worry erased her building excitement. "You don't think I'll get all—" She raised her hands, pretending to have claws, and bared her teeth. "*Grrrr!*"

The wolves and I laughed. She was about as vicious as a newborn chinchilla. Danny covered her hand. "Your werewolf tendencies and your human ones are probably just trying to adjust to each other. You may have a shorter fuse—similar to younger wolves—but I don't expect you'll become volatile."

The waitress brought over a bucket of Coronas. Bren handed me one and grabbed one for himself. "And you're probably more hot-headed considering the *were* equivalent of Cujo passed you his essence."

Shayna giggled. "Oh, my puppy's just a big love."

Bren stopped in the middle of dividing up the remaining beers. "Your puppy scares people shitless."

The rest of us agreed in a collective shudder. Shayna laughed and squirmed excitedly in her seat. "Do you think I'll *change* soon?"

Bren wiped his scruffy beer after chugging his beer. "Nah. If you were going to, you would have following the first full moon."

Shayna pouted—she would have loved a tail and some fur. Emme leaned forward. "But, Shayna, what you have is so incredible. Your sense of hearing is heightened. You can heal. You can scent—"

"You're a freak," the werehyena chimed in.

Her comment caused the group of *weres* at her table to erupt with laughter. My tigress stretched inside me in anticipation of a fight. Taran cracked her knuckles and flashed them an evil smile. We waited for their next move. Bren wasn't so patient. He was probably one of the greatest friends I've ever had. He was funny, loyal, and affectionate—he also didn't take any shit. He stood, towering above us, and trained his eyes at the werehyena. "You know what? You're really starting to piss me off."

A wereox who had also laughed stood and moseyed over to Bren. "Oh, yeah?" Like a moron, he poked Bren in the chest. "What are *you* going to do about it?"

Bren smashed our beer bucket right in the guy's face. "The same thing I did to your mother."

The werehyena launched herself at Shayna. I caught her in midair and used her momentum to slam her against the wall. She broke a beer sign into about a thousand pieces with her back and landed with a loud thump on our table. Taran loomed over her. "Not laughing now, are you, bitch?"

Weres brawled. A lot. As a result, a law had been established years ago for such behavior. So long as no one died and humans didn't become aware, the North American Were Council was fine with the occasional smackdown.

Shayna merged the utensils at our table and transformed them into two long ninja staffs. She let out probably the saddest excuse for a wolf howl I'd ever heard and attacked. Bren broke out laughing for some reason and just missed getting hit with a barstool. Taran scrambled out of the booth and jolted anyone she could with lightning. I took on a werekangaroo. His blows came fast and he kicked with both feet simultaneously. I missed most of his shots. He wasn't as lucky.

The wereox gained consciousness and charged toward Emme. She held out her small hand. "I don't want to hurt you, but I will if you take another step . . ."

The wereox stopped midstampede and smiled. "You're cute. How 'bout some head?"

Like the rapid fire from a machine gun, Emme slammed about a dozen beer mugs into the ox's groin. She frowned at him. "*Jerk.*"

There was some high-pitched screaming near the bathrooms where a woman dragged poor Danny away by his hair. I knocked out the kangaroo with a kick to the face and chased after them. I raced down the hall to the restrooms only to be intercepted by a wereyak barreling out of the men's room.

We grappled. Stupid move on my part—his human form was stronger than mine. I fell through the ladies' room door with him and *shifted* through the floor before his weight could squash me. I surfaced with an uppercut to his jaw. His head snapped back and he staggered into the sink. When his face met mine, he froze. Slowly, he peered over my shoulder. The anger twisting his face melted into horror and his olive skin paled to green.

My body shivered liked I'd been dumped naked on an icy tundra. Something wicked had appeared. Behind me. All the hair on the back of my neck shriveled into my skin. A sharp pungent smell burned my nose and made my stomach pang with the urge to vomit. I'd smelled that baneful odor once before.

Demon.

Not demon children. Demon children were a hybrid of demon and human blood. This . . . *this* was the straight-from-hell kind that didn't belong on earth. I turned slowly toward the scent, even though every part of me screamed to run. My tigress surprised me with a roar that vibrated in my throat; my human side very much wanted to cry and hide under the nearest bed.

On the windowsill sat something resembling a toad, only sickly white with gray spots and a fat humanoid head. Bright pink eyes blinked back at me. Its body was only about the size of a loaf of bread, but it didn't need to be bigger to scare me.

The wereyak backed away, crossing himself, the aroma of his fear mixing with mine. "Holy *shit*," he whispered. He slammed into the doorjamb in his haste to scramble away, leaving me alone with this *thing*.

The brawl continued in the dining area, but the bathroom turned hauntingly quiet. The demon opened his mouth and extended his thick gray tongue, tasting the air and possibly me.

I ripped the condom dispenser off the wall and smashed him with it. The first few blows felt as if I'd hit a wet balloon filled with water. I pounded him with more force until I heard a *splat*. The room filled with more of that horrible scent, propelling me to strike harder and harder.

My hands slicked with my blood against the warping metal. *Die, die, just die!* I jumped when Danny placed his hand on my shoulder. Still, I continued to pulverize what remained.

"Oh, my God. Celia, stop—*Celia!*"

"De-de-de." I was so terrified I couldn't bring myself to say the word, so I hit harder.

"It's okay, it's okay. I'll get rid of it."

I dropped the twisted metal dispenser on top of it. My feet automatically scurried away as Danny moved it aside. We both gagged at the smell. It looked like someone had poured bubbling white slime on the floor. Chunks of flesh floated on top, swirling together as if attempting to rejoin. *Five minutes.* Aric had once told me that only the strongest demons could leave hell. And five minutes was usually their curfew. My body convulsed with terror. It had at least three minutes left.

Danny took a small tube of water from his back

pocket and poured a few drops on the leftovers. The drops sizzled. Sparks of blue exploded and engulfed the slime in a magical mini wave, cleansing the floor and purifying the air.

My body relaxed slightly from breathing in the sudden freshness. "Holy water?" I stammered after a few moments of silence.

Danny shook his head. Dry blood caked his lips and several contusions covered his face. "It's water from the lake. The magic in Tahoe is mostly pure. I've been trying to analyze it at the lab." He shrugged. "I don't know. I just had a feeling it would help."

I gripped the edge of the sink, unable to stay upright on my weak legs. "What if the water hadn't worked?"

Danny smiled a true, genuine Danny-ish smile. "The power of good keeps demons from staying on earth. Even if the water failed to have any effect, that thing wouldn't have lasted long against your light."

CHAPTER 14

"You know, this really isn't necessary," I said to Hank.

He jogged alongside me, huffing and puffing like a two-pack-a-day smoker. "Celia, the Tribe is getting desperate to off you if they're sending demons your way. Pardon the fuck out of the master for trying to protect you." He spat on the asphalt. "Do you think I want to run? It's idiotic. I don't understand why you do it."

"It's not idiotic. It helps my stamina and calms my tigress."

"So does sex — and it's much more pleasurable. I don't understand why you keep denying the master."

Vampires were all about overindulging themselves — whether with money, sex, or feedings. How could I have possibly reasoned with such selfish beings?

People driving in the opposite direction gawked at us. It was a clear forty-degree day. I wore a baseball cap and sunglasses, but they weren't staring at my pitiful disguise. Nor were they stunned stupid by the gorgeous guy in the ridiculous seventies jogging suit running next to me. They stared at my security team, courtesy of my guardian angel master vampire.

Long gone were the days I raced along the lake trails by myself. Now every time I ran it was between two town cars full of combat-ready vampires. That was bad. The helicopter hovering above us? Much worse. Everyone in the Tahoe City area probably thought some eccentric billionaire was out for a stroll.

Hank grew impatient. "Well, are you going to tell me?"

"Tell you what?"

His expression told me he'd like to use my eyeballs to play Ping-Pong. "Why you don't bed the master? It's not like you're some shy virgin or something. That idiot Liam told me you and the pureblood were always getting it on."

My face flushed and I picked up my pace. "Hank, I am *so* not having this conversation with you."

He ignored me. "Not having sex is just unnatural, even for a weird-ass chick like you."

"Hank, you're really starting to piss me off."

"Just admit it—you want to have sex."

"I don't have to admit anything. And if you open your trap one more time, you're going to be sorry."

Again, he ignored me. "The master is reasonable. He'll probably allow his ears to be scratched during your lovemaking, if that's the sort of shit that turns you on."

As my speed increased, the cars in front and behind us accelerated. "Hank, don't bring Aric into this—you know nothing about him or our love life."

"What love life? You have nothing with that mutt. Look, I'm not trying to pressure you, but the others and I have a pool going. The pot's getting high and I don't want to lose."

"You're betting on whether Misha and I are going to do it!" The revelation only made me run faster.

"Not whether you'll do it—*when*. Edith and Liz are already out twenty grand. You have to please the master by Valentine's Day or else I'm out fifty."

"You're such an asshole, Hank. I can't believe you'd bet on me."

"I wouldn't have if I'd known how difficult you'd be. Shit, Celia. I knew you were stubborn, but this is bad even for you."

Hank was now wheezing. Vampires were fast, but not

designed to race for such long distances. We'd hit the ten-mile mark before I really began to sweat. I pushed faster. Hank tried desperately to catch me and lost his concentration. He slid on some gravel and took a dive. There was a loud grunt when the car behind us ran over him. *Serves him right.*

Tim stuck his shaved head out of the car in front of us. "Damn it, Celia—slow the hell down. The humans are going to suspect something."

I don't think so, Tim. I went up the next side road at the last minute. The car ahead kept going, but the car behind me made a sharp turn and tried to follow. They were keeping up pretty well until I *shifted* underground and turned up in someone's backyard.

The helicopter circled above me, searching. I giggled when the vamps started swearing. I continued to *shift* and kept to the shadows beneath the trees. Danny had convinced me demons—the real ones—couldn't appear so close to the lake. It made sense, given that the only ones I'd seen had been far from Tahoe's power. I continued to move. It wouldn't take long for the vamps to pick up my scent, and in the meantime I wanted a moment away from the annoyingly undead.

I finally appeared on a high hill that overlooked Tahoe and dropped down to a small patch of beach. The aroma of its magic brought me a sense of calm and assured me I was protected. My tigress purred and relaxed, allowing me to stretch before taking a seat on a large rock. I peered out at the water. Hank was right. I did want to make love, but it wasn't with his master. *I miss you, Aric.*

Aric and I always went to bed fully dressed, though it never lasted. Before meeting him, I used to be highly protective of my personal space. But once we were together, physical distance failed to exist between us. I always woke with his arms around me. Sometimes I faced him; other times my back was to him; there were also days when he lay on top of me—exactly where he'd fallen asleep. Regardless of the position, it always felt right. I'd only ever known true peace in his arms.

With Barbara having moved on to the next pureblood

she could sink her fangs into, I'd begun to fantasize more and more about making love to Aric. When I'd last spoke to Liam, he told me my encounter with the demon had pushed Aric to his breaking point and that he'd gone berserk trying to hunt down the Tribe in order to keep me safe. My touch, my presence, my body could soothe him and humanize his wolf again. I had no doubt.

The problem remained, though: sex wouldn't extinguish Aric's pack obligations or make the Tribe go away. It would calm his beast temporarily, yes, but our human sides would ultimately suffer. The kiss we'd shared at Shayna and Koda's wedding stemmed from longing and the desperation to be with each other. It hadn't solved anything. And it hurt so much afterward when we parted. If we made love, it would only reopen those horrible wounds from our first breakup. So then what?

The fluttering of wings interrupted my thoughts. A beautiful snow white owl landed on the low limb of the nearest tree. My tigress woke up. She probably wondered why this nocturnal bird had taken to flight during the day.

It stared at me. Its head tilted at an inquisitive angle, its round yellow eyes unblinking. A breeze blew softly, allowing me to catch the owl's aroma. It smelled of feathers, dry leaves, and pine trees. There was also the vaguest hint of something else. I took a deep breath, trying to figure it out. *Hmm, is it . . . copper?*

The owl flapped its broad wings and landed on a withered log next to me. The smell of copper intensified, quite subtle but unmistakable. My tigress didn't like the bird so close and grew uneasy. I concentrated on blocking its spirit in case it continued to advance. It turned its head toward me and opened its beak.

"*Celia Wird*," it said in a demonic voice.

The cocking of guns snapped me out of my shock. I dove off the side of the cliff as a stream of bullets littered the sky. I *shifted* to break my fall and surfaced behind a large boulder, where I poked my head around. The owl flew around at an unholy speed, dodging the spray of bullets from the snipers in the helicopter. It flew toward the horizon, continuing to chant, "*Celia Wird. Celia Wird. Celia Wird,*" until it disappeared into the sun.

The helicopter didn't follow, veering back. Misha's vampires had found me. Hank paced at the cliff's edge swearing like a maniac. Tim also yelled, his fingers gripping his bald head. "Mother's ass, what the hell are we going to tell the master?"

Another vamp appeared and looked out over the cliff. He shrugged. "The truth. You killed Celia."

There was a disturbing gurgling sound as Tim grabbed the vamp by the throat. The vamp foamed at the mouth when Tim tightened his grip and shook him. "I did not! That crazy bitch jumped off the cliff."

I stepped into view. "The crazy bitch jumped because you jackasses fired at me!"

Tim dropped the vamp down the side of the hill. He rolled with flailing limbs as more vamps rushed to the edge. They were all initially shocked to see me still alive, then relieved, and finally royally pissed off. In a flash, both Tim and Hank were in my face. "What the hell is wrong with you?" Tim hollered. "Do you have any idea what the master would have done to us if Drago killed you?"

"Drago?"

"Yes, Drago," Hank snapped. "Taking on a shape-shifter is just plain suicide!"

I glanced back at the horizon like an idiot. "That owl was a *shape-shifter*?"

Hank and Tim just shook their heads at me, probably wondering how I tied my own shoes.

"Would you stop looking at me that way? I'm not stupid! I didn't grow up in the supernatural community— there's still a lot I don't know."

"No kidding," Hank muttered.

He crumpled to the ground when I kicked him hard in the shins. "That's for insulting me and being involved in that stupid bet." I turned to glare at Tim. He took a step back. "Tell me about Drago."

Tim scowled but did as I demanded. "He's one of the oldest and deadliest of the shape-shifters. He's rumored to have made tens of thousands of blood sacrifices in order to gain his ability. He usually takes the form of a winged creature—that's why we think it was him."

"He smelled like a bird."

Tim rolled his eyes at me. "That's because shape-shifters assume the scent of whatever they *change* into. Their only constant underlying aroma is copper."

Okay, so I was right about the copper. "He watched me for a while. If he's so deadly, why didn't he just kill me?"

Hank staggered to his feet. Tim rolled his eyes at him this time and continued. "He's likely heard about you, too. The only reason you're still alive is he probably thought you weren't worth killing."

"Why?"

Walt, another vamp, descended the hill. "She's not very bright, is she?" He talked about me as if I wasn't even there. He was one of Misha's newer vampires and spent most of his time trying to buddy up to Hank and Tim. It didn't work, and I didn't appreciate him trying to earn a laugh at my expense.

Tim looked from Walt to me. "I suppose he didn't recognize you as a challenge."

Although the Drago creep had wigged me out, I couldn't help feeling slighted. "Why the hell not?"

Walt chuckled. "Because you're not. Near as I can figure, you're the master's charity case."

"Excuse me?" My hackles rose and a growl built deep in my core. The vampires in general weren't exactly kind to me, but this loser had just catapulted right over the piss-me-off line.

Hank and Tim knowingly took a step back from us, then another. Walt's smirk told me my inner beast had failed to intimidate him. He circled me, eyeing me like he wanted to take a bite. "I think for once your idiocy worked to your advantage."

My claws protruded as I felt him stalk around me. I wasn't scared. But he should have been. "You insult my intelligence one more time, Walt, and I swear I'll rip your arms off."

Walt loomed over me, bending his large frame to bare his fangs near my throat. "You forget yourself, Celia. You may be the master's plaything, but *I* am a member of his family. He would understand if I was forced to kill you in self-defense."

"So what was Walt trying to say before?" I asked Tim in the car.

Tim shifted nervously in his seat. "Ah, because you didn't know what Drago was, you didn't know enough to be afraid. He gets off on fear and pain. You failed to demonstrate either and therefore failed to excite him. And since you didn't attack, he didn't see you as an immediate threat."

I sat back against the black leather seat and adjusted my legs. "Drago called me by name. How is it that shape-shifters know me, too? I've done some damage, but not enough to get this level of attention."

Hank stopped trying to wipe Walt's blood off his polyester suit. I didn't like the grave expression that fell over his face. "For whatever reason, all the dark ones have gotten wind of you, Celia. Shit, I don't know why." He exchanged glances with Tim. "But someone has obviously told them about you and sent them your way."

"Misha said I'm supposedly the key to destroying one of the dark ones. I assumed it was the Tribe, since that's the group I've been training to kill. Now, after this, I'm not so certain."

Tim shook his head. "It could still be the Tribe. They and the shape-shifters deal with hell all the time. Tribe-masters because they're fathered by demons, and shape-shifters since, well, they carry the power of hell within them."

This was not the pep talk I needed. My fright likely played across my face like my own personal march to death row. All I needed was an impending-doom sound track.

Hank and Tim stared back at me with empathy—well, as much as they were capable of. Hank even tried to make me feel better . . . in his own Hank-ish way. "Consider it a compliment. You're a mutant who's kicked a lot of ass."

I slipped out of the car the moment we pulled into Misha's compound. The Catholic schoolgirls immediately surrounded me. Maria sucked on a lollipop suggestively. "Celia, we are going to de Naughty Time Boutique. Want to come?"

Considering the company, the destination, and the bet they'd made, I didn't have to think twice. "No, thanks."

Edith stepped back so one of the vampires could haul Walt out of the other car. "Oh, but, Celia, it's such a fun place. It's more than just lingerie. They have games and toys."

"Uhh, it's not really my thing."

The trunk popped open and someone retrieved Walt's arms.

"Here." Tim handed Liz a few bills. "Pick up some edible underwear for me. Two of my regulars really enjoy them."

"What flavor?"

"I think they like strawberry."

"Crotch or no crotch?"

"I don't care. Surprise me."

Agnes adjusted her glasses and scowled at me. "What's with you?"

Hank answered. "She was approached by Drago." The girls all gasped. "And he knows her by name."

I was bombarded with questions. The commotion ground to a halt when a certain someone spoke out in a deadly voice. "And just how did that interaction take place if she was in the company of so many escorts?" Misha asked.

It took a lot of begging and pleading, but no one was killed. Well, except for Walt, but he was annoying anyway. It helped that Misha was both distracted and disturbed by Drago's familiarity with me. At his request, I followed him inside and into the great room. We sat beside each other, facing the fireplace. He was unusually quiet. His fingertips touched in a praying position while his elbows remained on his lap. His unease worsened mine. I was sort of counting on him to raise my spirits.

Virginia entered carrying a large tray of food. She placed it on the table beside me and knelt before Misha. She unbuttoned her blouse and exposed her neck, along with one and a half breasts. Misha continued to stare straight ahead. "Not now, Virginia."

She left without bothering to button her blouse, yet her lack of modesty wasn't what needled me. Virginia knew the vampires had been ordered not to feed in front of me. The fact that she offered herself to Misha while I sat next to him was her way of telling me I didn't matter.

"I had expected those who oppose us to become aware of you and your sisters," Misha finally said. "And the magnitude of your collective power."

I fought to keep my claws from protruding. "You think whoever is after me will go after my sisters?"

"Once it eliminates you, yes." He paused and angled his head toward the large picture window. The breeze from the lake increased, hard enough to slap the branches of the closest fir against the pane. He rose from his chair and pushed open the thick lead glass. I followed him, watching as he lowered his lids and inhaled the mesmeric aroma of Tahoe's magic. He nodded subtly, as if listening to a conversation. I mimicked his movements and strained my ears to hear . . . Nothing, just the wind, the flicker of branches, the light snow that swept up to splatter the glass.

When Misha acknowledged me, his beautiful face contorted with worry. "You remain the key to its end, Celia—not your sisters. This . . . *enemy* is convinced you will see to its destruction . . . and to those who follow it."

My head spun, searching for what or who he could mean. A shape-shifter? Likely not. No one seemed to think I could kill one on my own. And how would killing one stop those that remained? A Tribemaster was more likely, but I'd have to kill a hell of a lot more to put an end to their reign. I ran a hand through my hair. *Crap*. This was not the uplifting talk I'd been hoping for. "How can I stop an invisible enemy? And how the hell could I possibly be the key?"

Misha took my hands and squeezed them. "I don't know. But until we learn more of what seeks you, you are not to attend another mission." I nodded, remaining quiet and lost in my thoughts. Misha lifted my chin to meet his face. "If it fears you, that means you can and will destroy it."

Yeah, I thought. *Unless it kills me first.*

Misha let me drive to Dollar Point in the reinforced Ying-Ying mobile without escorts. It must have packed a hell of a punch if he deemed me safe to ride alone. Fear tensed my shoulders and threatened to chew on me like a bag of tortilla chips. I reached for my tigress, refusing to let it cripple me. Misha was right. If this unknown predator considered me such a menace, then maybe I could overcome it. As for the shape-shifters, I believed Tim was right. Drago and his pals likely didn't see me as a threat . . . for now.

I heard Shayna howling in that pitiful way of hers and the wolves' uproarious laughter the moment I pulled into the neighborhood. Taran greeted me with tears glistening in her blue eyes. "What did she say that time?" she asked the wolves behind her.

Liam roared and held his sides. Even the more sympathetic Danny and Gemini couldn't control their hysterics. Bren had turned purple from lack of oxygen and Koda shoved a pillow over his face in an attempt to muffle his laughter.

"She said, 'The hog in my kitchen ate my steering wheel,'" Liam sputtered.

Emme covered her mouth to hide her grin. "Shayna, what were you trying to say?"

Shayna pouted. "There's a demon child in my house."

Taran snorted. "Damn, Shayna. That wasn't even close, girl."

Bren tried to compose himself. "You should have seen her at the steakhouse. She howled, 'There's a pig wearing my panties!' and then charged."

Shayna's face turned a color of red usually found only

on Emme's face. "Dude! You promised you wouldn't tell them!"

"The wolves are trying to teach Shayna how to *call* for help," Emme explained at the same time Taran asked what the hell was up with Shayna and pork. Everyone else exploded with laughter.

"Maybe you should just teach her the word 'help,'" I offered.

Bren stopped laughing when he caught sight of my face. I hadn't laughed or even managed a smile. "What's wrong, kid?"

I leaned against the door to affect a more relaxed pose. "Have you guys ever heard of a shape-shifter named Drago?"

Shayna slumped on Koda's lap. "What do you think I'm doing wrong, puppy?"

Koda, like the rest of the wolves, had lost his amusement. His voice dropped deeper than usual. "We'll work on your *calls* later, baby." To me he said, "Tell us."

I relayed the morning's events, including Misha's chat with the lake. Danny paced, as he often did when he thought about things. "He left without attacking you or the vampires. That in itself is encouraging. But, like you, I don't think a shape-shifter is what's after you."

"If it was, you sure as hell wouldn't be standing here," Bren ground out. He crossed and uncrossed his arms several times. His beast wanted to come out and gnaw on something. I hadn't seen him so worked up in a long time. "Shit, Celia. Fighting those prick Tribesmen is bad enough, but those shape-shifters carry hell within them."

Emme's face blanched. "Th-they're more powerful than Tribemasters?"

Gemini nodded. "In providing the blood sacrifices, they're gifted with the might of their dark deity. Shape-shifters are the hardest of all evil beings to destroy."

I pushed off from the door. "If they're so badass, why would they care about me?"

Bren looked at me square in the eye. "Because you're not supposed to have what they have." He swore again when he caught my surprise. "Ceel, these mofos go through a lot of shit to gain the ability to assume any form. All you have to do is rub up against the nearest critter."

"But I can't control it!"

"They may not know that. But even if they did, it wouldn't matter to them. You're a threat!"

Gemini walked toward me in the heavy silence that followed. "Bren has a point. But I don't believe the shape-shifters are the immediate enemy. Typically, these dark forces don't align unless there's something in it for them. Something is influencing them toward your direction."

My gaze returned to Bren, his face strained with the effort to hold back his wolf. Good thing Danny was naturally calmer, and the others had my sisters to soothe them. A pack of agitated werewolves was the last thing I needed to deal with. "That's what the vamps are saying, too."

Shayna played with her fingers nervously while she continued sitting on Koda's lap. "Do they have any idea who would send these creatures your way?"

I shook my head. "The Tribe still remains suspect number one."

Bren walked over to hook an arm around me. I let out a small breath, thankful he'd finally managed to reel in his beast. I smiled warmly at him. He was a great friend to care so much. "Misha's postponing my assignments for a while. I've wondered, though—if I lie low, will Drago target someone else?"

"With any luck, hell yeah," Bren muttered.

I swallowed hard. "Not necessarily."

Gemini watched me with interest, suspecting, I imagined, where my thought process was headed. "You're worried about your sisters." I nodded. "And Aric." I didn't have to answer him. He knew he was right. He sighed. "Aric is regarded as one of the most powerful *weres* in history. He remains the only one among our kind to have achieved his first *change* at less than two months of age. However, the level of his supremacy is yet to be recognized. When it is, then, yes, he will be stalked by the dark ones as well." He returned to Taran and drew her into his arms. "And so will your family."

"But in addition to his own strength, Aric has us to protect him," Koda said. "Just as we'll protect our mates and you as his."

I squirmed uncomfortably. Like I said, until Aric called me his mate directly, I wouldn't accept it. I gained some composure and met their worried stares with a small smile. "Don't worry about me. I have the Catholic schoolgirls on my side." They failed to consider my humor. I couldn't blame them. Until we knew who or what sought me, none of us was safe.

CHAPTER 15

"Anara has given up on trying to marry off Aric."

Yippee.

"Now he just wants him to breed," Liam continued on the phone. "He's throwing every hot *were* he can find at him. Wolf or not, pureblood or not, he doesn't care. All Anara wants is for our kind to multiply. And you should see some of these girls, the way they act and how they dress. There was this one—just today, as a matter of fact—who walked up to him *completely naked* trying to seduce him. She'd written Aric's name across her belly with an arrow pointing to her—"

"Thanks for the info, Liam." *Now I'll have nightmares.* "Please put Emme on."

"But, Celia, there's more. Turns out she's a wereminx and, *damn*, is she flexible. She went up to Aric when he was lying on the bench press and—

"*Put Emme on now!*" I rubbed my eyes. "Please," I added a little less psychotically. Dear Lord, sometimes I wished Liam came with an off switch.

"Liam, sweetheart, please stop. You're upsetting Celia," Emme said on the other end of the line. "Sorry about that, Celia. Liam sometimes gets carried away."

"I've noticed. Look, I'm late for my workout. I just wanted to let you know I'll be at the gala tomorrow night."

"That's wonderful, Celia. It'll be great to see you. What changed your mind?"

"I want to see Aric." Although I didn't want to see him with another female, knowing I wouldn't react . . . *diplomatically*, shall we say. And disemboweling some *were* hoochie on the *weres'* sacred turf struck me as a big no-no. I disconnected with Emme, then took a moment to rub my shoulders. I'd spent the last few weeks getting the snot knocked, twisted, and cajoled out of me by Ying-Ying and Kuan Jang Nim Chang. Although I was lying low for a while, I couldn't do so for long. I would soon come face-to-face with the Tribe or whoever the hell was behind the attacks. When the time came, one of us would have to die. I wanted to make sure it wouldn't be me.

I placed my cell phone on a small table near the entrance to the dojang and slipped off my shoes. Instead of finding Ying-Ying standing with one leg behind her neck over a bed of cacti, I found Misha with a mystified bald eagle perched on his arm.

"What's this, Misha?"

"I thought it would be best if I worked with you this afternoon, instead of Ying-Ying."

I glanced at the eagle and then back at the exit. "I don't know . . . I wouldn't want to disappoint Ying-Ying."

My yogi appeared behind one of the woven bamboo doors that led to a back storage room. She glided across the light wood floor with a little extra twitch to her step, smiling alluringly as she passed us.

Misha's grin matched hers. "Do not worry for Ying-Ying. I assure you she is quite satisfied."

"Slut," I muttered under my breath.

Misha quirked an eyebrow. "I'm surprised to find you think so little of her."

I gave him a hard stare. "I was referring to you, Misha."

My comment earned me a wicked smile and a deep chuckle. "Touch my bird."

"Excuse me?"

"The eagle, kitten. Come touch the eagle."

I threw out a hand. "Misha, did you learn nothing from the dog incident?"

"Actually, kitten, I believe I did. My theory is since your other self is a predator, you would do better controlling the form of another beast of prey."

"Dogs are predators—they're related to wolves. And you saw how well that went."

"Kitten, a Cavalier King Charles spaniel is so far removed from a wolf you insult the lupines by even making such a suggestion. I initially believed if we started out with a small creature, we would have better results. But perhaps we need to be more aggressive. Now, if you don't mind, let us begin."

"Actually, I do mind very much. Did you have fun watching me drool all over your bed when I had the seizure?"

"No, I would simply enjoy you naked on my bed." He thought about it. "And screaming with ecstasy as opposed to drooling."

My face flushed with color. "Are you done?"

His grin told me no. "I also enjoy watching your areolas tighten whenever I stare at your breasts." He glanced down. "Just as they are now."

Tears actually leaked from my eyes from the heat building around me. I covered my telltale girlfriends and stormed toward the door. It seemed master vampires also came equipped with magical nipple-stiffening power.

"Kitten, wait—it was all merely in jest."

I turned to face him. The eagle shook from Misha's pathetic attempts to hold in his laughter. "Yeah, you're just hilarious, aren't you?"

I almost rammed into Hank on the way out. He greeted me with—yup, that's right, an arrogant smirk. "See, it's just like I said. You want the master. Now go back inside and get the job done. My money is at stake here, Celia."

"For the last time, I don't want Misha!"

"Oh, yeah?" He elongated his incisors. "Let's have a look at those nipples."

Hank was refastening his jaw when I screamed at him, "Fine. I'll go back in just to prove I don't want him. Kiss your fifty grand good-bye, Batman!"

Misha had calmed when I went back in, but his amused grin remained in place. I stomped to his side, pointy boobies and all. "Let's do it, then." He raised his eyebrows in surprise. "I mean your damn science experiment, Misha!"

Misha, although seemingly disappointed that his eagle wouldn't witness our fornicating on the floor, commenced his twisted exercise. "Take a breath and raise the shields that surround your spirit."

My eyes closed and I breathed deeply, allowing my protective aura to fall like a velvet curtain.

"Very good, Celia. Now, allow my bird to enter you."

I cracked open one eye just to be sure he was still clothed. He smirked. Against my better judgment I laughed. "Does everything have to be about sex with your kind?"

"Forgive me."

"I always do, Misha."

We began. I focused on blocking the eagle's spirit before reaching out to the entranced bird. The feathers of the majestic beast were unbelievably soft, but beneath his plumes strong muscles waited to propel him into the sky. I breathed deeply, trying to take him in without seizing.

"Step back," Misha said quietly. My soles slid across the smooth floor. "Now *change* into the eagle."

I searched within me for any trace of the bird. I couldn't perceive so much as a quill. "Misha, I can't."

"I disagree. Try harder."

I focused on the eagle's white head, his satin brown feathers, and how tight he gripped Misha's arm. I concentrated on his scent and the details of his form. Nothing happened. Misha had me repeat the steps over and over. Each time I tried to withdraw my shields a little more. I startled about an hour later when I landed hard on my butt. At first I thought it was the beginning of a seizure, but when I looked at my toes, instead of feet, I bore talons. When I tried to wiggle my new appendages, they *changed* back to human.

"Well done, my darling. Now try again."

I repeated the same steps that had brought on the talons, this time without success. It was extremely frustrating, but I continued, motivated now that I'd experienced an inkling of progress. After another hour of hard work, I saw my pinkie toe nail elongate and turn black. The moment I touched it, it dissolved into my flesh and resumed its normal appearance.

My muscles felt ready to slip off my bones and land with a splat. Sweat dripped between my shoulder blades and breasts. I sucked in a breath, surprised how much my concentration physically taxed me.

"You seem weary."

Misha sensed my obvious fatigue, but my stubbornness and the excitement that accompanied my newfound talent motivated me to continue. "I'm okay."

"No. You have done enough for the day. Come, let us dine. We will continue our practice tomorrow."

"We? All you did was hold the bird."

He smiled. "Nonsense. You wouldn't have achieved that level of success had it not been for my encouragement."

"You're just a regular cheerleader, aren't you? Okay, grab the pom-poms and let's go."

"She wants him to grab her pom-poms," Edith whispered excitedly from the door.

"What de hell does dat mean?" Maria hissed, her annoyance deepening her Brazilian accent.

"It means they're going to bang like shudders during a tornado. Pay up, O naughty ones."

Liz poked her head in briefly and scowled. "I'm not paying you shit, Hank. They still have their clothes on. And what the hell's up with the bird?"

Misha and I reached the entrance in time for Edith to open the door. She smiled at Misha with so much sizzle, I thought his black cashmere turtleneck would burst into an inferno. "Oh, Master, what sort of mischief have you been up to?"

Misha returned her grin. "Tell Chef to prepare Celia her dinner and fetch me an equally deserving feast."

The vamps took off.

"Does it bother you that they have this whole bet thing going?" I hadn't known if Misha was aware, but I supposed it was his job to know all of his family's bizarre antics.

"No. It's similar to children at play."

"Children don't often bet on whether their parents are going to have sex."

Misha's sly grin slid across his face like a seasoned figure skater across ice. "Does this mean you consider yourself their mother?"

"Mom to the fang-banging Brady Bunch? Oh, hell no. Besides, they barely tolerate me." My voice softened. "If I ever do have children, I hope they would at least like me."

He slipped his free arm around me and the deep twinkle of mischief in his eyes dissolved into tenderness. "They would love you, Celia."

My heart melted at the softness of his words. I buried my head into his shoulder. "Thank you, Misha."

We practiced again on the following day, stopping only for meals.

"That is barely a wing."

I flapped out the half wing I managed from my elbow down. The breeze tickled my underarm briefly before the whole thing vanished. I rubbed the sweat off my brow. "No kidding."

I managed a beak, a few talons, and some eagle eyes, but no matter how hard I tried, I couldn't keep the form for long. Just before it was time to get ready for the gala, I *changed* completely into an eagle. It lasted only a few seconds, long enough for me to see my reflection in the mirror the vamps had brought in. Not to brag, but my eagle form was magnificent—and immense. Like my tigress, it was about four times bigger than my human self.

My human body returned in one painful rush. I collapsed, panting and exhausted on the floor, surrounded by the tattered remains of my clothes. Misha perched the eagle on his stand and quickly knelt next to me. "Are you hurt?"

I shook my head. "No, mostly just tired. I'll be fine in a moment."

Misha smiled. I wasn't sure whether he was proud of me or whether it was because I was naked. I grabbed at my torn rags and tried my best to cover myself. He inched his way closer, his face moving toward mine. Whatever he'd planned was interrupted by wretched screaming.

The little Russian dressmaker hurried in, the *tap, tap, tap* of her pointy black shoes echoing in the room as she launched into one mean-ass fit. She waved a garment bag above her head, all the while shaking her bony finger at me. She motioned to Misha, spurting angry Russian like venom from a cobra. Finally she shoved the bag into Misha's hands and whirled off like a hurricane.

I narrowed my eyes. "What did she say?"

"She said your dress is ready."

I *changed* into a tigress so I wouldn't be naked, abandoning Misha, who continued to laugh out loud. The interaction between me and the old twit had entertained him tremendously. Goody for him. I returned to my quarters to shower her bitchiness off my skin.

My muscles ached. The hot water helped relax them. It failed, however, to wash away my nerves. I was going to see Aric. And he would be in a tux. My hands skimmed over my body as I applied lotion, remembering the first time I'd seen Aric in a tuxedo. He hated opera and didn't care for any type of classical music. But he knew my love for Il Divo and surprised me with tickets on a romantic getaway to Sacramento. My olive skin was deeply tanned from our time on the lake. I'd slipped into a strapless canary yellow cocktail dress in the bathroom of our hotel room. When I stepped out into the master suite, Aric had just finished adjusting his bow tie. We gawked at each other for roughly three-point-five seconds before he pounced. We never did see Il Divo. Not to mention my dress lay in pieces and he lost the deposit on his tux.

"What's with the stupid grin on your face?"

Leave it to Liz to buzz-kill my memory. She and Edith lounged on my bed like lazy heathens. They were dressed in sexy black plaid dresses that still screamed uniform. I pinched the bridge of my nose. Maria and Agnes probably wore the same getup. "What are you doing here?"

Liz tossed back her ice blond hair and narrowed her eyes. "You will be representing *our* house tonight. We're here to make you look decent, for once in your life."

Edith smiled and I instinctively covered my liver. "Don't fuck this up for us, Celia."

Liz agreed. "Yeah. Don't fuck it up."

There were three reasons I allowed their "help." The first was that they didn't have anything sharp or pointy in their hands. The second was that, as much as they made me want to gouge my own eyes out with a spoon, hair and makeup was their thing—not mine. And the third reason—albeit the most selfish on my part—was that if they somehow messed me up, Misha would kill them. That in itself was worth the chance.

Edith did a nice job of giving me a cascade of neatly flowing curls. When it came to my makeup, Liz applied eyeliner, blush, and lip gloss. She very much wanted to add some eye shadow for a smoky effect, but I wouldn't allow it. That earned me a death glare and a few mutters about what an ingrate I was. And here I'd thought the vamps weren't any fun.

Edith unveiled the Russian couture dress, shocking me with its elegant beauty—and length. The silk ivory halter dress sparkled with tiny little clear crystals and creamy pearls. The shoes matched the dress perfectly. They were made of the same silk and had the same beading sewn in. The crazy old lady had even provided matching earrings. I put them on, along with a skimpy pair of panties, and stepped into the dress and shoes.

The skirt was so short there was no way I would be able to bend over. Good thing the wack-job seamstress had strategically added pleats. I'd still be able to kick up past my head if I got into any trouble. And while I normally wouldn't have chosen a dress this sexy, the thought of what Aric would say warmed my cheeks with anticipation.

I adjusted my breasts in the halter while looking in the full-length mirror. The style enhanced my cleavage, but obviously not enough for Liz's taste. She handed me what resembled raw chicken cutlets. "You'll need these."

"What are they?"

"Adhesive silicone bra cups."

I wrinkled my nose. "Can't I just go braless?"

"No! It's bad enough you refuse to wear the silk stockings."

"I don't need them."

Edith licked her lips. "She does have great legs." She assisted me in attaching the bra cups—I suspected more to cop a feel than to help. When she finished, I filled out the dress significantly more.

I gaped at myself in the mirror. "Um, don't you think this is a little much?"

Liz was seconds from taking a bite out of me. "*No*. It's *not*. If anything, you should consider getting them professionally done. Here. Put this on. The master is waiting." She handed me what looked like a white mink coat.

I held my hand up. "Sorry. I don't wear fur."

Liz scowled. "Celia, it's a fake. It's been magicked to resemble the real thing." She held out the coat for me to examine. It felt real to the touch. I sniffed it, satisfied only once I smelled the polyester. "We need to go. I can feel our master growing impatient."

We hurried to the house. Edith and Liz strutted the length of the stone pathway, wiggling their hips and throwing back their hair in perfect choreographed movements. I stumbled behind them, trying not to fall on my face in the sinfully high shoes. Their steps increased when we entered the house. Misha's growing irritation must have beckoned them forward.

I sighed and gave up trying to chase them down. They abandoned me in the kitchen in their haste to meet their master. I entered the foyer alone, smiling when I saw Misha.

Stunned silence greeted me. My steps slowed and my

smile faded. He and all the vampires stared at me like they'd never seen me before. I turned around, certain someone else had caught their attention.

"You look beautiful, my sweet," Misha said quietly, bringing my focus back to him. He wore an amazing black tuxedo that hugged his muscular body to perfection. His ivory shirt and vest were made of the same silk as my dress and shoes. And although they lacked the beading, they somehow matched the style of my dress. "May I see the rest?"

Everyone took it as their cue to depart. Misha slowly slipped off my coat. The soft edges of the fur tickled my arms and slid down in a seductive caress. He circled me, very much like the predator he was, and examined me carefully. The sizzle in his eyes made my heartbeat accelerate. I wanted to take a step back from him and knew I should. My tigress believed otherwise. He was a predator, but so were we, she reminded me.

Misha's lips parted slowly, like those of a lover before the start of a long, deep kiss. And while his fangs didn't elongate and his tongue failed to beckon me for a taste, I felt his vampiric charm inviting me to him. He watched me, expecting me to react to one extreme or the other. I remained where I stood. He was my friend. I wouldn't desert him. But I also wouldn't welcome him to my bed.

When I didn't react, Misha helped with my coat and pulled out my hair trapped beneath it. His hand ran down the length of my tresses and his skin radiated with the promise of seduction. "You look beautiful," he said once more.

My voice cracked when I tried to speak. I cleared my throat. "Thank you, Misha. You look nice, too."

Misha offered me his arm and we made our way to his Hummer limo. All four Catholic schoolgirls, Hank, and Tim waited in a row outside the colossal vehicle. They scrambled back when I reached the door. Hank opened it and ducked behind it, using it as a shield should things go *boom*. Although Ying-Ying had reinforced and booby-trapped all the vehicles against sabotage, I suppose they weren't taking any chances.

"Allow me," Misha said, annoyance at his family clipping his words. He slipped into the limo ahead of me, ignoring the audible gasps from his family. He then reached for my hand, pulling me in before I had time to panic. Nothing exploded, sizzled, or jolted. I didn't so much as feel a zing. I took my seat beside Misha, thankful the coat hung longer than my skirt and that it kept all my important parts covered. The vamps piled in. At Misha's nod they poured champagne and passed it around. I didn't take any. I might not have been blown to bits this time, but that didn't mean I was safe.

The other vampires laughed, gossiped, and drank the entire way to Squaw Valley. Misha and I barely said a word. When I thanked him for the clothes, he only smiled in response. In his silence I wondered what else he had planned for the night and what awaited me in the unwelcome territory known as the Den.

CHAPTER 16

When I'd first heard the term "Den," a vision of a cold, damp cave came to mind. So did a giant bear nursing her cubs. What can I say? All the Animal Planet specials had led me astray. I hadn't pictured the behemoth and sacred compound that awaited us where Aric served as the chancellor of students and oversaw the young *weres* training to be Guardians of the Earth.

The helicopter filled with snipers that had hovered above abandoned us at the base of Granite Chief Peak. We didn't need them to follow us to the top, where the Den lay surrounded by snow-draped pines and firs and a Goliath stone wall. The local clan of witches had placed magical defensive wards following the first demon children attack and extended them after the disastrous Tribe invasion. Now the wards covered almost the entire mountain and snaked their way through several hidden paths along Squaw Valley.

The hum of witches' magic buzzed around us when we passed through the border of the first ward. It irritated my skin as if it disapproved of my presence, but couldn't harm me since I meant no ill will against the *weres*. The second ward—the one closest to the Den—shoved me with an invisible force and momentarily stole my breath. I shook it off quickly. Although the *were* magic reinforcing it made it clear I didn't belong, again it couldn't harm me. The vampires swore and swiveled in their seats. They'd felt it, too, though not to the extreme that I had. Misha? He had barely blinked.

We passed through the giant wrought-iron gates and into the virtual fortress. The entire campus consisted of massive three-story lodges mimicking an exclusive ski resort. The main building housing the gala was the largest and most impressive, boasting polished cedar floors, granite pillars, and floor-to-ceiling windows with breathtaking mountain views.

We arrived to a packed house. I took in a breath, hoping to catch the scent of my family, friends, or Aric. I detected no one. It bothered me. My insecurities burned a hole into the pit of my stomach. I needed my sisters and friends. Galas and charity balls were not my thing, but then again, I would have felt intimidated at a prom. Yes, I was with the vampires, and, yes, I knew them, but they would never comprehend my discomfort. This was *their* thing. They loved rubbing elbows, flirting, and flaunting their power. It helped that they also had the goods to back it up, and they damn well knew it. The good Catholics tossed back their hair and flung their hips seductively as they strolled ahead, just as they had at the house, only with a little more sass and a hell of a lot more attitude. Hank and Tim swaggered in like they were doing everyone a favor by showing up. Their smug smiles screamed seduction. My brain screamed for them to give it a rest.

Arrogance was never a quality I found attractive. Confidence, yes, but cockiness was hands-down unappealing. To other vampires it was something of a turn-on. Even a few of the witches in attendance showed interest. There was one who gave Tim the once-over. He nodded toward her, flashing his gleaming white fangs. "Genevieve."

Genevieve was the Tahoe region's head witch. A position I'd helped her secure, though it hadn't been my intent. She was a beautiful woman with dark brows, waist-length ebony hair, and blue eyes that glowed like melted sapphires. When she walked into a room and raised her arms, I could swear doves and butterflies flew out of her armpits. When I raised my arms, it was usually in defense of the evil creature trying to chew them off. She matched Tim's smile. "Maybe," was all she told him.

Misha escorted me along the entrance hall while we waited to enter the ballroom. He had been right about the attendants; all the major players from the supernatural world mingled around us. Besides his master, Uri, and the Elders, I didn't know any of them. But I felt them. Their command brushed against me. It was an unpleasant feeling—challenging in a way, as if their inner entities flexed their muscles in my face. I took comfort in knowing I wasn't the sole target. Everyone seemed to be involved in pleasant conversations while subtle power struggles occurred amid the laughter and phony smiles.

"Come, my love. There is someone I'd like you to meet."

I knew who Misha wanted to introduce me to even before we approached her. She was a vampire—an extremely powerful one who matched Misha in strength despite her blatant lack of soul. Aside from Uri, who surpassed Misha's power only slightly, I'd never sensed a vampire strong enough be his equal. Most masters lacked Misha's vigor. This vampire lacked nothing but clothing. She was tall and voluptuous with gorgeous light brown hair that fell perfectly straight just below her shoulders. Her bronze skin shimmered as if brushed with glitter, while her glacial blue eyes practically chilled me in place. Humans would have mistaken her for a twenty-year-old girl. Those capable of scenting potent magic, like me, realized she was well over five hundred years old. A vampire that strong had to have been *turned* a long, long time ago to have gained such supremacy.

Her hairstyle was simple. One length, parted down the middle. That's where her simplicity ended. She wasn't wearing any jewelry. She didn't have to. Her skirt consisted entirely of diamonds, sewn in like the pearls on my dress. I say "skirt" because she wore no other fabric. Her breasts and part of her stomach were covered in an intricate pattern of diamonds and precious stones that appeared to have been glued on. She must have spent the entire day getting ready. I'd barely taken an hour.

She pushed her hair aside, with her perfectly manicured diamond-encrusted nails. Her smile was pleasant, childlike in a way. But this was a woman who loved attention and had absolutely no problem getting it. Male and female suitors surrounded her. Some admired her with blatant lust while others regarded her with reverence. It was easy to tell that, unlike me, this girl had never spent a dateless Saturday night shoving ice cream down her throat.

The moment Misha approached, her suitors scattered. Misha didn't hiss, didn't challenge, and didn't demonstrate any show of force. Misha just was. The seemingly innocent creature turned to him and offered her hand to be kissed. "You look ravishing, my dear," he said to her.

"As do you, beloved." Her voice was extremely feminine, thick with a Russian accent, and highly suggestive.

Their eyes locked. Any moron could see a lot more than the exchange of pleasantries taking place. Misha glanced at her breasts, just long enough for her to notice. I looked, too, just to see whether he affected them the way he did mine. He did. Bastard. And although he wasn't even looking at me, mine tingled slightly. When the powers that be handed out the vamp mojo, I didn't understand how or why "capable of stimulating nipples" needed to top their superpowers list.

Misha stood and continued to hold her hand. I felt like an idiot when I realized I was still attached to his arm. I tried to leave, but yippy skippy, he stopped me. "Ileana Vodianova, I would like to present you to Celia Wird."

She smiled at me and dropped Misha's hand. Her eyes sparkled as she took me in, and appeared genuinely amiable and caring. I would have been a fool to believe it. "Hello, Celia. How good to finally meet you."

I released Misha's arm and grinned back, mimicking her phony enthusiasm. My fist knocked her in the shoulder with an obnoxious punch. "How's it going, kid?"

It's not that I lacked couth; I could actually be the couthiest. I wanted to make it clear that, despite all her diamonds and preternatural power, she didn't intimidate me. *That's right, sweetheart. I could* so *take you on.*

Misha raised an eyebrow, chuckling slightly to demonstrate I was merely joking. Ileana seemed thrilled, excited even. She clutched Misha's arm and jumped in place like an overly enthusiastic Girl Scout. "Yes, beloved. Celia will definitely do!"

My smile dropped. "Excuse me?"

Misha snaked his arm around me. "Ileana is pleased by you. She approves of our . . . connection."

"Uh-huh." Misha and I were *so* going to have a talk later. His half-truths pricked at my skin like needles and alerted my beast. Something was rotten in Fang Land.

Another vampire approached us. His hesitancy demonstrated his lower position in the vampire hierarchy. "Forgive the interruption, Sir Aleksandr. Baron Vladimir would like a word with Countess Vodianova."

Ileana trailed her perfect left hand up my arm while her right slipped over Misha's. Her smile was delicate and saintly. Her hands told a different story. They told me I'd relish in the pain she was capable of delivering. I disagreed and let her know by jerking away from her. My rejection of her advances delighted her. She beamed at me. "Forgive me, but I must attend to the baron."

"I'm sure you must."

She lowered her lids seductively, as if I'd offered to record their romp. "Will you spare some time for me inside?"

"Nope."

Misha ignored me. "Of course we shall."

She and Misha exchanged a very short but very steamy kiss. When her lips tried to meet mine, I shoved my hand in her face. "I don't think so."

She threw her head back and laughed. "Oh, Misha. What a tigress indeed!"

With a small wave, she made her departure. Misha didn't miss a beat and led me through the crowd. "What was your impression of Ileana?"

I shrugged. "About the same as all the other vampires I've ever met."

He chuckled. "All of them?"

"Most of them anyway. You're lucky—you can make me laugh and know how to tell a good story."

"Ah, so it's my persona you find so appealing." He stole a glance at my breasts. Even with the damn silicone, he could probably tell they were saluting him.

"You're pissing me off, Misha."

He laughed quietly. His glee ceased the moment he spotted another powerful vampire. This one I knew from my past, and he was one I had no desire of encountering again. My hackles rose.

Misha sensed my anger. "You know Angelo Cusamano?"

"We've met," I answered stiffly.

"He holds my position on the East Coast."

"Does he?" *Why am I not surprised?*

"There is a matter I need to discuss with him." Misha glanced at my protruding claws. "But perhaps I should do so alone?"

"For his sake, that would be best. I think I'll try and find my sisters."

Misha kissed my head. "As you wish. I will join you shortly."

I was probably the shortest female there, and although Misha was no longer escorting me, the guests parted from my path. They stared at me as I passed. Some smiled politely while others watched me carefully. No one seemed overly friendly or aggressive, but I didn't like being noticed and would have preferred them to ignore me.

I was halfway through the foyer when an outlandish, remarkable scent caught my attention. A tall, muscular *were* leaned lazily against the mantel of an immense granite fireplace while two females clung to his every word. The jacket of his charcoal tux hung open and he hadn't bothered with a tie. The white blond hair skimming his shoulders and his deeply tanned skin suggested surf bum, not member of mystical royalty. His stunning blue eyes shot in my direction as I neared. He ignored the females to fire an alluring smile and one hell of a dimple my way. I averted my eyes. *No, thanks, pretty boy. I already have enough trouble.*

I hurried along, pausing when I noticed Genevieve's "maybe" had turned into a "yes." Tim had one hand against the wall while his other played with her hair. A smile curved her lips. Her lack of fear around Tim impressed me. Then again, the magical whoop-ass staff she clutched against her could probably blow him to smithereens.

"Witch" appeared to be the preferred flavor for the evening. All the Catholic schoolgirls had found one to make out with. Edith cuddled hers near one of the eighteen-foot windows. She held a glass of champagne in one hand while a tall dark-skinned enchantress ran her lips along Edith's throat. Edith elongated her neck to give her date better access. She also elongated her fangs, lust stimulating her thirst. Agnes walked by with her own new friend and elbowed Edith hard in the ribs. Edith hissed, but retracted her fangs all the same.

Misha appeared by my side without warning, slinking an arm around my waist. His discussion with Angelo hadn't taken long, making me believe the chat must have been more a passing insult or some supersecret vamp exchange. He whispered closely in my ear, "I see Uri's favorites dressed up for the occasion."

Male underwear models always served as Uri's escorts. Seriously, they were gorgeous and wore only underwear. Tonight they'd upgraded to black silk boxers and bow ties. I covered my mouth to suppress a laugh. My giggle was cut short by a throaty growl. Aric scowled at us from a few feet away. I didn't get a good look at him. The two scantily clad *weres* clinging to him like giant pieces of duct tape blocked my view. I couldn't get over the way they were dressed. My dress might have been sexy, but it carried an elegant beauty. Their ensembles resembled something street prostitutes would consider too risqué. They pulled him into the ballroom and away from me. I'd caught enough of his expression to know he was angry. Well, that made two of us.

Misha's grip tightened. I hadn't even noticed my claws shoot out or my body lurch forward. "Do not start the evening by scuffling with *weres* on their premises," he whispered tightly.

"I wasn't going to scuffle." *I was going to throw down and feed those sluts their small intestines.* Acid boiled in my stomach like building lava as I watched them disappear with *my* wolf.

"Celia!" Shayna called.

"Ignore the wolf and enjoy your family." Misha nudged me over to where my sisters and friends were coming at me full speed before disappearing to speak with yet another master. Shayna greeted me first. Her long black hair was pulled into a beautiful chignon and a plum satin dress clung to her thin frame like a second skin. A strapless red number hugged Taran's curves. Gemini hugged her waist just as tightly. He snarled at a passing vamp who licked his lips when he stole a glance at my sister. Calm spirit or not, Gem would make a ski cap out the vamp's stomach if he trekked too close to his mate.

Emme's pink cocktail dress made her the belle of the ball. My God, she looked *lovely*. All the wolves sported black tuxes of varying James Bond style—even Bren.

The sight of those who loved me extinguished my anger. We greeted one another with warm hugs and excited smiles. "Here, Celia. Let me take your coat," Danny offered. Their jaws collectively dropped when Danny slipped the fake fur from my shoulders. My insecurities brought a flush to my cheeks, but the howls and whistles from the wolves heated my entire face.

Liam hooted. "Aric is going to lose it when he sees you."

Koda winked. "Hell yeah, he is!"

Apprehension erased my cheer. "It didn't seem that way just now. He growled at me—*growled*."

The wolves exchanged worried glances before Gemini stepped forward. "Aric's wolf has been especially . . . irritable lately."

"Irritable?" Bren snapped. "The werecougar rammed

up his ass is using his colon as a scratching post—and he's invited friends!"

Gemini narrowed his eyes. "Aric's frustrations with his situation, his anger at the Tribe for targeting you, and his need to be with you have surged his animal instincts as of late." He leaned forward to speak low in my ear. "Your presence will give his wolf the alleviation that he desires. I'm sure of it."

"I hope you're right."

Gemini's reassuring grin morphed into a scowl at Misha's arrival. That only made Misha flash a gleaming incisor and slip his arm around me. "Come, my love. It's our turn to be presented."

I glanced nervously between him and my sisters. "Um, *presented*?"

Shayna grinned and pinched my backside, making me jump. "It's just a formality, Ceel. Don't worry—we'll see you inside."

Misha whisked me away and placed us before a set of large ornate wooden doors carved with images of wolves during a hunt. His vampires positioned themselves directly behind us. I fidgeted a little in my shoes. Damn, a formal presentation was so not my idea of a good time. "You appear nervous," Misha whispered.

"That's because I am. Can't we just walk in through the back?"

Misha chuckled and offered me his arm. I clung to it like a drowning woman. "Fear not, my love. You are the most desired woman in attendance. Enter knowing every male seeks your company."

"You've been sucking on crazy if you think that's going to make me feel better."

His chuckles turned into full-out laughter just as two Den students in dark suits and white gloves pulled opened the brass knobs. Misha yanked me forward when I failed to move. A *were* roughly the same age as dirt cleared his throat as if choking on his own lungs. Unless they died in battle or from loss of their mates, *weres* lived until the first full moon after their one hundredth birthday. That wolf looked a dozen moons past his quota. "I present Sir Misha Aleksandr, Lady Celia Wird, and family."

I didn't know how I ended up with a title, but crap, I'd be sure to return it the moment this gala was over. All I wanted was to *shift* out of the room and out of the limelight . . . until I caught my first real look at Aric. My heart stopped. All the attendants vanished except for him. I walked forward, drawn by the pull of his wolf and the urging of my tigress.

He stood behind a large granite table. His dark Irish skin appeared tanned against his black silk shirt and tie. He wore his chocolate brown hair just the way I loved it, short all around except on top, where long strands hung slightly over his light brown eyes. Aric's damn sexy face and body sizzled to smoking-hot proportions in that tux. I stopped breathing for a moment just to take him in.

The surfer-looking *were* I'd seen leaning against the stone fireplace stood next to him, along with the Elders, Uri, and some other higher-ups in the supernatural world. Aric's lids peeled back. He lunged toward me, hard enough to shove the heavy granite table blocking his path. My tigress clawed inside me with excitement, trying to reach him, knowing his wolf had tried to reach us. My hips swayed harder as I neared. I nibbled on my bottom lip. We were almost to him. I smiled and he . . . *scowled.*

I stopped dead. *What the hell?* Aric was livid. The aroma of his fury sliced around his aura. I watched him for a few moments of stunned silence until his glare and my anger at his response made me give him my back. The tension between us beat against my skin. I waited numbly while his Warriors and my sisters were introduced next.

Taran's steps slowed when she caught a gander at His Royal Pissiness. She inched her way to my side and frowned. "Why the hell is he so premenstrual?"

I forced back my protruding claws. "Oh, don't worry, Taran. It's not him—it's just his wolf." Beast rising to the surface or not, I was miffed at both of them.

I stared straight ahead. The elderly *were* continued

announcing the honored guests until only one remained. "And last, but certainly not least, I present . . . Destiny."

Taran and I jumped—she into Gemini's arms and I against Misha. Aric's deep warning growl made it clear I should have leapt elsewhere. Perhaps off the mountain. I couldn't help it. I didn't frighten easily, but Destiny scared the bejeebers out of me. Taran and I had had the oh so jolly experience of meeting Destiny in vampire court. Destiny had the ability to transfer people's memories onto a screen by merely placing her hands on their heads. Neat trick, huh? Well, not so much if you were the poor schmuck on the receiving end. Taran and I had been exposed to her hauntingly agonizing, vomit-inducing touch. The process had felt like barbed wire scraping along my brain. I'd never wanted to see her again—*never*—much less mingle and share hors d'oeuvres.

Destiny stood on the tippy-toes of her zebra-print cowgirl boots and waved excitedly like we were old pals. Her fashion sense hadn't improved since our last meeting. Tonight's ensemble consisted of a shin-length fuchsia dress with dark brown furry polka dots. Destiny *loved* polka dots. They matched what resembled a dead weasel wrapped around her neck.

I blinked several times. *Oh, good Lord, that* is *a dead weasel.*

A lime green bow anchored her librarian bun. Matching lime eye shadow covered her lids, clashing with her neon pink lipstick. Damn. Seriously. Damn.

Destiny barreled toward us. Taran made a break toward the exit. Misha pulled me to him when I attempted to skitter after her. Amusement trickled into his Russian accent. "Do not fear, kitten. I will keep you from harm."

A horrible crunching noise had me veering backward. Aric stood with a large chunk of the granite table in his arms. The menace of a thousand barbarians marched across his face, hardening his features. He snarled once and tossed the massive hunk of rock. It landed with a loud bang at Misha's feet.

My eyes bulged with alarm. Misha flashed him a sinister smile and tightened his grip around me. For a moment, no one so much as breathed. Silence spread through the entire ballroom. Those in attendance waited to see who would strike first: the vampire or the wolf.

Makawee, the Omega wolf of the pack Elders, wouldn't allow it. She stepped toward Aric and smiled, releasing the calming energy of her magic. It stroked against me as soothingly as a mother's touch. "Perhaps we should all take our seats now," she said quietly. "Destiny can tell us her predictions later."

The crowd before us dispersed and took their seats. And although Aric had been the one to cause the outburst, I was the one many of the *weres* glowered at. "What predictions?" I asked Misha in an attempt to ignore them.

Misha's voice grew dangerously quiet and his eyes fierce. He was angered by the negative attention the *weres* had slapped me with. "Destiny can also foresee the future." His vampires gathered around us and bared their fangs at those who continued to glare at me. Misha's hand found my lower back. "Perhaps it's best you stay close to me tonight."

My tigress eyes replaced my own. She appreciated dirty looks and underlying threats about as much as I did. "It's okay, Misha. I'll be fine. I'm not afraid of these idiots." I responded loud enough for the furries to hear me. "Besides, I want to spend time with my family."

Misha gave me a slow nod. "Very well, but do not hesitate to find me if you continue to feel . . . unwelcome."

"Thanks, Misha."

He kissed my forehead, earning me yet another growl from Aric.

CHAPTER 17

Since the vampires had dined previously, they mostly danced, socialized, and made out. Makawee had been kind enough to seat me with my sisters and friends. It helped to have them close, seeing as Aric continued to glower at me all through the main course. Cranky inner beast or not, I was ready to smack him upside the head. *I* should have been the angry one. Those sluts repeatedly fondled him and kissed his cheeks. And while they sat a few tables down from us, I heard everything they said to him loud and oh so clear.

"Oh, Aric," one of them cooed. "You smell *sooo* good."

I threw the knife I'd been holding on my lap onto the table. My jealousy and fury had allowed me to easily bend it into a circle. Still, it did little to suppress my need to kill something. Bren tried to ease my temper. He nuzzled my neck, imitating the tramp's lusty voice. "Oh, Celia, *Celia* . . . You smell *sooo* good, baby. May I straddle you like the whore I am?"

We all thought it was funny. Aric didn't. He growled yet again.

"Where would you like me to touch you?" The other *were* purred at him.

My claws whipped out like deadly blades. I shoved them under the table before I attacked her. The wood slivered and cracked as my hands raked back and forth against the dense mahogany, leaving gouges deep enough to poke my fingers through.

Taran didn't hear the *were*'s comment. Shayna did and told her what she'd said. Taran smiled gleefully and rose, tossing her napkin on the table. "Excuse me. I'll be right back."

Gemini chased after her, his voice panicked. "Sweetheart, where are you going?"

Taran sashayed her way to Aric and his groupies. Gemini was at her heels begging her to return to the table. Taran ignored him and whispered something to Aric so low, none of us heard it. Whatever it was must have been a doozy. Aric's eyes shot open. He grabbed the *weres* as they launched themselves at Taran while Gemini hauled her back to our table.

Shayna sat at the edge of her seat, bouncing with excitement. "Dude! What did you say?"

Taran flicked her hair back when Gemini released her, seemingly pleased with herself. "I merely said if they needed pointers they should talk to Celia. She knows exactly where to touch Aric."

A slow grin spread across my face. Aric didn't growl that time.

By the time dessert passed, Aric's bimbettes halted just short of having sex with him. He remained unaffected by them, sitting still as stone watching me. But just because he failed to respond to their advances didn't mean I enjoyed the show. I finally had enough and, as petty as it was, I decided to get some revenge. Music by Flo Rida provided me with the perfect opportunity. "Let's go dance," I said to my sisters.

They followed me without thinking twice. I tapped into the smooth, silky movements of my inner cat and went wild. Taran didn't miss a beat and joined me, matching my provocative moves with a few of her own. The last time I'd danced that way it had been for Aric, and only Aric, alone in our room. Just before he tackled me to the floor.

Taran dazzled me with one of her more evil grins, encouraging me to be more daring. "Come on, Ceel. Is that the best you got?" My competitive streak took over and so did hers; we kept trying to outdo the other. I lowered my lids and imagined Aric watching me from our bed. My hips rocked and my body swerved in long, sensual, snakelike movements to the beat of the music, teasing the Aric in my mind with my form. When I opened my eyes, the crowd of *weres* that had glared met me with impish smiles and steamy glances. I ignored them. They didn't matter. Only Aric did.

Shayna and Emme didn't last long, their wolves whisking them away for a little alone time after the first song. I fought back a laugh when I caught Gemini's face. The poor guy practically drooled watching Taran. A bunch of *weres* had snuck their way to her. He robotically shoved them out of the way to reach her.

Taran gave him a look that could only be described as a promise for a long night. "Hi, baby," she whispered. "Do you like what you see?" His growl and grab told me yes. They disappeared along the crowd.

The moment the second song ended, I left the floor, grateful for the exaggerated cat walk my tigress gifted me with. I had more than made my point, but still needed to add a cherry to my seduction sundae. I sauntered past where Aric continued to sit with his gal pals, tossing my hair alluringly so he caught a strong whiff of my scent. Judging by his familiar moan of longing, I still had the goods to stimulate his beast. I continued forward, passing a few more tables until the surfer guy stepped in front of me, blocking my way.

He glanced down at me, making sure to fire another dimple my way. "So, you're Celia, the tigress I've heard so much about."

I shrugged. "I suppose." My tigress found him curious and tried to figure him out. "And what might you be?"

"Take a guess."

My tigress urged me forward. Her interest in him surprised me, but something about him tugged me closer. I leaned forward, stopping about six inches away from his chest to inhale deeply. I rolled my eyes at Aric's audible growls. *Hypocrite.*

The *were* smelled feral, like the Serengeti. I scented trees, tall grasses, and dry scorching air. It intermixed with a hint of musk and a stronger smell of salaciousness. I knew then why my tigress had taken an interest in his aroma, and the realization made me smile. I'd met another big cat. "You're a lion."

"No, sweetheart. I'm *the* lion."

I raised my brows. "Oh, and a modest one at that."

He analyzed me from big hair to pointy shoes, his cocky grin becoming wider. "You're a lot smaller than I thought," he said. "How could a little thing like you piss off the Tribe enough to command your death?"

Hmm. Interesting. Even the lion believes the Tribe is the culprit. I didn't answer him and removed my shoes. He watched me, the gleam in his eyes suggesting I remove a little more than just my footwear. I *shifted* quickly and surfaced behind him, poking him with my right toe to get his attention. He whirled around, admiration easing the surprise on his face. *Thanks, Ying-Ying.*

I lowered my foot back down slowly. He followed it down with his gaze. Aric's growls escalated, bordering on murderous. The lion ignored him, keeping his attention on me.

"Looks can be deceiving," I said with a grin.

"And sexy," he added with a playful smile. "I'm Tye Gris de Leone. Would you like to dance with me? You know, one cat with another?"

Aric no longer growled. His sounds were more like deep sadistic rumblings, similar to clouds before the thunder cracks. I angled my gaze around Tye, convinced Aric had gone full-out wolf. His human side remained intact . . . although the human appeared ready to munch on lion. *Damn.* Tye seemed neither upset nor worried. In fact, amusement played like a fiddle across his features.

I'd only just met the guy, and while his arrogance didn't sit well with me, he seemed decent enough. It wouldn't be right if Aric, like, killed him. I smirked. "I'd better not. My ex-boyfriend is a lunatic."

Aric's murderous snarling only reinforced my point.

I slipped into my shoes and went to the restroom to freshen up. Aric was standing outside the ladies' room waiting for me when I exited. I scanned the area. Good thing for those sluts of his they'd stayed behind.

"I see your list of admirers has grown," he said in a really nasty tone.

I frowned. "Why do you care? You have the naked tramp twins following you around."

"Would you prefer we all dressed the same way, like you and *Misha*?"

Okay, Aric. You and your crazed beast are going down. I ran my fingers playfully between my full breasts, then slid my hands down my body, paying close attention to my waist and thighs. My lips pouted and my voice came out in a purr. "What's wrong, wolf? Don't you like my dress?"

Aric's eyes traveled slowly from the center of my halter and down to my legs. He swallowed hard before answering. "No. I don't."

I smiled bewitchingly. "Really? Well, you could have fooled me. You looked at me like you wanted me. Just like you used to before Boobless came along."

"Who the hell's 'Boobless'?"

"You know—*Barbara*, your former fiancée?"

As furious as Aric was, he couldn't suppress that grin I loved so much. And as hard as I tried, I couldn't help smiling back. We locked eyes, and for a moment it was as if we'd never been apart. He stepped closer. When I didn't move away from him, he took another step, and another. He was so close I could feel his heat, the same heat that intensified in my presence and soldered us together. His eyes softened. "I never wanted her. Or anyone else. You know who I want," he murmured.

A burning sensation built deep within my core. "I

miss you," I whispered. I covered my face with my hands. "I'm sorry. I shouldn't tell you this, but I do."

Aric clasped my wrists and gently pulled them down. "Don't hide your beautiful face or your feelings from me. I can't stand being without either."

His touch sent enticing chills across my skin. My heart drummed madly. This time I stepped forward, close enough that my breasts grazed his hard chest.

"Aric?"

Martin's baritone voice echoed the length of the long hall. Instead of jerking away from me in the presence of his Alpha and Elder, Aric released my hands slowly. I inched away from him, guilt heating my face despite that we hadn't done anything wrong. Or maybe we had. Sweat glistened Aric's forehead and my entire body tingled with anticipation and need.

Aric's timbre was as cool as a March breeze. "Yes, Martin?"

The angles of Martin's face reflected his serious tone. I couldn't scent anger per se, but his displeasure at finding us alone tensed his shoulders like a burdensome load. "Perhaps it's best that you visit with our honored guests in the ballroom. Don't you think?"

"Of course, Martin."

Martin had helped raise Aric, and became a father figure when Aric lost his. Their current state suggested they'd never been close or exchanged a kind word. It saddened me, knowing I'd caused this rift between them. My inner beast chuffed. The strain between them made us restless.

Martin nodded in my direction. "Celia."

"Hey, Martin." I waved awkwardly, not knowing what else to do. Shaking his hand didn't seem right and I wasn't what anyone would call a "hugger." I didn't mean to act like a dweeb, but sometimes my inner nerd shoved my tigress aside and took over. Aric grinned. The most subtle twitch of a smile curved the edges of Martin's lips before he turned on his heel and left.

I didn't want to leave Aric just yet. It soothed my essence and enlivened my soul to be near him. And if he could do that for me with just his presence, his riled beast must have felt a sense of relief around me, too. Already his temper had hushed and the ire surrounding him had dispersed like dry leaves in a storm. I took a chance. "Aric, would you like to—?"

"Yes," he answered in a hoarse whisper.

CHAPTER 18

I laughed a little. "You didn't let me finish."

"I know."

Aric's gaze was so intense, my mouth tried to remember how to speak. "Will you sit with me, even for a little while?"

His crooked smile held more mischief then I'd ever seen. "Oh, that. Sure, I could do that."

Aric had expected me to ask him to do more than just sit and chat. I tugged at my bottom lip nervously with my teeth. He released the softest of groans. I staggered away before I succumbed to the urge to rip off my clothes and his. He followed close behind me, placing his hand on the small of my back when we entered the ballroom. My body stiffened with surprise. Perhaps he wanted to present me as his, but the rest of his kind clearly wasn't ready to receive me.

Glares and whispers followed us as we made our way to where my sisters and friends waited.

"Problem?" Aric asked a werebear who shot us a particularly nasty scowl.

The bear dropped his gaze, but his bitter words cut us both. "We're counting on you to keep our species from dying out, Aric. I haven't turned my back on my responsibilities and neither should you."

The she-bear next to him idly rubbed her small pregnant belly. She didn't acknowledge us, or her partner. They were together, but not a couple—pures, I assumed, brought together by obligation, and not by love.

I hurried ahead, giving Aric ample space to change his mind and return to his pack. He paused briefly. The aroma of his rising frustration and anger reached my nose from afar. His warmth also reached my skin when he'd caught up to me. He didn't want to abandon me. It should have thrilled me. Instead guilt warred with my happiness, making it difficult to relax once we reached my table.

Unlike the *weres* we passed, our loved ones greeted us with warm and pleased smiles. Gemini nodded at me, giving me the impression he sensed a different quality to Aric's beast.

Liam pulled Emme on his lap so Aric could sit next to me. I crossed my legs and adjusted my skirt. Taran motioned to Aric when she caught him staring at my legs.

"You don't have to be here," I told him. "I'll understand if you can't stay."

"I don't want to leave you. We've been apart enough."

I pursed my lips. "Not wanting to" and "having to" were two different things. I squirmed uncomfortably. The werebear was proof I'd been foolish to ask Aric to accompany me, especially here among the elite of his pack.

Danny arrived, interrupting Aric, who seemed to want to say more. My longtime friend shook, and breathed as if he'd been chasing cars.

"Where have you been?" I asked, worried something had happened to him.

Danny coughed into his hand. "Um. Heidi is on security detail. I, ah, just went to bring her something to eat." It was then I noticed his wrinkled shirt and that the buttons weren't lined up correctly. He'd hooked up with the Pamela Anderson of werewolves—again. He coughed, more and more as we all stared.

"You really like her, don't you, Danny?" I asked.

Danny dropped his head and nodded. I was happy he'd found someone. I just hoped she wouldn't break his heart. Heidi had a reputation for being lethal, earning her place as one of Aric's Warriors. She also had a rep for sleeping around. And that was what worried me.

Bren leaned back in his seat, reeking of witch's brew and slurring his words. "I can't believe you banged someone as gorgeous as Heidi."

Danny's head shot up. "I've dated hot women before."

"No, you haven't, Dan. Aside from Celia, Heidi's been your only decent lay."

That's when the world stopped.

Aric crushed the water goblet in his grasp like a withered twig. His Alpha glare honed in on Danny, making him jump. "*You* were with *my Celia*?"

Danny jerked toward me. "You never told him?"

Oh, no.

Aric dropped the fractured pieces of glass onto the table. They fell like broken icicles. His hand showed no signs of injury, but his face shadowed with fury and betrayal. "You went after Celia the moment my back was turned, knowing I was goddamn miserable without her."

Danny's voice quavered. "Aric, I didn't. Honest I didn't. You have to believe me."

Bren, of course, just had to jump to our rescue. "Come on, Aric. They only slept together a few times."

Aric rose slowly. Koda and Gem stood with him, placing themselves on either side of him.

"Aric, you need to calm down and take control of your wolf," Gemini said.

"This isn't the time, Aric." Koda's voice was just as stern as Gem's. "Reel in your beast."

Aric ignored them both. He trembled, and his voice was barely restrained. "This . . . *happened more than once*?" He wouldn't even look at me, despite my frantic pleas to calm and Taran's threat to jolt him with lightning. His wolf was focused on Danny—his prey.

I clutched his hand. "Aric, please—you don't understand. This happened years ago."

Aric left Danny to focus on me. He stopped shaking when I touched him, but his fury still heated the air around him. "When did it happen?"

"We were young, Aric. Just kids."

"*Kids?*"

I held out my hand. "That's not what I meant. It came out wrong."

Liam closed in on Aric palms out, stepping over Bren, who'd passed out drunk on the floor. "Come on, Aric. So what if he popped Celia's cherry?"

My sisters and I gasped. I couldn't even believe we were having this conversation.

Koda snarled through gritted teeth, "*Liam*, stop trying to help!"

I blocked Aric's way when he lunged at Danny, and grasped both of Aric's hands in mine. Gemini and Koda backed away. They knew Aric wouldn't risk hurting me just to pound Danny. My gaze pleaded with him. "Aric, this is a senseless discussion. It happened before I ever met you. I swear we haven't been together since."

Aric's heartbroken expression wrung my insides. "Why didn't you ever tell me? You led me to believe you were only friends."

"We are only friends, love."

My term of endearment tamed Aric's beast, but only momentarily. Once more the air around him fired with his anger. "Just like you and Misha are only friends? How many *friends* are you getting naked with and kissing?"

I'd forgotten Liam had told Aric about the kiss. I was driven with need to explain this and a lot more, but Aric's words struck me like a blow. I shoved his hands away from mine. "It's not what you think. Misha was trying to bring out my abilities and—"

"Oh, I bet he was," Aric growled.

Aric had been growling all night. Whether it was his fired-up beast or not didn't matter. I'd reached the end of my patience and so had my tigress. "Well, now you know everyone I've ever slept with: you and Danny. That's two guys. How many girls have you been with, Mr. Pureblood? Can you even count that high?"

"That's different. None of them ever meant anything to me."

"And that makes it better?"

"Yes, it does. *You* can't seem to let go of anyone you're intimate with. After all, here you are with Danny *and* Misha—"

"*And you.*" That stopped Aric right in his tracks. I stared at him, trying hard not to cry. I'd missed him so much and all we'd done was fight. My voice broke. "You're right, Aric. I can't seem to let any of you go."

Makawee's essence swept in like a gentle rain, extinguishing the majority of my wolf's rage, but not all of it. She interrupted calmly. "Aric, please come with me. This is a time for celebration, not anger. And, Celia, Uri would like a word with you."

Aric and I glared at each other the entire way to the main table, where Misha and Tye also waited. Tye flashed me another dimple and waltzed his way between us to stand next to Aric. "How's it going, man?" he asked him.

"Shut the hell up," Aric snapped.

Uri's hands clasped my elbows and led me to Misha, passing Anara and the hateful "hello" scowl he sent my way. "Oh, lovely Celia, it's so good to see you again," Uri said. "The Elders and I were just discussing how vital you have been to our cause."

Martin's deep baritone voice resonated with a kindness I hadn't expected. "You and your sisters have been most extraordinary."

"Thank you," I stammered. Martin had never been cruel to me. But seeing how he'd encountered Aric and me alone in the hall, his pleasantness surprised me. I looked around. The Elders and Uri all watched me. Even Anara regarded me with interest. They'd obviously been discussing me, which was bad enough. But I just about hurled when Makawee spilled the deets.

She clasped her hands and nodded approvingly when Misha slipped his arm around my shoulders. "We're looking forward to seeing what gifts your children will possess."

Aric shifted his gaze from me to Misha. "*What?*"

This isn't happening to me.

"Misha and Celia have been talking about starting a family," Uri explained like it was obvious.

Oh, sweet heaven, this is so not happening to me.

I threw my hands out like I was trying to stop a Mack truck. "Um, no— Wait!" I looked to Misha for help. Fang-ass had the nerve to smile angelically. "This whole . . . thing is being . . . misinterpreted." It was no use; Aric's face had darkened past red into vicious "I'm going to eat you" purple. And *crap*, his growls were worse than when I'd been with Tye.

Destiny popped out of nowhere, giggling like a toddler. "Uri, you have it all wrong. The tigress and the *lion* will mate." She motioned to me, and to where Aric and Tye stood directly beside each other with a dramatic wave of her arms. "*Their* children will be the ones to keep the world safe from evil."

She smiled with glee following her earth-shattering revelation, evidently believing this was the greatest prophecy *ever*. I stood there like someone had walloped me with a sledgehammer covered in poo. Tye danced his brows and gave me a wink. And at that moment, I thought both Aric *and* Misha were going to lose it.

Makawee angled her head inquisitively. "That is the future you have foreseen, Destiny?"

Destiny's response was more enthusiastic than Tim's at an edible underwear competition. "Oh, yes! It's almost completely certain, Makawee."

I wanted to run away screaming from this disastrous evening. Instead I excused myself like the lady I pretended to be and dashed for the bathroom. 'Cause that's what women do when they're faced with something they can't deal with. My sisters chased after me. When they reached me they found me gripping the jade granite countertop and trying not to hyperventilate. It took me a few moments to enlighten them on my latest debacle.

Taran paced back and forth. "Son of a *bitch*. You're supposed to make cubs with that werelion?"

"So says my Destiny," I answered almost numbly.

Shayna focused on the stall in front of her as if the

answers to my woes were etched into the door. "But you
don't even know him, like, at all!"

"Nor do I want to."

Emme's soft green eyes glistened with sympathetic
tears. "I always thought you and Aric would find your
way back to each other . . . no matter what."

The ache in my throat intensified. "Yeah, I was kind
of hoping for that, too." My sisters watched me for a
while, unsure what to say. Their kindness meant the
world to me, but I'd taken enough of their time. They
could still enjoy their evening. "Go back to your wolves.
I'll be out in a minute."

They didn't want to leave me, but seemed to recognize I needed a moment to catch my breath. When I finally deserted the bathroom, I couldn't bring myself to
return to the gala. I wandered through the foyer and
onto the stacked-stone porch, where I took a seat near
one of the outdoor fireplaces. Flurries continued to fall
and the bitter cold chilled my bare legs. Yet the warmth
from my inner beast and the fire made it tolerable.

Around me couples cuddled in corners. A few swept
down the steps in their haste to find privacy. They had
someone to keep them warm. Aric had more than a
someone. He had two. I caught his scent and that of his
dates as they led him past me. Their arms wrapped his
waist and their bodies snuggled tightly against his. He
might not have returned their affection, but he sure as
hell wasn't beating them back. He paused with his back
to me, obviously having caught a trickle of my aroma.
"Wait by my quarters," he told them.

They kissed his cheeks and strutted off, stopping only
to beam at Aric wickedly. He faced me then, his expression a horrible mixture of hurt and defeat. "I need to get
over you. Don't I?"

Tears burned my eyes as I rose. "If you do, you're certainly giving it your all."

He stepped toward me. "Don't look at me that way—"

"What way, Aric? Like I expected more from you?
Well, maybe I did!" I glared into the night where his
tramps had flounced off. "Maybe I'm the one who needs

to get over you. You're not the man I thought you were. Not like this." I swallowed hard. "It was my mistake to love you . . . and to think that you really loved me."

I veered quickly and slammed right into Tye. He was happy to see me and yanked me into a tight embrace. The feeling wasn't mutual and his words disgusted me. "There you are, dovie. Since we'll be making babies soon, maybe we should get to know each other."

I shoved him into a wall when he bent to kiss me. "If you think I'm going to sleep with you because some geek with hideous fashion sense said so, you're out of your mind! Keep your goddamn hands to yourself before I ram them down your throat!"

I barreled down the steps and cut through a walkway between two smaller buildings. I wasn't sure where I was going. I just wanted to get away from Tye *and* Aric. The walkway seemed endless. I don't know how long I stormed down the path before it finally curved and led into a large garden.

The leaves had shriveled from the trees and stout bushes. I didn't care about the barrenness and welcomed its solace, just like the large gulps of air I struggled to take. My back fell against a retainer wall. The cold granite was like a slab of ice against my exposed back, yet it didn't bother me enough to move. My body trembled from my raw emotions and my tigress fought to emerge, to protect me from the pain of the evening and manage the hurt that always seemed to haunt our lives. I tried to settle her. It was hard. The mysticism of Tahoe brought my beast a sense of peace, both energizing and harmonizing my inner magic. We belonged in Tahoe, and in a way we were a part of it. It wasn't that way in Squaw Valley. I was hated here, and there was nothing I could do to change that.

My anxiety and sadness surged. I needed a distraction before my tigress tore free. I concentrated hard on the branches of one tree. A slight breeze caused the tips to dance and drop icicles onto the snow like frozen tears. It comforted me in a way to have something symbolically cry for me. If I allowed myself to weep, I wasn't sure when I'd stop.

My tension began to lift a little just when someone approached. Aric had tracked me. He moved toward me slowly and leaned against the wall beside me. We both stared straight ahead and didn't speak for a long time.

I hated standing next to him like that, without talking, without touching. How had the relationship I'd once so cherished ended like this? "Don't you have someplace else to be?"

"No."

A growl burned my throat. "You could have fooled me."

Aric let out a long breath. "You know what would have happened if I'd met those females—*nothing*. My beast rejects anyone who's not you, and the man in me doesn't fight to change his will. Except tonight." He stared out hard into the darkness. "My Elders came down on me just now, and threw everything in my face—Destiny's prediction, my obligations to my pack, and the annihilation my kind faces if we fail to reproduce. I finally surrendered and gave up any hope between us . . . and then I saw you on the porch. All it took was feeling your spirit beside me to know that I can't be with anyone else." He turned to me then. "No matter what anyone tells me."

I angled my head to the side, not wanting to expose the rip in my heart.

"What about you?" he asked when I failed to speak.

I wiped my eyes. "What about me?"

"Do you want Tye?"

I couldn't believe he even had to ask. "Of course not."

"Or Danny?"

"No."

"Or Misha?"

Tears streamed down my cheeks in tandem when I faced him. "How can I be with Misha or anyone when all I think about is you?"

Aric reached for me, holding my face with his hands and wiping my tears with his thumbs. "Don't cry, sweetness. Please don't cry."

Aric's eyes met mine, the way they had so many times in our past. There was no anger, no bitterness, no distance. Only compassion and tenderness remained. I held his hands with mine. "I can't help it, Aric. I love you. I'd give anything to be with you."

"You don't have to." He kissed me, *hard*, just as he had a thousand times in my dreams. The warmth we shared spread through me like a wave of soft water. I didn't want to stop, but I knew I had to. Whether I loved him or not, the world needed him, and so did his pack. The werebear and his pregnant wife had shown me as much. I struggled against him and finally managed to pull away.

It hurt to move away from him so forcefully. My tigress rushed to the surface, trying desperately to pull us back to him. He had felt so *good*. The rest of me tried to beat her back, knowing I couldn't handle it if he abandoned me again. "Aric, what about your commitment to the pack?"

Aric backed me up against the wall, pressing his body firmly against mine and gripping my hips with his large hands. His pounding heartbeat threatened to explode between my breasts. "I don't want to talk about that now," he murmured in my ear. "You just told me you love me — prove it. Prove that you still need me. Prove that you still want me, because I sure as hell want you."

Aric smashed his lips against mine. This time, I didn't resist. I drove my tongue into him, making him groan. My arms wrapped around his neck. His hands moved from my waist and traveled beneath my skirt to caress my backside. I let out a cry filled with anticipation. Aric became more insistent; he wasn't going to stop. But even if he did, I wouldn't have let him. I kissed him across his jawline. When I found his ear, I licked it in the way that drove him crazy and grazed the lobe with my teeth. A deep growl thundered in his chest and his growing need hammered against my stomach.

Aric reached into the halter part of my dress and peeled away the stick-on bra. He cupped my breasts possessively, smoothing his rugged palms along the curves. My lids fluttered from his touch and eagerness, but when he tugged at the tips, I couldn't stifle my mews.

"That's better," he muttered through clenched teeth.

The warmth between us spread into a burning fire. We didn't have much time, and fear of being discovered kept me from ripping his clothes free of his hot form. So I kissed and nibbled while my hands worked to unbuckle his belt and pants.

Our groans were loud and our gasps harsh. His neck craned when I took hold of him, the cords straining as I stroked and pulled exactly how he liked. I slid to my knees to put him in my mouth, only for him to haul me back up. His need was too great; then again, so was mine. He fastened his arm around my waist and pinned me against the wall. I spread my legs for him and moved the crotch of my panties aside—there was no time to take them off. He held me close and used his free hand to ease himself inside of me.

Aric's size always made him work to enter me. My body was excited to receive him, but it still wasn't enough and I'd grown impatient. I fastened my ankles around his back and forced him into me.

We both let out howls of pleasure mixed with pain. For a moment neither of us moved. We locked eyes and continued to pant as my body relaxed and fully accepted his. Then something in him changed, a feral hunger that needed quenching. He kissed my lips just once and began to thrust. The ache was incredible and the position allowed him access to the perfect spot. He unsnapped the halter of my dress and played with my breasts while I bit back my screams and rocked my hips.

Aric and I had always had a spicy love life. But the possibility of being caught along with trying to hold back our cries added to the intensity. We both climaxed quickly. He wouldn't release me after he finished. As we continued to kiss, I decided to put all the hours of yoga training to good use. I pulled away and whispered, "Hang on."

I placed my ankles on either side of his head, lighting the fire in Aric's bedroom eyes. He released a hungry growl and powered into me once more. It hurt, but it was a good kind of pain. I whimpered while his deep, agonized moans filled the night. This time was longer and needier.

We finished together, barely managing to keep from screaming. My head fell against his shoulder when he lowered my legs to his waist. I breathed him and our lovemaking in, wishing more than anything our time didn't have to end so soon. We kept our stance until we caught our breaths and then slowly he released me.

Aric watched me re-dress while he fumbled to fasten his pants. I giggled when he slid on a small patch of ice in his haste to return to me. He grinned, gathering me in his arms. His lips met mine softly with a taste so addicting my soul begged for more. As our kiss ended we smiled and focused on each other in silence. Sometimes words weren't so important.

Our brief happiness was interrupted by the familiar ringtone on his cell, announcing he was needed by his Elders. Aric ignored it, but the insistent ring forced the smile from his face. Sadness consumed the air around us. Nothing had changed. We still couldn't be together.

The phone continued to ring and I knew we could pretend no longer. We hugged tightly, taking a moment to breathe in each other's scents. I didn't speak. Because speaking meant saying good-bye, and I couldn't do it again. So I took the opposite path and walked away from him quickly. As I made my way up a small hill, the sound of breaking glass had me veering back.

Aric was gone. On the ground, in small shattered pieces lay the remains of his phone.

CHAPTER 19

I never made it back to the ballroom, and bumped into my sisters in the foyer. They explained that the wolves had gone to prepare the pack for an emergency mission.

Emme approached me cautiously, her face distraught with worry. "Celia, there's something we need to tell you."

Their stress fired up my beast. "What's wrong?"

She turned to Taran. Taran stepped forward and looked me directly in the eyes. "Celia, Aric is majorly pissed and being a prick. He's all upset over that freak's prediction, and he's convinced you want to make vampire babies with Misha."

I nodded and tried to choose my words with care. "Okay," I managed.

My sisters blinked back at me, obviously confused I wasn't more upset. Shayna placed her hand on my shoulder. "He left with those slutty girls, Ceel. We think he's with them." I didn't react. "You know, with them in his room." She gaped at my unfrazzled expression as if I'd lost my mind. "Right *now*."

"I see." My reaction to their news was clearly not what they had expected. They looked at me like I'd been cracked in the head with a few bowling pins and possibly the ball.

Taran flicked her carefully manicured nails. "All righty, then . . . So, where the hell have you been?"

"I went for a walk." I cleared my throat. "And, um, got some air."

Emme frowned. "In this cold?"

"It wasn't so bad." *In fact, it was really hot.*

Shayna stared at me, but it wasn't just because of my loopy responses.

"Something wrong?" I asked her.

She leaned in and took a sniff. "You smell different."

I backed away slightly. "What do you mean?" I asked, even though I knew exactly what she meant.

"I'm not saying you smell bad, Ceel, just different." She took another whiff and nodded pensively. "Hmm, it's a familiar scent, though. No—wait . . . It's not just one aroma you carry, but two. Hmm . . . what is that? It's kind of like warm musk . . ."

Panic spread like a rash across my face. Emme and Taran exchanged glances, confused by my flushing cheeks. I grabbed Shayna by the arm and squeezed tight. "Shayna, zip it. Zip it now!"

"Ouch! Celia! What's the big deal? I'm just trying to—" She clamped her hands over her mouth and muffled a scream. When her eyes bugged out, I knew for sure she had figured things out.

Yep. That's right. I smell like sex and Aric. My gaze locked on hers. She nodded once, finally comprehending that now was definitely not the time to talk.

"Celia!" Hank called from near the door. He held my coat and waved me forward. "The master is waiting for you."

I said good-bye to my sisters and exchanged one last look with Shayna before leaving. There was no way to camouflage my aroma and I worried how Misha would react.

All heads snapped in my direction the moment I entered the limo. Misha's vampires looked at me, then at him, and vanished. There was a slight breeze when doors shut behind them, but then nothing. Only an icy stillness remained. I sat in the seat facing him.

His fangs protruded and clenched so tight I thought they'd snap. His glare was threatening, malicious, and so very cold. I used my coat to shield his stare. Not because I was afraid—and *not* because I was ashamed. I couldn't quite place what I felt then. I'd seen the fury in Misha's eyes countless times before, although it had never been directed at me. Perhaps he felt I deserved it. If so, he was wrong.

It was a long drive back to the mansion. Misha continued to stare at me and not speak while I continued to avoid his eyes. The moment we arrived, I jumped out of the Hummer and left for the guesthouse. I removed my dress and shoes and placed them on the bed. I washed off my makeup and then slipped into a tank top and some underwear. I didn't want to shower, hoping to keep Aric's scent on me as long as possible.

When I came out of the bathroom, Edith was sitting on my bed, trembling with her hands clamped tight. "The master wishes to see you," she mumbled.

It wasn't a request. I threw on a robe and a pair of slippers and followed her back to the house. Edith's swagger was long gone. Her shoulders hunched the entire way to the house. She led me to the library and quickly disappeared. I paused before entering. Misha's growing anger bubbled around him and stirred my beast. She believed it was best to come out. I kept her in place.

Misha leaned against the huge mantel, staring at the massive flames. A strange smell wafted from the fireplace and encompassed the room. I walked to him, realizing the scent was that of burning silk. My dress and shoes had been thrown into the fire. "Sit down," he said in a low voice.

I didn't argue and chose one of the armchairs closest to him. The chessboard rested on the table next to me. I fiddled with the pawn as I waited for him to make his next move. He was angry. I had caused him pain. But I didn't belong to him and nothing he could say would make me regret my actions. By the time he addressed me the marble chess piece had grown warm in my hand.

"Were you with the wolf tonight?"

My voice was quiet yet strong. "Yes."

His voice turned deadly. "Why?"

I didn't blink. "Because I love him, Misha."

Misha swatted the chessboard across the room, embedding the pieces into the wall. His hands gripped the sides of my chair and his nose was inches from mine. "Am I not worthy of your love?"

I was so shocked words initially failed me. But my surprise quickly morphed to fury. Did he think he could scare me so easily? Did he think I was one of his servants and would just cower at his feet? *Oh, hell no.*

"How can *anyone* love you when you're not capable of loving in return?"

Misha hissed. "What do you know of what I am capable of?"

"More than you think — I see it every day. You sleep with anyone you want and indulge yourself in any way that suits you. Have you ever committed to anyone — or given someone every part of you?" Misha continued to glare, but wouldn't answer. "I didn't think so. So until you know what I'm going through, don't pretend what you offer is enough for me or anyone else." I pushed him away and stood to leave. "If you wish, I'll still fight for you, but I refuse to live here. I'll take my chances with what hunts me. At least it doesn't pretend to be a friend." With those final words, I stormed out of the room.

Three voice mail messages from my sisters waited for me when I returned to the guesthouse. The first one was from Shayna. "Ceel, you and Aric like totally did it! Call us back and tell us what happened."

The next one was from Emme. "Oh, Celia, why aren't you calling us back? We want to know what happened. We're so happy that you and Aric reconnected . . . Well, you know what I mean." I didn't need to see her to know she'd blushed when she said this.

Taran, who was not known for her patience, left the last message. "What the hell, Celia? Are you *still* having sex? Oh, shit! That's it, isn't it? You're getting nasty. Call back when you're done. Damn it — details, I want details!"

I yanked off my robe and kicked off my slippers, pacing as I fiddled with the phone in my hand. My thoughts urged me to call them back, but the rest of me remained shaken from my encounter with Misha. I jumped when the phone buzzed in my hand and Gemini's face appeared on the screen. He never called me. "Gem, what's wrong?"

"It's me, sweetness." My heart leapt into my throat. It was Aric. He must have borrowed Gem's phone.

"Hey, wolf," I answered, almost crying.

"You're upset. What happened?"

"Nothing. I just really miss you." *I also just had a bad fight with Misha.*

"I miss you, too. Celia, I'm sorry things ended tonight the way they did."

"It's okay—"

"No, baby. It's not right that I'm not with you now."

I wiped a trailing tear. "There's not a lot we can do about it, love."

"You're wrong. Come to your bedroom window."

I stared at the screen briefly before racing from the kitchen to the bedroom. I tossed my phone on my armchair and yanked open the blinds. Aric perched on the long sill. He'd already removed the screen and opened the window. He tucked the phone in his jeans and grinned.

"Hey. I know I shouldn't be here, but—"

I grabbed him by his shoulders and hauled him inside, using a little too much force. Aric landed on top of me, making me purr.

"Hello, beautiful," he murmured.

Aric stroked me gently with his tongue and nibbled lightly on my lips. Every bit of Aric was delicious, but his taste made my body ache with need. He lifted me into his arms and carried me to the bed, lying next to me. He stopped our kiss and swept his hand through my hair. I melted against him. Aric represented home, security, and love—my answer to my loneliness.

I took in his face with my eyes and his body with my hand. All I felt was hard stone beneath the softness of his skin. He had always been muscular like a boxer, but now Aric's physique resembled more of a wrestler's.

His chest rose and fell slowly and his face flushed. "I've missed your touch."

I continued my slow caress. "You've really bulked up."

He took my hand and kissed it. "I spend most of my time hunting the Tribe, training, and fighting—working out my frustrations so I can better manage my wolf." He smiled when I continued to play. "Do you like it?"

I shrugged, to me he'd always looked good. "So long as it's what you want. I just like you."

Aric's hand slipped beneath my tank top and slid over my side and tummy, frowning when his fingertips skimmed along my waist. "You, on the other hand, are even smaller. Hasn't Misha been feeding you?"

"Yes, Aric. I actually eat more now." I snuggled against him and released an extremely content purr. His laugh rumbled against me. I placed my hand over his heart, to feel it beat and as proof he was lying next to me. It was warm, comforting, relaxing. But it didn't last.

Aric's Alpha wolf voice replaced his soothing timbre. "We need to talk." He lifted me with ease so we could face each other, keeping his hand tight against my hip. "What do you know about what's after you?"

I shook my head. "Nothing. Just that whatever it is sees me as the one who'll destroy it and those it leads."

"Considering what you've been into, everything points to the Tribe."

I watched him carefully. Our relationship had lasted mere months, but they'd been the most intense months of my life, filled with powerful moments that had left me breathless. I knew this wolf enough to know there was more. "You're not convinced it's the Tribe."

"I'm convinced enough to slaughter them every chance I get."

"But you still have doubts."

Aric nodded and palmed my backside. "I can see them portraying you as an enemy of evil and influencing other dark forces to annihilate you. And I can see why they'd want you out of their way." He growled. "But the why of it doesn't make sense. What's this damn key you supposedly possess? Could there be a hidden power we still don't know about?"

"I suppose. Mish— I've been working on my ability to *change* into other animals, but my efforts are pathetic at best. My power to return a vampire's soul was something I didn't know I had, so it's possible there's some other freak talent I possess."

Aric stiffened. "How many beings know you've been practicing *changing* into other creatures?"

"Just the vamps."

Aric snarled. "You can't trust these assholes, Celia. If the damn shape-shifters get wind of this, they will try to destroy you. They see themselves as the only beings powerful enough to command any form. To them you're competition, regardless of your inability to heal." He swore up and down. "I'm leaving on my last mission tonight. When I come back, I'm going *lone* and getting you out of here."

I stared at him, unable to blink. After my shock wore off, I flipped out. "Are you nuts? Aric, you can't abandon your pack. You once told me you're nothing without them."

"Celia, things have changed. You're the one I'm nothing without. Don't you see? This is the only way we can be together."

I touched his stubbled jaw with my fingertips. "Not like this, baby. There has to be another way."

Aric shook his head. "Celia, tonight you shone like the amazing beauty you are. It should have been me escorting you—not Misha. I should have been the one you turned to when Destiny frightened you. I should be the one asking you to dance, not that goddamn lion. I should be the one who talks to you about starting a family, not anyone else." He waited, taking in my thunderstruck reaction. "And I should be the one protecting you from whatever seeks to harm you."

Aric had warred with his inner animal to stay in control, but the man in him still hurt despite his beast's best efforts to protect him. "Don't let your jealousy cloud your judgment, Aric. And take back authority over your wolf. He doesn't need to fear being without me. So long as you want me, I swear never to leave you."

"How can you doubt that I want you?" Aric cupped my face. "And how can you fail to see what you mean to me? You are my mate. I live and breathe for you, Celia. My heart and soul are soldered to yours for eternity."

Aric had shown command in his gaze before, but all those times paled to how he looked at me then. My heart thumped like the slow beat from a heavy mallet. I took a moment to allow the depths of his words to sink in. When they did, it felt as if I'd broken through the snow after being buried in an avalanche. Mate, he'd said. I was Aric's *mate*. I quivered from the tears that threatened to fall. "Why didn't you ever tell me? I never knew how you felt."

Aric's face split with sadness and guilt. "Because as pureblood I wasn't supposed to love you, but as man I can't stop."

He kissed me. It was so different—new in a way. Our passion exploded so quickly we yanked each other's clothes off. His left hand stroked my breast to tease my nipple with his thumb. The other hand traced down my stomach until he found my building moisture. My back arched and I grunted while his hands rediscovered me inside and out. The salt from his skin made me hungry to taste other parts of his body. My tongue slid down his chest. Aric was in such need. He thrashed and grunted, completely turning me on. My mouth hadn't been around him long before he pulled me on top of him and I began to move.

CHAPTER 20

Water slid down my arms. My cheek and breasts cooled against the slick tile as I panted. Aric kissed his way along my shoulder. "Are you ready?" he asked breathlessly.

I didn't want him to separate us, but nodded. Dawn was quickly approaching. He needed to return to his pack and leave for the mission. I'd convinced him not to go *lone*, at least for now.

His groan matched mine upon his release. I opened the glass door and staggered out of the shower, aching in all the right places. "You'd better get my scent off you." The twinkle in Aric's face made me laugh. That's exactly what I'd said before he'd yanked me into the shower to wash the latest aroma of our lovemaking.

Aric lathered his skin, watching me slip into my robe. "Four times in one night. Brings back some sweet memories."

I shuddered from his deep murmurs and from the rush of images his words flashed across my mind. My brain reasoned my body should be more than satisfied, but my tigress insisted we hadn't made up for lost time. I sat on the edge of the bathtub and admired his luscious physique. "Do you think your Warriors know you're here?"

"Koda and Liam don't. Gemini must. He didn't blink when I asked to borrow his phone. While he recognizes the importance of continuing our race, he also knows I love you. He told me tonight that, for once, he's happy not to be of pure blood. He said he didn't know how I'd been able to stay away from you and that no one would keep him from Taran."

Aric's hands passed along his chest as he washed, just not with the same enthusiasm I'd demonstrated. "At least he's supportive," I said.

"As much as he can be. He knows being away from you has tortured me. I'm pissed all the time and I've been a bastard to be around." He placed his hands against the tiled wall and dropped his head. "I can't believe I ever left you. I couldn't even bring myself to touch you that day. If I had, I wouldn't have been able to do what I thought was right for the sake of my race." His bruised gaze met mine. "I'll never forgive myself for hurting you."

I hugged my arms and turned away for a moment. The pain I experienced that day still affected me. And it still wasn't behind us. "What happened when you met with the Elders tonight?"

Aric stepped out of the shower and took the towel I handed him. "It was damn obvious we'd been together. I couldn't hide our scent, nor did I want to. We . . . had words, and Anara ordered me never to see you again."

I frowned, confused. "As Beta, Anara closely matches Martin in *were* magic."

"Yeah, he does." Aric answered as if he didn't care, and that the Elders' supremacy meant nothing.

"Then how are you here, especially after a direct order to stay away? I thought that whole blood bond wolf mojo thing prevented you from disobeying."

He toweled off, smirking. "There are certain loopholes to the blood bond. When Anara ordered me to take Barbara as my fiancée, I had to obey. During the ceremony, my bond to you as my mate helped me resist."

"But the Elders are aware of the loopholes, right? I would think they would have tightened them somehow." I scoffed. "Especially given all the power they can draw from the pack."

Aric wrapped the towel around his waist, his grin widening. "They're aware. And I'm sure they used some of our collective magic to help strengthen the order. But I don't think they realized how strong I've become, and I'm not planning on telling them."

I reached for him, but thought twice before touching him. "What happens if Anara or the others discover you disobeyed them?"

Aric stopped smiling. "Let me worry about that."

"Aric . . ."

"Celia, I hate hiding our love like it's something wrong. If they find out, I'll deal with it." Aric's eyes held the strength and determination that first attracted me to him. "I'm going to fix this, Celia. Somehow I'll find a way for us to be together."

I returned with Aric's clothes after running them through the dryer with a softener sheet to remove my scent. I watched him dress, my growing need to hold him worsening. We were together again, but still so much apart. "Be careful," I said softly.

Aric slipped his long-sleeved black shirt over his eight-pack. He leaned forward. "I'm going to come back to you. Don't worry." He stilled. "In the meantime, I want you to stay sharp. The only reason I'm not dragging you out of here is that, assholes or not, the vamps have the muscle to protect you and keep you safe in my absence."

My body tensed. This was so not the moment to tell Aric I was jumping off the S.S. *Bloodsucker*. Maybe I could crash at Bren and Danny's. *Two wolves and a tigress should be enough to thwart scary monsters, right?*

"Okay, love. I promise to keep my eyes open." I walked him to door, smiling when his lips found mine. He licked his own lips, camouflaging my scent and having one last taste of me.

No sooner did he disappear into the breaking dawn

than the snow began to fall and Maria appeared at my door.

She followed me into my bedroom. I ignored her and hauled my large suitcase from beneath the king-sized bed. Her walk lacked her usual shimmy and she kept quiet despite her typical tendencies to say something wretched. "You are really leaving, aren't you?"

"Yup."

"It will not be de same without you. You are crazy bitch weird and all, but okay." She made an irritated gesture with her hand. "Just okay."

I couldn't help but smirk. "Gee, thanks, Maria."

A breeze slapped me in the face and I felt someone behind me. "Do you need something, Liz?" I asked.

She flung her ice blond hair back and started filing her nails. "Chef prepared you some breakfast. You should go eat."

It was too early for the vamps to be up, including Chef. Misha's anger must have kept them up. "Is Misha there?"

She stopped filing. "No. The master is not there now."

"But he will be."

She tried to sound indifferent. "Yes, most likely he will be."

Misha and I would have to talk eventually, and I'd never been one to walk away from a fight. When I entered the kitchen there was a whole spread laid out. The vampires I was most familiar with loitered around, watching me with solemn faces and unusually quiet mouths. I tried to smile encouragingly, although it was foolish of me to do so. They were annoying, oversexed, selfish, and downright vicious. Still, I didn't want the so-called creatures of the night to feel bad.

I thanked Chef and proceeded to eat like I was going into hibernation. I was almost done when Misha appeared with Virginia in tow. "Leave us," he said to the others in the kitchen.

Everyone scattered like dropped marbles. Misha sat at the table and watched me as I drank my orange juice. Our eyes met with equal stubbornness, but I didn't want to play "who blinks first." I wiped my mouth and threw my napkin on the table. "I'm sorry about what I said last night, Misha. I was angry, but I didn't intentionally mean to hurt you."

"What do you hope to accomplish by seducing that mongrel?"

"*What?*"

"Are you trying to convince him to leave his pack?"

My hackles rose and my tigress readied us to strike. "Misha, you're way out of line."

"Do you know what happens to a *were* of his stature who decides to turn his back on his race?"

I stood, knocking my chair back. "You don't know what you're talking about." My body shook. "I suggest you *shut the hell up*!"

Misha's stare fired with malice and his voice thickened with spite. "*Yes, I do.* The reputation of your wolf's family will be destroyed. All his finances *and* those of his closest relatives will be depleted—"

"Misha, stop it."

"He has an elderly mother, does he not? Are you prepared to take her home from her? All her valuables—"

"*Shut your fangs now!*"

"They will all be disgraced and shunned. All because of you—"

My hammer fist strike to the table quieted him. The table split in half and all the contents splattered to the floor. I threw the sections aside and went after him. "You want to do this?" I shoved him through the door. "*Fine. Let's go.*"

The snow fell in large thick flakes, coating my long hair almost instantly. The sky had darkened and thunder roared in the distance. I continued to push Misha until we reached the large section of lawn separating the garden from the main house. Misha's vampires gathered, forming a wide circle around us. I expected them to hiss and attack me. Instead they stood silent, watching us closely while their rising anxiety danced around me.

Misha's eyes never left mine. He stooped in a crouch

and charged. He was fast, but not fast enough. I spun him past me and sent him face-first into a dirty pile of snow. The vampires gasped. Misha rose surprisingly slowly and turned to shoot me a death glare. Slush dripped down his perfect face to stain his white silk shirt.

"Not as fast as you thought, are you, old man?"

The vamps jumped at my words with their mouths covered. Misha seemed oddly amused and laughed. However, it wasn't a "golly, aren't you funny?" kind of chuckle. It was more like an evil scientist laugh complete with thunder crackling above us. Like shot from a gun, Misha attacked.

This time he was prepared. He turned his momentum in the opposite direction at the last minute and tried to flip me. I grabbed his hair and we both went down, hard. We wrestled in the snow, digging our feet into the ground for leverage and kicking up dirt. We were soiled and saturated within minutes. It was a mean, dirty, ferocious match. But as mad as we both were, neither of us exchanged blows. We grappled and twisted and even yanked hair, fighting to pin each other.

Large hills of dirt and snow formed every time we shoved and slid across the lawn. Misha was stronger, but I was faster and used all my training against him. I snatched his wrist into a lock. His slippery skin allowed him to break free. He tossed me across the lawn. I landed on my feet, searching for an opening. "What's the matter, kitten? Too weak to hold an old man?"

I dove across the lawn and *shifted* beneath him. I surfaced in a high leap and snagged him in a choke hold. "You're calling the wrong cat a kitty, Goldilocks."

He forced an arm through my hold and yanked hard. I landed on my butt and scrambled to my feet. Misha tackled me before I found my footing and sent us rolling down the small incline. We barreled into the garden and right smack into one of the stone waterfalls. I landed on top and slammed him against the granite slab with the might of my arms. "Nice try, Rapunzel, but you won't beat me that easy," I growled.

Misha exposed his incisors and flipped me over, pressing his weight against me. "Our encounter the other night in my bed should tell you I am all male. Or need I remind you?"

I shoved him off me and *shifted* him down, burying him up to his neck. Misha's face deepened to purple as he thrashed about. "*This is how you choose to treat me after all I have done for you!*"

I staggered back. Being the mature gal I was, I pointed an accusing finger at him. "You started it!"

Misha broke through the frozen ground and sloshed to me. "No, *you* did. I merely elucidated that your actions are severely misguided."

He encircled my waist, but I hooked his leg with mine and twisted. We fell and rolled back, all the way to the guesthouse. The minute Misha hit the side of the house I released him and hurried back. The snow fell hard. It felt good against my heated skin. Again, we faced each other.

"You're wrong about Aric. He's not going *lone*. I won't let him."

Misha grabbed me in a painful arm lock. "And why is that?"

I twisted and flipped, grabbing his neck in a scissor hold with my legs and bringing him down with the brunt of my weight. "Because I love him, damn it. It would hurt him to leave his pack."

He entwined his arm in between my legs and broke free. "I know. You've made it clear that it's *him* you love."

We were a few feet from each other, trying to catch our breaths. I paused to take in his face once my brain listened to what he had to say. *Really* listened. Misha was angry—furious even, but there was something else. Not resentment. Not bitterness. Not even arrogance. No. Misha was . . . *heartbroken*. His brows curved as if he was in agony, and the creases in the corners of his eyes expressed his lack of sleep and torment.

I threw my hands in the air. "Is that what this tantrum is about, Misha? You think I don't love you?"

He took a step toward me. "What are you saying?"

Mud dripped down our panting faces and our drenched clothes clung to our forms. Misha continued to frown, but his pained expression had softened. I wiped my face and gradually ambled toward him. My shoulders dropped with a heavy sigh and I shook my head. Without giving it much thought, I extended my hand and touched his cheek. Slowly, he covered it with his palm. "I do love you, Misha," I said softly. "It's just not in the way that you want me to." The frown erased from his features and the familiar tenderness returned. "I don't want to lose you. But if you're expecting more than my friendship, I have to walk away."

Horrible screaming interrupted before he could answer. Virginia broke away from the crowd of vampires and rushed me. Misha yanked me behind him.

The gleam in Virginia's eyes bordered on psychotic. She lunged at Misha and clawed at his chest. I gasped, knowing it was me whose skin she wished to rip apart. Maria and Agnes yanked her from him, hissing and snarling through their fangs.

"Take her away," Misha ordered. His voice remained strangely calm, but his stare stayed on Virginia as if encountering another preternatural. Maria and Agnes lifted Virginia with ease as she sobbed and kicked all the way back to the main house.

I watched her go, disturbed by her volatile response. If she hadn't been obsessed before, she certainly was then. Misha took my hand and led me to the front door of the guesthouse. More yelling echoed from the house. We turned to find Kuan Jang Nim Chang racing barefoot through the mess we'd made of the garden, wearing nothing more than his gi to protect him from the heavy snowfall. He smiled wide and waved the broken leg from the kitchen table at us. He jabbered on in Korean before finally pointing and motioning me toward the dojang. He then practically skipped toward the building while I blinked back at him like the nutcase he was.

I turned to Misha. He wiped some of the muck off the

back of my hand and kissed the tips of my knuckles. "Chang hopes that you will stay. I hope that as well. Now, if you will excuse me, I must take my Metamucil."

As I watched Misha march through the mounds of destroyed landscaping, I wondered if I should just leave. I'd already hurt him once. And I knew more pain was yet to come. I just didn't know I'd receive the brunt of it.

CHAPTER 21

"Shit. You're staying?" Taran asked.

I dodged the electrically charged balls Kuan Jang Nim Chang launched at me, shifting right, then left, then dropping into a split. "I don't know. I'm not sure what to do."

Shayna's sleek black ponytail whipped back and forth as she watched Chang and his bouncing balls. "Dude, what the heck are those things anyway? They look like they have little lightning bolts in them."

"Oh!" my sisters yelled when one hit me.

A shock ran up my spine and my hair sizzled. I hadn't rolled fast enough. *Damn it.* I groaned and flopped into a kneeling position. "As a matter of fact, they do have little lightning bolts in them."

Kuan Jang Nim Chang fired a string of rapid Korean before laughing hysterically.

My eyes narrowed. "I am so trying!"

"You understood what he said?" Emme asked.

"Not a word." I stood and tried to beat down my hair. It didn't work. "He laughs more when I mess up. I think it's his way of saying, 'If you'd try harder, you wouldn't get hurt.'"

"Do you think the little man will mind if I try?"

I couldn't face Shayna directly. Chang continued to

fling his balls, all the while inspiring me with comments like, "Tribe coming. Faster. They eat you. They kill you. You die like dog not tigress."

Heaven forbid he stop his oh-so-fun training session just so I could engage in conversation with my sisters. "Shayna, that's not a good idea. I don't want you to get hurt."

"No worries. I have werewolf blood pumping through my veins." She flexed her string bean arms. "See? I'm just as tough as you are now."

That made me smile. "Is that right?"

"I sure am! Plus, it looks like fun."

Was she kidding? "Fun? Did you say 'fun'? Okay, Shayna, be my guest."

"Um, I don't think you should let her do this," Emme warned.

Taran flashed a wicked grin. "Aw, hell. I think you should. It might knock her off that high horse she's been straddling."

It took us less than seven minutes to return to the guesthouse. Shayna zinged, zapped, and pa-chinged the entire walk back. Snot ran down her nose like a leaky faucet and her once pin-straight black hair stood out like a large Afro. "Whaaaat the heckkkkk isss wrrrronng with that maaaann?" she asked.

Taran and I led her to the kitchen using the rubber gloves Hank had scrounged up. He assured us Shayna would be fine in another hour or so. His reassurance did little to ease my guilt. I never should have turned her over to Kuan Jang Nim Chang's evil clutches.

"... and then heeeeeee jjjjussst laughed annnddd pp-pointed."

"I know, Shayna. I know. I'm so sorry."

"So what the hell are you going to do about the whole Misha situation?" Taran asked.

I shrugged. "Part of me wants to move back home and just commute to train."

"So, damn it, why don't you? Gemini texted me earlier to say Aric's calling in a favor. The local witch bitches are supposed to place a new ward around our house in case anything nasty shows up. I think it's similar to the one Ying-Ying put on your car—strong enough to keep things out until help arrives."

Emme shook her head. "What if help is delayed like last time? Celia can't take on a Tribemaster by herself."

Taran rammed her fists on her hips. "She doesn't have to, Emme. We'll stay there with her and keep each other safe."

"Wwweeee can't—the wolves wannnt usss to stay at the Dennnn."

Taran huffed. "Damn it, Shayna. I hate the Den. It's not our home. The only reason I'm there is to be with Gemini, but now he's gone. We're not under the Elders' rule. They can't make us stay."

I thought about it. "Why don't we compromise? While the wolves are away, we'll stay at the house. When they're back, you guys return with them to the Den and I'll stay with Misha."

"Or Aric?" Taran asked smiling. "I bet that's another reason he had Genevieve ward the house. So you two can have your own safe little love nest."

I bit my bottom lip nervously. "So long as we don't get caught."

Taran's smile turned wickedly curious. She circled me, very much in the way I did a steak. "Speaking of getting caught, where were you exactly when you got it on with him?"

I averted my eyes. "You know where we were. We were at the Den."

Taran arched a brow. "Celia. You've been away from that wolf for months. Don't play off your hot and beastly hump-hump like some kind of cute romantic interlude. Tell us *exactly* what happened!"

My cheeks instantly heated. "Taran, I told you what happened. I was upset and Aric found me. We kissed and got a little carried away."

Taran smirked. "That's not good enough. Spill deets, Celia."

My jaw dropped open. "And why exactly should I do that?"

"Cannnnn IIIIII hhhhhhavvve ssssommme wa-water?"

"No, you'll just electrocute yourself," Taran said, then turned back to me. "Shit, Celia. You don't know what you and Aric have put us through. The least you can do is give us a little dirt."

"Celia doesn't have to tell us anything," Emme said quietly.

Although Emme had insinuated my privacy should be respected, the anticipation brightening her green irises and the flush to her fair skin told me she was dying to hear every last little detail. I groaned. "What do you want to know?"

Taran grabbed my arm and shook it. "For one, where the hell were you? Did you go back to his quarters?"

"Um, no. His dates were there."

"Were yyyyouuu innnn his cccarrrr?"

"No."

Taran shook me harder, her excitement building. "Did you go back to his office? Damn, that's hot. I seduced Gemini in there once. Just don't tell Aric."

"Ah, no. We weren't in his office."

"Jjjusttt tttttellll usssss, ddduuuuddddde."

I let out a defeated sigh. "It was in a large garden a few blocks away from the main building."

My already pink cheeks burned when I saw their stunned faces. Taran threw herself on top of me and hugged me warmly. "I'm so proud of you, Ceel."

Emme seemed confused. "But there's no place to sit or anything."

"Emmmmeeee's rrrright. Hhhow ddddid you . . . ?"

Taran gasped; being the adventurous sort, she had figured it out. "You, like, did it standing up, didn't you, you little hussy?"

My face dropped into my hands and I nodded. When I glimpsed up, Emme's face was redder than mine. "Oh, my," she said. "You really did get carried away."

"Can we talk about something else now?"

Taran continued to smile wickedly. "I can't think of a damn thing I would like to discuss more."

"I can," Emme said quietly. Something in her demeanor had changed. And I could tell by the way her sadness seemed to overtake her petite stature that it had nothing to do with me or Aric. "I'm breaking up with Liam when he gets back."

"Wwwhhhyyy?"

Tears streamed down her face. I put my arm around her, only to have her tears run faster. "Liam finally admitted to me that I'm not his mate."

Emme swallowed hard as she took in our astonishment. "He's the best man to ever come into my life. But I'll never be the best thing in his."

"Buttttttt he lovessss youuuuu."

"It's not enough," Emme whispered through her sorrow. "Shayna, you and Koda are mates. No one else will ever mean what you mean to each other. Liam can't make me that same promise." She lowered her chin. "Just like he can't promise he won't leave me if he finds his destined match."

I brushed her hair back from her face, struggling to find words that could comfort her. "Maybe you are and he just hasn't realized your connection."

"Don't bullshit her, Celia." Taran's words were harsh, yet her tone carried a softness and a strong sense of comprehension. "Gemini knew I was his. Just like Koda realized what Shayna meant to him following their first night together." She walked toward the door as if retreating, but turned back and faced me, her expression strangely bruised. "Aric is risking heaven and earth to be with you—regardless of how it affects the freaking *world*. Don't you think Emme deserves that, too, rather than someone who can't promise he won't dump her? *Weres* need their mates, Ceel." She rubbed her eyes. "Gem's made that clear more than once."

Emme wiped her cheeks and turned away when someone knocked on the door. Edith strutted in and froze upon taking in Shayna's condition. She threw back her head and laughed. "What the hell have you freaks been up to?"

"Shut your hole before you end up the same way," Taran snapped.

Edith ignored her and choked back another cackle. "The master would like you and your sisters to join him for dinner. This way, losers."

Taran sent her flying out the door with one of her own bolts of lightning. I rushed out as she pushed herself up on her arms and hissed. The ends of her dark hair smoked. Taran hadn't quite achieved Chang's look, but she made a damn good effort. I blocked Edith's path when she lunged at Taran. "Now may be a good time to remind you my family is under your master's protection." Emme sniffed behind me. "And that today is not a good day to piss me off."

Edith retracted her fangs and angled her head. I usually ignored the vamps' little digs. They typically didn't bug me enough to retaliate. But where my family was concerned was a different matter. Edith nodded and motioned for me to follow. I didn't know whether my threat or the knowledge that Misha would kill her gave her pause. Nor did I care. She needed to leave my sisters alone, especially given Emme's fragile state. I stayed between Edith and my sisters the entire walk to the house.

When we entered the lavish dining room, an army of servants waited to tend to us. Misha was nowhere to be found. "Where is he?" I asked Maria.

"De master is in de library. It would please him if you joined him."

I strolled down to the library and swung open the door. Misha was parked in a high-back leather chair with his hands clasped behind his head and his eyes closed. I would have thought he was sleeping, had it not been for the stiletto-clad feet sticking out from beneath the desk.

I jetted out of the library and smashed into Maria. "I thought you said he was available!"

Maria frowned as if I'd stolen her whip. "No. I said it would please him if you joined him."

"You may enter, Celia," Misha called from the room.

I poked my head in. Virginia stood next to him, pulling her dress back on. She stopped for a moment just to scowl at me. "I wanted to talk to you, but it can wait," I told him.

"As I said, you may enter." He gestured for Virginia to leave. I ignored the urge to snap her neck when she narrowed her eyes at me. I never understood how Misha could possibly be attracted to both her type and mine.

Misha gave me a small smile and motioned for me to sit. It was awkward. I sat in the same exact seat I'd been in when he went ape shit over Aric. "Is it still your plan to leave my residence?"

"I think it's best if we distance ourselves, at least a little bit." He watched me quietly but didn't respond. "I'll be staying in Dollar Point with my sisters when their wolves are away." He nodded slightly, yet still said nothing. "If it's okay, I'll still continue to stay with you upon their return."

He remained quiet, almost too quiet. Finally, he smiled. "Very well, if that is what pleases you."

"It does. Thank you." I stood to leave. I'm not sure why, but I gave him a quick peck on the cheek and high-tailed it out of there, not bothering to see his reaction. And although I'd failed to mention that Emme would be staying as well, I didn't think he'd mind.

Misha caught up to me easily and we entered the dining room together.

"*Merde*," Chef hissed upon seeing me. I took my seat, well aware of his death glare. It was just loads of fun at Camp Fang and Bang. How could I have even considered walking away from all this? He raised his arms, signaling his band of waiters to unveil the silver platters in unison. Apparently my absence had stalled his big reveal.

My sisters glanced at their pretty salads briefly before digging in. I sniffed and grimaced at the sour stench of vinegar. My stomach churned. Misha paused in the middle of lifting his fork. "Something wrong, my darling?"

"I'm sorry. I don't think I can eat the salad."

"*Merde*," Chef hissed again before disappearing with my food in a huff. Virginia strode in a few minutes later and placed a bowl of seafood bisque in front of me. Chef must have been severely irate I'd passed on one of his creations.

Misha entertained us with stories of his youth. We'd almost finished eating when Shayna's phone buzzed. She smiled. "The wolves are back." Her smile faded as she scrolled down the screen. "The Elders want us to return." She looked at me then and swallowed hard. "They're requesting your presence."

Emme was nervous the entire drive up. She hadn't expected Liam to return so soon. Not to mention she and my other sisters were panicked over what awaited me at the Den. I tried to calm them, but, considering my nerves were shot to hell, I failed miserably. The Elders must have discovered Aric had disobeyed their orders by seeing me. Would he be punished? If so, they'd likely choose to do so in front of me. Well, screw that. No way would I let him endure anything alone. Whatever he faced, we'd do it together.

The wolves and the Elders met us in the foyer of the main building along with Tye. Makawee rushed toward me, only to stop and cock her head when I fell into a fighting stance with my claws out. "Something wrong, my dear?"

Aric's eyes bulged. I'd never seen him so alarmed. I retracted my claws and fixed my posture. "Um. No."

Tye winked at me, complete with another flash of that dimple of his. The dimple may have worked on other females, but my narrowed eyes made it clear it didn't work on me. My reaction seemed to simultaneously surprise and offend him. He straightened. *What did you expect, jerk?*

Martin moved forward. He and Makawee engaged in polite conversation with my family and me and even discussed the details of the successful Tribe raid they'd returned from. It was only then that the rest of us relaxed. My tigress, though, continued to pace. The Elders had obviously not summoned me to say hello, so then what was up?

Liam approached Emme and gathered her in his arms. He stilled upon seeing her eyes shimmering with tears. He growled, "What's wrong? Did one of those leeches hurt you?"

"No, Lee." She looked to me. Her poignant expression told me she was going to break up with him. I wanted to stop her and talk her out of it. But it wasn't my decision or my heart at stake. "Can we go somewhere?" she asked him. "I need to speak to you alone."

Liam exchanged glances with Koda and then reluctantly led Emme through the large glass front doors. There was a brief moment of tension among our group until Makawee approached me smiling. The long strands of her white hair drifted like a sheet around her dark skin. "Celia, I would like to thank you for coming. Based on the occurrences of the night of the gala, the Elders and I wanted to extend an open invitation to you at our Den."

Huh?

"We realize this might come as a shock," Martin said when I stood there with my mouth open. "After all, we have not been as hospitable to you as we could have been." He and Makawee both glanced at Anara.

I blinked back at the others, my face reddening when I thought of "the occurrences" between Aric and me in the garden. Aric beamed as if he'd spray painted our exploits on the damn garden wall we'd made love against. Tye—oddly enough—appeared as confused as I was.

Anara addressed me then with a stiff nod. It was strange not to have him scowl at me. Hell, I'd almost gotten used to it. "We realize we shouldn't interfere with destiny," he said.

"Destiny?"

The Elders laughed. I failed to get the joke.

"Yes, dear," Makawee said. "You both are meant to be together. The very least we can do is facilitate the union by allowing you to visit."

"You want me to visit him here," I repeated slowly.

Makawee started to regard me the same way the Catholic schoolgirls did. "Yes, child. He'll stay here while he continues to help train our young wolves. Eventually, though, we hope you will reside together and begin your family."

My sisters and friends stood motionless, their eyes

widening. "Son of a bitch," Taran muttered. Still, it was more polite than what spewed from Bren's lips.

I took in the Elders one by one. "Is this some kind of trick?"

"Celia, I assure you, this is not a trick. We don't wish to toy with you or your emotions," Martin added patiently.

"So you're saying we—he and I"—I motioned to Aric—"should be together, and have *babies*?"

Anara threw what little patience he'd managed right out the window. "Who else would we be talking about?"

For some reason Tye blew up. "Now wait just a goddamn minute!"

"Silence," Anara snapped.

Tye growled deeper. Aric ignored him to encase me in his arms. "So, dovie, what do you say?"

Tye lunged at us. The aroma of *were* magic sizzled against my skin as Anara threw out an arm, leaving Tye suspended above the wood floors, barely able to move. By calling upon the power of the pack, Anara had stopped him midair.

Tye struggled, his muscles twitching. In the distance a pack of wolves erupted in howls.

I returned my focus to Aric when he caressed my back, encouraged by Makawee and Martin's smiles. I continued to stand there like an idiot while my brain whirled with confusion.

Aric grinned from ear to ear. "Well? Do you want me or not?"

My chest erupted with pure joy. I grabbed Aric and kissed him—something I never would have dreamed of doing before in the presence of the Elders. He paused before responding with one hell of a deep kiss. My tigress rose inside me, but it wasn't to meet Aric's wolf. She insisted something was wrong; I ignored her. What could be wrong? Aric had found a way for us to be together.

The loud snarls from Tye forced Aric to break our kiss. The lion was absolutely out of his mind. I couldn't comprehend his fury. Had something happened that I wasn't aware of?

Aric held me tighter and smiled. "Damn, girl. That was one hot smooch. I wasn't expecting that, especially after the other night."

I angled my head. Aric's manner of speaking was so unlike him, and his comment made no sense. "I would think you would," I whispered.

Taran rammed her way between us, forcing us apart. "Celia, what the hell are you doing?"

"Hey, get away from her." With her newfound strength, Shayna shoved Aric away past the granite fireplace and farther down through the entrance hall.

"What? *No!*" I tried to follow them. "Don't take him away from me!"

Gemini and Koda stepped in front of me, blocking my view of Aric. I pushed my way through them.

"Gemini, Miakoda, stand down," Anara commanded when they attempted to restrain me.

Taran clasped my wrist with both hands and dug her heels into the hardwood floor. I yanked my arm hard enough to send her sprawling across the floor. She screeched when her back hit the wall, but I didn't care enough to look back. Aric was getting farther away the more Shayna continued to shove him.

Bren and Danny snagged my wrists when I charged after him. The desperation to be with Aric overwhelmed me. I struggled and fought to break free. Their tightening holds fueled my hostility. Instead of just trying to escape, I attacked, not caring whether I hurt them.

"Ow! Celia, calm down," Danny said.

"Watch her hands and feet," Bren snapped. "Her claws are out."

"Let *go* of me, damn it. Let go of me *now!*" I hissed.

I could no longer see Aric, only hear him down the large expanse of space. I kicked Bren in the face and smashed Danny's nose with a head butt. I lurched forward, my legs strangely weak, and ran for all I was worth.

Bren tackled me before I could make it very far. My breath released in short pained gasps, as if I couldn't breathe without Aric. I needed his scent, his taste, his warmth around me. What remained of my sanity rushed out in an agonized scream before my body lost control and I began to hyperventilate. Bren loosened his hold. "Jesus, Celia. Breathe, kid. Just breathe."

My elbow nailed him hard in the temple and I clawed away from him. I staggered to my feet, my tigress eyes fixed to where Aric's heated voice continued to fight with Shayna. Bren and Danny grabbed my arms once more, their faces battered and dripping with blood. I broke away so forcibly my body flew through a wide French door leading into an office. Taran screamed. Glass cut my body, stinging my arms, face, and neck. Warm fluid dripped down my chest and soaked my stomach, but I didn't matter. Only Aric did.

CHAPTER 22

Bren's and Danny's injured faces paled with horror and panic. They approached me cautiously, their palms out pleading. I crawled backward through the glass, slipping on my blood as I moved.

"Celia, honey, please look at me," Danny whispered anxiously. "I need you to focus. Please look at me."

My hand clutched a large piece of broken glass. "*No. You won't keep me from him!*" My chest ached with every sob. "I need him! I can't live without him! I *won't* live without him!"

"*Celia!*" Taran screamed.

Something shattered and Anara roared in pain. The shard of glass I held rested just above my heart, piercing through my thick sweater. Tye had stopped me from stabbing myself. His hand clamped my wrist, he dripped with sweat, and he worked to catch his breath. Bren lay across my other arm, and Liam and Danny restrained my lower body. Slowly, my fingers uncurled against my will and the glass within my grip floated away.

Emme had appeared. She discarded the piece along with the remaining shards surrounding me with the power of her *force*. Her face had blanched. Taran stood beside her crying.

Martin and Makawee slowly rose from the floor. Martin staggered to Anara, who lay unconscious several feet away. Martin shook his head. "Anara will be all right. He just failed to shield himself properly. I suppose he never expected Aric to break his hold." He looked over at Aric. "And neither did I."

At the mention of Aric's name, I struggled again. This time the wolves made certain I couldn't move.

Shayna waited by Aric with her arms hugging her thin frame and her voice shaking. "What about my sister? Is she okay?"

Aric's eyes scanned the area before falling back on me. "What the blazes happened?"

"Let me go!" I sobbed. "I want to be with Aric—just let me be with Aric!" My cries grew hysterical and again I struggled to breathe.

"Sweetness, I'm right here. I'm right here, baby," Tye said.

I screamed at him when he tried to hold my face. "Don't touch me, you stupid goddamn lion!" With the exception of Makawee and Martin, everyone looked at me as if I'd gone insane. Maybe I had.

Makawee stroked my forehead. I shrugged her off; the only touch I wanted was Aric's. "Celia has been poisoned," she said gently. "Release her and I will try to cleanse her body." Everyone climbed off me except for Tye. Makawee placed her hand on his shoulder. "Do not fear, dear wolf. No harm will come to her."

I rushed to Aric the moment Tye let go. I managed only a few paces before Makawee caught me and restrained me with a strength that belied her petite stature. She held me by my arms while waves of nausea slammed into me like an angry tide. Cold sweat rushed down my body and the room spun. I started to faint. Strong arms caught me before I hit the floor. Makawee carried me to a bathroom and placed me in front of a toilet just in time. I threw up violently. Instead of the sickening smell of vomit, the scent of dark magic filled the air. My body shuddered with weakness. The moment I finished, I slumped into someone's arms. "I've got her, Makawee,"

Shayna said. Her voice trembled over Taran's and Emme's sniffling.

"Emme, fill the tub with warm water and then help Taran and Shayna take off her clothes. We need to bathe her. I will return shortly. I must gather some herbs to purify the water."

"I need to heal Celia, Makawee," Emme pleaded. "She's still bleeding."

"In sealing her wounds, you'll trap the poison inside her. The yellow dock I'll add to the water will help cleanse her blood, but we must hurry. We're running out of time."

My eyelids closed tight and my head throbbed over Tye's loud bellows. "Let me through—I need to see her!"

"No, Aric," Makawee answered. "Celia is too vulnerable. We can't risk her trying to hurt herself again."

Tye swore in frustration. Martin's deep baritone voice boomed in the foyer. "Aric, you are keeping Makawee from helping your mate. Move out of the way." He growled. "You will also do well to watch your tongue when speaking to your Omega."

My ears picked up on the sound of shuffling feet outside the door before Makawee's soft voice spoke once more. "Young Daniel, come with me, please."

I drifted between sleep and wakefulness. The tub closed around me like a snail shell. Warm water lapped at my skin as my body floated around the spirals. Growls echoed in the distance, both lion and wolf, together as one. Aric's and Tye's voices had united. I wanted to sleep, but I feared drowning. *Will the snail let me drown, Aric?*

"I'm not looking, Aric. I swear I'm not looking," Danny kept saying.

Makawee stopped her chanting. I couldn't even recall when she'd come back. My thoughts were muddled, and I struggled to make sense of what was happening. "Young Daniel, I would like you to watch what I'm doing. As a blue merle werewolf, you may be gifted with the ability to heal others. Kindly open your eyes." Her chanting resumed.

A pop followed a sizzle. "Ow! What the heck, Taran?" Danny said. "Makawee made me look."

"She said 'watch' not 'gawk,'" Taran snapped. "Reel in your damn hormones before I zap you again."

More growls erupted.

"Aric, calm down," Bren said. "It's not like he's never seen her naked before."

There was a sudden upsurge of breaking, smashing, and more snarling. Once again, Makawee stopped her chanting. "Aric," she said calmly, "please allow your Warriors to escort you outside and away from the building." Her soothing essence floated above my skin. The silence on the other side of the door was immediate. "Now, young Daniel, take the black cohosh and sprinkle it over Celia while I finish the ritual."

"What will that do?" Emme asked meekly.

"It's the final herb to destroy the poison."

The scents of licorice and rose water tickled my nose before the aroma of sage clouded the room. My mind flooded with visions of Native Americans dancing to the beat of a soft pounding drum. I coughed, through my mouth and through my cuts.

"Oh, shit," Taran whispered.

"Do not fear. The dark magic is leaving her body."

I coughed several more times. My skin felt like a sponge being squeezed, but with each cough it became easier to breathe.

I left the Native Americans and slipped back through the snail shell. I blinked my eyes open during my last few coughs to find my sisters staring back at me. Shayna lifted me from the water and helped me to sit. Danny hurried to the corner, giving his back to me.

Makawee nodded. "It is done."

Emme healed my wounds following Makawee's cleansing ritual. They burned my clothes along with the remaining herbs, forcing me to borrow a tunic and jeans from Shayna. I tried to apologize to Taran for hurting her, but she wouldn't hear it. When I emerged from the bathroom, I couldn't look anyone in the face. Even though I knew magic had influenced my behavior, humiliation heated my body. It had bothered me to be vulnerable. I could handle most things, but being defenseless wasn't one of them.

Makawee explained I had ingested a poison that caused me to switch Tye's and Aric's entities. The magic was so strong Tye and Aric took on each other's looks, scents, and apparently their tastes as well. The way his lips and tongue had swept against mine should have warned me something was different, but in retrospect my thoughts seemed so jumbled, focused only on taking in Aric. She also told me the poison had amplified my feelings for Aric, turning me dangerously obsessive and suicidal. I couldn't argue with that. *Shit*. I'd almost killed myself.

Shayna slung an arm around me. "It's okay, Ceel. Don't be embarrassed."

Taran rubbed at her face. "I'm sorry I knocked you out, Makawee. And please extend my apologies to Martin. I was trying to put Celia to sleep, but I was so scared for her I didn't aim my magic in the right direction."

Makawee smiled gently. "Not to worry, Taran. These things happen."

I kept my eyes on the floor. *Oh, yeah. I'm sure they happen all the time.*

Makawee turned to leave, but I stopped her. "Thank you for helping me, Makawee. I don't know what would have happened to me if you hadn't been here."

She patted my shoulder. "You're welcome, Celia. Try to rest tonight."

Gemini, Koda, and Bren regarded me with their arms crossed over their powerful chests. Aric was nowhere to be found and neither was Liam or the remaining Elders. I could barely catch a trace of their aromas.

My hands squeezed Bren's and Danny's arms. Dried blood caked their faces and hair from the injuries I'd inflicted. My shame made it hard to meet their gazes. "I'm so sorry I hurt you."

"We know, honey," Danny said quietly. "It's okay."

No, it really wasn't.

"Who did this to you, Celia?" Gemini asked. His voice wasn't so quiet.

"I don't know."

Koda's upper lip curled into a snarl. "Didn't you just have dinner with the bloodsuckers?"

"Misha wouldn't do this," Danny answered. He was the only wolf not scowling. "He wouldn't want Celia to be with Tye any more than Aric."

Bren narrowed his eyes. "Maybe not Misha, but how 'bout one of his other leeches?"

Shayna encircled Koda's waist to calm his increasing growls. "Misha's vampires are terrified of him, puppy. I don't see any one of them risking their hides to harm her."

Emme clutched my hand with hers. "Misha's vamps adore Celia." My head slowly turned toward her. She blushed. "Well, I mean, in their own special way."

"We're going to figure this out, Celia," Gemini said. "In the meantime, I'd like to speak with Makawee about allowing you to stay here tonight."

I shook my head. "The Elders brought me here with the purpose of hooking me up with Tye. I don't want him. I want Aric. My inebriation proved as much. They're not going to want me around now. Hell, you might get in trouble for even suggesting I stay."

Gemini didn't respond. He knew I was right.

Bren cracked his knuckles. "The Elders don't require me and Dan to live here. We're going back to our apartment. Come with us—you can crash at our place."

"Thanks, Bren, but I feel safe enough going back to Misha's."

Taran and Shayna remained shaken by the events of the evening. They wanted to return to Misha's house with me or back to Dollar Point. I insisted they stay with their wolves and appease the Elders. No one seemed happy, but their worry increased when Emme climbed into the car with me. It was then that everyone seemed more aware of Liam's absence.

Emme drove behind Bren and Danny, passing through the large stretch of Den grounds. I stared at Emme, who kept swallowing hard and taking deep breaths. As we passed through the wrought-iron gates, the dam burst and she broke down. I had her stop the car before we crashed. Bren rushed over to us to see what was wrong. "What the hell happened?"

"She and Liam broke up," I answered quietly. I slid out of the car and went around the other side.

Bren wrenched the driver's-side door open, fired up. And yet when he reached for Emme, he was incredibly gentle. He gathered her into his arms and kissed the top of her head. "Do you want me to kick his ass?" he offered.

I hurried around the other side and clutched his arm. "It's not like that." I sighed, not wanting to announce my sister's business to the world but worried Bren would go after Liam if he thought he'd hurt Emme. "Liam told Emme that she's not his mate."

Hearing the cause of their breakup in words was the emotional kick to the shins Emme didn't need. She sobbed into her hands.

Bren looked down at her, then at me, then called for reinforcements. "Dan! Hysterical female, you need to handle this."

I led Emme into the backseat and tried to comfort her while Danny drove our Legacy. Bren was better off driving alone in his Mustang. The moment he slammed his door shut he blasted Metallica. He didn't do well with crying women, emotional breakdowns, or drama. He did only bar brawls, babes, and beer. And yet he'd done his best to soothe Emme's pain.

Emme choked through her words. "Liam didn't take our breakup well, and begged me reconsider." She wiped her tears with the sleeves of her pink sweater. "When I asked him if he was certain I wasn't his mate, it took him a long time to answer. I kept waiting for him to give me hope. But he wasn't able to. Instead he promised to love me as much as he could."

My heart panged. "As much as he could" wasn't good enough, no matter how much Liam meant it to be. I didn't want their relationship to end. But I also wanted what was best for both of them.

"We didn't say anything more once we heard the

screaming inside." Emme leaned heavily against me. "I've never loved anyone else, Celia. And I don't think I ever will."

I held her close and thought of Aric. If her mate wasn't Liam, then it was someone else. If so, she would love another.

Bren and Danny left us at Misha's after Bren explained the effects of my poisoning in graphic detail. Misha seethed with a rage I'd never seen. Like the wolves, he'd concluded one of his own had poisoned me. It made sense. My last meal and drink had been in his home. And the witch fire . . . yeah, that had occurred under his watch and on his turf as well. It went without saying something was rotten in Dracville.

Emme and I passed the line of vampires waiting to be interrogated on our way to the guesthouse. Most of them shook in fear of Misha's wrath. But none like Chef. Sweat cascaded down his face in rivers and he crumpled his hat with trembling hands. "What's going to happen to Chef?" Emme whispered when we stepped outside.

"I don't know," I answered. But I did. Vamps could sniff lies, but they weren't immune to illusions or conspiracies. If Misha suspected Chef's involvement, he wouldn't last the hour.

"It's hard to believe Misha would kill his own."

I opened the door to the guesthouse. Someone had lit a fire in the family room's small fireplace. The glow greeted us in the otherwise dark house. I flipped the lights on in the hall. "Vampires live by different rules, Emme. Disobedience isn't tolerated. Otherwise vamps would roam the earth hurting humans and making them aware of their presence." I focused on the dancing flames. "I'm not saying it's right. But it is their way."

"D-do you think Chef did it? Do you think he's been the one trying to kill you?"

"Considering I was poisoned, he seems the most likely suspect. Still, I don't see how he can possibly see me as the key to ending the vampire race." I pursed my lips. "I wouldn't want to be the one deciding his fate. I just hope Misha's decision is the right one." I grabbed a set of towels and placed them in the bathroom for Emme to shower. I was handing her a T-shirt when my phone rang.

"Hello?"

Aric growled on the other end, the rage evident in his words. "Are you okay?"

I stepped into my bedroom and closed the bathroom door behind me. "I'm fine. Gosh, Aric, I'm sorry about tonight."

"None of this is your fault."

"You just sound so angry."

"I am—but not at you. I blame myself."

"*Why?*"

"If I hadn't claimed you as my mate, the obsessive trait of the spell wouldn't have been as severe. I almost killed you."

"*No*, you didn't. Please don't say that."

"Celia . . . I'm going to have to break our mate bond."

My heart sank. "You want to sever our bond. The very one you started and never told me about? No. That's unacceptable."

"Celia, I know I should've explained our matehood sooner. Forgive me for keeping you in the dark. That night I was out of my mind for you and your body. My animal instincts took over and drove me to claim you. I should have held off, knowing you weren't aware of what we were sealing between us."

I remembered that night so well. Aric wasn't the only one hungry to make love. And while I didn't know what was happening between us, it didn't take away from what we'd created. It remained one of the best moments of my life.

My voice quavered. "If you break our bond, you'll have to obey Anara. We won't be able to see each other. Don't you think we've spent enough time apart?"

Aric let out a long breath. "I don't want to be without you. But I'd rather keep you alive than risk another turn of events like tonight. If I hadn't broken out of Anara's hold . . ."

I paced the room, my entire being on edge. "Aric, I've finally accepted that I'm your mate. And it's wonderful, and amazing, and it's given me more joy than I ever could have imagined. Please don't take that away from me."

"Sweetness, I don't want to do this to us. I'm just trying to protect you. I don't know what's after you. But whatever it is wants you gone. You're not safe anywhere, baby."

"Isn't that more of a reason to stay connected to me? Our bond is getting stronger, Aric. I can feel it. Hell, I can feel *you*. You know when something's wrong, don't you?"

He hesitated. "Yeah, I do."

"Then keep what we have and don't let go."

Aric's deep voice lowered into a rumble. "What if you're poisoned again?"

"Misha assured me he'd take care of it."

Aric growled. "That's great, seeing how he's done such a banner job so far."

I sat on the bed and tried to change the subject. "What happened when you met with the Elders?"

"In breaking free from Anara's hold I basically demonstrated how much power I'd amassed. Anara feels I'm out of control and in need of discipline."

I stood, trying to relax my grip before I crushed my phone. "Were you punished?"

"No. Makawee and Martin overruled him. They said I'd done nothing wrong; all I did was save my mate's life."

My fingers dug through my hair. "If they know I'm your mate, why the hell would they try to bring me and Tye together? Especially in your presence?"

"Because they trust Destiny and her predictions. Our *were* race has dwindled. In Destiny saying your children"—he ground his teeth—"with Tye will help protect the earth from evil, it's given them hope. Hope for our world and for our species. Mates or not, my feelings for you don't come first in their eyes."

I leaned against the windowsill and looked out, afraid to ask Aric what I needed to. "And what do you believe?"

Aric started to growl again. "I believe I need to choke the shit out of him. He agrees with the Elders and feels he should . . . get to know you."

"Aric, I want nothing to do with Tye." I rubbed my eyes. "And damn, I cringe when I think about how I kissed him—while you watched! My God, I would've ripped out someone's spinal column."

"Believe me, the thought crossed my mind, but . . . it helped when you called him a stupid lion."

I laughed and he did, too. "What can I say? I'm in love with a wolf."

"I love you, too. Always."

In the background, a wolf howled in mourning. I looked out into the night. He sounded so close. "Is that Liam?"

"Yeah, he's really upset over Emme. He went wolf and disappeared. Koda and I are going out to look for him. I have a feeling it's going to be a long night."

Emme stepped out of the bathroom then, her eyes swollen from crying. "Yeah . . . same here. Good night, Aric."

"Good night, sweetness."

Emme collapsed in my arms, sobbing. I helped her to bed and cuddled up next to her. My heart broke for her. I stroked her hair until drifted off into a deep slumber.

I woke with a start, scanning the darkness of my room. My body shuddered with cold, fear, and pain. But the feelings were not my own. Misha's fading voice called to me, *Celia . . .*

I shook Emme hard. "Emme, wake up—something's wrong."

Emme rose, yawning. "Wwwhat?"

The cries of battle thundered outside, shaking the plate glass. Something large hit the far wall, crumbling the Sheetrock and shaking the foundation. I grabbed

Emme and yanked her to her feet as the wall and part of the ceiling gave in with a detonating blast. Agnes, Edith, Liz, and Maria crashed onto the floor hissing and clawing at the enormous bloodlust vamp they were fighting.

Bloodlust-infected vampires were strong and hideously vicious. Fortunately, so were my Catholic schoolgirls.

"*No, Celia!*" Liz screeched when I tried to help. "The master's in trouble!"

That's all I needed to hear. I leapt through the hole in the wall and raced toward the house. Chaos erupted around me as Misha's vampires battled a large band of Tribesmen. I shoved my way past them, not bothering to fight. My bare feet had just touched the back lawn when Tim soared from Misha's bedroom window. Chunks of bone exploded from his chest when the iron light post punctured through his back and out his chest.

Blood spilled from his mouth like a geyser as he choked out his words. "Hurry . . . save the master."

I bolted and threw myself onto the side of the house, using my front and back claws to scale it. My fingers pierced through the wood as I raced, the pained roars ripping through the air urging me to climb faster. I leapt through the demolished bedroom window ready to kill, only to scream when I saw what remained of Misha.

He'd been ripped in half. His hips and legs lay a few feet away from his torso. A tangled mess of intestines scattered between the separated parts. Blood spilled from the slowly beating heart dangling outside his chest, held in place by only one of the great vessels. His eyes widened as they took me in.

Misha's hand slipped from his chest and reached out to me. He couldn't speak, but his stare pleaded with me to save him. Hank twitched next to his master, his severed limbs tossed like logs around him.

The Tribemaster from Nicaragua loomed above them, laughing. "I found you, bitch," he hissed in Spanish.

I launched myself at him with more hatred than I knew existed. I kicked him in the groin and tore out a chunk of his larynx in one motion. He lifted me by my throat and squeezed. I scissor kicked with my back claws, partially disemboweling him. His howls of agony climaxed when my front claws punctured through his eye sockets. He flung me across the room, demolishing part of the wall with my head and back. I rolled forward, struggling to my feet while the room spun around me.

A kaleidoscope of stars blinded my vision. They barely dissipated enough to see him charge. I scrambled out of his path just in time. He rammed his tusk into what remained of the wall, wedging himself between two support beams. I broke the leg off a bedside table and aimed for the back of his skull. He dislodged his face and whirled with such velocity, I stabbed his chest instead. My strike wasn't hard enough. I missed his heart and was thrown again. This time I slammed to the floor and didn't move.

The Tribemaster stampeded toward me like a speeding bus. He may have been blind, but my groans of anguish led him to me. I thought I was dead until invisible arms slammed into him and shoved him back. Emme had found us. She used her *force* to propel him back. She whimpered and screamed as he collided against her power. She skidded backward, unable to hold him. I lurched to my feet as a horde of Misha's vampires stormed in, followed by Chang and Ying-Ying. They plowed onto the Tribemaster, but they were no match for him.

He needed to die.

I sprinted toward them, roaring with the might of my beast. "*Move!*"

My jumping, spinning back kick decapitated him. I landed hard, but leapt up instantly and crushed his head with the heel of my foot. I fell back to the floor next to his skull and ripped out his brain. His body buckled at once. Around me, the vamps holding him collapsed into a bloody, sweaty pile.

We all lay there, panting and wheezing heavily until Virginia screamed. Blood dripped onto her face from the deep laceration across her scalp. She ran at me wielding an ax. Maria yanked it out of her hands and knocked her unconscious before she could strike.

I blinked back at her limp form. "I don't think she likes me," I muttered.

"*Celia*. I can't heal Misha—he's dying!" Emme cried out.

My eyes widened at Misha's graying form. I crawled toward him. Oh, my God. His heart shuddered, no longer beating.

"He's lost too much blood," Hank sputtered.

Misha's fingertips traced down my cheek, causing the huge lump in my throat to crack. I couldn't let him die, and only one thing could save him.

I cradled him against me and pushed my hair away, leaning my neck against his lips. "Bite me!" Misha didn't respond. I shook him fiercely. "Damn it, Misha—this is no time to be a gentleman. *Bite me!*"

At first when his fangs grazed my neck nothing happened. Suddenly he let loose. The initial stabbing pain was temporary, but the pleasure was not. Images of Aric on top of me overtook my reality. I moaned loud and strong, my body arching and surging with each orgasm he brought me. I fell back to feel a hand caress my face, neck, and shoulders. Deep within my mind I heard Misha, his groans hungry and lustful. My lids fought to open as my conscious broke through the fog. This wasn't Aric and me making love. It was Misha, *feasting*.

Jesus.

I no longer held him. He held me. My limbs draped against the wood floor like wet socks. I couldn't move and could barely breathe. I was . . . dying.

Someone shook him. "Master, *stop!*" Maria pleaded. She shrieked and something hard hit the wall.

"You're taking too much, Master!" Liz yelled.

Our bodies shuddered aggressively as more and more vamps begged him to release me and struggled to pry him off me.

Emme screamed, "Misha, you're killing her—*you're killing Celia!*"

Strong arms abruptly released me. My eyes blinked open. Misha's sickly pallor had deepened to gold and his lower body was crawling to him. The room tilted and everything blurred. I remember Emme's healing light surrounding me as Misha shouted orders over the dimness claiming my sight.

Aric . . . Aric, I need you . . .

CHAPTER 23

"She's waking up," Shayna whispered.

Bren growled. "It's about damn time. She scared the shit out of me."

"I better call Aric," Danny said.

"Let me do it," Emme offered. "I don't want you to get in trouble with the Elders."

"Nah, that asshole Anara doesn't recognize us as part of his pack. He's got no hold over us."

I pushed up on my elbows, stiff but surprisingly all in one piece. In fact, I felt exhilarated . . . and hungry. It took me a moment to realize I was in the upstairs apartment of the guesthouse. The bedroom was smaller and decorated with white, silver, and rust accents. My mouth had the worst taste, despite the IV running in my left wrist.

"How are you feeling, sweetie?" Emme asked.

I rubbed my eyes. "Hungry. How long have I been out?"

"Three goddamn days!" Taran snapped. She hit the button for the main house and ordered me food.

Chef answered with a resounding "*Merde!*"

It was strangely comforting to know Chef was still alive. I tugged at the IV in my wrist. "Was this just for hydration?"

Shayna helped me remove it. "No, Ceel. We had to give you Emme's and Taran's blood. We weren't sure how my furry side would affect you, but it looks like you didn't need it anyway."

I started to remember the details of the fight. "Is everyone okay?"

Shayna placed gauze over where my IV had been and held pressure. "For the most part. But some of Misha's vampires didn't make it. The weaker ones were taken out before we arrived."

"We?"

Bren sat on the bed next to me. "Aric sensed you were in trouble and *called* us. We got here almost at the same time everyone else did since he let Shayna drive."

I walked to the bathroom and turned on the shower. My sisters followed me in. "Tell me what happened."

Taran watched me brush my teeth, as if she expected me to pass out. "The attack was sloppy, just like when the other asshole Tribemaster invaded the area. What Misha's vamps didn't kill, we slaughtered when we arrived."

Emme stared at her hands when I slipped into the shower. "I don't think as many of Misha's vampires would have died had the stronger ones not been fighting to protect him."

Taran rolled her eyes. "Or trying to save you from him. Aric flipped when he found out Misha fed from you."

"It was my idea," I mumbled.

Shayna watched me thoughtfully. "That's what Martin said, too. Which is why he ordered Aric not to fight him."

I stepped out of the shower and dried off. "Why was Martin here?"

Taran shrugged. "Misha is an Alliance leader. I guess he felt obliged to help. He also knew you were here and that Aric would lose his shit if something happened to you. Poor sap."

I yanked on a pair of sweats, pausing when I slipped a tank top over my head. "Poor sap? You can't mean Aric."

I stepped out into the bedroom to find Bren laughing. "No, she means Martin. The old bastard never had the . . . *pleasure* of riding in a car with Shayna. It took him a few moments to gather himself before he could climb out of the car and take on evil."

Shayna knitted her brows together. "It wasn't that bad."

"Yes, it *was*," Taran snapped.

Danny entered the room and jerked a thumb toward the living area. "Food's here."

Everyone followed me into the kitchen, gasping when they saw the giant buffet that awaited. My empty stomach growled and cramped when I began to fill it, but the loss of Misha's family made me sad. I finished quickly and slumped on the sage-colored couch, tucking my legs beneath me. "How many of Misha's family died?"

Shayna exchanged glances with Taran, who jutted her chin. "She needs to know. The sooner we tell her the better." Taran looked at me square in the eyes. "Eleven vampires . . . and Virginia."

My spine straightened. "Misha killed Virginia for attacking me?"

Bren scoffed. "*And* for poisoning you *and* for planting the witch fire."

Taran cut him off, appearing more furious than I'd seen her in a long time. "Misha questioned the bitch with his mojo after they revived her. She admitted to paying a Tribe witch a shitload of money to make both. When the fire didn't take you out, she slipped the poison in your bisque, knowing it would drive you to kill yourself." A spark of blue flame crackled over her head. "But that wasn't all. She's also the one who sent word to the Tribe *and* the shape-shifters, painting you as the perfect weapon . . . and one that needed to be disposed of."

Shayna played with the edges of her long ponytail. "When the poison didn't work, she made one last desperate call to that witch who'd helped her. The Tribemaster was supposed to come for you and you alone." She let her hair go. "She hadn't counted on the army he brought with him or that they'd also target Misha."

My jaw tightened. "She let them through Misha's wards." My sisters nodded. I shook my head in disbelief.

Virginia had hated me—that was obvious—but to risk Misha's life to come after me skydived right into psycho.

Bren leaned back into the sofa, placing his hands behind his head. "What I don't get is why the hell you didn't just feed Virginia to Misha? Seriously, kid, did you have to give yourself to that asshole?"

"I wasn't really thinking, Bren. I just reacted. I mean, crap, he was going to die." I rubbed my hands against my knees and tried to think things through. "It seems strange that Virginia would make me think Tye was Aric."

"Ceel, you're forgetting the poison was designed to make you crazy obsessive. You couldn't fixate on Tye like that unless you truly believed him to be Aric." Shayna leaned forward in her seat. "Remember how you told us Virginia was constantly lurking about? She probably learned of Destiny's prediction. Think about it. Would anyone question you wanting Tye based on what Destiny said?"

What she said made sense. And yet, Virginia's actions didn't seem quite right. My mind struggled to work things through. "But wouldn't the witch Virginia used need something of Aric's or Tye's to make the magic target them specifically?"

"The most powerful ones can do with just a photo, Celia," Danny answered. He'd been quiet, listening carefully to what everyone had said. "And Tribe witches are exceptionally lethal—that's why the Tribe recruits them."

"Okay, I guess that wouldn't be so hard to do." I glanced out the window when I heard someone outside. "How are the other vampires doing?"

Bren chuckled. "Those losers are fine. The healthier ones gathered a bunch of clubbers in South Tahoe and brought them back to replenish themselves. The next day they hit the casinos and had some Mexican."

I quirked a brow. "Mexican?"

"His name is José," Danny explained.

Emme walked to the window. "José and his friends were looking for work so Maria brought them back here."

"To *eat*?"

Shayna nodded. "Yeah, Ceel. But they're also helping to repair the damage to the house. Misha is paying them a heck of a lot more than we make. We should have been carpenters."

Aric burst through the door and barreled toward me. He scooped me into his arms before I could greet him. "What are you doing out of bed? You should be resting."

I kissed his pursed lips and smiled. "I've been resting for three days. It feels good to be up."

Aric sat on the couch, keeping me on his lap. He ran his fingers against my neck and carefully examined it. His eyes softened once he realized I wasn't going to keel over. "Thank God you're safe."

I snuggled against him and took in his scent. "I'm fine, wolf."

Bren rolled his eyes. "Get a room."

Taran flashed a wicked smile. "Or a garden," she sang.

My face flushed and so did Aric's. "You told her?" he murmured in my ear. He tickled me with his nose, so I knew he wasn't mad.

I played with the buttons on his shirt. "She pretty much figured it out on her own."

Misha came in then, followed by Liz. "Hello, my darling."

"Hey." I was relieved to see him safe and healthy. So why did my body heat up and why the hell was I panting? I was surprised by how my body responded to seeing him, and so was Aric. He released me gently, then lunged at Misha. He didn't get within three feet of him before hitting an invisible wall.

Misha flashed him a little fang, the arrogance he was infamous for soaring to the surface. "Tut, tut, tut, wolf. You know what Martin said."

My nipples hardened at the sound of his voice, and damn, he hadn't even glanced my way. I tried to cover myself with my arms. My aroused scent filled the room, and everyone with a supernatural nose noticed. I just about begged God to kill me when they all gawked.

Bren burst out laughing. "Oh, shit. This is going to be good."

"*Ceel*, cut it out!" Shayna admonished.

As if I had any control over it.

Aric's growls struck the air like a raging wind. "*What are you doing to her?*"

Misha quirked a brow, his devilish grin widening despite his obvious surprise. "Nothing, I assure you."

Danny cleared his throat, leaning close to speak softly. "Since he fed from you so deeply, your subconscious is associating him with, um, you know . . . climaxing."

"But I was thinking about Aric the whole time," I answered like a dumbass.

"It should fade soon." Danny cleared his throat again. "I hope."

"You *hope*?"

Liz continued to file her nails, unaffected. "It's also because of your engagement."

I righted myself, certain I misheard. "Aric and I aren't engaged."

Liz dropped her arms and shot me another one of her "boy, are you dumb" scowls. "I'm talking about you and the master. In allowing him to almost drain you, you and he triggered the engagement bond. You'll be married by the next full moon."

"*What?*"

I exploded in a stream of feathers. Everyone jumped and gasped. No one said anything until Bren finally spoke. "Your nipples are *huge*," he said in awe.

"Screeech?"

I looked in the glass reflection of the fireplace and realized I'd *changed* into a bald eagle. I literally was bald. I had no feathers. Just a bird body . . . and large breasts with protruding nipples.

Emme gasped and covered her mouth. "Oh, my . . . *goodness*."

My humiliation and anger surged. Around us, anything that wasn't pinned down levitated and exploded with blue-and-white fire. Taran ducked and just missed getting hit with pieces from a ceramic pot. "Shit!" she screamed.

Danny's head jerked from side to side. "Celia, Taran's and Emme's blood is affecting you. You have to calm down. You have to—" A flying breakfast quiche nailed him in the face.

It was chaotic. Aric lunged at Misha, swearing and threatening him as he pummeled the invisible force field. Shayna batted the flaming objects with a fire poker, sending them to explode inside the fireplace. Emme and Taran tried to help me. Emme found a blanket and threw it on me, blocking the objects flying around the room with her *force*. Taran did a lousy job. She ripped into me, demanding I calm the hell down. Bren—well, he just sat on the couch watching the commotion like it was the greatest movie ever made.

When things finally stopped exploding, Shayna, Emme, and Danny busied themselves with picking up my feathers and the broken objects off the floor.

I fired a stream of obscenities at Misha, but they all came out in bird. The egotistical son of a bitch had the nerve to chuckle. "Now, poopsie, don't upset yourself so. None of this was intentional."

I *changed* again, this time into the Cavalier King Charles spaniel—with breasts. *Poopsie? Did you just call me poopsie? Do you think this is funny? You bastard! That's the last time I save your pathetic bloodsucking ass. I can't believe we're engaged!*

"Growl, bark, yip, yip, growl, woof, bark!"

You'd better wipe that damn smile off your face before I tear your throat out. You're going to wish the Tribemaster finished you after I'm done with you.

"Bark, bark, growl, yap, growl, yip, woof!"

Liz rolled her eyes. "I'll go get the friggin' biscuits." She left, but not before giving me one last annoyed look, as if everything was my fault.

Aric's growls bordered two steps from murder. Danny approached him with his hands out. He whipped them back when Aric appeared ready to chew them off. "Aric, calm down. I'm sure there's a way to fix this. I don't think it's official until they . . . ah . . ."

Aric paused from trying to kill Misha. His deep timbre fell several octaves. "Until they *what*!"

"Consummate their union," Danny mumbled.

An icy menace chilled the air. Aric met Misha's eyes. "*Over my dead body*."

Knowing Aric felt threatened by Misha bothered the hell out of me. If I was engaged, it should have been to him. I whined to get his attention and wagged my tail when he lifted me wrapped in the blanket. My fuzzy head nuzzled his neck as I took in his scent and that wonderful heat that surged between us. I hadn't recognized it for what it was, our connection as mates. Slowly my body *changed* into my human self once more. "Take me to the suite," I whispered.

Aric carried me to the room, setting me down after he shut the door. I let the blanket drop to my feet. "Now take me to bed."

Aric and I lay facing each other a long while later soaked with sweat. I continued to writhe from the effects of our lovemaking. "That was unbelievable."

He smiled and played with my hair. "Yes, it was. I like that thing you do with your legs."

"I could tell." I huddled close to him and squirmed at the sound of his racing heart. "Aric, you were even louder than usual. Was that because you really enjoyed it or was that all for Misha's sake?"

Aric answered with a sly smile.

"*Aric!*"

He climbed on top of me. "It was both, baby." His grin faded. "I'm not sure whether I should leave you here."

I pushed his dark hair away from his sweet baby browns. "Aric, I'm not marrying Misha."

Aric shook his head. "It's not only that. It's about this whole shit with Virginia. I'm not buying she was the mastermind behind all of it. She sounds too unstable."

A strange chill wiggled its way along my back despite

how warm I felt with Aric against me. "Yeah. Neither am I. If she believed I was stealing Misha from her, I could see how she'd perceive that as the key to her destruction, especially because she lived and died for him. But the second part of that—the one that says I'll also destroy all those it leads—doesn't fit. Virginia didn't lead anything. She was a one-woman psycho ward. The vampires had little to do with her."

Aric growled. "So we're back to square one. You not being safe."

My fingers stretched down the strong muscles of his back. "Not necessarily. She's no longer around to let the bad guys in or make me out to be the ultimate weapon."

"Doesn't matter, Celia. She fed the dark ones enough shit about you. Shit that became truth when you destroyed yet another Tribemaster." He quieted while he thought things through. "This may still be the safest place for you. Regardless of that damn engagement the vampires think you're a part of."

"You know that's not true, don't you?"

Aric's thumb passed over my bottom lip. "I do. But only because if you're going to be engaged . . . it's going to be to me. I want to marry you, Celia."

Tears streamed down my face as I smiled. "I want to marry you, too, Aric."

We kissed. A lot. The moment we stopped, he reached for the phone to call the house and asked to speak with Misha. "Hey there, Meesh. Your wife and I have worked up quite an appetite. How about you fix us some grub?"

CHAPTER 24

Aric was moon-called to meet with the Elders shortly after Misha hung up on him. It was actually a good thing since I didn't want the whole situation to turn into another one of their pissing contests. We emerged from the bedroom holding hands to find several garment bags draped over the sage couch and shoe boxes stacked on the floor. Aric frowned.

I knelt to examine the shoes. They were all made of elegant satin varying in shades from stark white to deep ivory. Pearls embellished some while rhinestones sparkled the tips of others. All came in my size, but they weren't mine. I shook my head. "I have no idea what this is about, wolf."

He shrugged. "Crazy leeches."

I stood and squeezed his hand. "Don't be mean. Annoying as they may be, those crazy leeches helped save my life."

He gathered me in his arms, growling something indiscernible. I stopped him by brushing my lips against his. I leaned against him the entire way to his Escalade. "I wish you didn't have to leave."

"I know, baby. But you have my word—one day we'll never know a night without each other."

I kissed him one last time and watched him drive

through the gates. I hoped he was right, but the demands of his Elders made me worried he'd have to go *lone* to keep his promise. I wrapped my arms around myself and returned to the guesthouse, hoping to track down Emme. I found her sitting in the garden next to one of the carp ponds. Fresh snow covered the area around her. My beast, sweater, and jeans kept me warm, but the thin suede jacket Emme wore didn't seem like enough to protect her petite frame. "Emme, what are you doing sitting out here by yourself?"

She smiled. "I wanted to give you and Aric privacy. I realize your moments together are brief."

"Thank you, but I don't like that you've been out here alone."

"I haven't been by myself long. I walked back to the house with Misha and the others. Ha-Hank kept me company."

I blinked at her a few times. "*Hank* was with you?"

"Yes. I left him so he could eat. He's ravished considering he's had to grow back his limbs." Her cheeks turned pink. "Celia, why are you looking at me that way?"

I drummed my fingers against my arms, feeling my muscles tighten. "I'm just a little surprised Hank would make an effort to be nice."

"I—I used to think he was elitist, but he was very kind to me just now."

Hank, kind? No. Horny, yes. Annoying, ditto. But nice? Something was up. Hank and his buds had never been welcoming of me or my sisters. After saving Misha, I thought I'd finally earned his respect, and probably his trust. Emme's interaction with him had been limited at best. "Did he try anything with you—make a move, cop a feel, try to bite?"

"No, no, of course not. He was a total gentleman."

"Hank" and "gentleman" went together about as well as "venomous snake" and "cuddly." Emme's demeanor also freaked me out. She was typically timid around others, but not so much around her family. "Emme, why are you blushing?"

She shrugged. And her blush deepened. "It's just been a while since I've had a guy look at me. Liam usually scares anyone senseless who tries."

"Hank was checking you out?" I shuddered. Help me, Obi-Wan, Lassie's fallen down a well.

"I don't know . . . maybe."

With her soft blond waves and her Natalie Portman face, Emme had the whole pretty-girl-next-door thing going for her. Hank was a vampire, and in this world vampire equaled hotness. I wasn't blind. I knew Hank was attractive. But Hank was an asshole who frequently engaged in assholeish behavior. And can anyone find someone like that sexy?

My sister was smaller than me by a few inches and several pounds. She wasn't physically strong—she couldn't even open a damn jar of spaghetti sauce. And while her gift made her a formidable opponent, her naïveté could get her into trouble with someone like Hank. Part of my protectiveness related to her breakup with Liam. I loved Liam. He would've died protecting her. Hank . . . not so much. That moron would use her as a human shield without thinking twice. I groaned and rubbed my eyes. Could she *really* be interested in *Hank*? Like Liam, Hank had that bad boy image going for him. Liam was all image, though. Hank actually *was* a bad boy. I'd seen some of the girls he'd been with. The guy was downright naughty.

"Emme, I know you might be feeling lonely right now . . ."

Her eyes filled with tears. "Celia, don't—just . . . don't."

"I'm sorry, sweetie." I hugged her. "I didn't mean to upset you."

My muscles twitched when I scented a vampire approach. "Maria is coming," I whispered. Emme probably needed a good cry, but she wouldn't want to do it in front of the good Catholics. She quickly wiped her face and turned away.

A beautiful champagne gown draped Maria's statuesque figure, and her hair was piled in an elaborate twist. I wondered where the hell she was going.

She traced her free hand down her body as if admiring herself and swirled the wine she held in her opposite hand. The slit in her dress ran the length of her left thigh; one false move and it would tear past her hip. "Sorry to interrupt girl time and all. But de master would like you to join him for dinner in de solarium as soon as you are ready."

I thought I misheard. "Why in the solarium? I thought he only used that space for special occasions?"

Maria huffed and pointed into the sky toward the full moon. "It *is* a special occasion. It is your goddamn wedding reception!" She stormed down the slate walkway muttering in Portuguese before I could formulate a response. Emme stumbled back into the stone bench. Her shocked expression no doubt mirrored mine.

"Did she just say my *wedding reception*?"

Emme nodded, unable to speak. I grabbed her hand and led her back to the guesthouse. After I found my suitcase, I filled it like I was helping Mrs. Mancuso pack for a one-way trip to hell.

"Celia, what are you doing?"

"We have to get out of here, Emme. I can't deal with this."

"What about the attempts on your life?"

Compared to what possibly awaited me inside the house, death threats and scary monsters didn't sound so bad. "Emme, I can't see Misha right now."

"Why? You need to straighten him out and tell him you're not married."

I glimpsed down at my already stiff nipples. "Look, whatever happened when he sucked me dry has affected my body. It's not being reasonable. What happens if my mind goes next? I don't want to be shipped off to Transylvania on a honeymoon."

Emme smiled at me gently. "Celia, you'll be fine. You're in love with Aric."

It must have been a beautiful, magical place inside Emme's head. I almost told her to give Tinker Bell a shout-out for me. "Emme, vampire magic remains foreign to me. I don't know what it can do or even if it can compel me to do something against my will. Look at me—my body is already reacting. I don't want to risk hurting either Aric or Misha."

Emme clasped my hands. "Celia, you have to face him. He needs to know that no amount of blood draining or vampire magic will allow you to betray Aric." She squeezed my hands. "Don't worry. I'll be with you."

Emme was right. I needed to kick this marriage thing in the virtual ass. "Okay, but whatever you do, don't leave us alone." I stalked toward the main house with Emme at my heels. I couldn't run from Misha. I always faced my fears. Why should this be any different? I tried to picture Misha in my head just to mentally prepare myself. All it did was tighten my twins further. I worried they'd snap off from the stress by the time I saw him.

Aric's aroma remained embedded on my clothing. I took a strong whiff from my sleeve before entering the brightly lit kitchen. His scent helped me relax. We walked through the house and into the solarium. I stopped beneath the grand archway and swore under my breath. An orchestra, complete with a maestro, performed classical music for the elegantly dressed mob of vampires. I recognized some of the out-of-towners from the gala.

I couldn't believe how quickly the entire shindig had been thrown together. White roses and garlands hung from the ceiling. Long-stem candles in crystal candelabras illuminated the gold table linens and place settings with a subtle glow. Dazed and overly smiley waiters snaked their way between the guests carrying champagne flutes filled to the brim.

Edith Anne, Agnes Concepción, and Liz dressed in a similar gown as Maria and expensive tiaras topped off their glamorous French twists. They were red carpet ready, aside from the scowls on their faces. They pounded toward us, ready to kick some nuts.

"Celia, for the love of all that is sacred, what the hell are you wearing?" Liz demanded.

My nerves were already on edge. I was in no mood for her rants. "Jeans, a sweater, and UGGs," I answered stiffly.

Edith stomped her feet like they were on fire. "It's your damn wedding celebration! Why didn't you put on one of the dresses we left you?"

My fangs protruded without my consent. "It's *not* my reception because I'm *not* married!"

"Yes. You. Are!" Liz hissed. "I told you back at the guesthouse that you'd be married by the next full moon." Like Maria, she pointed to the moon. It gleamed back at me through the glass ceiling as if mocking me.

Liz whirled and turned her anger on Maria. "Didn't you tell her we were celebrating her marriage to the master?"

"Of course I did." Maria swept her hand dismissively in the air. "But you know how she is."

Agnes scowled at me and adjusted her librarian glasses. "It appears we should have sent in reinforcements."

I clenched and unclenched my fists. The time had come. I was going to kill them. "You know, I'm really sick of your bitchy attitudes. I helped save Misha and *this* is how you repay me?"

Liz waved her arms dramatically around the room. "No—*this* is how we repay you."

I glanced at the ceiling. *Dear God in heaven, please stop me from staking the schoolgirls.*

Emme's eyes danced to each one of them. "Why are you all dressed the same?"

Agnes bent forward to get in her face. "Why wouldn't we be? We're her best friends."

Edith hissed. "Who the hell else would be her bridesmaids?"

Emme's lip pouted down to her toes.

I slapped my hands over my head. "Emme, *don't* look at me that way! None of this is real. If it was, you, Taran, and Shayna would be my bridesmaids."

Maria gave me a hard stare. "Are you saying we're not good enough for you?"

I locked gazes with her. "Yes, *and* that you're a bunch of delusional freaks."

The orchestra played a beautiful new melody and an

excited murmur spread through the crowd. I thought they'd dropped off a busload of virgins by the way everyone responded, but I was wrong. Boy, was I wrong.

Misha entered in a black tuxedo with tails and a white silk shirt and bow tie. His long blond hair cascaded around his broad shoulders like a waterfall flowing with sin. He strode across the solarium, commanding those before him to take in his beauty. Not only did all admire, they bowed regally from the might of his sexual hot stuff–ness. My heart initially stopped at the sight of him. Now it raced full speed ahead, pounding in time with my happy place to the beat of the music. He took in my appearance and flashed me a wicked smile. A smile that clearly said, *It doesn't matter what you're wearing; you'll soon be naked anyway.*

Every last female part in me tingled, danced, and pointed his way. My only comfort was Emme by my side. Emme wouldn't let me down. Emme was my sister, my friend, my conscious, my rock. Emme was . . . *drooling*— and—and covering her breasts with her arms.

Damn.

I sniffed frantically at my skin and hair, hoping Aric's scent would slap the horniness right out of me.

It didn't work.

Misha bent gallantly. "Good evening, my darling—"

"I want a divorce!"

I had a major freak-out. I had to admit, it was downright embarrassing. Misha cleared the solarium. Everyone regarded me like the slow village girl Dracula had unwittingly been stuck with. Misha received several sympathetic glances and even a few offers to put me out of my misery. He ignored them and surprised me by continuing to smile. I couldn't wait to get out of there. Emme, however, convinced me to stay and have dinner since food always had a magical way of comforting me. She also didn't want us to appear rude. Emme was all about manners. It kind of sucked.

We sat down with Misha and were joined by Hank. Yippee. By the second course I'd begun to breathe normally.

Until I caught Hank staring at my sister. "Quit looking at her, Hank."

"Not until you stop smelling yourself. That's really annoying, Celia."

"Your mother is really annoying."

"Yeah, she was. What's your point?"

Emme placed her hand on Misha's arm. "Excuse me, Misha, but I think you need to consider Celia's feelings on this, er, union."

"I have, sweet Emme. She doesn't recognize us as husband and wife—"

"That's because we're not," I snapped.

Misha smirked. "So then none of this matters. The marriage between us can only be complete through mutual consent." He danced his eyebrows, setting my girl parts off to do the limbo. "And by consummating the union."

Emme took in the over-the-top decorations and the orchestra that continued to play. "Then why go through all the trouble of having this reception?"

Misha leaned back in his seat, smiling. "My original intention was to celebrate Celia's awakening and our survival. My family believes the start of our union was triggered the night I fed from Celia and therefore felt the marriage should be commemorated. It seemed important to them, so I allowed it."

I leaned forward, resting my arm against the table. "I thought you didn't care what others think?"

"Normally I do not allow the influence of others or my emotions to rule me. If I did so, not only would I be an ineffective leader, but also an irresponsible one. Thus, the happiness of my family can never be at the forefront of my decisions. However, if an opportunity arises where I can grant them a bit of joy, I do."

"They didn't look joyful when they left," I muttered.

"That's because you're an ungrateful psycho," Hank mumbled.

I sighed. On second thought, maybe I hadn't earned his respect.

Misha and Emme gave Hank just enough of a glance

to make him squirm. Oddly enough, he seemed more affected by Emme's response than Misha's. Staff members appeared to remove the plates and offered sorbet in preparation for the next course. Misha took a few bites to cleanse his palate before continuing. "My family searches for any opportunity to throw an event. This was yet another reason for them to dress elegantly and socialize. Planning everything in mere hours gave them an unexpected thrill they are unaccustomed to. When we're done with our dinner, they will continue the festivities. If you wish, you are welcome to partake, but I assure you, my kitten, you're under no obligation."

I pushed my hair aside. "I don't want them to get the impression I am a willing participant in all this, Misha. Staying here would only reinforce their beliefs that I'm your wife. It's not fair to allow them to think that."

Misha watched me carefully before rising and motioning me toward the stone terrace. "Kitten, step outside with me a moment. There is something I wish to discuss with you."

Two servants opened the floor-to-ceiling glass doors. We stepped out to a spectacular view of Lake Tahoe, deep blue beneath the clear starry night. Four outdoor fireplaces warmed the area despite the frigid cold. I followed Misha to the edge and so did my shadow, Emme. He did a double take when he saw her, but her presence somehow managed to delight him.

"No offense, but I don't trust you." I crossed my arms and so did Emme. She tried to appear tough, but still wouldn't have scared off Porky Pig.

The gleam in his eyes made my happy place throb all over again. "It would seem it's you who does not trust herself around me." A slow, sultry smile eased across his face. Suddenly, it wasn't so cold outside. Misha closed the distance between us and reached out to touch my face. I swayed a little, mesmerized by the vampiric magic around him, amplified by the mysticism of the lake. I couldn't move. My body took over and shoved all conscious thought aside. *Oh, no. No*.

Emme yanked on his sleeve. "Misha, stop that." He

ignored her and stroked my cheek. She stamped her little foot, but I barely heard it. A strange cloud numbed my senses and reason. She tugged him harder. "Stop it, I say!"

My face melted against his hand and Emme panicked. Rather than using her *force* to push him away, she slapped his hand and broke her own in the process. She yelped and jumped up and down from the pain. It scared me and snapped me out of my stupor. I reached for her. "Emme! Are you okay?"

Hank appeared and wrapped his arm around her waist to still her. "*Querida amor*," he whispered in her ear. "*Cálmate, mi vida, cálmate*." His silky voice was tranquil, seductive. The prick had never used such a gentle tone with me. I didn't even know he spoke Spanish. And what was all that "my love, my life" crap?

Hank's calming words allowed her to relax and focus. She used her gift to heal herself. Still, once she mended, Hank refused to release her. I could smell the heat rising between them and stepped toward them to break it up. Misha grabbed my hand and pulled me back. When I turned to protest, he fell to one knee.

"Wwwhhhaaat are you *do*ing?" I sounded like I'd been zapped by too many lightning balls.

"The celebration tonight was not only about your return to health, my love."

My already sensitive girl parts tingled with every word he spoke. "Ahhhhh."

The surge from his power and whatever link I'd created by allowing him to feed from me threatened to disintegrate my clothes. I didn't want Misha. I didn't love him. But something in my mind snapped and robbed me of my will. I tilted a little from side to side, just like a human trapped in a vampire's hypnosis. *Sweet Lord*. Misha had me within his cerebral grip. And there was not a damn thing I could do about. My soul screamed, trying to fight and gain back control.

Misha angled his head, confused by the daze I'd fallen into. Vampires couldn't control other preternaturals and yet he had me just fine. His eyes widened when he realized I'd succumbed to his power. He passed a hand in front of my face. And just like that, my will returned and the sizzle coursing through my feminine regions dissolved.

He kissed my hand, his soft gray irises meeting mine. "Celia, you almost died for me the other night. You did so not because you are bound to me by blood, but because of the type of being you are." His stare traveled the length of my figure. "I know that your body is ready to yield itself to me." He sighed. "But I also recognize that your heart is not. When you are ready—in heart, soul, and body—I shall be waiting."

Misha rose and held my face in his hands. His eyes sparkled with tears as he took in my face. The desire I'd felt just moments earlier seemed like something in an impossible dream. In seeing the extent of his gratitude, it was all I could do not to cry.

"Thank you, Celia, for coming into my world. Thank you . . . for saving my life."

Misha took me into his arms and held me close. I returned his embrace with newfound affection. He had me for the taking. Instead he released me, choosing to prove his love.

CHAPTER 25

"Come inside, Liam. I'll fix you something to eat."

I'd planned an early dinner with Aric at our house in Dollar Point. I was shocked to find Liam in wolf form lying on our porch. His ears drooped against his head and he barely blinked my way. The railing did little to hide him. Since I didn't see any police cars or animal control vehicles, I assumed the neighbors hadn't noticed the 450-pound brokenhearted wolf lounging on our doorstep.

I lifted the charm Aric had given me, courtesy of Tahoe's head witch. The simple pebble fixed to a leather string with wire hummed, releasing the protective ward around the house so I could pass through the door. My muscles relaxed a little. The weeks that had passed had been quiet. No attempts or threats on my life had occurred, but that didn't mean I'd let my guard down. I constantly looked over my shoulder in public, watching and waiting for my nemesis to appear. He or she was out there. Aric was right. Virginia couldn't have acted alone.

Liam followed me in. I breathed in the welcoming scent of my home. It felt good to know I could still be safe here.

Liam nudged my hip, reminding me of his presence. I adjusted the bag of groceries in my arm and led him into the kitchen. I threw four large steaks on the grill for him and steamed a few potatoes, then got busy preparing the roast I planned to have with Aric. Before the wolves met us, meat and potatoes were all they ever ate. Over time, their tastes broadened from eating our eclectic cooking. Based on Liam's despondent state, today wasn't a stuffed-peppers kind of day.

Liam whined as I finished preparing his lunch. I stopped to pet his brown furry head. "I know you miss Emme. She misses you, too."

Liam gave me an indignant bark.

"She does *too* miss you. This was a very difficult decision for her."

"Grrr."

"Don't get cranky, Liam. You might not believe me, but part of the reason she broke up with you is because she loves you."

"Woof."

I sighed. "Liam, not being your mate both frightens her and breaks her heart. In leaving you, she's giving you the opportunity to find your destined partner. If that's not love, I don't know what is."

"I love her, too. It's stupid for us to be apart."

Liam stood in front of me. Human and naked. I jumped so high I almost dropped the bowl of potatoes I was mashing. I averted my stare. "It's not stupid if you'll leave her one day for someone else."

"I'm not going to dump her for another girl!"

"Even if that girl is your wolf's mate?" Liam grew quiet, shutting his mouth tightly. "I know you love Emme as much as you can right now. But I also know in the end it may not be enough. I don't want her hurt, Liam. And I know you don't want that, either."

He hauled me into a tight embrace. "But I want her back."

"Um, Liam—"

"She's my angel, Celia. I've never met anyone like her."

"Liam, I—"

"You know how she never kissed guys on the first date?"

"Yes, but—"

"We kissed the same night we met and made love against a tree a few days later."

TMI. "That's nice. You should—"

"Doesn't that say how much we want each other?"

"Um, I—"

"And it only got better from there. I love her, Celia." He embraced me tighter against his chest and his man parts. "I really do."

I tried to breathe—and avoid shuddering. "I'm so sorry, Liam. But maybe you should go put on some pants now. Lunch is ready."

Chad Kroeger's strong and raspy voice sang softly through my iPhone as I slipped into a shapely burgundy dress. My lids lowered and I sighed softly at the sound of familiar footsteps walking upstairs. Aric entered my room holding a gorgeous bouquet of flowers. A dark blue sweater hugged the extra-large muscles of his chest and arms and his tan slacks covered a backside I couldn't wait to get my hands on. He grinned and brushed his long dark hair away from his eyes, knowing perfectly well it drove me wild. The distance between us quickly disappeared. "You look beautiful," he whispered.

"Thank you, love."

Aric handed me the flowers and stepped toward my music system. "Good song." He played with the playlist until he found the one he wanted. "This one's better."

A guitar strummed over the speakers as Aric faced me once more. He took my flowers and placed them on the dresser, then gathered me to him, encircling my waist while my arms slid around his neck. Our bodies swayed, moving to the evocative melody of "Into the Mystic."

It took only the first lyric for the heat to rise between us.

"You're pretty romantic, aren't you, wolf?" He answered me with a very slow and sexy kiss, giving it the attention it deserved. I moaned, encouraging his hands to wander up my skirt. He growled deeply when he discovered my garter belt hidden beneath the stretchy fabric. The vibration in his throat sent me into a tailspin of yearning. Our passion grew. Aric practically ripped my dress yanking it off and I half strangled him when I tried to disrobe him. Our hands moved quickly. The moment my bra hit the floor his mouth found my breasts. My grunts from the pleasure turned into screams when his hands wandered between my thighs.

He backed me into the bed, refusing my touch, to taste my body. I watched his head turn in circles as he explored my most tender region. Tears of bliss streamed down my face. I wanted him and I told him so. He wouldn't release me. His tasting became more frantic when I climaxed. Finally he pulled me off the bed.

We made love standing up, on my leather chair, against the dresser. His movements were hard and quick and his face grimaced with want and pleasure. Every ripple of emotion on his handsome face encouraged me to bear down. Sweat trickled down that perfect chest as he groaned, growled, and moaned. But when I tightened and forced him deeper inside me, he roared.

We collapsed on our bed. "I am the king of orgasms." He breathed against my neck, mimicking Darth Vader's voice. "Worship me."

I laughed and pulled him against me. It felt unreal to lie with him in our bed. We continued to kiss while he played with my breasts. I swore in my head when my cell phone alarm rang reminding me it was time to return to the kitchen. Although I didn't want to, I ended our kiss. "I'll be right back, love."

Aric brushed my hair aside and kissed my neck when I tried to wrap my silky robe around me. "Where are you going?"

"I have to finish dinner."

He tugged off my robe and ran his tongue down my back. I shuddered. "Stay with me," he said between licks. "We'll order in."

I faced him to give him a short, sweet kiss. "I want to do something special for you."

"You just did," he replied in that bedroom voice of his.

The aches from our lovemaking throbbed in the most delicious way. I smiled and stroked back his hair away from his eyes. "It's important to me that we share a sense of normalcy. Otherwise, our lives seem too chaotic. Let me do this for you, and for us."

He closed his eyes and breathed deeply before kissing my lips. "Okay."

I slipped the robe on again and left the room. The smell of the crown roast filled the house, but it wasn't strong enough to camouflage Aric's scent or the scent of our intimacy. And I was glad of it.

As I placed the baked brie onto a serving dish, an evil gaze fell upon me. I jumped. Mrs. Mancuso scowled at me from her kitchen window.

My hair was Jersey big and love bites covered my neck, but she didn't have to look so mad. I glanced down, realizing my left breast was exposed. I covered it quickly, only to have Mrs. Mancuso reward me with a stiff middle finger.

Aric came up behind me and kissed the base of my ear. "You said you'd be right back." Unlike me, he hadn't bothered to cover his naked body. He pulled open my robe and cupped my breasts before I could stop him.

"*Aric!* Mrs. Mancuso is watching us!"

Mrs. Mancuso's neck skin brushed against the windowsill when her mouth fell open. Talk about wanting to die. Aric simply smiled and waved. I backed him away from the window before I could catch her reaction. We were both still laughing when we stumbled back into our room.

I told Aric about Liam's visit during our candlelit dinner. "Yeah, it sucks about him and Emme," he said. "She's such a great girl. I can't picture him with anyone else."

"Is there any chance she could still be his mate?"

Aric finished filling my wineglass and placed his hand over mine. "No. His wolf would have told him by now if she was."

I turned my palm to link our fingers. "Why didn't he tell her sooner? Or break up with her before things grew so serious between them?"

"Because Liam does love her and wants to continue being with her. It's just not enough. As much as he loves Emme, it will pale in comparison to how he'll feel toward his mate."

I didn't want to be right about them, but I guess I was. I focused on our clasped hands. Aric and I had something so special. Emme needed to have it, too. "If he weren't a *were*, do you think they would have made it?"

"Most likely, yes. The majority of humans don't ever come close to having the kind of relationship Liam and Emme shared, and yet they still marry and do just fine. But he's a *were* and *weres* need their mates." He released my hand to feed me a bite of roast from my plate. "Sometimes it takes years for mates to find each other. They may not always be on the lookout, but their inner beasts constantly are. Before the war began, most found their mates sometime during their lives." Aric rubbed his eyes. He seemed so tired then, as if the mere mention of the war exhausted him. "We've lost so many *weres*. I'm afraid most won't meet their mates until the hereafter."

"What if Liam's mate is no longer living? It would be sad if he never marries or has a family."

Aric regarded me with a flicker of sadness. "It would be worse if Liam's mate does exist and he and Emme eventually marry. There have been multiple instances of when the human side of a *were* has tired of searching for his mate and settled into a relationship with another. The results have been disastrous for the *weres* and their families when they discover their mates after the fact. Most *weres* leave their spouses heartbroken. Some stay out of obligation, living a life of misery because of their desire to be with their mate."

I stared down at my plate. "In being forced apart, this almost happened to us. You would think the Elders would care about leaving so much emotional devastation."

Aric leaned back in his seat. "For years they didn't have to worry as much. *Weres* had become plentiful. The war changed everything. Now their focus is on maintaining the race. The Elders aren't made of stone, Celia. But they won't allow their emotions to interfere with what they believe must be done."

I understood the Elders' reasoning. Hell, in their place I probably would have made the same decisions. The circumstances surrounding my upbringing never allowed me to be selfish. Everyone and everything came before my own needs and happiness. But in choosing to continue my relationship with Aric, I was being selfish. Perhaps that's why the pangs of guilt made it difficult to finish my meal. "Aric, do you think we shouldn't—"

Aric's response was stern. "No, Celia. There's no doubt that we should be together. I can't and I won't be with anyone else. I'll continue to guard the earth. But I won't abandon you for it."

I believed his words. And I desired the same. But sometimes the obstacles we faced made our relationship seem impossible to maintain. He must have sensed my concern, because he quickly changed the subject. By the time we finished our dessert, we were laughing again.

Aric carried me to the couch and placed me on his lap. He rubbed his nose against mine. "I should have told you I loved you long before this. If I'd just listened to my wolf, we would be married now. Nothing could have come between us."

My hand slid over his chest. "Your wolf told you to marry me?"

He chuckled. "No, but he howled to me you were my mate that day we met on the beach. I didn't know what the hell had happened. I'd heard stories of mates recognizing each other—crap about gazing at each other across a crowded room. I always dismissed them as bullshit exaggerations." He shook his head as if trying to clear it. "I never expected that—hell, I never expected you. Everything about you struck me right away—your eyes, your face, your body, your scent—but when you flashed me that sexy smile it was all I could do to hold my wolf back. He wanted to chase you down. I just wanted to not look like a stalker."

I threw my head back laughing. "Aric, you don't even know how pathetic I was after I met you. I ran on the beach sometimes three times a day, hoping to see you again. One day I ran five times." I held out my hand. "*Five times.* Only to see you with that wereslut a few days later."

A spark lit Aric's light brown eyes. "I'd made the date with her before I saw you. I only kept it because my Warriors made me."

"They *made* you? I doubt that." I smirked. "I saw what she looked like and what she was wearing."

Aric's hand slid over my knee. "They thought something was wrong with me. I couldn't focus and I could barely put two words together. I started to believe them. Then I saw you again and that squashed any doubt that remained."

He kissed me then, his soft lips and sweet taste as welcoming as the first time we touched. We were both breathing heavily when he finally pulled away to pass his lips over my neck. "My father told me I'd go through a lot of females. He warned me not to marry until I found my mate. He didn't explain how I'd find you; he just knew I would." His hand wandered farther up my thigh. He growled when his fingers found the strap to my garter belt. I was so turned on I didn't know if I'd be able to stop. "You had to go and wear this, didn't you?"

I was panting heavily but forced myself to glance at the clock. My heart worked to beat. "It's time," I whispered.

Aric played with the lace. "The pack can do without me tonight."

I rubbed my face against his. "No, they can't, Aric."

His hand tightened around my thigh. Then, very slowly, he released me. I rose, embracing him closely when he straightened. He tightened his hold and placed his chin on my head. "It shouldn't have to be like this. We should be together all night."

"I know."

We kissed one last time before finally stepping away. I grabbed my purse, flowers, and keys. Aric walked me out to the car. The ward buzzed behind us as we passed through, rubbing against the small hairs on my arms and letting me know it was ready to blow anything threatening to smithereens if it approached.

Aric kept me behind him while he scanned the area. My predator's eyes replaced my own, searching as he did for what awaited in the darkness. In leaving my house, we were leaving our escape from our worries. Outside, the reality of my life-and-death struggles and his demands as a pureblood resurfaced with a vengeance.

He opened the door to the Ying-Ying mobile and waited for me to slip inside. "I'll follow you back to vamp camp. If you sense anything unusual, flicker your lights."

"I will."

Aric watched me for a moment before shutting my door. "Happy Valentine's Day," he said quietly.

"Happy Valentine's Day, love."

CHAPTER 26

Aric's phone rang.

I was topless and his hand was inside my pants.

Aric's phone rang again, and again, and again.

The Elders were calling him, but he couldn't seem to stop. I'm sure it didn't help that I was screaming like a banshee and thrashing about, having lost all control.

I finished. For a moment, there was only the sound of our pounding hearts and ragged breaths. The windows of Aric's Escalade were fogged and I'd dug holes into his leather seats with my claws.

His phone rang again. My lips swept over his. "We need more time."

Aric growled. "We *always* need more time."

He hauled himself off me and opened the door. I caught a glimpse of the hard-falling snow before he slammed the door.

Aric and I had barely seen each other over the last several weeks. The Elders continually sent him on missions or kept him busy at the Den. They suspected our relationship and these maneuvers served only to keep us apart.

My hand slid down my breasts, still moist with perspiration from Aric's heat. We were parked in the forest at the base of Squaw Valley again. I didn't mind so much; it was important to see Aric any way I could.

What I did mind were Anara's calls, and how they affected Aric.

"It's none of your business where I am or who I'm with, Anara. I'm a *Leader*, not your goddamn servant."

"Watch your words, boy," Anara snapped on the other end of the line. "I remain your Elder, or perhaps you've forgotten?" Aric tried to suppress his growls, but his beast side threatened to take control. "Return to the Den *now*. Or face the consequences of your insubordination."

Anara hung up. Aric exploded in a series of curses and growls. When he climbed back in, melting snow dripped down his face and bare chest. I was just as he'd left me: partially naked, sweating, and panting. He leaned over top of me. Despite the cold outside, his skin felt warm. "I have to go, sweetness."

My eyes traveled the length of his hard chest. His excitement at hearing my cries continued to be obvious. I lightly touched the outside of his jeans. "Can't you just let me please you, even a little bit?"

Aric swallowed hard and his light brown eyes glazed with ardor. "It won't be enough. I need to take you completely."

I unbuckled his pants and reached in, my eyes returning to meet his. "Then do so."

Aric lost it. He tore my jeans and panties off in one motion. He entered me, thrusting savagely. I climaxed quickly as he growled my name. It was rough, hard—and *astounding*. The entire car shook wildly as he exploded inside me.

The knock on the guesthouse door saved me from explaining to Emme what my jeans were doing in the garbage . . . and why they were ripped in half. Aric had apologized afterward for "getting carried away." I made it clear he never had to apologize for mind-blowing sex.

I opened the door to find Misha with Tim and Hank

directly behind him. Misha stepped forward. "Kitten, we are needed at the Den. The matter is of tremendous urgency." He glanced past me to where Emme had been emptying the trash. "My dear, your presence is also requested."

I gripped the knob of the open door. My first guess was that Anara had discovered my rendezvous with Aric. But then, that didn't make sense. For Misha and also my sister to be summoned meant the Tribe had struck once more. We marched out of the guesthouse and followed the vampires into the BYTEME Hummer.

None of us spoke on the ride to the Den. Misha seemed unusually distant despite maintaining his focus on me. "Do you know what's up?"

He leaned forward, frowning slightly. "No. Only that I may not be able to protect you from what's coming."

Emme gasped. I tried to smile reassuringly. "Isn't this the reason you've trained me? So I wouldn't need protection?"

Misha regarded me closely. "Not the only reason," he answered quietly.

The moment we arrived, Misha grabbed our hands and led us swiftly into the main building and into a large meeting area. The grand open space reminded me of a supersized family room. A large bookshelf comprised one wall, stuffed with old leather-bound novels, while the opposite was made almost entirely of glass with magnificent views of the setting sun. A few plush red couches wrapped around a large granite fireplace. But no one sat. Everyone was on their feet and tension thickening the air would likely keep them that way.

My sisters and the wolves were already present along with Tye and the Elders. Their presence didn't surprise me. Uri's did. I was also shocked to see Bren and Danny. Anara refused to recognize them as Aric's Warriors and never allowed them to attend any meetings. *God, what's happened?*

Aric glared at Misha when he caught him holding my hand. I released Misha's hand as subtly as possible. Misha smiled at Aric, gave him a wink, and then wrapped his arm around my shoulders. I elbowed him. "Don't antagonize him, Misha."

Taran and Shayna slipped next to us. Their beautiful faces creased with fear and worry. "You're not going to like this shit," Taran muttered.

Martin acknowledged us with a slight tilt of his head and spoke. "Thank you all for joining us. We have unfortunate news that we need to act upon. The depletion of their numbers has forced the Tribe to take more desperate measures. In an effort to destroy us, the most formidable among the Tribe have sought to raise Ihuaivulu." I didn't know who or what Ihuaivulu was, but judging by the grim faces of Uri and the Elders, the news was worse than I could have imagined. Martin gestured to Aric. "Please ask your Warrior to explain."

Aric looked to Danny and motioned him forward with a jerk of his head. "You're on, Dan."

Danny remained where he stood, trembling. We waited, but he wouldn't speak or move. Aric nodded encouragingly. Still nothing happened. Bren gave Danny what he'd probably intended to be a soft nudge. Unfortunately, it sent him flying forward. He stumbled and slid across the polished wood floor and just barely missed barreling into Anara.

Koda grabbed him by the collar and lifted him to his feet before any of us could blink. Danny was nothing short of a hot, frazzled mess. Sweat dripped down his shivering form as if he were fighting the flu. If so, the flu was winning. He cleared his throat a few times before finally speaking. "A Chaitén volcano recently erupted after being dormant for a millennium. I found it suspicious considering this same volcano is said to house Ihuaivulu—a seven-headed fire-breathing demon." He paused to wipe his hands against his slacks. "I brought my concerns to Aric. He thought it was worth investigating and encouraged the Alliance to send spies to Patagonia—"

"Where the hell is that?" Bren muttered. I was glad he asked. Geography and I were mortal enemies.

Danny regained his confidence—academic matters had that effect on him. He smiled. "Patagonia is a region that encompasses Chile and Argentina—that's where Chaitén is located. Our spies discovered the Tribe found scriptures to raise the demon." He stopped smiling then. "That's why the volcano erupted. They've awakened Ihuaivulu."

My mouth went dry. *They awoke a seven-headed fire-breathing demon?* Was he kidding?

Misha stiffened next to me. "Can we halt the demon's rise?"

Danny shook his head. "We're too late. Ihuaivulu has already broken through the first part of the mountain.

Bren held out his hand. "Wait—did you say he broke through a *mountain*?" Danny nodded. "How big is this asshole?"

Danny scratched at his moppy curls. "I'm not sure. Maybe the size of an average office building?"

My heart skipped a beat, then a few more. Seven-headed demons would do that to a gal. "So he could be bigger?" I asked.

Danny nodded and Taran swore up a storm. Around us, the pack of wolves growled. Aric stepped forward. "How do we kill Ihuaivulu?"

"He can't be killed, Aric."

Emme moved next to me and took my hand. She was scared—rightfully so. Some scary monster that couldn't die had just been roused from sleep. I squeezed her hand tight. "What can we do then?" I asked, hoping there was something.

"There are two ancient rocks called the Sacred Stones of Mughal. They both need to hit Ihuaivulu at least once."

Gemini rubbed his goatee. "Do they need to hit at the same time or in the same area?"

"No, but the second must hit him within twenty-four hours after the first. The first stone is only meant to weaken Ihuaivulu. The second will force him back into a dormant state for at least the next millennium."

"Do we know where to find Mughal's stones?" Bren

asked. He chuckled slightly when he thought about what he'd just said. That earned him a smile from Makawee and a dirty glare from Anara.

"The Tribesmen who performed the awakening are guarding one in Chaitén, believing they can control the demon with it." He shook his head. "But they can't. No one can."

"Where's the other stone, Dan?" Aric asked.

"It's at the Ngorongoro Crater in Tanzania. They have to be stored far apart—on separate continents—otherwise they blow up like atom bombs if they're not used for their purpose. The Tribe is trying to locate the one in Tanzania to keep it from us. But the map that describes its location is written in ancient Mapudungan and difficult to translate. According to what the spies uncovered, I believe they have the wrong location. It gives us time to find the second stone."

I grinned at Danny. I couldn't even repeat the name of the language he mentioned. But I knew he could, and a lot more. "You know where the second stone is."

Danny's obsession with ancient magic, myths, and languages was paying off. He raised his chin in all research-geek glory. "Yes, Celia. I know exactly where it is."

Makawee tilted her head, bowing respectfully. "Well done, young Daniel."

Martin faced Aric. "You will take your Warriors to Chaitén and obtain the first stone."

Uri in turn addressed me. "Celia, we're counting on you to locate the second stone. Young Daniel will accompany you. The Elders have also agreed to send one of their fiercest *weres* to aid you on your quest."

I looked to Koda, Gemini, and Liam, expecting it to be one of them. I wasn't expecting nor happy to see Tye step forward, flashy dimple and all. "What's the matter, dovie? You can't go to Africa and not get some lion action."

"*No.*" Both Aric and Misha growled at once.

"We're not asking for your permission or advice," Anara snapped at them. "This is the plan whether you wish it so or not."

Makawee placed her hand on Aric's shoulder as he continued to growl. "Tye has been chosen based on his fighting abilities and his many talents. He is among our most valued Alliance members and will no doubt be a tremendous asset to Celia."

Misha's blatant disapproval swept into the room like a breeze—a really annoyed, possibly menopausal breeze. "I insist on accompanying Celia."

Uri adjusted his ridiculous opera cape without bothering to acknowledge him. "No," he said simply.

"Then one of my family, Grandmaster."

I now pictured myself hiking across the plains of Africa with Catholic schoolgirls in tow. It wasn't a pretty picture. Neither was the way Misha continued to argue with Uri.

Uri's stare softened, to my relief. Misha's actions could have been interpreted as a challenge. I considered the extent of Uri's power. Whether he had a soul or not, I wasn't positive Misha could take him. Uri grasped Misha's shoulders. "My son, no vampires shall accompany Celia on her journey. Many days may pass without any human contact. I will not risk one of us acquiring bloodlust, nor can I allow those on the expedition to be used as food. That is my final order."

Aric glowered at Tye with enough resentment to burn. "Celia cannot go with just Danny and . . . *him*. We don't know what she'll face and her safety is of tremendous importance."

Anara locked eyes with him. "Celia is welcome to bring any additional Alliance members she wishes— *except you*."

Taran tossed her hair back. "She doesn't need Alliance members. She has her sisters. *We'll* go with her."

Their wolves tensed. Koda and Gemini appeared on the verge of *changing*. The muscles in their faces twitched, but both managed to keep their control. I started to object, only to have Makawee interrupt with her soft, reassuring voice. "Taran, I deeply admire your love for your sister and ask your forgiveness for the request I am to make of you." Taran relaxed her stance—

whether to be respectful or from surprise, I wasn't sure. I only knew Makawee appeared to appreciate her less defiant posture as she continued. "I wish to ask you to join Aric and his Warriors on their mission to Chaitén. We have learned that one of the Tribesmen guarding the sacred stone is an extremely powerful witch. While our Warriors are gifted in many ways, sorcery eludes them, and so does the fire. The demon wields flame as a weapon. I fear we need a fire wielder of our own to assist them. You would be a tremendous advantage, and I have no doubt that, with Gemini as your mate, you will be kept from harm."

Taran looked from me to Gemini, her torn expression obvious in the way she took us in. I refused to allow her to choose between us. "Go ahead, Taran. If you're going to do this, it's best you stay with Gemini."

Emme wrung her hands nervously. It was a rare occurrence for the four of us not to fight as a family. Still, she recognized the need for Taran's power on Aric's team. She tried to smile despite her obvious worry. Shayna slung an arm around Taran. "Go with them, dude. We'll keep each other safe."

Taran jutted out her chin. "Okay, Makawee. I'll accompany Aric's team. But only if Celia can take another of his Warriors."

Anara's teeth grinding made it clear Taran's request was out of line. She didn't seem to care, and neither did Koda. He stepped forward and bowed. "Great Elders, I respectfully ask to accompany Celia's team. Shayna is my mate and I would like to assure her safety and that of her family."

"No," Anara said stiffly. "She will only distract you from your goal."

Koda's tumultuous dark eyes blazed with volatility. Aric took hold of his arm. His actions, while assertive, did little to silence Koda. "You allow Gemini to stay with Taran, but you will not allow me to be with my wife?"

The sound of wolves howling followed the surge in Anara's power and anger. "Gemini has the ability to split into two wolves, one who can continue with the mission at all costs and one who can protect his mate. Unless you have suddenly developed this gift, you are to accompany Aric."

"Anara, my mate—"

"Miakoda, she voluntarily chooses to be with her sister. No one is forcing her to do anything. I will hear no more on this subject." Like the flick of switch, the song of wolves ended.

I seriously thought Koda was going to attack Anara, and apparently so did Shayna. She left Taran to wrap her arms around him. He returned her embrace. While it did not completely soothe his rage, it calmed him enough not to make a move against his Elder.

A bunch of swearwords ran through my head. Damn, I *hated* Anara. He returned my glare with equal loathing and likely a little more. Any sane person would have dropped her eyes immediately. It was a shame I sometimes felt sanity was overrated. "Is there something you wish to say, Celia?"

Uri placed himself in front of me. I stumbled back a little when a touch of his vampiric magic brushed against my shoulders. He was flexing his power to both me and the wolves, despite his deceptively pleasant smile. "Leave her alone, Anara," he said. "Celia is family and friend."

"Among other things," Anara added scornfully. Aric bellowed a hideous growl, shaking the glass wall. Misha covered my mouth and hauled me to the door as Anara swerved toward Aric. "*You dare challenge your Elder?*"

Martin stepped between Aric and Anara, his dark face twisting with anger. "Do you expect Aric to ignore such blatant disrespect to his mate? Enough of this childish behavior, Anara."

Makawee's soothing power flickered and encased the furious wolves. It was Aric, though, whom she specifically addressed. "Aric, calm, please."

It was only because Aric's growls ceased that I allowed Misha to lead me outside. He released me once we reached the wide walkway at the bottom of the stone steps. "Anara only behaves this way as he is threatened by you. Do not give him the satisfaction of knowing his words affect you so."

"I don't care what that idiot thinks of me. But I do care about how he treats Shayna and Koda. It's as if their relationship doesn't matter. He's a bully and an elitist, and I can't stand him."

"You do not have to hold him in your favor." He smiled then. "But I fear your anger blinds you from seeing you have found the weapon to eliminate the very enemy who seeks your destruction."

I straightened at his words, unsure of what he meant. Then I remembered how desperate the Tribemasters were getting, and how the strongest among them had sought to raise Ihuaivulu. "The stone. The one I'm supposed to go after?" I grabbed Misha. "If I get it, I can take out the Tribe once and for all."

"Or at the very least cripple them beyond repair. Either way, you can see to the Tribe's destruction and those who follow it." Misha's humor dissolved and his stare turned forceful. "This corroborates that they were the ones who sought to kill you. If they'd schemed to raise Ihuaivulu, then they'd know we'd send you to retrieve the element that could stop him."

Especially since Virginia portrayed me as the vampires' linchpin. Knowing I could finally end this war fired up my desire to find that damn stone. "I can do this," I said aloud.

He pushed my hair off my shoulders. "I know you can."

Misha's smirk and his show of affection made me uncomfortable. I caught Shayna's and Koda's scents and used that as an excuse to turn from Misha. They sat near one of the outdoor fireplaces on the massive porch holding each other. Koda stroked Shayna's ponytail so that the long strands slipped between his fingers. From the gentle way he showed her affection, no one would suspect how easily he could kill. "I don't want you to go with

Celia," he said. "We don't know what you'll find and I can't focus if I'm worried about you."

Shayna smiled, but her grin lacked its usual brightness. "Puppy, I can't sit by while you and Celia are away, any more than you could. I promise we'll be careful."

"It's more than that, baby. I want to be with you."

Shayna continued to smile despite the tear that slid down her cheek. "I would love to fight alongside you. If it wasn't for that loser—"

Koda cut her off with a kiss. His original intent was likely to keep her from insulting Anara within hearing distance. The kiss, however, turned into something more . . . a lot more. My own temperature rose considerably when Koda swept Shayna into his arms and disappeared to say a proper good-bye.

Misha placed his lips near my ear. "I see passions run deep in the Wird family."

I took a few steps away from him. "Stop it, Misha."

The aroma of angry lupine had me glancing toward the top of the steps where Aric stood. He stalked down and handed me a stack of documents without meeting my face. "These are your passports and medical records. I understand the vampires already provided you with the necessary immunizations." He spoke as if discussing business with a complete stranger. I searched his features for a hint of the man I loved, yet he continued to avert his gaze.

I cleared my throat. "I was vaccinated months ago in preparation for my foreign missions." Aric nodded, refusing to look at me directly. "Which Warrior do you suggest I take with me?" I asked in an attempt to get his attention.

"Liam volunteered to go. Based on what's happening between him and Emme, I advised against it. It's best that they spend some time away from each other. Out of everyone I'd want Gemini to assist you, but it's not fair to oblige him since Taran will be with us."

"What about Bren?"

Aric leaned back on his heels. "Bren isn't respected by

the Elders due to his lack of education in our pack and because of his former *lone* status. I had to fight to include him in the meeting today. But despite his weaknesses, I know he's loyal and a fierce fighter." He ran his hand through his hair. "The problem I face is trying to convince the Elders."

"Kitten, is Brendan who you desire by your side?" Aric glared at Misha. He hated when he called me "kitten."

I not so casually stepped between them. "Only if he wants to go."

He flashed Aric a little fang. "Then you shall have him. I will inform Uri and he will make it so."

I pinched the bridge of my nose. *And let the pissing contest begin.*

Tye strode down the steps as if he owned them. "You must be quite the little hellcat to captivate a wolf *and* a vampire." The corners of his mouth curved. "I'm looking forward to getting to know that side of you. That kiss alone wasn't enough."

Aric's unholy growl only slightly overpowered Misha's deadly hiss. I narrowed my eyes at Tye. "Look, moron. The only reason you even got that kiss was because I mistook you for Aric. Keep your head out of your ass and focus on the mission. And if you dare make a move on me I'll knock the living shit out of you!"

My predator eyes still flashed when Aric and Misha faced me. They both smiled and Aric even chuckled. Tye's expression went from slightly surprised back to alluring. "You're a feisty one, aren't you?"

Aric switched back to Big Bad Wolf mode. "You'll never know just how much."

Makawee swept down to us, her lovely white hair trailing like a bridal veil behind her. "That is enough out of all of you," she said calmly. "It's time to ready yourselves. You leave in a few hours. Tye, come with me, please."

Misha lowered his head. "Pardon me, great Omega of the Elders. Celia wishes for Brendan to accompany her on her mission. I ask respectfully that you grant her this request."

Makawee clasped her hands in front of her and considered his appeal. "Very well, Sir Aleksandr. Inform your grandmaster. If he agrees to allow it, then so will we."

Misha winked my way as Makawee disappeared with Tye. "I will see you back at our home, *kitten*." Aric didn't react. I thought for sure the "our home" combined with his pet name for me would set him off. It didn't, and in a way disappointed me. Aric didn't seem to care about anything, me included. Misha hurried into the main building, passing Taran, Emme, and our remaining friends on his way to speak to Uri.

"Bren, do you want to accompany Celia to Africa?" Aric asked.

Bren immediately perked up. "Hell yeah! We'll tear those Tribe bitches up." He grabbed me in a choke hold and messed my hair.

I shoved him off me and pushed my hair out of my face. The wolves' darkening faces focused on Bren. "Don't be an asshole, Bren. Aric isn't just talking about slaughtering Tribesmen," Liam said. He glanced at Emme. "You need to take the entire mission seriously."

Bren got in Liam's face. He continued to smile, but his eyes shadowed with all the seriousness of a predator. "No shit, Liam. Do you think I'd let anything happen to them? I'd die first, man."

Taran grabbed Bren's hand before I could and pulled him away. Bren wasn't challenging Liam per se, but it was never a smart idea to allow two *weres* to make eye contact. "Damn, Bren. We love you, too. Now be a good little beast and stop talking about dying."

Emme shuddered. None of us wanted to think about not coming back, yet it would have been foolish to think it wasn't a possibility. I smiled a little and tried to lighten the mood. "I think you wolves forget we're not exactly delicate little flowers."

Gemini glanced at Aric before speaking to me. "You may not be pack, but you're part of our family, Celia. It bothers us when we can't protect our own."

I bit the inside of my cheek. My sisters and I had gone most of our lives without anyone. To know we finally had family was both beautiful and frightening. I shook off my girly emotions and tried to grin. Instead my face dropped when Liam gathered Emme in his arms, allowing her to release her pent-up tears. "Just because we're not together doesn't mean I won't always love you," he told her.

Taran fell against Gemini. He smoothed her hair as her emotions unraveled. "Son of a bitch—enough with the mushy shit."

Aric's fists clenched as he stared intently at the building opposite. He couldn't openly show me affection, but at the very least I wanted him to acknowledge me. Instead he gave me his back when I tried to touch his fist with my fingertips.

Taran's and Emme's sobs echoed around us. If it hadn't been for Bren, I think I would've started crying, too. As I mentioned, Bren didn't do well with sappy women. To distract us, he told us the most disgusting joke ever involving a weremuskox and a Chihuahua in heat. While it was a joke I'd never repeat, it did sidetrack us. Taran slapped his arm. "You're so nasty." She was right, yet she still cracked up and so did the other wolves.

Emme's face scrunched. "Is that even possible?" she asked me in a low voice. Why she thought I'd know was beyond me. Everyone else roared with laughter, having caught sight of my burning cheeks.

"Anything is possible with a little imagination, a dash of determination, and a tube of petroleum jelly—"

I held out my hand. "That's enough, Bren. No more." There was a lot I didn't need to know about Bren's creative thoughts.

We continued to chat until Shayna and Koda joined us. Night overtook the mountain and darkness crawled along the sidewalks, reminding us our time was up and we had to say good-bye. We embraced and wished one another well. Aric and I were the only ones who failed to touch. He stormed away before I could tell him I loved him. My sisters watched him leave, taken aback by his rebuff. Regardless of the hurt he'd caused, I wouldn't allow it to interfere with our farewell to Taran. I opened my arms to them and we held each other. Taran's teeth clenched while she fought back tears. "Don't get yourselves killed, all right?"

Shayna squeezed her tighter. "And don't you join the Mile-High Club."

Taran's siren grin gleamed in the increasing gloom. She tossed Gemini a wink over her shoulder. "Too late for that, sister."

We left, not knowing when we'd speak again. The wilds of Africa weren't known for their terrific cell phone reception, and finding the stone could take weeks. Emme drove us in silence while I sat in the back riffling through the paperwork Aric had given me. I jumped out of my seat when I saw he'd also left me a note. "Shayna, do you know where they keep the landscaping equipment when it's not in use?"

Shayna turned around from the front, clasping the side of her seat. "It's outside the Den walls in an old barn. Why?"

"Take me there."

I raced through the cold, snowy woods in the direction Shayna pointed. The barn door swung open when I was mere feet away. I leapt into Aric's waiting arms. He kissed me wildly as he ran his fingers through my long hair, holding me tight and speaking between ragged intakes of breaths. "I'm sorry about this, Celia. I just couldn't stand not being able to say good-bye as lovers."

I rested my face against his chest. "When you wouldn't look at me, I thought you were mad at me. Why did you treat me that way?"

"Sweetness, I *couldn't* look at you. It's getting damn near impossible to control my wolf around you. All that part of me wants is to be with my mate no matter what. My animal side doesn't care about the consequences, and now I don't know if my human side does, either. I can't keep away from you much longer. This bullshit is driving me crazy."

I thought about what Misha said would happen to Aric's family if he abandoned his pack. "Aric, please don't do anything rash. I don't want anyone hurt because of our desire to be together."

Aric cupped my face in his large hands and fell into a deep silence. He shook his head. "I don't know how much longer I can keep my promise, love."

CHAPTER 27

It was hard to say good-bye to Aric, but the thought of an indestructible seven-headed fire-breathing demon on the loose proved adequate motivation. I allowed Shayna to drive to make up for my time spent with Aric. The ride was frightening to say the least. Emme spent most of her time screaming while I dug holes into the dash with my claws. I don't know how Shayna did it, but we managed to beat Misha back by at least fifteen minutes. If she ever tired of our "ridding the world from evil" gig, driving in the Indy was definitely in her future.

When we arrived, three small backpacks with the essentials had already been prepared for us by the schoolgirls. I was almost afraid to peek inside and hoped they'd opted to fill it with protein bars and matchsticks as opposed to edible undergarments and ball gags. We had a quick meal and then headed for the airport. Misha accompanied us to the landing strip, where a lavish private plane awaited. "Safe journey," he told us.

Emme stepped out first. "Thank you, Misha," she said softly. "We'll see you soon . . . hopefully."

"Thanks, dude." Shayna skipped toward the plane as if we were going to a party.

There was a lot I wanted to say to Misha then, but there was also a lot that could be misinterpreted. I thought I could get away with giving him a quick hug, yet he clutched my arm, refusing to release me. "Please wait. There is something I wish to discuss with you."

Shayna rushed back to the limo when she heard Misha beckon me to stay. She stopped skipping and creased her brow when she saw Misha holding me. "I'll be on board in a minute. Go on," I insisted when she didn't move. She left slowly after Hank shut the door.

Misha stared at me, all of his usual wicked humor absent from his face. "I would like you to drink my blood."

"Huh?"

He smiled. "You heard me."

"Ah . . . *why*?"

"What awaits us in Chaitén could mark the end of the war. I am needed." He drummed his fingers on the armrest. "Tahoe's magic abandons me from such a great distance. I cannot take its power with me, but you can take mine with you. Ingest my blood, Celia. It will transfer you a portion of my strength. I must warn you—it will last only a few days."

"But won't that also transfer some of your essence?"

His smile widened. "Yes, and therefore more of my strength."

"Misha . . . I don't think this is a good idea."

"Celia, I cannot accompany you to help keep you safe. At the very least allow me to provide you with a little more . . . command, shall we say?"

Why the hell did everyone feel the need to protect me? Hadn't I kicked enough of evil's ass? "I can take care of myself, Misha. Trust me."

"You don't know what you'll face. Why would you deny yourself something that may make a difference in saving your life or that of your beloved sisters?"

I smirked. "You really know how to make someone feel guilty. Did you have an Italian grandmother for lunch or something?"

Misha laughed. "Yes, and she was also Catholic."

"Will this create another bond between us? Seriously, we just pooh-poohed the marriage one. I don't want to have to divorce you again." He didn't answer me. "*Misha?*"

"Yes, but like the bond *you* created it will dissolve itself in a few days."

I willed myself not to strangle him. "Damn it, Misha. That's not the point. I can't do this. Aric will rip out your innards!"

Any other preternatural would have thought twice about angering my boyfriend. Then again, Misha wasn't just your run-of-the-mill bloodsucking master vampire. "The wolf will excuse your actions should my blood protect you."

I swore up and down. In the end I gave in. Misha was right. I needed all the help I could get. And I needed to protect my family. "*Fine*. What do I have to do?"

Misha's smile was so sinful, I absentmindedly covered my nipples. "Bite me with your fangs and drink from me. The more you take, the stronger you shall be."

My stomach did a mini flip, and possibly a split. Despite the constant presence of my inner tigress, I didn't crave blood. In fact the scent repulsed me. I grimaced the more I thought about it. "Okay . . . I'll try—but don't expect much. Tasting blood gives me the willies."

"I assure you, you shall be willy-free." His eyes danced down my body. "Unless you prefer otherwise."

I rubbed my face. "If you're going to be a pain in the ass, I'm not going to do this."

Misha chuckled and unbuttoned his collar just enough to expose that sculptured chest of his. He pulled me onto his lap. When he pushed his long hair away from his neck, I realized none of this would make Aric happy. In fact, he'd probably prefer I take my chances. I jerked away from him and rose as much as the limo would allow. "Call me crazy, but I don't think it's necessary to straddle you. I'd rather do it standing up."

The gleam in Misha's gray eyes made me want to bolt. "Whatever position suits you, my darling."

Aric's growls echoed around me. My gaze searched for him, expecting him to have magically appeared in the Hummer. Instead, an image of his rabid beast filled my thoughts. I misinterpreted it as guilt until Misha smirked. "Your connection to that mutt has strengthened. His wolf recognizes that another seeks you as his, and is making it clear you belong to him alone."

"If you know this, it's more a reason to let go of me and find yourself a nice girl to settle down with." I thought about it. "Preferably someone less sluttish than you're used to."

Misha ignored my comment and addressed my mate-hood with Aric. "You are neither *were* nor human. Did you ever think that just because you are the mongrel's mate, he may not be yours?"

That was a slap in the face I didn't need. My tigress eyes fixed on Misha. "There's no doubt in my mind I belong with Aric. No matter what happens."

"Then prove it." Misha leaned back into the leather seat, exposing his neck and chest.

I concentrated hard on my emotions and imagined my hands smoothing over the thick dark fur of Aric's beast. *I'm doing this only to help me on my quest and to return to my lover's arms.* The growling stopped, but his wolf didn't appear any less ferocious. *I love you, Aric, and your animal side. Trust me to do the right thing and my tigress and I will be with you soon.* Ever so slowly, his wolf's vicious image disappeared. I'd like to say it was replaced by a vision of a happy wagging wolf. Then again, I'd also like to win free Doritos for life.

I sighed and tried to relax. "Okay, Count Chocula. Here I come."

I leaned over Misha and exposed my fangs. My body trembled with fear despite my best efforts to convince myself Misha's blood could mean the difference be-tween life and death. I took a breath and plunged my fangs deep into Misha's neck. Misha gasped as a small trickle of blood dripped into my open mouth. I forced myself to taste it.

Oh . . . my . . . stars!

Misha was *delicious*! Every decadent dessert I've ever had coated my tongue with each sweep—brownies with ice cream, death by chocolate, New York cheesecake . . . Oh, and fried Twinkies. My fangs dug deeper and my tongue moved fast, refusing to allow one drop to escape.

Misha writhed and moaned beneath me. My sugar high reasoned that he liked those desserts, too.

Somehow I ended up on top of him with my knee pressed firmly against his groin. The reason I knew this was because the feel of his erection growing against my leg snapped me out of my foodie-induced insanity. I retracted my fangs and scrambled back to the other side of the limo. Both our faces flushed and we breathed heavily. The tremendous bulge in his pants warned me, though, that it was obviously for very, *very* different reasons.

The rest of Misha's shirt had been torn open. I prayed up and down that he'd done it himself. That probably wasn't the case, given the fiery red claw marks raking across his muscular chest. *Shit.* It was like Misha's blood was catnip and his body the damn scratch post. I watched with horror as the grazes closed and the fang marks healed. Then I scowled and pointed at him accusingly. "You knew this was going to happen, didn't you?"

Misha continued to stare at me with feral eyes. "Had I known, I would have taken the Italian grandmother for lunch much, much sooner."

"I have to go." It was horrible. I couldn't believe I'd let Misha talk me into this, this S&M blood-slurping fiasco. I leapt toward the exit and inadvertently ripped the handle and part of the door off when I wrenched it open. I gawked at the parts like an idiot and then at Misha. He stared at the remains of his door. "It appears the process worked," he mumbled.

I slipped out and tried to fix the door back into place. Instead, I accidently broke it free from the hinges. Rather than wrestling with it and risking more damage, I shoved it into Hank's not so willing arms. He hissed at me — surprise, surprise. I ignored him and faced his master. "I'm so sorry, Misha. You can take it out of my paycheck."

Misha suddenly stood on the asphalt with me, holding my face gently in his hands. "Do not apologize. Just promise you will return to me safely."

Misha was many things: selfish, overconfident, and kind of a man-whore. Obvious erection aside, he was also my friend and honestly cared for me. "I promise I'll do my best."

He kissed my forehead and I waved good-bye.

When I entered the plane, I was momentarily taken aback by its extravagance. Unlike the plane we'd taken to Nicaragua, this was designed for the very rich. A set of four lavish chairs faced another set, with a table in between. Plush couches snaked around the perimeter and a minibar took up the far right corner. The light cream, sage, and burgundy decor suggested tranquillity and relaxation, while the rest screamed party time—both welcome feelings considering our destination.

My sisters and wolves engaged in a conversation about the plane and all its perks, buzzing about all the high-tech gadgets and who'd sleep in the large bedroom at the rear of the plane. The excitement of traveling in such luxury thrilled my loved ones and momentarily extinguished their anxiety.

Tye, if anything, appeared bored. He stretched his long body on one of the couches as if sunning himself on the boulder where Rafiki presented Simba. His white blond hair fanned out over the microfiber and his chest rose and fell as he napped. *Typical lion.*

The captain and copilot were a nice couple who came out to greet us and explain our flight plan. When they disappeared, Bren cornered me. "What took you so long?" He sniffed. "And why do I smell Misha all over you?"

I'll just tell them the truth. After all, I've done nothing wrong. It's not like I had sex with the guy—hell, I hadn't even kissed him. All I did was try to give us some leverage on this suicide mission. What's wrong with that? I mean—

"Sweetie, what's wrong?" Emme asked.

"I drank Misha's blood."

That drew everyone's attention; even Tye sat up. Their brows creased in unison. I steeled myself against the inevitable bombardment of questions, screams, and "Why did you do it?"s. Danny came to my rescue before the first stone was cast. "That's a great idea, Celia. It will help make you stronger on the trip."

Thank the Lord everyone considered Danny a supernatural expert. His comment mollified everyone's fears. I sat and attempted to join their conversation. Danny and Emme invited Tye to join us. They were nice like that. I wasn't.

Tye of course parked his cocky ass right next to me and flashed one of his sexy grins. It was all I could do not to smack him with a barf bag. My claws protruded when he inched closer and leaned into me. Had it not been for the sound of the plane door opening, I would have sliced that damn dimple clean off his face. I almost fell off my seat when I saw who stood there.

Misha had sent reinforcements.

Ying-Ying and Kuan Jang Nim Chang boarded the plane with backpacks and wide grins. Ying-Ying said something in Mandarin at the same time Chang fired off some Korean. Everyone looked to me as if I was the translator.

Shayna bent forward and whispered frantically in my ear. "Do you think he brought his balls?"

"We all need balls to survive this mission," Bren answered for me.

I stood and bowed to them. "Welcome. Please join us." I motioned to the chairs with a slight giggle. Team Aric comprised of Taran and the *were* equivalent of Special Forces. Team Celia consisted of a brand-new wolf, a former *lone*, a horny lion, three weirdos, and two non-English-speaking sadists.

And let the adventure begin.

We departed Tahoe sometime after eight. The flight to Amsterdam alone would last nine hours. Bren suggested a poker game to pass the time. I hated playing poker with him because he always won. This time, Tye gave him a run for his money and so did Ying-Ying. It was a real exciting game and kept everyone involved even after most of us folded. Kuan Jang Nim Chang repeatedly gave Bren advice in Korean.

Bren pointed to his cards. "That shit won't work, Chang. If I place these down, he'll get me here." Chang squinted at his cards and patted Bren's back apologetically.

Shayna stopped looking at Ying-Ying's cards to crinkle her pixie face. "You understood him?"

Bren scratched his scruffy beard. "Hell no. But I got the gist."

Shayna's phone rang, and I didn't need to hear Koda's voice to know it was him. Her smile lit up the cabin right before she stole into the back bedroom to speak with him.

I couldn't believe my eyes when Bren tossed his cards on the table. He took Shayna's place and sat next to Ying-Ying, at first to help her with the game. It didn't take him long to flirt, tease, and charm her. Ying-Ying giggled at Bren's attention. I shook my head. Leave it to him to charm the yoga pants off someone without even speaking her language.

Emme sat next to Tye. He patiently explained his strategy to her while she listened closely and tried to understand. He wasn't being inappropriate with her, so I couldn't be mad; in fact, he was actually very nice to her. He caught me watching and smiled. I ignored him to stalk to the refrigerator and grab us more drinks. I'd just filled my arms with water bottles when an uproar erupted from the table. Ying-Ying had won with Bren's tutelage and walked off with over two hundred dollars.

"Great job, Ying-Ying," I said. She asked me something in Mandarin. All I understood was Bren's name and made the mistake of nodding. Her whole face beamed and she bowed back excitedly. I realized I'd done something terribly wrong when she grabbed Bren and led him to the rear of the plane.

Bren saluted me before they disappeared. "Thanks for the good word, Ceel."

Shayna screamed and raced back to the main area with her hand clasped over her mouth. "They're, like, going to do it."

I ignored Emme's blush and handed Tye a water bottle. "You don't drink?" he asked.

I shrugged. "Occasionally, but since we're headed for Africa I figured we need to hydrate."

"Nice to see all the Girl Scout training has paid off."

"Mmm. I was never a Girl Scout. We've never even been camping."

Tye almost choked on his water. "Tell me you know how to build shelter and fire."

"Nope."

"You do hunt, though, right?"

"No. I eat meat, but I like animals too much to kill them."

Tye glanced around the cabin, horrified. "What can you do, then . . . any of you?"

My tigress barreled to the surface. "Who the *hell* do you think you are?"

Emme frowned. It always impressed me how she oozed cuteness even while fuming. "I'll have you know we're all excellent fighters—"

"Well . . ." Danny interrupted.

Emme's blush returned. "Except for Danny, but he's smart and an excellent researcher."

My head jerked toward the bedroom. "Um . . ."

"And, well, Ying-Ying, too." Emme's blush deepened.

Tye appeared ready to vomit. "Ying-Ying can't fight, either?"

Shayna held her hands out. "No, man. But her yoga skills are . . . superb."

"She's here to do *yoga*?" Tye let out a string of swearwords. "This is a nightmare! How are we going to get the stone if I'm busy babysitting?"

"We're not inept," I hissed. "We've fought our way out of many dangerous situations."

"I'll believe it when I see it, sister."

"I am *not* your sister."

Tye growled. "No. You're not. You're just the one I'm destined to be with."

Tye grabbed a blanket and pillow and threw himself across the couch with his back to us. Turned out he wasn't so impressed with me after all.

Chang muttered something in Korean as he watched Tye get comfortable. I nodded at him, agreeing. "Yeah, I know. What a total asshole."

I turned on my heel and prepared for bed. Sometime

around one in the morning West Coast time, I woke up. Emme and Shayna lay in bed with me. To my surprise and relief, Shayna hadn't woken up screaming. She sometimes twitched and whimpered, but she would settle and return to sleep.

I moved slowly to avoid waking my sisters and slid open the window shade. From what I could see out the window, it appeared we'd just landed in Amsterdam. A team of men in safety orange suits rushed to the plane and prepared to refuel the jet. Our captain stepped out and spoke to one of the workers, smiling. His pleasant demeanor reinforced that all was well.

Next stop: Tanzania.

"Why do you sleep with them?" Tye sat on the couch opposite us, his clear blue eyes appearing to glow from the subtle light in the cabin.

I didn't understand why he was asking, but I answered anyway. "There's not a lot of room considering Bren and Ying-Ying hogged the back." I covered Emme's back with the blanket when she shivered. "Besides, it's not a big deal. We grew up sleeping together."

Tye leaned forward, causing the sheet around him to slide to his waist. "Didn't you have your own rooms?"

"No. Our parents slept in a pullout sofa in the living room when we were little, while we shared a bed in a small bedroom. In our first foster home we were separated . . . but that just made us want to be together more." I didn't elaborate and hoped he wouldn't ask for details.

"You were in foster care?"

I nodded.

"What happened to your parents?"

"They were killed during a home invasion."

Tye's frown relaxed into something that resembled shock. I guess no one had bothered to tell him anything about me, except that we should have cubs together. "You said 'our first'—how many foster homes did you end up in?"

"Just one more. Ana Lisa, our foster mom, kept us and gave us a real home. Her house had only two bedrooms so we went back to sharing a room." My fingers traced along the sill in an attempt to distract myself from my rising discomfort.

"Four girls in a room together and you didn't kill each other?"

"No, we've always been close." I scooted off the couch and disappeared into the bathroom, well aware of Tye's gaze following me.

I waited outside the bathroom door when I finished. Tye now lay across his bed, supporting his weight on one elbow. He watched me, as if expecting something extraordinary. I returned to bed without a word, hoping he'd get the hint that I no longer wished to discuss my past or anything else. He continued to regard me with interest. I ignored him and tried my best to fall back asleep.

Our plane soared through the skies for ten more hours before landing in a small airport in Arusha, Tanzania. It was eleven in the morning in Tahoe, but nine at night in Arusha. Evil, it seemed, had no sympathy for jet lag. We grabbed our packs and hurried off the plane. Just because it was night didn't mean we could stop to rest.

I rubbed my skin, feeling sticky from the dry heat digging its way through my pores despite the absence of sunlight.

"How far is it to Ngorongoro Crater from here?" Danny asked Tye.

"Pretty damn far. We have another plane ride to the Manyara airstrip and then a two-hour drive on gravel roads to the park."

Shayna threw her pack over her shoulder and peered at Misha's jet. "Why don't we just refuel and keep going?"

"The jet's too big and too damn obvious. The Alliance greased a lot of palms to avoid stopping at Kilimanjaro International, but we still need to be smart and lie low."

Emme ran next to me in order to keep up. I placed my arm around her lower back to help her along. We stopped in front of a small white plane, large enough to seat about ten passengers. My eyes scanned the desolate hangar. "Where's our pilot?"

Once more Tye's dimple made an appearance. "You're looking at him, dovie. Like Makawee said, I'm a *were* of many talents."

My sisters and I exchanged glances before following him onto the small aircraft. It wasn't a new plane, nor was it fancy or sleek like the jet. But it seemed in working order and thankfully rust-free.

Tye asked me to ride shotgun. I obliged in an effort to be civil, but didn't plan on socializing much. I relaxed when I saw how he flipped the switches with ease and adjusted the controls as if he'd done it a thousand times. My anxiety returned as the small aircraft sped down the runway and ascended into the pitch-black sky, leaving the bright lights of the runway behind. I had no clue how he knew where to go. Despite my tigress eyes I couldn't detect anything in the horizon.

Tye laughed. "You didn't strike me as the nervous sort until now."

I disregarded his comment and tried hard to find a landmark. "How do you know which direction to fly?"

"My grandmother used to fly all over the world. She started teaching me around the time I was six. I know my way around the air, sometimes even better than on land." His fingers fiddled with a knob before turning the control and tilting the plane slightly toward the right. "Africa and I are old pals. I've flown here at least a dozen times."

I watched his motions closely, knowing if it was up to me to fly the small aircraft we would all just have to die. "Why?"

"Because I enjoy it."

"No, I mean, why Africa specifically?"

"I'm a lion, dovie. I wanted to trace my animalistic roots. Haven't you ever thought about returning to the motherland?"

"My motherland is Jersey."

That earned me another laugh. "So there's a personality deep beneath that tough exterior."

"I'll have you know I'm pretty hilarious once you get to know me."

"So are you saying we'll get to know each other after all?" He waggled his eyebrows.

"Not in the way Destiny intends."

"You don't believe in Destiny?"

"It's hard to believe in someone who wears a dead weasel around her neck and zebra cowgirl boots."

Tye grinned. "She's not so bad. She's actually a nice girl, just a little quirky."

"You *know* her?"

"Yeah, we grew up together."

It was hard for me to picture Destiny as a child, although she seemed very infantile in her own way. "So in addition to Africa you're also old pals with Destiny?"

"Yeah, we are." He smiled fondly as if remembering, but then his smile vanished as he spoke. "My parents are pures and have always rubbed elbows with the elite. Destiny's parents are famous witches. When she was born, they knew right away she was a Destiny."

My head angled toward him. "You mean they knew Destiny should be her name?"

Tye regarded me like I'd missed something important. The creases in his brow softened when he realized I was genuinely awaiting his response. "Destiny is not her name," he said slowly. "It's what she is. About once every century an especially gifted baby girl is born from a union of two witches—a sort of soothsayer. The extra talents she'll possess vary from each individual, but the common trait is her aptitude to predict the future. It's tradition to name her after the original soothsayer, but she's always referred to as Destiny."

I adjusted my position as much as the small area would allow, but the so-called cockpit was too cramped to permit much movement. "That's kind of strange. If she has a given name, why don't people use it?"

"Because it's Trudhilde Radinka." He shrugged. "If it were me, I'd sure as hell go by Destiny."

I blinked back at him. "No kidding."

"Give her a chance, Celia. She's a good girl with a heavy burden on her shoulders. Since her birth, her parents have always thrown her power in people's faces. It's been hard for her to make friends."

I never thought I could relate to Destiny, but I did then. Friends weren't a gift that came easy for me. I hadn't stopped to think how someone like her would fare. "She seems so peculiar. Between her style of dress and my experience with her in vamp court, she's not someone I've longed to approach. But . . . if you consider her a good person, I'll make an effort to be nice if I see her again."

"I'd appreciate that," he said quietly. The fondness in his tone returned and his expression softened, but it didn't take long for an underlying hint of mischief to brighten his features. "So, dovie, now that you know more about Destiny, are you more apt to believe what she says?"

"Not when she's talking about us."

He smiled at me with curiosity. "Why are you so certain?"

I smiled back and crossed my arms. "Why are you?"

"For one, Destiny's predictions are never wrong." His voice dropped an octave and his playful demeanor vanished. "For another, I've been attracted to you from the first moment I caught your scent."

I inched away from him. "I think it's just a cat thing. I don't find there are many of us around."

"You're . . . *blushing*." He sounded surprised.

I shifted nervously, except there was no place to go but down.

"How can someone who's mated to a wolf and living with one of the earth's deadliest masters be so shy?"

My body heat rose the more Tye continued to watch me. "Don't look at me that way."

The timbre in Tye's voice lowered to a bedroom whisper. "Why shouldn't I?"

I focused on the control panel. It was better than the alternative. "Tye, I'm not used to this kind of attention. It makes me uncomfortable. You have to understand, Aric and Misha are among the rare few who have given me more than a passing glance."

Tye started to say something, but instead paused to sniff the air around me. His expression changed from someone ready to make a smart-ass comment to an individual who knew compassion and carried it well. "You're serious, aren't you?" I nodded with my now crimson face. He scoffed. "I had you pegged all wrong, girl. Here I thought you were another stuck-up princess. In truth, you're just a timid little bird."

I couldn't argue. Aside from my relationship with Aric, I knew nothing when it came to romance. I barely understood the male species, and had absolutely no desire to learn more.

I'd seen Tye-the-player and Tye-the-jerk in action, but at that moment, he showed me a different side. Instead of continuing his banter, he spared my feelings and described some of the animals we'd see on safari.

We talked for about an hour until the plane struck some kind invisible wall. It didn't make sense. The plane continued to speed forward. But then it jolted as if rammed by something hard, and the controls went haywire. Lights blinked off and on and several alarms blared a warning. The nose dipped and the steering mechanism wrenched free of Tye's grip. My stomach lurched to my throat as the plane plunged downward in a spiral. My sisters screamed. Tye fought to regain our altitude, only for us to be jerked back down. Again, he managed to level the plane, but just barely.

"The Tribe knows we're here!" he shouted. "Get ready to jump!"

CHAPTER 28

Everyone in the back scrambled for parachutes. I unbuckled and hurried to help, while Tye fought to keep our plane in the air.

We turned the plane inside out, only to find one chute.

"*Shit!*" Bren growled.

I scanned the compartment filled with terrified faces, desperately trying to figure a way out of this. Only Chang and Ying-Ying remained surprisingly calm. I thought it was because they didn't comprehend what was happening. I swallowed a lump in my throat. How could I possibly explain we were all about to die? Charades at a time like this seemed completely inappropriate. I opened my mouth to say something when Ying-Ying pointed to the plane door. I didn't move, so she pointed again. "Bren," she said.

Emme clutched the headrest in front of her, her fair skin pale with fear. "I—I think she wants one of you to open the door."

Bren and I tried to explain that we couldn't open the door when Chang stood. He calmly strapped on two backpacks and grabbed a blanket from one of the storage compartments. A huge smile lit his face as he kicked open the door. Gusts of wind overtook the small cabin, smacking my hair into my face. I pushed it out of the way in time to see Chang grip Shayna's arm and leap out with my poor shrieking sister.

Bren and I rushed to the door in a panic. I gasped when I caught a glimpse of a white parachute. Chang had somehow magically converted the blanket. "Holy *shit*!" Bren yelled.

Bren and I continued to gawk while Ying-Ying slinked her way through the small space. He freaked out when he saw she was carrying two packs: hers *and* his. "No. No, no, no, no." He held out his hands trying to block her. I watched in horror as the tiny yogi shoved my extra-large friend into the air before diving after him. Her maniacal laugh exploded out of her, drowning out Bren's hollers as she flew toward him.

Tye grunted. "I can't keep the plane up. *Get going, now!*"

Danny had just finished securing the parachute to Emme. "Celia, grab Emme and go—the parachute will hold you both. Tye and I will jump before the plane crashes."

"Screw that!" Tye shouted. "Go with Emme, Dan. They're going to need you to find the stone. Celia will just go eagle and fly us out."

"Good idea!" Danny yelled and leapt out, clutching Emme.

Good idea? GOOD IDEA!?

"Tye, I don't think I can—"

Tye grabbed our packs and flung us out the door.

I didn't have time to think or attempt to calm the hysterical female shrieking inside me. The wind whipped against my body and the earth spun below. I gritted my teeth and called forth my will to survive.

But then my call turned into a screech—the mighty screech of an eagle.

My legs shrank and my arms lengthened, sprouting feathers from one breath to the next. I righted myself and glided into the night with a grace and speed I'd never known. My sharp vision fixed on Tye, who was hurtling toward the ground at an alarming rate. With one, two, three flaps of my powerful wings I had him.

I dug my talons into his shoulders and cried out in triumph over the sounds of the plane exploding below. My new form felt natural, as if I'd done it a million times. Unfortunately, this was my first flight, and if it hadn't been for the tree we smashed into, I wasn't sure how we would've landed.

The pain broke my concentration and I *changed* back to human. We swore and groaned as we hit just about every damn branch on our way down. I landed on my back and rolled into Tye, who lay sprawled trying to catch his breath. A family of very pissed-off monkeys shrilled and scurried around us, completely disgusted that we'd disturbed their sleep. Leaves rained down on us and collected into several small piles before either of us moved. Tye let out the mother of all swearwords before turning to glare at me. "What the hell kind of eagle are you anyway?"

I sat and wiped the dirt from my arms and shoulders. "I never claimed to be an eagle! I only ever managed the full form once and even then it was only for a few seconds."

"My boy Uri said—"

"Your boy Uri likes to exaggerate the truth!"

I scrambled to my feet and tried to pick the leaves and twigs out of my hair. I was pulling what I hoped was a giant seed from my curls when I noticed Tye's expression had morphed from furious man to hormonal teen. He stared at me smiling. It hit me too late that I was standing there naked.

I jumped behind the tree. "Throw me something from my pack," I demanded. He went through my pack and tossed me a pen. "Damn it, Tye—you know what I mean. Give me something to wear!"

He stood and strolled toward the tree. "It's hot. You'll probably be more comfortable this way."

Before I could pound the crap out him, Danny's wolf howled. My head whipped in the direction of his *call*. "They're in trouble!"

I *changed* into a tigress and bolted. Tye sprinted behind me, but he couldn't keep up. I swerved through a maze of trees until I reached a clearing of flat earth and drying patches of grass. The crumbling blades crunched beneath my feet as I stalked.

Emme and Danny stood back to back, cowering and trembling as about twenty weresnakes slithered around them with flicking tongues. The snakes were at least twelve feet in length and twelve inches in diameter. The closest ones struck over and over, their speed unearthly and eerily mesmerizing. Emme kept them back with her *force*, but she couldn't keep their fangs from meeting their flesh for long.

My deep growl announced my arrival and so did Tye's roar. The snakes hissed and spat venom from their full dripping mouths before parting, allowing a dark figure swathed in a red cape and hood to glide through their wall of sliding bodies. Dark magic swirled around her as she levitated above the soil and drifted toward us.

She licked her thin lips as if ravenous. "Celia Wird," she whispered in a thick foreign accent.

Great, another fan. The whole "let's get Celia" campaign had pounced on my last nerve.

Drool trickled from her mouth to sizzle against the crackling dirt. "You don't want to anger my friends. They're hungry and you're keeping them from their feast."

Our growls grew deadlier as Tye and I prowled forward. *Celia, the green ones are boomslangs and the others are black mambas—both poisonous, but there's no cure for the boomslangs' venom.*

Although Tye's voice jarred me when it echoed in my head, I didn't dare avert my eyes from the snakes. We separated to circle them just as Bren arrived with Ying-Ying hovering in lotus pose on his back. She slid off his fur almost silently and rushed to my side.

One of the snakes lunged toward Tye. I didn't see what happened—the movement was too fast. But in the next moment Tye spat the large reptilian head at their mistress's feet. The hissing grew louder, but the snakes failed to attack. The cloaked figure raised her arms and chanted as a red mist enclosed the field. One by one the snakes disappeared.

Our heads jerked, searching and sniffing for any trace of our enemy. Bren's snarl twitched his nose. Their scent remained. They were here. But where? Ying-Ying left my side and calmly stepped toward where the witch had stood. She kicked a few pebbles away before falling once more into lotus pose.

I didn't bother exchanging "look at crazy Ying-Ying go" glances with everyone. Our enemies remained somewhere near, angry and ready to puncture our flesh.

The ground beneath me barely trembled before the first one attacked. It launched itself straight at me in 3-D. Others followed, springing from beneath the soil like demented jack-in-the boxes. They were fast, but so was I. I dodged out of the way and bit one's head off before it struck again.

Pandemonium erupted. I crouched, sprung, and clawed, evading strikes. The snake-charming witch started to chant something else, but then stopped abruptly with an ear-piercing scream.

Bren and a blur of white passed in front of me with blinding speed while I faced off with another weresnake. This one was bigger. It danced around me with hypnotic grace and flicked his tongue in a disgustingly sexual way. My claws sliced through his eye when he struck. I pounced and went for his throat when another knocked me to my side and coiled its body around me.

My right claws punched through its jaw and snapped them shut as we wrestled and barreled into anything that stepped in our way. My back arched and twisted, trying to keep the other snakes from lunging at me. The snake holding me squeezed tighter, robbing me of oxygen and weakening my screaming muscles.

The pressure in my head built to a dull throb. I was losing consciousness when Shayna arrived. Her small thin frame leapt in the air wielding two spinning swords. One severed my attacker's head. The other jabbed through another's open maw. With a flick of her wrist and a grunt, two heads landed in the dirt one after the other. I wriggled free and kicked the dead snake off me.

She jetted after the black mamba chasing Danny with a boomslang at her heels. I snapped her pursuer in half as it leapt onto her back and reached for her throat.

Our group repelled the enemy with vicious grace. Blood darkened the soil while chunks of flesh splattered and stuck to large boulders. Roaring, hissing, and slithering sounds drowned my snarls as my fangs pierced through smooth reptilian skin to crunch on bones.

Shayna's strikes whistled in the night like high-pitched fireworks. She grunted as her spiraling blades cut through the thick, tough hides of the black mambas and the points stabbed and gouged the boomslangs.

Chang fought three massive snakes like an extra from *Crouching Tiger, Hidden Dragon.* He spun and leapt in the air as if on invisible wires. Perhaps that was next week's lesson. The snakes worked together to kill him, but failed to match his ghostlike speed. He evaded them, landing a rapid array of blows and kicks before flipping backward to descend on the back of another. Sparks flew with each blow until he beat the serpents unconscious. He held no weapons, and yet he chopped the heads from their motionless bodies with thrusts from his bare hands.

Danny's and Bren's wolves teamed up to play tug-of-war with the serpents, ripping the snakes in half. Blood pumped out of the lifeless remains, riling Bren's wolf and making him howl.

I'd finished clawing through a black mamba when the white blur slowed in front of me. Behold, Tye the white lion. His fur sparkled like fresh-fallen snow in the moonlight. He paused from continuing his carnage just to flash me a lion's grin and flick his tail teasingly in my face.

I batted his tail away and raced to find Emme. He chased me and just about ran me over when I skidded to a halt. My bashful and kindhearted little sister had battled the witch and won. She'd manipulated vines with her *force* and entwined them around the powerful enchantress, wrapping them around her mouth and preventing her from casting another spell. Tye did a double take, stunned that Emme was restraining her while holding two more snakes for Bren and Danny to kill. Ying-Ying, on the other hand, remained in lotus pose as the anarchy continued around her.

I fought my way to Ying-Ying to protect her, tearing off the heads of two boomslangs along my path. We continued our onslaught until only one snake remained, a boomslang. Tye fought it, slashing and pouncing with lion's speed, but the snake surpassed his strength and power. It flung Tye against a large boulder. His ribs snapped with a hair-raising crunch. Emme held tight to the witch while I left Ying-Ying to help Tye.

My whiskers tingled with the rise of dark power. The boomslang's leathery skin thickened and elongated with every brush of magic against my fur. It dropped open its mouth, spilling venom as the witch's dreadful voice echoed from deep within its throat. Despite Emme's hold, the witch had managed to transfer her essence into the weresnake. "Make no mistake, Celia Wird," she spat. "We will kill you *and* your destiny."

Her deadly voice brought me chills, yet also fueled my rage. It also fueled the rage of my friends. We attacked as one. I launched myself on the snake and dug my fangs into the back of its head. It shrieked as I raked and stabbed its cold skin. It flung me like a rag doll until, collapsing with a hard thump, I released it. Shayna had delivered the final blow by piercing its brain with one of her swords.

She dripped with sweat and panted with exhaustion, but hell, so did the rest of us. We'd fought long and hard. Everyone was breathless. Well, except for Ying-Ying.

I thought only the Tribe witch remained. But I was wrong. A final weresnake rose from the earth in front of Ying-Ying, who continued her meditative state. My claws dug into the earth, kicking up soil as I sprinted toward her. My speed was fast, yet not fast enough. It struck. There was a sickening crunch and then it was over.

Ying-Ying didn't need me. The decapitated snake head joined the rest surrounding her. I was confused by what happened until I saw her happily munching away. She smiled at me with full cheeks. Danny and Shayna hurled behind me. Bren and I gagged when an eyeball popped out of her mouth, but we managed to keep it together. Chang laughed happily and pumped his fist, as if Ying-Ying had told a funny.

Tye *changed* back to human. I quickly averted my eyes from his naked body. Every *were* I'd ever met—no matter what kind—was always hung like a damn bear. Tye, it seemed, was no exception. He laughed and came to face me. "Don't worry, dovie. We haven't time for anything else . . . At least not at the moment."

I kept my lids rammed shut, until Emme called to me. She pointed to the witch's limp form. "I think she invaded that other snake's soul. She must have died when Shayna killed it," she whispered.

Bren growled in human form. "Doesn't matter. We would have killed her anyway." The threat against my life had angered him. Hell, it angered me, too, and reinforced that the Tribe wanted me dead.

Even though we'd fought a tough battle, the witch's words had a more profound effect. Shayna stroked my back. "I don't like how all these dark critters seem to know you, Ceel."

Yeah? Well, me neither.

Emme hurried to my side. She didn't say anything, but the scent of her fear smacked me in the nose. I rubbed my head against her to comfort her and almost knocked her frail form down. Tye caught her against his naked body. It was dark, and Emme probably couldn't see much, but she knew Tye wasn't wearing so much as a fig leaf. Her cheeks could have started a wildfire and she quickly scurried back to me.

Tye smirked, pleased with his ability to make the Wird girls turn red. "Come on," he said. "We need to keep moving." He paused to look at me. "Don't worry, Celia. I won't let those assholes kill either of us."

We ran all night in our beast forms, carrying our two-legged friends on our backs. Tye led the way to the crater. The terrain was littered with sharp stones, debris, and enough dust to coat our throats. I used Aric's image to propel me forward, and ignored Tye when he attempted to communicate through his thoughts. He believed himself my destiny, and the Tribe's latest target. My heart told me he was wrong.

As dawn broke through the horizon, a sign alerted us that only five kilometers remained until we reached the crater. We *changed* back to human, unsure who we'd stumble upon.

Tanzania was beautiful; I only wished I could have enjoyed it more. The light blue sky held no clouds, just a bright sun that beat against our backs. Bren carried Emme most of the way; her lack of athleticism hindered her especially given the rough terrain. Shayna struggled to keep up the pace, and so did Danny. But their werewolf essence gave them enough of a boost to follow close behind.

We hiked along a dirt road and passed a lake filled with flamingos. They took flight when we approached, frightened of the predators they sensed within us. A couple of hippos peered at us from the water, just as natural here as ducks back home. We even caught a beautiful lioness and three cubs crossing the path before us. Everyone *ooh*ed and *aah*ed except for Tye. He played it cool, but the sparkle in his grin exposed his love of the land.

"I wish Koda were here," Shayna whispered to me. She smiled as she said it, but sadness and worry dulled her eyes. I knew how she felt. As much as I tried not to, my fear for Aric and the others preoccupied my thoughts.

Maybe Aric and I could come back here on our honeymoon.

Bloodcurdling screams halted my steps and thoughts. I bolted to a small gravel path and froze.

Demon offspring attacked a band of Tanzanians. They flew through the air and swept down to grab the villagers. The women cowered over their young as the men fought bravely to spear their attackers. I didn't think about the consequences of our discovery; I just acted. I *changed* and sprinted toward them.

I flung myself at a demon attempting to rape a screeching young girl and rammed my claws through its chest. His innards spilled and slithered away like mucus-covered snakes, only to shrivel in the scorching sun. The girl screamed in horror and her mother threw herself on top of her. Blood oozed from the multiple cuts on the woman's skin, yet it didn't stop her from trying to protect her daughter.

Another demon targeted the same family. I sliced through its neck before it reached them. The mother's and daughter's blood must have aroused the creatures. Six smaller demon children closed in, thick black saliva dripping from their long yellow fangs and greedy mouths. I positioned myself between them and unleashed a ferocious growl. No way would I let these assholes harm this family.

They jumped on me at once, raking their claws against my skin. I flipped over, slamming them repeatedly into the earth, then tore their heads off one at a time.

Demon parts pelted my fur as my mighty *weres* shredded body parts like bloody Triscuits. A few of the villagers glanced from what remained of their attackers, then back to us. Their faces slowly changed and their eyes widened. They knew we were trying to save them. Hope gave them strength. They picked up their spears and fought back with pure ferocity.

A group of young children watched in awe as Shayna transformed an abandoned shield into a razor-edged disc. She flung it like a Frisbee, decapitating a demon with ease and digging it into the chest of another.

Bren and Tye leapt on top of the demons that were attempting to fly away with children and tore off their wings. The demons fell writhing to the ground, meeting their ends when the natives stabbed them to death with their spears.

Ying-Ying collected weapons from those too injured to fight. She carried them to Emme, who was protecting a small band of women, and an already injured Danny, who struggled to stand. Emme gathered her *force* and launched all ten spears at the demons who had escaped Bren and Tye. They fell to the dry earth, moistening it with their splattered entrails.

Ying-Ying contorted herself into some kind of ball

and used her body to knock the demons down like bowling pins. Chang and I pounced, beheading their stunned forms. "Celia!" Chang called, pointing wildly at a demon flying off with a crying baby.

I darted toward the baby but was intercepted by a mound of yelping beast and wings. Danny had tried to rejoin the battle and now a demon had him. Blood saturated his fur as he tried to fight off the giant brute. Yet despite being *were*, Danny could not match the demon's strength. I scrambled forward and tackled the demon, sending us both down the ravine.

Gravel and sharp dried branches pummeled and punctured my skin the entire way down. I hit the bottom with an excruciating jolt, cracking my skull against a large flat rock. Fluid seeped from my ears and mouth and my stomach lurched from the cold rush of nausea. I wanted to scream from the paralyzing agony, but could barely gather a breath. Something was wrong—very wrong. I'd never felt pain like this. I lost my concentration and *changed* back to human.

It took me a long time to gather my resolve and attempt to stand. When I finally tried, my limbs failed. I gave up for the moment and tried to regulate my breathing. That's when Aric appeared. He clutched my broken body in his powerful arms and comforted me with his soft sweet words. He promised me a lifetime of togetherness, but I had to stay strong and survive. I held on to his words. He was right—I had to live. Although at that moment I wasn't sure how.

Neither the demon nor I moved for a long while. I sprawled completely helpless, praying he was dead, but my prayers were not answered. The moisture from my sweat and blood chilled my skin as the demon slowly stood and limped his way toward me. He stretched his leathery wings and smiled with shattered fangs.

Aric's hideous growls fired all around me, but he wasn't actually there to help me. I struggled to move, and once again failed. My body trembled as the demon crawled on top of me. His long forked tongue slithered out with a hiss and black drool splattered my face. He drew back his claws and aimed them toward my heart. I flinched at the expectation of my death.

It never came. He slumped on top of me, dead.

Above me, the mother whose child I had saved held the spear that pierced his skull.

A group of men sprinted down the side of the hill and hauled the creature off me. "Thank you," I mumbled when they helped me to my wobbling feet. They caught me as my knees buckled. I couldn't stand while human. I needed the strength of my beast. I gathered what focus remained and *changed* back to tigress, much to the wonder of the Tanzanians.

My body stumbled and swayed. The only reason I wasn't dead was the same reason I'd managed my eagle form. Misha's blood had made me strong enough to cheat death twice.

Tye met me halfway up the ravine and stroked his face against my neck. *Damn, Celia. How bad are you hurt?* He rubbed his body against mine and urged me up the mountain. *Talk to me, dovie. As cats, we can speak to each other. Just concentrate and allow your tigress to take over.*

I collapsed and threw up in response. The pain worsened as blood from my stomach spewed out. When I was done, Tye nudged me to my feet and up the ravine. The Tanzanians walked on either side of us, their spears out and ready to protect us from any threat. It wasn't necessary. When we reached the top, it was clear no demon had survived. The waiting crowd parted and allowed us through. We must have been quite the sight, a golden tigress and an albino lion walking side by side.

I tried to reach Emme, but didn't make it. What little strength my tigress had given me to make the climb ran out. I fell on my face and *changed* back. Shayna screamed and Bren swore when they saw me. Someone threw a blanket on top of me while Bren yelled for Emme. Ying-Ying and Chang spurted rapidly in their respective languages; both were cut and bleeding, but they didn't seem to care about themselves.

Emme had just finished healing the baby that had

been rescued and immediately hurried toward me. She touched my face. Her gentle yellow light surrounded me and her sympathetic tears wet my cheeks. We both cringed at the popping sound my skull made as it readjusted itself and I bit back a shriek when about four ribs abruptly snapped back into place.

"I can't watch," I heard Bren say over the buzzing in my ears.

The image of Aric's face appeared in my mind and his deep timbre filled my head. *I love you*, he said. *It's almost over.* I focused on his words. It took Emme a long time to mend me. The severity of my wounds far surpassed what I'd ever endured. Slowly, my strength returned and my nausea disappeared.

I spit out the blood that remained in my mouth and stood. I would have rather lain on the ground and slept, but I needed to reassure myself and everyone I was safe. Shayna helped adjust the blanket around me while Tye spoke with several of the men, communicating in a language I couldn't identify.

Tye stalked over to us, his brows set in a deep frown. "The Maasai say all the neighboring parks had been evacuated due to what they believe were leopard attacks. They were fleeing when they encountered the demon children. The Tribe is obviously near. False info or not, they're getting close to that damn stone. We need to get to the blasted crater before it's too late."

The beasts among us immediately *changed*. Tye was right—we were running out of time. Emme climbed on my back and held tight to my fur. The others sped off ahead of us. I paused to look back at the woman who had saved my life. She clutched her daughter against her. These Tribe assholes wanted me dead and I hated them for it. But I hated them more for all the lives they'd claimed along the way. It was time for them to die.

Emme stroked my head. "Are you all right, Celia?"

I chuffed a yes before running full out to join my team.

CHAPTER 29

I ran my fingers through my unruly curls and tried not to melt from the wretched humidity. "And how exactly did you learn to hot-wire a car?"

Shayna's tiny butt shimmed and twitched as she toyed with the SUV's wiring. "Koda taught me. He said, 'Baby, every gal needs to know how to do three things: defend herself and hot-wire a car.'"

Emme fanned herself with her hand. "That's only two things. What's the third?"

Shayna slipped from beneath the dash when the engine roared to life. Her blush and grin told me more than I needed to know. "I'll tell you later, cutie."

We jumped into the Range Rover that we'd, er, *procured* at the entrance to the crater. Tye had wanted to drive. Much to Emme's displeasure, I insisted Shayna take the wheel. I hated to admit it, but, as crazy as she drove, her reflexes and speed were unmatched.

I tried to focus on the scenery in order to avoid screaming like poor Emme. We sped through jungles and open plains prowling with leopards, through swamps busting with black rhinos and warthogs. But when we encountered a herd of elephants, I knew I'd found the perfect weapon. "Shayna, pull over." I leapt from the vehicle before she finished skidding to a smooth stop.

Tye chased after me. "Celia, what the hell are you doing?"

I ignored him and crouched down a few yards from the majestic beasts. Slowly I crept, closing in on them as much as I dared. "Damn it, this is no time for sightseeing," Tye growled.

My eyes never left the herd. "I'm hoping this will come in handy."

"*What?*"

I *shifted* underground and surfaced behind the largest male. My fingertips gently touched his wrinkled belly. He flicked his tail but otherwise didn't respond. I concentrated on absorbing his essence, just as Misha had taught me. Something triggered inside me, similar to the feeling I'd had when I first connected to the eagle. I sighed with relief. *Thank you, big guy*.

I withdrew my hand, feeling pretty pleased with myself, until the elephant noticed me. Turns out pachyderms aren't the most forgiving of creatures. He swung his massive trunk at me and just missed crushing me with his mammoth feet. I *changed* and took off running.

Tye's eyes shot out of his face when he saw us barreling toward him. "Oh, shit!" He kept his human form as he hauled ass and dove into the car.

My four-hundred-pound self couldn't fit inside a crammed Range Rover so I *changed* as I leapt through the moving car window. Shayna floored it and—surprise, surprise—I landed naked on top of Tye. Everyone urged Shayna to hurry while Chang hung out the window snapping pictures with his iPhone.

Emme's head whipped back toward the charging beast. "Oh, my goodness. Celia, I hope that was worth it."

Tye grinned as I scrambled to pull on a shirt. "Yes, yes, it was."

Danny whipped through his notes and directed us to the crater. Even with Shayna driving, it took almost two hours to reach the base. When we finally reached our destination, we shot out of the SUV as if it had caught fire. Danny ran ahead and searched the high walls after another glance at his notes. "We need to find a small cave about twenty meters up—it's shaped like a dragon's mouth. The stone is supposedly tucked in a ridge, close to the cave's entrance."

Bren scratched his scruffy beard as he took in the enormous crater. "I know we should have probably asked a long time ago, but what the hell does the stone look like?"

Danny stuffed his notes into the back pocket of his worn jeans. "According to the scripts, it's green in color and we'll recognize it by its splendor when we see it. Come on, this way."

We jogged around the perimeter for about half an hour until Tye spotted the cave. I expected it to look like a narrow protruding snout, but instead it resembled an open serpent mouth with jagged teeth. The roar of a small aircraft halted our climb. We ducked into the brush as it passed over us. We didn't move until the engine faded in the distance.

Tye emerged from the dense vegetation with Emme in tow. "It might just be park rangers checking on things, but let's not wait around to find out." He stripped and threw his clothes on the ground. "Celia, you and I will go up. The rest of you keep watch." He *changed* and climbed swiftly along the crumbling crater wall. I kicked off my sneakers and protruded my front and back claws. He did a double take when I caught up to him with ease, returning my grin with that of his beast. I laughed. Even his lion had a dimple.

A short distance away we heard the plane return. And land. We exchanged quick glances and scaled the wall faster. The cave was in reach when someone fired a shotgun. Tye threw back his head and snarled, his light blue eyes firing with agony. A cursed gold bullet had struck his hind leg. Smoke billowed where it had burned through his flesh. We scrambled the last few feet as the fight between our side and Tribesmen erupted below us.

I fought my way through a nest of spiderwebs and almost cracked my head on the jagged ceiling. Danny wasn't kidding; the ridge was only ten feet from the entrance. I swept my fingers along the edge. Something with lots of little legs scurried over my hand. I jerked my hand back and shook it violently. Lara Croft I wasn't. I took a breath and tried again. This time, my fingertips slipped over something large, cool, and smooth. I grabbed it in both hands, ill prepared for what I saw. An emerald the size of two softballs lay in my palms. I hurried out and presented it to Tye. His huge maw fell open, but then he veered toward the edge of the cave and growled.

Four bloodlust-infected vampires scurried toward us at high velocity, their bodies shuddering with the need to feast. At the base our group huddled against the crater, fighting off the Tribesmen who'd cornered them.

Tye panted from pain yet crouched and prepared to attack the bloodlusters that were almost upon us. I yanked at his mane. "Tye, listen to me. Close your eyes and hold your breath." He snarled when I shoved the stone in his mouth. I hung tight to his fur and winked. "Trust me, Mufasa."

The first bloodluster smacked his clawed hand in front of us as I *shifted*. Our bodies broke down into minute particles, allowing us to pass down and through the crater with ease. I surfaced at the bottom as an elephant. A very hungry, sleep-deprived, and cranky elephant. My massive trunk slammed a bloodlust vampire into the wall, hard enough to splatter the putrid green fluid bulging her muscles. I lifted on my hind legs and crushed a cluster of Tribesmen with my front. The element of surprise helped me do some damage, but we were seriously outnumbered and needed to get the hell out of Tanzania. My legs trampled and my trunk walloped, giving Team Celia time to jump on me. I *shifted* us out, emerging a good distance away and momentarily confusing the Tribesmen.

My elephant form disappeared as soon as I resurfaced. It was strange, but I knew I'd never possess it again. It was either too strong or too large for my spirit to maintain. Yet there was no time to grieve the loss.

Shayna leapt on Bren's wolf body and pointed straight

ahead. "Their plane landed over there. Come on!" She hauled Emme with her and Bren sped off. Danny chased after him, carrying Ying-Ying and Chang. I *changed* into a tigress and carried Tye the naked human on my back. I plowed through the vegetation, but the shots fired behind us motivated me to dash faster.

Tye panted in my ear. "This isn't how I pictured our first time together. I mean, I knew I'd be on top, but this is just weird."

I wished I could communicate with him just to tell him to shut the hell up. But unlike Tye, I didn't seem to possess that ability.

We reached a clearing and spotted the plane. Tye tossed Bren the stone and we all scrambled aboard. I took in all the bells and whistles on the console and jerked my head toward Shayna. "Did your puppy happen to teach you how to hot-wire a plane?"

"Not necessary." Tye hit a few buttons and kicked the engine into gear. We taxied along the flat grass field as the propellers gathered momentum. Tribesmen emerged from the jungle before we could take off, lugging some sort of rocket launcher. May God forgive me for the words that flew out of my mouth.

Now, I didn't speak a word of Korean, but I believe Chang said the equivalent of "Screw *this*!" He flung open the door and pitched several objects from his pack. One hit the Tribesman carrying the rocket launcher before he could fire. The guy sizzled as if jolted by an electric current as a flash of silver ran up his arm and into the weapon. It exploded with a thunderous rumble splattering chunks of dead Tribesmen against the side of our plane.

Shayna raised her arms. "He brought his balls!"

Chang continued to hang out of the plane as we flew past the remaining Tribesmen. His hysterical laugh echoed over the whirl of the engine while he merrily waved his middle finger.

Tye used Shayna's cell phone to arrange for Misha's plane to meet us at the Manyara airstrip. We no longer cared about going unnoticed. We just needed to get to Chaitén.

The moment we boarded, Shayna and I prepared to remove the gold bullet from Tye's leg. I don't know whether it was the fever burning through his body or whether it was because he watched Shayna sharpen a spoon into a scalpel, but all his arrogance dissolved like ice cream in a frying pan. His pupils dilated and he practically shook right out of his seat. "Have either of you ever performed surgery before?"

Shayna lengthened the pointy end of the scalpel to a finer edge with her gift. "Well, no. But Ceel and I are labor nurses and we've watched C-sections performed about a million times."

Tye clutched the arms of his seat. "I don't have a goddamned uterus. Leave me the hell alone!"

I almost told Tye I'd once removed about half a dozen bullets from Gemini's body. But then I thought about the comment he'd made about "our first time" and "knowing he'd be on top." So instead of trying to ease his anxiety, I looked to everyone else. "Get him."

Everybody pounced, even Emme. Tye wrenched and twisted his body, swearing like a drunken sailor during Fleet Week. Everyone held tight. I gave him a nice smile and stroked his long mane away from his face. "I thought you were the king of beasts, not the lord of chickens."

My touch and grin distracted him . . . a little too much. He flashed me one of his sexy smiles. "So, what do I get if I let you— *Son of a bitttccchhh!*"

I tossed the extracted bullet into a cup. "Absolutely nothing."

I stood and washed my hands while my pals climbed off him—except for Emme, who helped him heal. The little whiny feline was as good as new in under a minute. He rose from his seat and padded over to me, leaning in close to place his hands on my shoulders. "That wasn't nice," he murmured.

I shrugged his hands off. "You're welcome."

Tye immediately clasped my shoulders again and locked his gaze on mine. "I like you, Celia," he whispered. "How about, if we make it out of this alive, you let me take you to dinner?"

Tye said "dinner" the way most males said "bed." I backed away from him as a deep sadistic growl tore through my mind. By the smirk on Tye's face, he'd heard it, too. A white haze surrounded me, making me glow. I freaked out. "What the hell?"

Everyone gawked at me except for Tye. "Looks like Aric's bond with you just kicked up a notch." He let out a small laugh. "So, how about dinner?"

CHAPTER 30

"Celia, wake up."

I stretched my arms slowly, only to sit up abruptly when my stomach lurched. Crap, I was nauseated.

Tye frowned. "You okay?"

"Yeah, just jet-lagged." My thoughts led to Aric. I rubbed my face, chest, and arms, expecting them to hurt for some reason.

Tye watched my movements. "We're an hour from our last stop. I need everyone ready before we land. I've arranged for a helicopter. It's the quickest way to get to Chaitén."

I nodded and gently nudged Shayna. "Puppy?" she mumbled.

"No, babe, it's just me." I didn't like the deep-set wrinkles crinkling her forehead. She appeared to be in pain, but then she grinned and propped herself up. I stretched again and searched for some crackers to settle my stomach. If I didn't get some decent sleep soon, my body was going to turn on me.

Shayna's phone rang in her pack as I found some saltines. She fumbled through it until she found it. "Koda?"

"It's me, Taran." My heart sank when I heard her trembling voice. Something was wrong. Shayna's hands shook as she put the call on speaker. "Please tell me you're all right and please say you have the stone," Taran begged.

Shayna stilled, barely blinking. Emme sat down next to her and clutched her hand while I spoke. "We're fine and we have the stone. We should get to you in about an hour and a half." Taran's cries rang through the phone and stung my ears. I swallowed hard. "Taran, what's happened?"

"We can't defeat Ihuaivulu. He's too strong. We had to use the first stone to weaken him. Aric and Koda were the only ones able to get close enough to cast it." Her voice cracked. "They're hurt . . . It's really bad."

Taran's sobs cut through my heart and sent chills rushing down my spine. Bren pulled me against him and held me tight. There was fumbling on the other end before Gemini came on the line sounding miserable and exhausted. "Aric and Koda were severely burned." He let out a breath. "Their injuries are not healing . . . but they're still able to fight."

I broke out of Bren's hold, yelling over Shayna's cries. *"You're telling me they're injured and they're still being sent to fight?"*

"There's no choice, Celia. We've been fighting Ihuaivulu for the last twenty hours since Aric hit him with the stone. All we've managed to do is keep him at the volcano. Alliance members from all over Central and South America have joined us, but we're still no match for him. You have to get here—you're our last hope."

What sounded like a large screeching bat echoed through the phone with enough force to send it spinning off the table. I covered my ears and screamed for Taran, but the line went dead.

The silence that filled the air threatened to choke me. Tears streamed down Shayna's face and her eyes pleaded with me to tell her she'd misheard—that Taran was safe and our mates hadn't been harmed. I knew this because I wanted to hear it, too. I wanted it all to be some horrible dream. But it wasn't. Her love and mine were in pain, and our sister was in danger. They suffered alone and there was nothing we could do . . . for now.

Shayna's face blanched. "What if they die, Celia?"

I refused to spill any tears at Shayna's words. Aric couldn't die and neither could Koda or Taran. Aric and I were supposed to get married and spend our lives together. No, I would not cry. Crying meant I already believed them dead and that my time with Aric was over.

I stormed into the bathroom to splash cold water on my face. Tye followed me. "Are you all right?"

I stared at my pale skin in the mirror, gripping the sides of the sink before I smashed my reflection to bits. "No," I answered. "No, I'm not."

The last few minutes were the longest of our trip; even Ying-Ying couldn't keep still. We were anxious, infuriated, and ready to fight. The moment our plane rolled to a stop, we sprinted toward the helicopter with Tye leading the way. No one was there to greet us; only a note taped to the window with coordinates to Chaitén anticipated our arrival.

What we found in Chaitén was devastation befitting a world war. A thick cloud of gray ash resembling fallen snow covered the entire town and coated the air like a fog. Tye ascended up the mountain where all the vegetation lay completely destroyed. Rows and rows of demolished and still burning trees rested on top of one another like discarded Lincoln Logs, casting light onto the charred remains of dead *weres* and the darker clumps of ash that had once been vampires. Some trees stubbornly remained erect, like giant black candles continuing to smoke.

The terrible batlike screech drew our attention toward the volcano, where fire shot into the heavens from several different directions.

"I *really* hope that's just the volcano erupting," Bren said.

"If only," Tye muttered. "Shit, and supposedly he's weaker now."

Tye continued upward. Remnants of motorcycles and helicopters littered the area like a metal graveyard amid a burning world. Only one patch of hidden forest remained untouched: the Alliance base camp. We'd arrived.

I didn't see our wolves or Taran, but several members tending to the injured stood and pointed frantically toward the volcano.

Tye adjusted his transmitter and gave me a tight smile. "Looks like we're on. Anyone who's not ready needs to get off now." He hovered above the camp while I scooted into the back and opened the door.

I motioned toward the exit and then to Chang and Ying-Ying to make them understand. "This is your chance to save yourselves. We're going after Ihuaivulu now." They smiled kindly, yet stayed put. I clasped my hand over my eyes and tried to snuff my welling tears. Chang and Ying-Ying had been my teachers and tormentors, but they'd also become my friends. All my life I'd carried the weight of protecting my sisters on my shoulders. Now I carried theirs as well. I dropped my hand and clenched my fists. "This is not your fight. You should go." They stood together and maneuvered around the seats. But instead of jumping, they bowed.

Chang patted my shoulder. "Proud," he said.

Ying-Ying nodded. "You good girl."

They returned to their seats and tightened their belts. I shut the door as Tye took us to the skies. My gaze took in the determined faces of those I loved.

Bren and Danny comforted Emme and Shayna. I wanted to tell them they didn't have to do this, that I would gladly die for them instead. I also thought to inspire them somehow. They had, after all, jumped on board the Team Celia train. Without hesitating and without so much as a glance back, they'd followed me into danger. They'd trusted me to lead them and yet I couldn't form the words to tell them what their actions meant to me.

"I . . ."

Danny's eyes glistened. "We love you, too, Celia."

I leaned my palms against the door and dropped my head. *God, please keep them safe. Don't take them yet. The world is a better place with them here.*

Tye took a sharp right turn—hard enough for me to clutch the seat—and spoke into his mouthpiece. "I want to stay as far away from Ihuaivulu as possible. Emme, when we get near him, use your *force* to launch the stone." She nodded and reached into her pack to retrieve the stone. I joined him in the front and wiped my sweaty palms against my tank top. He smiled and flashed his dimple. "Don't worry, dovie. We're going to make it. Our cubs are destined to rid the world of evil. That means we get to stick around to conceive them."

I shook my head and sighed. Tye was in for a rude awakening, regardless of whether we made it or not.

The terrible bat screech bellowed with enough power to shake the helicopter. All hell broke loose at the summit. *Weres* thundered over the ground, attempting to herd what could only be described as, well, a seven-headed fire-breathing dragon. *Oh, my God.* Ihuaivulu's immense form trumped most three-story buildings and his long lizard necks made him seem larger yet. Red flames funneled from some of his mouths while the others swallowed the guerrilla-looking vamps shooting at it.

Ihuaivulu whipped his tail and struck the rider of a dirt bike. The rider flew and slammed into the side of the large hill, his broken body unmoving. I screamed when I realized it was Misha . . . and that Ihuaivulu was closing in fast.

The two Geminis and Liam arrived in wolf form and tried to intercept the winged demon. If the wolves were afraid, they masked their fear well. They fought with ferocity and rabid fury, nipping and ramming Ihuaivulu in an attempt to distract him and get him to chase them. But it was no use.

I lurched toward the back and wrenched open the door. "I need to get off *now*!"

Tye maneuvered the helicopter toward Misha. I leapt out the moment we passed above him. My body dove straight at him with my hands outstretched. The moment my fingertips felt the tease of his leather jacket, I *shifted* us through the hill and up to the top.

Misha sputtered out dirt when we surfaced. He stared

at me, momentarily stunned until his arms locked me in a tight embrace. "You came back to me," he whispered. The ground rumbled beneath us and knocked us on our sides. We scrambled to the edge. Below us, Ihuaivulu tore his head free from the hill where Misha had lain unmoving.

He pulled me to my feet. "We must leave—now," he urged.

My jaw clenched tight. "Not yet."

Tye maneuvered the helicopter for a second pass. The fire-breathing mouths followed, snapping their omnivorous jaws in search of more prey. Tye dodged and veered his way around the flames, but his jerking motions worked against us. Emme fell out of the front, where she had prepared to launch the stone from. It plummeted from her grasp when she grabbed onto the skids. Bren climbed out to help her, but she couldn't hold on. With lightning speed Ying-Ying dove after her. She contorted herself around Emme and bounced away from Ihuaivulu like a rubber ball.

They were safe, but the others were not. Ihuaivulu slammed one of his heads into the helicopter and catapulted it out of control. Bren, who was hanging to the skids, *changed* and leapt to the ground after the fallen stone.

The helicopter crashed away from us yet didn't explode. The main rotor continued to spin as Tye and Danny emerged as beasts with Shayna and Chang on their backs. They zigzagged to avoid Ihuaivulu's flames, but they'd landed too close to him and needed help. I was about to charge toward them when a stream of blue and white fire shot at Ihuaivulu with the fury of hell.

Taran emerged on a hilltop opposite us, hovering above the ground with her crystal eyes fixed on Ihuaivulu. She screamed as meteors of fire tore from her core and at her target. The demon caught the balls of fire and swallowed them whole. Taran was in trouble.

And Emme was there to save her.

My youngest sister raised the large hunk of twisted metal that was once that copter with the full gamut of her *force*. She grunted and screamed with her hands above her head. Blood trickled down her nose and tears streaked her deep purple face as she levitated the aircraft above the ground. Ying-Ying jumped wildly and fired out words of encouragement as Emme's burden shook from her strained efforts. With one last primal scream, Emme thrust the helicopter at Ihuaivulu. The spinning rotors took off three of Ihuaivulu's heads moments before the rest exploded on top of him in a giant burst of light.

The excited hollers and howls of Alliance members were short-lived. The remaining heads ignited the entire area into a raging inferno. "*Retreat!*" a vampire screamed just before flames engulfed him.

Misha grabbed my hand and we raced back toward the camp. We swept in about the same time Gemini and Liam charged in. The others hadn't returned.

Gemini's two wolves became one. He and Liam *changed* and rushed to us. "Celia, where is everyone?" Liam asked.

"I don't know. We got separated."

Gemini's dark gaze whipped back toward the smoking forest. "I'm going back."

Misha intercepted him. "Don't be a fool. The entire area is on fire. If they survived they will return in time."

Misha's words, although true, did nothing to calm me. My eyes darted around frantically. I didn't see anyone I recognized. Just when I thought I would lose it, Taran appeared. The blue and white flames protecting her form withdrew back into her core, allowing Gemini to gather her in his arms. She wept openly while Gemini led her to me.

Taran threw her arms around me. "Oh, my God, Celia. I thought I'd never see you again!"

My voice shook. "Taran, did you see anyone else?"

She glanced over her shoulder at Gemini. "No one else came back?"

He placed his arm on her shoulder. "No, but we need to give them time."

I pushed my hair back and paced, trying to avoid staring at the *weres* around me. Horrid scars covered the vast majority. Some had limbs completely burned off while others were swathed with heavy dressings to protect their fresh wounds. The few vampires that remained appeared unharmed. They must have dodged Ihuaivulu's deadly fire. Had the creature's flames even grazed them, they would have joined the heaps of ash surrounding the mountainside.

The injured watched me, fear and pain claiming their distorted features. None of them seemed familiar. None were who I longed to see. A horrible sense of dread claimed the pit of my stomach and twisted my gut. "Are Aric and Koda . . . ?"

"They're alive, Celia," Gemini answered me quietly. "The ones with the greatest trauma have been moved into the tents."

My knees buckled when I once again took in the *weres* with the missing limbs. They waited out in the open, not in tents . . . which meant they were the ones in better shape.

Taran draped her arm around my shoulders. "I'll take you to them. But Aric especially is not . . . well." She led me to the rows of tents, pausing outside one of the larger ones.

The flaps of the tent opened as the Elders exited. Anara regarded me with his usual distaste, while the others met me with a mixture of sadness and compassion. I took a deep breath before stepping inside and tried to imagine the absolute worst.

Nothing could have prepared me for this. I gasped in horror. It was all I could do not to scream.

Half of Koda's body blazed with angry red blisters ready to burst, but the rest of his body was in far worse condition. His right side resembled thick charred leather, patterned much like the scales of a snake. His right eye had swelled shut and he'd lost an ear. And his hair, once long, thick, and silky, now lay singed or was missing from the sections of his burnt scalp. He hunched over in agony.

And still he'd fared better than Aric.

The top and sides of Aric's hair had vanished, devoured by the seared indentations speckled across his scalp. His face, neck, chest, and arms were brutally damaged. He'd lost the first two layers of skin in some parts, and all three in others. His ears—*my God*—were nothing more than shrunken pieces of deformed flesh. And where his right eye had been, only a patch of burnt skin remained. His left eye moved to where I stood, shrouded beneath an alarmingly swollen slit.

The wolves watched me closely, but didn't move. Taran leaned in close to whisper. "Ihuaivulu's power was too great. They're slowly healing their infections and pain, but the scarring . . . appears to be permanent."

Shayna's heart-wrenching sob made me jump. She staggered past me to fall kneeling before Koda. "Oh, my God, no. Puppy, *no*!" Her screams pounded my chest like vengeful blows. She reached out to him, but pulled back. Her eyes swept over his burns, unsure whether to touch him.

Koda pulled her onto his lap, subjecting himself to obviously excruciating pain. Yet he didn't care. He just wanted to hold his mate. Shayna kissed his lips and cheeks, weeping hysterically. He tried his best to comfort her, but it was no use. She hurt as much as he did.

Aric's ruined face met mine, yet I couldn't bring myself to go to him. My hands balled into fists and tears leaked from my eyes. I trembled with the force of my rage—livid for the pain he'd endured and for how he would continue to suffer.

I wanted to scream from the injustice. Aric had honorably protected the earth, and *this* was his reward? *Fuck. YOU!*

My tigress eyes replaced my own and hatred filled my rampant heart, scorching the edges of my soul and demanding I destroy anything in my path. My beast roared inside me, clawing and biting at my rib cage. *Kill*, she demanded. *Kill!*

Taran gripped my wrist. "Celia . . . Celia, are you all right? *Jesus*. Celia, just breathe, honey. Just breathe . . . Oh, God. Honey, please calm down . . . I swear we're going to get through this . . ."

My own personal hell raged inside me. I didn't know how to control it, or whether I wanted to. And then the ground quaked, hard enough to shove my tigress aside and pull my human side forward.

Ihuaivulu, that wretched son of a bitch, was nearing.

Misha stormed into the tent and spun me, grasping my shoulders tight. I tried to toss him, but he held strong and thrust his face in mine. "Now is not the time for mourning, Celia. Bren is back with Emme *and* the stone." He shook me hard when I tried to break free. "*Listen to me!* We have the power to finish this. Do it. *Now*."

My mind struggled through the vile fog twisting and distorting my thoughts. *The stone. The stone is back.* I bit down hard on my lip until it bled and snapped me out of my misery.

I tore away from the tent, pumping my legs as fast as they'd carry me. Aric called to me. My God, his pained and garbled voice held no hint of his once deep and confident timbre. It was all I could do not to race back to him. I wanted to take him in my arms and never let him go. But Misha was right. I had to put an end to the Tribe once and for all.

The steps of those chasing me quickened, but failed to reach me. I focused on Tye, who stood at the edge of a cliff, waving the stone—the very weapon I needed.

"Time to go eagle!" he yelled before he jumped.

I exploded into my new form and dove for him. He cringed and swore as my talons once again dug into his shoulders. I flapped my powerful appendages and aimed for Ihuaivulu, who sped toward us with outstretched wings, hell-bent on murder. *Time to say good night, you evil bastard.*

I soared above Ihuaivulu with hopes Tye could just drop the stone on him. It would have worked had the creature not taken flight. *Damn it to hell.* I supposed it was too much to hope his wings were just decorative.

I dipped right, left, and down, trying to avoid the multitude of snapping jaws and sprays of fire. No way could I outfly him. So I had to fly smart. I nosedived into the outside of the volcano and *shifted* us through. I was almost out of air by the time we flew out the other side. Beneath me, the earth rumbled from the force of Ihuaivulu slamming into the volcano.

"*Celia*, I lost the stone!"

"Screeech?"

"It didn't *shift* with us. It has to be on the other side. Go back. *Go back!*"

I tilted my wings and circled around. My heart leapt into my throat when I saw what was happening at the farthermost edge of the Alliance camp. Shayna darted around the splintered chunks of ruined trees, converting the pieces into long silver spikes. The vamps and *weres*—including Aric and Koda, who grunted in anguish—impaled Ihuaivulu's tough skin and shredded his wings to worthless bits. He roared and tried to fly, only to collapse on the ash-coated ground.

My eagle eyes scanned the ground below and fixed upon the discarded stone. I dove toward it, ready to snag it when Ihuaivulu struck Tye with his tail. The blow propelled us into a distant tree. My sisters' screams were barely audible over the crumbling bark and crash of the falling timber.

We landed hard atop the smoldering trunk and flopped onto the heated soil. I lost my eagle form and couldn't reclaim it. I *changed* into tigress and lurched in time to avoid being fricasseed by Ihuaivulu. Heat from his flames scorched the earth, turning the mountain into his personal hell. My lungs contracted with the need for air. I couldn't breathe and began to suffocate, yet I compelled my body to plow through the battered terrain, willing my paws to ignore the mounting heat.

Tye's lion form jetted full speed for the stone. His white fur made him almost invisible against the ash, but it was only a matter of time before Ihuaivulu's remaining heads spotted him.

I needed to distract Ihuaivulu. So instead of running away from him, I charged right at him. My sisters and friends yelled at me to turn back. I ignored them and kept my head in the game. If it was my time to go, so be it—but Ihuaivulu was coming with me.

I jumped and darted away from his flames faster than

my tigress had ever moved before, seeing the streams of fire as merely larger versions of lightning bolts thrown from an overzealous martial arts master. My strategy worked, and so did my high-velocity dodges that managed to manipulate Ihuaivulu into burning his own tail. He roared and stumbled in pain, allowing me to launch myself onto one of his remaining snouts.

My back claws fastened onto his nose, my front claws gouged his eyes, my jaws broke through the thick scales and into bone. Warm liquid squirted against my claws and mouth, and his furious screams pained my ears, but I continued to unleash my wrath—for Aric, for Koda, for everyone who'd stood against him.

The last thing I saw was the second head rushing at me right before a deafening explosion fired me into the air. I landed as a human on a mountain of ash, choking and gasping next to Tye's naked form. We sputtered and coughed as dust settled around us while an outburst of excited cheers echoed through the valley. Tye kipped up and hauled me to my feet. "Motherfucker!"

That pretty much summed it up. The ruins and destruction of the mountain surrounded us, yet not a trace of Ihuaivulu remained. "Damn," I said quietly.

Tye didn't respond, choosing instead to rub his thumbs against my hands. Ash covered both our bodies. Unfortunately, it did little to hide my goodies. I yanked my arms back and *changed*. He shook his head once before resuming his lion form. We sprinted back to camp, his cheer making him playful. He rubbed up against me, tickling me enough to cause me to purr. I swatted at him and he nipped at me teasingly. We continued our banter all the way back. I took it as good-natured fun until we reached our friends and he *changed* back.

"Celia, if you ever change your mind . . . you know where to find me."

"Get in line," Misha hissed. He and my loved ones embraced me and patted my back. I searched for Aric, but failed to see or scent him.

Gemini bent to scratch my furry face and whisper in my ear. "He's in the woods immediately to my right."

I *shifted* and traveled as far into the forest as I could manage, then used my nose to track Aric. I found him wrapped in a blanket, staring pointedly at the ground. I *changed* back to human and hurried toward him. Tears dripped down my face as I took in his disfigured features. "*Aric.*"

"I'll understand if you don't want to stay with me."

My tears stopped their descent as I struggled to make sense of what he said. "What the hell are you talking about?"

He stepped away from me when I reached for him. *What?* All I wanted was to hold him.

"I'm saying you can choose Tye, Misha, or whoever else you desire. I just want you to be happy."

I stumbled backward into a tree, stunned and barely able to keep my wits. My fist found the trunk and struck. Blood poured from my knuckles. "I'm happiest with *you.* Don't you dare try to get rid of me again!"

"Celia, I know what I must look like—"

"Do you think your looks are all I care about? I love you, Aric—all of you." After everything we'd been through and all our time apart, now he was pushing me away. I cried into my hands, releasing the fear and sadness I'd carried since first learning of his afflictions. My sobs turned into gulps, frantic gasps for air. My chest ached from the sharp intakes of breath and from the cruel stabs of his words.

He stepped toward me slowly and placed his battered palms on my arms. His garbled voice cracked when he spoke. "You still want me?"

I yanked him to me and met his lips with mine. He grunted in pain, but I refused to let him go. Instead, my kiss turned more passionate.

Aric wrapped his arms around my waist and pulled me close, kissing me back with the love I knew so well. His skin scratched like rough and jagged plastic. He was no longer handsome or smooth or soft. The tease of tiny little chest hairs was gone, as was his sense of touch. There was no firm muscle, and he'd lost the mobility in his lips. He would never again greet me with the smile that made my soul sing. But he was still *my* Aric. His taste was just as sweet, his body just as warm, and his heart still beat for me.

He broke away, panting heavily, but this time not from pain. I stroked the side of his face as gently as possible. "I'll always want you," I whispered. "No matter what happens."

Footsteps approached from the dense wooded path behind me. Aric covered me with his blanket and pulled me close. Tye leaned against a tree, wearing a pair of shorts and a rather amused grin. "You really don't believe in Destiny. Do you, dovie?"

I tightened my hold on Aric and rested my head against his chest. "My destiny is in my hands, Tye."

CHAPTER 31

Makawee examined Aric's arms, her white brows knitted into a frown. "With Ihuaivulu's return to his dormant state, the effects of his power should have ceased." She shook her head. "I cannot comprehend why our *weres* are incapable of healing."

Emme had tried to help Aric and Koda. She took away their remaining pain, but their scars would not dissolve.

Danny watched Makawee release Aric. Regret and sadness dulled his young features, making him appear years beyond his age. "What happened to the Tribesmen who were guarding the other stone? Maybe they can tell us something."

Gemini stroked his thickening goatee with his thumb and forefinger. Aside from a few minor burns on his forearms and back, his body had been spared. "Most were incinerated by Ihuaivulu when they awoke him."

"The Tribe *weres* who survived were given to the vampires," Liam said, unable to hide his disgust.

"Hey, we were hungry," a vamp called from a few tents down.

I moved toward Aric, then thought twice. Makawee, while sympathetic, would likely object to any contact. My arms weighed heavily from the urge to hold him as I faced her. "What about the witch who helped raise Ihuaivulu? Could she have—I don't know—done something so they can't heal?"

"I killed her, Celia." Taran's eyes skimmed over Aric's and Koda's forms. "The bitch deserved a lot worse."

Shayna remained a permanent fixture on Koda's lap. She wouldn't talk, but when Koda lifted her chin, she flashed him a gleaming smile. It lacked its usual luster, yet was enough to curve one side of Koda's mouth.

We followed Makawee outside to join the crowd of Alliance members that had gathered. I held back a little so I could walk beside Aric. I waited until she joined the Elders and Uri on a small incline before I spoke softly, "I just want to be alone with you."

Aric lowered his head. "Now's not a good time, love. But I'll see what I can do."

I blinked back tears. Since we'd returned from the forest, Aric had kept his distance. I understood why. We didn't have the luxury to be together like Shayna and Koda. But he needed me at his side. Couldn't the Elders grant us that much? I brushed my hand over his before stepping closer to Emme. Aric glanced down at his hand. Though his damaged face gave no indication of whether he appreciated the gesture, I hoped he had.

I wiped my eyes only to smear more of that wretched ash continuing to fall. My tigress paced with the need to abandon this wasteland and return to Aric. It took me a moment to soothe her enough to focus on the leaders and the words they were sharing with the gathering crowd. Martin and Uri thanked the survivors for their courage and sacrifice. Their words were hopeful and uplifting, and most of all sincere.

The atmosphere changed when Anara took center stage.

His gaze scanned the crowd until it fell directly on me. I sensed the chill he brought with him, and his fury when he spoke. "We lost many great Warriors and friends today and I fear more than ever for the future of our *were* race. Only through *proper* breeding can we ensure the survival of our species." He shook his head from side to side, anger digging further into his hawklike features. "It *disgusts* me that even our own Leaders fail to see that the world will crumble without us." He looked to the *were* dignitaries of Central and South America, ignoring Uri and Misha beside him. "I plan to put forth a decree before the North American Were Council that will require all unmated *weres* to fulfill the same duties we demand of our purebloods. And I urge you all to ask the same of your governing bodies. The future of our kind depends on it!"

My gasp was barely audible over the uproar that ensued. Martin stormed forward and muttered low into Anara's ear, his angled brows illuminating his displeasure with Anara. Anara kept his attention on me, refusing to acknowledge a single word. Was he that arrogant? Pureblood Beta or not, Anara wasn't stronger than his Alpha.

Many *weres* disagreed with Anara, but a surprising number took his side. I covered my face and bit back a furious roar. The Tribe might not have succeeded in taking over the world, but it had succeeded in massacring the numbers of *weres* who guarded it. God *damn* Anara. He wouldn't stop with creating a law to force all *weres* to breed. He'd make sure my relationship with Aric was construed as a crime.

We separated into groups following Anara's rousing speech, waiting like cattle to be transported out of Chaitén. Aric was ushered out quickly, leaving me with Emme, Taran, Bren, Danny, and a couple of Alliance members I'd never met.

Bren took in the mess around us. "How the hell are they going to explain all this shit?"

"Most of it will be blamed on the volcano erupting." Danny wiped some of the ash covering his hands on his jeans and sneezed. He only succeeded in soiling them more. "The vampires in the South American Alliance are pretty high up politically. They feel a few hypnotic suggestions will take care of any loose ends."

Emme crinkled her forehead. "Is that all they plan to do?"

Danny scratched his coated curls. "The Alliance feels since they just saved the world from Ihuaivulu, the least the Chilean government can do is pay for the cleanup."

Taran agreed. "You're damn right they can." Her head jerked to the side, where a vampire stood waving from the bed of a battered pickup truck. "Come on—it's our turn to go." Although she was eager to leave the destruction far behind her, she waited for me to join her side. "How are you holding up?"

I watched as my filthy sneakers passed over the trampled ash-ridden soil, my head so heavy I couldn't lift my chin. "I don't know—angry, numb, seconds from losing my mind." My voice cracked as we passed a few *weres* lifting another who'd lost both his legs. Taran's hand gripped my arm as if to stabilize me and my volatile emotions. "This wasn't supposed to happen, Taran. The tribe was after me. *Me*. No one else should have suffered."

Taran whirled me around. "Don't," she snapped. "This bullshit is not your doing. These bastards go after everyone—the weak, the strong, it doesn't matter. If it wasn't you, it would have been anyone else who had the balls to stand up to them." Her tone carried such an edge, I didn't realize she was crying until I glanced up and caught the thick drops leaking from her eyes.

Her grip tightened. "And don't think it's over, Ceel, because it's not. We have majorly pimp-punched them and sent them running. But whatever remains of them still fucking remains. They'll continue to come after you. Be sharp, and stay strong." She motioned ahead to where Aric and Koda had disappeared. "And fight for those you love."

The ride down the mountain required us to wear masks. Between the breeze continuing to sweep the chunky powder off the leaves and the smoke from the smoldering forest, I didn't take a decent breath until we reached the airport. My silence, however, wasn't solely

due to my muffled mouth or the state of Chaitén. Tara
was right. The efforts of the Alliance had pummeled th
Tribe. But that didn't mean it was gone. I was safe—fo
now. Maybe even for the next week, or month, until th
legion of superscaries regrouped and remembered I'
helped bring them down.

And that I was indeed as formidable as they'd feared

We scrambled out of the pickup at the outermos
edge of the runway. The air remained thick and covered
but considerably lighter and more bearable. We walke
along the tarmac, carrying the tightly wrapped bags c
clothes the jeep driver had tossed us, and searching alon
the fleet of planes for our ride home.

Gemini rushed out from one of the private jets ahea
of us and raced to our side. He took Taran's hand an
motioned forward. "Come with me—hurry."

We moved fast. It wasn't fast enough. The Elder
caught me ascending the stairs as they boarded the plan
just to our right. Martin and Makawee averted thei
gazes. Anara didn't. His piercing dark irises raked a
mine like a branch of thorns. Never had anyone hate
me so.

We entered the plane, where Shayna, Koda, and Liar
waited in silence. My entire body tensed. "Where
Aric?"

Liam met my face with sad eyes. "He's in the back
Celia. I think he needs some space. Maybe you shoul
give him a moment."

I waited until we reached altitude. Then waited an
other half hour more. Aric never joined us. My anxiet
worsened and kicked my patience aside. I grabbed the
LOVE CHILE shorts and T-shirt set I'd been given and en
tered the small suite. All the lights were out. I didn'
bother turning them on. I knocked on the door to th
bathroom, once, twice. He didn't answer, but eve
through the door I could smell the lingering aroma of hi
burnt flesh.

I gathered my resolve and opened the door. Ari
stood before the mirror, unmoving and barely breathin
My stomach twisted hard enough to make me clasp m

hand over it. *Oh, God.* He'd finally seen the extent of Ihuaivulu's damage. And there wasn't a damn thing I could do to ease his hurt and shock.

I beat back my sorrow and took a breath. Aric didn't need my tears; he needed my strength. I shimmied around him and turned on the small shower. It wasn't until I started ridding myself of Taran's borrowed dirty clothes that Aric acknowledged me. "Celia . . . what are you doing?"

"We're both filthy. Come on, hop in with me."

Aric didn't make an effort to remove his clothes, so I did it for him. He stilled as I yanked his shirt over his head, but when I tried to unsnap his shorts, he clasped my wrists. "Don't, love."

His grip was tight, but loosened when I stared up at him and tried to smile. "Why? You like being naked with me."

Aric shook his head slowly. "Things are different now . . . My face isn't the only part of me damaged."

I unwittingly followed the trail of ruined tissue down his chest, past his belly button, and into his . . . *Jesus.*

I tried to tell him it didn't matter, only to stumble and stutter over lies he didn't need to hear. Of course it mattered. So instead of spewing foolish mutterings, I pulled him under the water with me. He just stood there watching me without moving, so I sat him down on the small bench.

There wasn't a lot of room. I placed my legs between his knees and washed what remained of his hair. My breasts hung near his face, but he kept his head turned away from me. When I was done, I kissed his lips and concentrated on the rest of his body. I tried not to react with grief as my fingers ran over the thick grooves in his skin pooling with water. "Remember the last time we showered? I do . . ."

Aric didn't respond. His only reaction was to turn back to face me. With his healthy eye, he watched the water slide down my body before turning away once more. I didn't like him looking away from me. Neither did my tigress. So following a little boost of her charm I

gave him my back and made a show of washing my hair
and curves. I continued until I felt his rising heat stroking
against my back. I slipped out and teased him with the
way I applied my lotion, careful not to make eye contact
until I heard him step out of the shower.

Aric had tossed his shorts and covered his waist with
a towel, a towel that did little to hide the growing strain
of his arousal. My fingertips slipped up and down the
length of the long lotion bottle and my husky voice fell
into a seductive whisper. "Come with me." I snatched the
bottle from the small counter and backed into the bedroom. Aric prowled toward me and followed me onto
the bed.

I warmed the lotion in my palms before sliding it
along his damaged skin. He tensed beneath my touch
until I began my deep massage of his shoulders. Heat
spread along my palms in almost visible circles, inciting
the bond between us. My hands drifted along his chest
until they linked around his neck. I kissed his cheek and
waited. He panted softly as if trying to hold back and
stay in control, but that's not what I wanted. My lips continued to sweep across his jawline. When I reached his
lips, he pushed my wet hair away from my face and drove
his tongue deep into my mouth.

Our passion escalated, urging me to roll on top of
him. I cried out when his hard length struck my tender
region. Maybe he was damaged, but everything seemed
in optimal working condition. My hands found him, playing and exploring until his growls and grunts rang in my
ears like a lustful melody. My heart thundered, yearning
with the desire to have him inside me. I needed to feel
close to him. And he needed me, too.

Aric reached for my breasts. I jerked a little when the
sharp edges of his damaged fingers scratched against the
tips. His want distracted him, and he failed to notice. But
when his hand slipped between my legs, I couldn't mask
the pain from his touch.

He pulled away from me, breathing hard. "I'm sorry,"
we both said at once.

He stared at his butchered hands before his frozen

expression ran the length of my body. The air left my lungs in a gasp. His caress had marked my skin with scrapes and scratches. Not enough to scar or bleed, but enough to halt our wandering hands and extinguish our fervor.

"I'm sorry," he repeated, with more regret dripping from his voice.

We watched each other for what felt like too long until my need to feel his arms around me shoved the strain of the moment aside. I lowered myself so we lay facing each other, and cuddled against him. He pulled me to him, but still I scented his apprehension and his fear.

He was afraid to hurt me.

We waited in silence, both of us searching for something to say. Yet not even our beasts could give us the knowledge to form the right words. Aric shuddered once before the aroma of his tears pricked at my nose. "Are you sure you want to stay with me?"

I kissed his chin before the start of my own sorrow. "I'll never leave you. I swear it."

CHAPTER 32

We both fell asleep. I awoke sometime later from the discomfort of dehydration. Aric draped his arm over his face. I imagined that without the ability to lower his lids it was the only way he could manage to rest. I decided against disturbing him and walked into the main cabin.

Everyone glanced up when they saw me. Their bleak expressions mirrored mine. My maternal instincts made me want to comfort them, but the emptiness in the pit of my stomach surpassed any emotions.

Emme squeezed my hand. "Celia, have something to eat."

My eyes skimmed along the table filled with chicken, vegetables, and rolls. A wave of acid burned my throat and made me grimace. I cleared my throat to prevent from gagging and placed my hand over my belly. "I'm not hungry. I still feel kind of ill."

Emme released my hand. "I'm feeling ill, too. I called Dr. Belman and set up appointments for us for tomorrow. I'm worried it's more than just jet lag."

Emme was right. God only knew what bizarre infections we could have picked up from all our globe-trotting. Africa alone had a growing list of frightening ailments.

Liam stood, frowning. "Why can't you just heal yourselves?"

"I can't cure diseases, Liam. Sometimes if it's related to a physical injury I can fix it, but that doesn't seem to be what's happening."

Liam placed his hand on Emme's shoulder. "But you'll be okay, right?"

Emme slipped her hand over his. "We'll be fine, Lee."

I grabbed a water bottle out of the small fridge. I'm not sure why such a simple task made me so emotional, but I started to cry after chugging half the bottle. My sobs made me spit out some of the water. Koda didn't care. He just wrapped his arms around me and pulled me into an embrace. "Stay strong, Celia. He needs you."

Taran eventually convinced me to eat. I managed to nibble on a few pieces of bread before preparing a tray for Aric. He sat up when I placed the food in front of him. His burned flesh had tightened and shriveled the muscle, making it arduous for him to chew and swallow. I shredded the chicken for him in smaller bites and mashed the potatoes and carrots for him with a fork. "I'd like to take you to a burn center. There's one in Santa Ana we could go to."

"*Weres* don't belong in human hospitals, sweetness." He scanned his injuries. "And there's no plausible explanation to justify the extent of my scars."

I returned to mashing the vegetables. "I just want to help you."

"I know," he responded quietly.

Aric and I barely spoke the remainder of the eighteen-hour flight. Mostly we just held each other and tried to rest. He'd fidgeted, unable to sleep until I moistened a washcloth and placed it over the hard slit covering his eye.

"Thanks, love," he murmured beneath the cloth.

Out of habit, I reached to stroke back the bangs he no longer had. I fought back my sorrow. It wasn't fair. Once upon a time, however brief, we were both safe, we were both whole. Now the scars enveloping his form marred and claimed us both. Happily-ever-afters in the mystical world didn't come without a hefty price. And yet it was a price I'd willingly pay. I crawled beneath the covers and found my place beside my mate.

Aric nudged me awake sometime much later. "We just landed in Tahoe, sweetness. The Elders are outside waiting for me."

The realization we would be apart jolted me awake. "Okay . . . but when will we see each other?"

Aric turned from me. "I don't know."

My hand covered his. "Aric, we're going to work through this, okay? You have to believe me."

He lifted my knuckles and tried to kiss them, but I barely felt the movement of his mouth. "I love you, Celia."

He said it, and maybe he meant it, but his words sounded more like good-bye. By the time I climbed into Misha's limo, I was an absolute mess. I wanted to be with Aric. I wanted to care for him. And I wanted him to know I'd never give up on us. Instead I had to watch him leave without me.

Emme tried to console me, but I couldn't stop crying.

Misha watched me. Initially he held back. Finally, I guess my despair became too much. He slipped onto the long leather seat beside me. "My darling, look at me." I was so embarrassed by the blubbering spectacle I'd become I couldn't do as he asked. "Kitten, please look at me."

He lifted my chin, taking care not hurt me. As soon as I met his soft gray eyes, I lost myself in their tenderness and beauty. A sense of calm surrounded me. My soul took a breath and silenced my tears. Emme's soft voice echoed from a faraway place. "What are you doing to her, Misha?"

"Just granting her some peace, sweet Emme."

"Will it be permanent?"

"No. My power is no match for her pain."

CHAPTER 33

I awoke in Misha's guesthouse. The first thing I did was check my cell phone for messages. There were none. Aric hadn't called. I took a moment to calm before I showered and started my day.

I drove to my house in Dollar Point to gather some personal items following my doctor's appointment. I was about to take a walk along Lake Tahoe to clear my head when someone knocked on my door. Anara waited on my doorstep holding a charm similar to the one I had to pass through the wards. My hackles instinctively rose. How did he have access to my house? "What are you doing here, Anara?"

A long vicious growl rumbled through his chest. "I'm here to tell you that if you ever see Aric again I'll—"

"You'll what? Kill me?" I was livid. How *dare* he come to my home and threaten me!

This made him laugh. "No, you stupid woman. I'll *kill him.*"

His response infuriated me. I crouched and readied myself to attack. "*Not if you're already dead.*"

Anara threw out his hand as if batting a fly, sending me slamming into the portrait-covered wall. Glass from the frames cut into my skin, stinging and piercing my flesh like the jagged teeth of a shark. Warm blood trickled down my back and soaked through my thick cotton sweater. He held me a few feet off the floor with just his will. I jerked my shoulders, trying to move, to kick—*anything* to break from his hold. My limbs failed me. I reached into my tigress for strength, but Anara's power caged her within me.

He walked inside, slamming the door behind him. Invisible fists struck my face with each step he took, each blow harder, magnifying my agony and making me scream. He broke my nose and bloodied my face without ever lifting a finger. My ears rang from the jolts and from the eerie call of howling wolves.

"Do you think me merely a vampire or a Tribemaster you can so easily defeat?" he spat. "I am an *Elder*. I can summon the power of the pack and use it to my liking. I can kill Aric and anyone I wish from miles away. No one can stop me—and no one can help you!"

My heavy lids widened. He was robbing the pack of its power just to come for me. Again, I tried to move my shoulders and pry free from the wall, but I barely managed to jerk my head.

Anara lifted his palm and squeezed his fingers, choking me slowly from where he stood and ceasing my frantic attempts. Spots speckled my vision. I thought he would kill me, until he dropped his hand and released the pressure burning my throat. He paced in front of me, seemingly pleased with the amount of power swirling at his fingertips. I spit out blood and tried to speak. "You're abusing pack magic. The other Elders will know."

"I've ensured that they won't." He closed the distance between us and leaned in close. "That half-breed Martin may lead as Alpha, but *I* possess his power." He stopped smiling. "I'll kill Aric, Celia. I will."

"Why?" I croaked.

His hot breath stirred against my face. "I will not allow an abomination like you to taint his bloodline. He is a king among wolves and you are nothing but a whore. I'd rather see him dead than have you ruin what remains of our eminence!"

His stare traveled the length of my body with the

deepest of loathing. He lifted the edge of my sweater before yanking it down with disgust. "I never understood what he saw in you," he scoffed.

Anara's hold continued as he stalked away. "My influence and control extend everywhere, Celia. I can manipulate anyone to do my will—just as I did Virginia and those she sent word of your power. I will know if you see Aric. I will know if you speak to him."

Virginia . . . the Tribe . . . the shape-shifters. *Jesus*, he'd deluded everyone—including his enemies—to view *me* as the threat. The realization struck me like a thunderbolt and washed my bleeding form with cold dread. *Anara* was the one who believed me the key to his destruction . . . and to all the *weres* he led.

He stopped at the door, the muscles of his back tightening until they bulged against his red shirt. "If you *dare* tell anyone about this, your sisters will share Aric's fate."

As a testament to his power, Anara didn't release me until about an hour after he left. I crashed to the floor coughing and shaking. The only thought racing through my head was the need to protect Aric, my sisters, and the baby growing inside of me.

Reader's Guide to the Magical World of the Weird Girls Series

acute bloodlust: Occurs when a vampire goes too long without consuming blood. Increases the vampire's thirst to lethal levels. Remedied by feeding the vampire.

call: The ability of one supernatural creature to reach out to another, through either thoughts or sounds. A vampire can pass his or her *call* by transferring a bit of magic into the receiving being's skin.

change: To transform from one being to another, typically from human to beast and back again.

chronic bloodlust: Results from a curse placed on a vampire. Makes the vampire's thirst for blood insatiable and drives the vampire to insanity. The vampire grows in size from gluttony and assumes deformed features. There is no cure.

claim: The method by which a werebeast consummates the union between his or her mate.

clan: A group of werebeasts led by an Alpha. The types of clans differ depending on species. Werewolf clans are called "packs"; werelions belong to "prides."

creatura: The offspring of a demon lord and a werebeast.

dantem animam: A soul giver. A rare being capable of returning a master vampire's soul. A master with a soul is more powerful than any vampire in existence as he or she is balancing life and death at once.

dark ones: Any creature considered to be of pure evil, such as a shape-shifter or demon.

demons: Creatures residing in hell. Only the strongest may leave to stalk on earth, but their time is limited; the power of good compels them to return.

demon lords (demonkin): The offspring of a witch mother and a demon. Powerful, cunning, and deadly. Unlike demons, whose time on earth is limited, demon lords may remain on earth indefinitely.

demon children: The spawn of a demon lord and a mortal female. Demon children are of limited intelligence and rely predominantly on their predatory instincts.

Den: A school where young werebeasts train and learn to fight in order to help protect the earth from mystical evil.

Elder: Werebeast clans are governed by three Elders, consisting of an Alpha, a Beta, and an Omega. The Alpha is the supreme leader. The Beta is the second in command. The Omega settles disputes between them and has the ability to calm by releasing bits of his or her harmonized soul, or through a sense of humor muddled with magic.

exceptis: A male born every three centuries from the union of two witches. Possesses rare gifts. Often volatile, selfish, and of questionable loyalty.

force: Emme Wird's ability to move objects with her mind.

gold: The element was cursed long ago and has damaging effects on werebeasts, vampires, and the dark ones. Supernatural creatures cannot hold gold without feeling the poisonous effects of the curse. A bullet dipped in gold will explode a supernatural creature's heart like a bomb. Gold against open skin has a searing effect.

grandmaster: The master of a master vampire. Grandmasters are among the earth's most powerful creatures. Grandmasters can recognize whether the human he or she *turned* is a master upon creation. Grandmasters usually kill any master vampires they create to consume their power. Some choose to let the masters live until they become a threat, or until they've gained greater strength to therefore take more power.

keep: Beings a master vampire controls, such as those he or she has *turned* vampire or acquired by destroying another master. They may also be humans the master regularly feeds from

Leader: A pureblood werebeast in charge of delegating and planning attacks against the evils that threaten the earth.

lone: A werebeast who doesn't belong to a clan and therefore is not obligated to protect the earth from supernatural evil. Considered of lower class by those with clans.

master vampire: A vampire with the ability to *turn* a human vampire. Upon their creation, masters are usually killed by their grandmaster for power. Masters are immune to fire and sunlight born of magic, and they typically carry tremendous power. Only a master or another lethal preternatural can kill a master vampire. If one master kills another, the surviving vampire acquires his or her power, wealth, and keep.

mate: The being a werebeast will love and share a soul with for eternity.

misericordia: A plea of mercy in a duel.

moon sickness: The werebeast equivalent of bloodlust. Brought on by a curse from a powerful enchantress, and causes excruciating pain. Attacks a werebeast's central nervous system, making the werebeast stronger and violent, and driving the werebeast to kill. No known cure exists.

mortem provocatio: A fight to the death.

North American Were Council: The governing body of *weres* in North America, led by a president and several council members.

potestatem bonum: "The power of good." That which encloses the Earth and keeps demons from remaining among the living.

purebloods (aka pures): Werebeasts from generations of *were*-only family members. Considered royalty among werebeasts and carry the responsibilities of continuing their species. The union of two purebloods is the only way to guarantee the conception of a *were* child.

shape-shifter: Shape-shifters are born witches. They spend years seeking innocents to sacrifice to a dark deity. When the deity deems the offerings sufficient, the witch casts a baneful spell to surrender his or her magic and humanity in exchange for immortality and the power of hell at their fingertips. Shape-shifters can command any form and are the deadliest and strongest of all mystical creatures.

shift: Celia Wird's ability to break down her body into minute particles. Her gift allows her to travel beneath and across soil, concrete, and rock. Celia can also *shift* a limited number of beings. Disadvantages include not being able to breathe or see until she surfaces.

solis natus magicae: The proper term for sunlight born of magic, created by a wielder of spells. Considered "pure" light. Capable of destroying nonmaster vampires and demons. In large quantities may also kill shape-shifters. Renders the wielder helpless once fired.

surface: Celia Wird's ability to reemerge from a *shift*.

susceptor animae: A being capable of taking another's soul, such as a vampire.

Trudhilde Radinka (aka Destiny): A female born once every century from the union of two witches. She possesses rare talents and the aptitude to predict the future. Considered among the elite of the mystical world.

turn: The rare ability to transform a human into a werebeast or vampire. Werebeasts pierce the heart of a human with their fangs and transfer a part of their essence. Vampires pierce through the skull and into the brain to transfer a taste of their magic. Werebeasts risk their lives during the *turning* process as they are gifting a part of their souls; should the transfer fail, both the werebeast and the human die. Vampires risk nothing since they're not losing their souls, but rather taking another's and releasing it from the human's body.

vampire: A being who consumes the blood of mortals to survive. Beautiful and alluring, vampires will never appear to age past thirty years. Vampires are immune to sunlight unless created by magic. They are also immune to objects of faith such as crucifixes. Vampires may be killed by the destruction of their hearts, decapitation, or fire. Master vampires or vampires several centuries old must have both their hearts and heads removed, or their bodies completely destroyed.

vampire clans: Families of vampires led by master vampires. Masters can control, communicate, and punish their keep through mental telepathy.

velum: A veil conjured by magic.

virtutem lucis: "The power of light." The goodness found within each mortal. That which combats the darkness.

Warrior: A werebeast possessing profound skill or fighting ability. Only the elite among *weres* are granted the title of Warrior. Warriors are duty-bound to protect their Leaders and their Leaders' mates at all costs.

Werebeast (aka *were*): A supernatural predator with the ability to *change* from human to beast. Werebeasts are considered the Guardians of the Earth against mystical evil. Werebeasts will achieve their first *change* within six months to a year following birth. The younger they are when they first *change*, the more powerful they will be. Werebeasts also possess the ability to heal their wounds and can live until the first full moon following their one hundredth birthday. Werebeasts may be killed by destruction of their hearts, decapitation, or if their bodies are completely destroyed. The only time a *were* can partially *change* is when he or she attempts to *turn* a human. A *turned* human will achieve his or her first *change* by the next full moon.

witch: Born with the power to wield magic, they worship the earth and nature. Pure witches will not take part in blood sacrifices. They cultivate the land to grow plants for their potions, and use staffs, amulets, and talismans to amplify their magic. To cross a witch is to feel the collective wrath of her coven.

witch fire: Orange flames encased by magic, used to assassinate an enemy. Explodes like multiple grenades when the intended victim nears the spell. Flames will continue to burn until the target has been eliminated.

Sacramento, California

The courthouse doors crashed open as I led my three sisters into the large foyer. I didn't mean to push so hard, but hell, I was mad and worried about being eaten. The cool spring breeze slapped at my back as I stepped inside, yet it did little to cool my temper or my nerves.

My nose scented the vampires before my eyes caught them emerging from the shadows. There were six of them, wearing dark suits, Ray-Bans, and obnoxious little grins. Two bolted the doors tight behind us, while the others frisked us for weapons.

I can't believe we're in vampire court. So much for avoiding the perilous world of the supernatural.

Emme trembled beside me. She had every right to be scared. We were strong, but our combined abilities couldn't trump a roomful of bloodsucking beasts. "Celia," she whispered, her voice shaking. "Maybe we shouldn't have come."

Like we had a choice. "Just stay close to me, Emme." My muscles tensed as the vampire's hands swept the length of my body and through my long curls. I didn't like him touching me, and neither did my inner tigress. My fingers itched with the need to protrude my claws.

When he finally released me, I stepped closer to Emme while I scanned the foyer for a possible escape route. Next to me, the vampire searching Taran got a little daring with his pat-down. But he was messing with the wrong sister.

"If you touch my ass one more time, fang boy, I swear to God I'll light you on fire." The vampire quickly removed his hands when a spark of blue flame ignited from Taran's fingertips.

Shayna, conversely, flashed a lively smile when the vampire searching her found her toothpicks. Her grin widened when he returned her seemingly harmless little sticks, unaware of how deadly they were in her hands. "Thanks, dude." She shoved the box back into the pocket of her slacks.

"They're clear." The guard grinned at Emme and licked his lips. "This way." He motioned her to follow. Emme cowered. Taran showed no fear and plowed ahead. She tossed her dark, wavy hair and strutted into the courtroom like the diva she was, wearing a tiny white minidress that contrasted with her deep olive skin. I didn't fail to notice the guards' gazes glued to Taran's shapely figure. Nor did I miss when their incisors lengthened, ready to bite.

I urged Emme and Shayna forward. "Go. I'll watch your backs." I whipped around to snarl at the guards. The vampires' smiles faltered when they saw *my* fangs protrude. Like most beings, they probably didn't know what I was, but they seemed to recognize I was potentially lethal, despite my petite frame.

I followed my sisters into the large courtroom. The place reminded me of a picture I'd seen of the Salem witch trials. Rows of dark wood pews lined the center aisle, and wide rustic planks composed the floor. Unlike the photo I recalled, every window was boarded shut, and paintings of vampires hung on every inch of available wall space. One particular image epitomized the vampire stereotype perfectly. It showed a male vampire entwined with two naked women on a bed of roses and jewels. The women appeared completely enamored of the vampire, even while blood dripped from their necks.

The vampire spectators scrutinized us as we approached along the center aisle. Many had accessorized their expensive attire with diamond jewelry and watches that probably cost more than my car. Their glares told me they didn't appreciate my cotton T-shirt, peasant skirt, and flip-flops. I was twenty-five years old; it's not like I didn't know how to dress. But, hell, other fabrics and shoes were way more expensive to replace when I *changed* into my other form.

I spotted our accuser as we stalked our way to the front of the assembly. Even in a courtroom crammed with young and sexy vampires, Misha Aleksandr stood out. His tall, muscular frame filled his fitted suit, and his long blond hair brushed against his shoulders. Death, it seemed, looked damn good. Yet it wasn't his height or his wealth or even his striking features that captivated me. He possessed a fierce presence that commanded the room. Misha Aleksandr was a force to be reckoned with, but, strangely enough, so was I.

Misha had "requested" our presence in Sacramento after charging us with the murder of one of his family members. We had two choices: appear in court or be hunted for the rest of our lives. The whole situation sucked. We'd stayed hidden from the supernatural world for so long. Now not only had we been forced into the limelight, but we also faced the possibility of dying some twisted, Rob Zombie–inspired death.

Of course, God forbid that would make Taran shut her trap. She leaned in close to me. "Celia, how about I gather some magic-borne sunlight and fry these assholes?" she whispered in Spanish.

A few of the vampires behind us muttered and hissed, causing an uproar among the rest. If they didn't like us before, they sure as hell hated us then.

Shayna laughed nervously, but maintained her perky demeanor. "I think some of them understand the lingo, dude."

I recognized Taran's desire to burn the vamps to blood and ash, but I didn't agree with it. Conjuring such power would leave her drained and vulnerable, easy prey for the master vampires, who would be immune to her sunlight. Besides, we were already in trouble with one master for killing his keep. We didn't need to be hunted by the entire leeching species.

The procession halted in a strangely wide-open area before a raised dais. There were no chairs or tables, nothing we could use as weapons against the judges or the angry mob amassed behind us.

My eyes focused on one of the boarded windows. The light honey-colored wood frame didn't match the darker boards. I guessed the last defendant had tried to escape. Judging from the claw marks running from beneath the frame to where I stood, he, she, or *it* hadn't made it.

I looked up from the deeply scratched floor to find Misha's intense gaze on me. We locked eyes, predator to predator, neither of us the type to back down. *You're trying to intimidate the wrong gal, pretty boy. I don't scare easily.*

Shayna slapped her hand over her face and shook her head, her long black ponytail waving behind her. "For Pete's sake, Celia, can't you be a little friendlier?" She flashed Misha a grin that made her blue eyes sparkle. "How's it going, dude?"

Shayna said "dude" a lot, ever since dating some idiot claiming to be a professional surfer. The term fit her sunny personality and eventually grew on us.

Misha didn't appear taken by her charm. He eyed her as if she'd asked him to make her a garlic pizza in the shape of a cross. I laughed; I couldn't help it. *Leave it to Shayna to try to befriend the guy who'll probably suck us dry by sundown.*

At the sound of my chuckle, Misha regarded me slowly. His head tilted slightly as his full lips curved into a sensual smile. I would have preferred a vicious stare—I knew how to deal with those. For a moment, I thought he'd somehow made my clothes disappear and I was standing there like the bleeding hoochies in that awful painting.

The judges' sudden arrival gave me an excuse to glance away. There were four, each wearing a formal robe of red velvet with an elaborate powdered wig. They were probably several centuries old, but like all vampires, they didn't appear a day over thirty. Their splendor easily surpassed the beauty of any mere mortal. I guessed the whole "sucky, sucky, me love you all night" lifestyle paid off for them.

The judges regally assumed their places on the raised dais. Behind them hung a giant plasma screen, which appeared out of place in this century-old building. Did they plan to watch a movie while they decided how best to disembowel us?

A female judge motioned Misha forward with a Queen Elizabeth hand wave. A long, thick scar angled from the corner of her left jaw across her throat. Someone had tried to behead her. To scar a vampire like that, the culprit had likely used a gold blade reinforced with lethal magic. Apparently, even that blade hadn't been enough. I gathered she commanded the fang-fest Parliament, since her marble nameplate read, CHIEF JUSTICE ANTOINETTE MALIKA. Judge Malika didn't strike me as the warm and cuddly sort. Her lips pursed into a tight line and her elongating fangs locked over her lower lip. I only hoped she'd snacked before her arrival.

At a nod from Judge Malika, Misha began. "Members of the High Court, I thank you for your audience." A Russian accent underscored his deep voice. "I hereby charge Celia, Taran, Shayna, and Emme Wird with the murder of my family member David Geller."

"Wird? More like *Weird*," a vamp in the audience mumbled. The smaller vamp next to him adjusted his bow tie nervously when I snarled.

Oh, yeah, like we've never heard that before, jerk.

The sole male judge slapped a heavy leather-bound book on the long table and whipped out a feather quill. "Celia Wird. State your position."

Position?

I exchanged glances with my sisters; they didn't seem to know what Captain Pointy Teeth meant either. Taran shrugged. "Who gives a shit? Just say something."

I waved a hand. "Um. Registered Nurse?"

Judging by his "please don't make me eat you before the proceedings" scowl, and the snickering behind us, I hadn't provided him with the appropriate response.

He enunciated every word carefully and slowly so as to not further confuse my obviously feeble and inferior mind. "Position in the supernatural world."

"We've tried to avoid your world." I gave Taran the evil eye. "For the most part. But if you must know, I'm a tigress."

"Weretigress," he said as he wrote.

"I'm not a *were*," I interjected defensively.

He huffed. "Can you *change* into a tigress or not?"

"Well, yes. But that doesn't make me a *were*."

The vamps behind us buzzed with feverish whispers while the judges' eyes narrowed suspiciously. Not knowing what we were made them nervous. A nervous vamp was a dangerous vamp. And the room burst with them.

"What I mean is, unlike a *were*, I can *change* parts of my body without turning into my beast completely." And unlike anything else on earth, I could also *shift*— disappear under and across solid ground and resurface unscathed. But they didn't need to know that little tidbit. Nor did they need to know I couldn't heal my injuries. If it weren't for Emme's unique ability to heal herself and others, my sisters and I would have died long ago.

"Fascinating," he said in a way that clearly meant I wasn't. The feather quill didn't come with an eraser. And the judge obviously didn't appreciate my making him mess up his book. He dipped his pen into his little inkwell and scribbled out what he'd just written before addressing Taran. "Taran Wird, position?"

"I can release magic into the forms of fire and lightning—"

"Very well, witch." The vamp scrawled.

"I'm not a witch, asshole."

The judge threw his plume on the table, agitated. Judge Malika fixed her frown on Taran. "What did you say?"

Nobody flashed a vixen grin better than Taran. "I said, 'I'm not a witch. Ass. Hole.'"

Emme whimpered, ready to hurl from the stress. Shayna giggled and threw an arm around Taran. "She's just kidding, dude!"

No. Taran didn't kid. Hell, she didn't even know any knock-knock jokes. She shrugged off Shayna, unwilling to back down. She wouldn't listen to Shayna. But she would listen to me.

"Just answer the question, Taran."

The muscles on Taran's jaw tightened, but she did as I asked. "I make fire, light—"

"Fire-breather." Captain Personality wrote quickly.

"I'm not a—"

He cut her off. "Shayna Wird?"

"Well, dude, I throw knives—"

"Knife thrower," he said, ready to get this little meet-and-greet over and done with.

Shayna did throw knives. That was true. She could also transform pieces of wood into razor-sharp weapons and manipulate alloys. All she needed was metal somewhere on her body and a little focus. For her safety, though, "knife thrower" seemed less threatening.

"And you, Emme Wird?"

"Um. Ah. I can move things with my mind—"

"Gypsy," the half-wit interpreted.

I supposed "telekinetic" was too big a word for this idiot. Then again, unlike typical telekinetics, Emme could do more than bend a few forks. I sighed. *Tigress, fire-breather, knife thrower, and Gypsy.* We sounded like the headliners for a freak show. All we needed was a bearded lady. *That's what happens when you're the bizarre products of a backfired curse.*

Misha glanced at us quickly before stepping forward once more. "I will present Mr. Hank Miller and Mr. Timothy Brown as witnesses—" Taran exhaled dramatically and twirled her hair like she was bored. Misha glared at her before finishing. "I do not doubt justice will be served."

Judge Zhahara Nadim, who resembled more of an Egyptian queen than someone who should be stuffed into a powdered wig, surprised me by leering at Misha like she wanted his head for a lawn ornament. I didn't know what he'd done to piss her off; yet knowing we weren't the only ones hated brought me a strange sense of comfort. She narrowed her eyes at Misha, like all predators do before they strike, and called forward someone named "Destiny." I didn't know Destiny, but I knew she was no vampire the moment she strutted onto the dais.

I tried to remain impassive. However, I really wanted to run away screaming. Short of sporting a few tails and some extra digits, Destiny was the freakiest thing I'd ever seen. Not only did she lack the allure all vampires possessed, but her fashion sense bordered on disastrous. She wore black patterned tights, white strappy sandals, and a hideous black-and-white polka-dot turtleneck. I guessed she sought to draw attention from her lime green zebra-print miniskirt. And, my God, her makeup was abominable. Black kohl outlined her bright fuchsia lips, and mint green shadow ringed her eyes.

"This is a perfect example of why I don't wear makeup," I told Taran.

Taran stepped forward with her hands on her hips. "How the hell is *she* a witness? I didn't see her at the club that night! And Lord knows she would've stuck out."

Emme trembled beside me. "Taran, please don't get us killed!"

I gave my youngest sister's hand a squeeze. "Steady, Emme."

Judge Malika called Misha's two witnesses forward. "Mr. Miller and Mr. Brown, which of you gentlemen would like to go first?"

Both "gentlemen" took one gander at Destiny and scrambled away from her. It was never a good sign when something scared a vampire. Hank, the bigger of the two vamps, shoved Tim forward.

"You may begin," Judge Malika commanded. "Just concentrate on what you saw that night. Destiny?"

The four judges swiftly donned protective ear wear, like construction workers used, just as a guard flipped a switch next to the flat screen. At first I thought the judges toyed with us. Even with heightened senses, how could they hear the testimony through those ridiculous ear guards? Before I could protest, Destiny enthusiastically approached Tim and grabbed his head. Tim's immediate bloodcurdling screams caused the rest of us to cover our ears. Every hair on my body stood at attention. What freaked me out was he wasn't the one on trial.

Emme's fair freckled skin blanched so severely, I feared she'd pass out. Shayna stood frozen with her jaw open while Taran and I exchanged "oh, shit" glances. I was about to start the "let's get the hell out of here" ball rolling when images from Tim's mind appeared on the screen. I couldn't believe my eyes. Complete with sound effects, we relived the night of David's murder. Misha straightened when he saw David soar out of Taran's window in flames, but otherwise he did not react. Nor did Misha blink when what remained of David burst into ashes on our lawn. Still, I sensed his fury. The image moved to a close-up of Hank's shocked face and finished with the four of us scowling down at the blood and ash.

Destiny abruptly released the sobbing Tim, who collapsed on the floor. Mucus oozed from his nose and mouth. I didn't even know vamps were capable of such body fluids.

At last, Taran finally seemed to understand the deep shittiness of our situation. "Son of a bitch," she whispered.

Hank gawked at Tim before addressing the judges. "If it pleases the court, I swear on my honor I witnessed exactly what Tim Brown did about David Geller's murder. My version would be of no further benefit."

Malika shrugged indifferently. "Very well, you're excused." She turned toward us while Hank hurried back to his seat. "As you just saw, we have ways to expose the truth. Destiny is able to extract memories, but she cannot alter them. Likewise, during Destiny's time with you, you will be unable to change what you saw. You'll only review what has already come to pass."

I frowned. "How do we know you're telling us the truth?"

Malika peered down her nose at me. "What choice do you have? Now, which of you is first?"

ALSO AVAILABLE FROM
Cecy Robson

SEALED WITH A CURSE
A Weird Girls Novel

Celia Wird and her three sisters are just like other 20-something-year-old girls living in the Lake Tahoe region—with one tiny exception: they're products of a backfired curse that has given each of them unique powers that make their lives, well, weird. Their powers also tend to get them into trouble with the local vampires, werewolves, witches, and demons. Especially after one of them accidentally blows up a vampire in self-defense, which is punishable by death... but that's just the beginning of their problems.

Available wherever books are sold or at
penguin.com

facebook.com/ProjectParanormalBooks

Penguin Group (USA) Online

What will you be reading tomorrow?

Tom Clancy, Patricia Cornwell, W.E.B. Griffin,
Nora Roberts, William Gibson, Catherine Coulter,
Stephen King, Dean Koontz, Ken Follett, Nick Hornby,
Khaled Hosseini, Kathryn Stockett, Clive Cussler,
John Sandford, Terry McMillan, Sue Monk Kidd,
Amy Tan, J. R. Ward, Laurell K. Hamilton,
Charlaine Harris, Christine Feehan...

You'll find them all at
penguin.com
facebook.com/PenguinGroupUSA
twitter.com/PenguinUSA

Read excerpts and newsletters, find tour schedules
and reading group guides, and enter contests.

Subscribe to Penguin Group (USA) newsletters
and get an exclusive inside look
at exciting new titles and the authors you love
long before everyone else does.

PENGUIN GROUP (USA)
us.penguingroup.com